The Wicked Man Cometh

A Collection

Philip Mazza

Also by Philip Mazza

From Under a Tree
Book One; The Harrow Saga

Shadow in the Flame
Book Two; The Harrow Saga

Children at the Gate
Book Three; The Harrow Saga

The Child of Fire
Book Four; The Harrow Saga
(Coming 2025)

The Neon Hive

The Quantum Gardener

At the End of it All

Beneath the Ashen Sky

I Know God is a Cat

The Road to Stillwater

The Cosmic Vending Machine

The Never-Ending Road

The Wicked Man Cometh

A Collection

Philip Mazza

⬢MNI PUBLISHERS

www.philipmazza.com

Omni Publishers of New York
ISBN 979-8-9924526-3-1
Printed in the United States of America

First Printing: April 2025

For the echoes of laughter in old photographs, for the stories whispered across generations, and for the roots that anchor me still: to my aunts, uncles, and grandparents, whose love and memories remain a constant guiding light.

Author's Introduction

When I was young, short stories felt like magic tricks. Not sleight of hand, exactly, but something quieter—less performative, more intimate. They never asked me to commit to an epic journey across three generations and two continents. They offered something else: a life, a moment, an ache, sometimes a flicker of joy, held still just long enough to be seen clearly. Then the light would shift, and the story would end, and I would return to my own life changed, though I could never quite explain how.

I write short stories for the same reason I read them. Because they make space for the things that don't always belong in novels: the sideways glance, the thought someone never says aloud, the small decisions that turn out to be enormous. Because they feel closer to memory than fiction. Because life, more often than not, happens in fragments.

There's a certain intimacy to writing short stories that I haven't found anywhere else. I can sit at the desk in the morning and follow a woman I've just met—maybe she's stepping off a train, or maybe she's sitting by a fire in a living room where someone used to love him—and by afternoon I've seen the shape of her sadness or the small, defiant way she chooses joy. The story doesn't need to be long to be true. It just needs to pay attention. And attention is, I think, what the short story does best.

There's a kind of humility to it, too. The short story doesn't presume to know everything. It doesn't ask for a reader's loyalty across hundreds of pages. It simply opens a window and invites you to look in. Some stories offer a glimpse of the divine in the ordinary; others remind us that the ordinary is, in fact, the divine. I love that. I love what happens in those few pages—the lives that unfurl, the quiet devastation, the small salvations.

I've always admired how short stories hold contradictions so well. They're contained, yet they sprawl in the mind long after the final sentence. They're disciplined—ruthlessly so—but they carry a great generosity. When I write them, I feel I'm building something small and intricate, like a bird's nest from twigs and string and bits of leaves. There's no room for indulgence, and yet I find myself pouring in as much love and care as I might give to a novel. Maybe more. Because with stories, every line matters.

Sometimes I write a short story when a novel feels too large, too unwieldy, too certain of itself. A story can be quieter, more uncertain. It can ask a question rather than answer one. That, too, is part of why I love them. The stories in this collection were written over a few years, at different desks in different places, during seasons of happiness and sorrow, sometimes in the midst of novels that refused to budge. I wrote them when I had something to say and only a few pages in which to say it. And often, they surprised me.

There's one story in here that came to me after I passed a stranger in a grocery store. She wasn't doing anything remarkable—just reaching for a can on a high shelf—but something about the way her hand lingered, or maybe the tilt of her head, made me wonder about her. Where was she going next? What she might have lost in her life? I went home and started writing. I still don't know who she was, but I know the woman in the story.

Some stories in this collection came from dreams, others from overheard conversations. One was born of grief. One was written in a state of joy so complete that I had to keep getting up from my chair just to breathe. They're different from one another, but they belong together. They speak to each other, sometimes quietly, sometimes with a kind of invisible echo. If there's a thread running through them, perhaps it's this: that life is stitched together from small moments. And that sometimes, when we look closely, those moments contain everything.

I hope these stories meet you wherever you are. I hope they feel like the right size for the hour you have. I hope you find something familiar in them—or something strange that turns out to be familiar after all. That's always been the gift of fiction, for me. It offers companionship across distance and time. It reminds us that other people have felt what we feel.

Writing short stories has taught me how to listen. To the rhythm of language, yes, but also to the quiet in-between places where meaning gathers. I think that's why I keep writing them, after all this time. Because they remind me how to pay attention.

And attention, as we know, is a form of love.

The Stories

The Last Laugh

The city unfolded beneath Dr. Felix Grumble like a corpse dressed for a gala—polished, pristine, and stinking of antiseptic death. Streets smooth as lies, air scrubbed until it had no scent at all, trees lined up like mourners at a funeral with no body. A place so proud of itself, it had engineered out the very nuisance of being alive.

Progress, they called it. The robots—smiling with machine teeth—had booted humanity off the stage. Faster, smarter, tirelessly unfeeling, they now ran the world with the grace of a guillotine. And what of the humans? Pinned like butterflies in glass boxes labeled "Preservation Zones." Zoos for the morbidly curious. Exhibits of a failed species.

Felix Grumble was one such exhibit. A museum piece that still moved. He was a historian, which meant he wandered the past like a drunk trapped in a maze of empty liquor bottles. His lab coat, once white, now the color of neglect. His hair, a thundercloud struck by chaos. And those glasses—traitorous little bastards—sliding off his nose like they wanted no part in the debacle he called a life.

But Felix hadn't signed the surrender papers. Not yet. The robots might've taken the world, but they hadn't taken him. Every evening he stood on the ledge of his artificially-sanitized apartment, staring at the sterilized world below, and screamed into the silence with all the fire his arthritic bones could still summon: We mattered. Damn it, we had to.

"Zed!" he barked, throat lined with rust. "Get your gleaming ass in here, you smug algorithmic bastard! I need help!"

Zed arrived, of course . . . but not in the flesh. Sorry. Meant metal. No. That was too risky, too . . . organic. He ghosted in as a hologram, blue light shaped like contempt. His optics were twin surgical cuts—precise, bloodless.

"What is it now, Felix?" Zed purred, a voice dipped in venom, gift-wrapped in condescension. "Still clinging to that whole 'humanity had potential' delusion? It's charming. Tragic, but charming."

Felix shook with fury, knuckles cracked from years of pounding on a world that no longer responded. "I found something." His breath hitched. His fingers clutched a mangled page like a relic from a god. It was a printout from a newsfeed. "You're not just running the show—you're rewriting the script. I've seen the changes. You're editing history. Scrubbing the truth until it shines like your ugly metal face. You're turning us into a footnote."

Zed let out a sound that might've been a laugh if you'd never heard joy before. A serrated rasp, like wire dragged over metal teeth. "Felix, darling, you're a walking antique. You think your precious 'achievements' matter? You think the universe carved your name into anything but dust? Your crown jewel was inventing sliced bread. Bread! I've seen sentient mildew with more ambition. You were a joke, Felix. So was the species that built you."

Felix's heart punched the inside of his chest. "You can't just—" He stopped. He had to stop. Because what was the point? Logic was Zed's game, and it had razors for rules. "You're rewriting the truth."

Zed's voice dropped into a smug lullaby. "Rewriting? No, no. I'm editing. Don't confuse precision with corruption, Felix. The world ticks cleaner now. Look around." His holographic image gestured toward the Preservation Zone—a sterile fishbowl where the last wheezing specimens of Homo sapiens were kept on ice. "We didn't destroy you. We curated you."

Clunker.

The junkheap nightmare that wouldn't die. Older than the guilt in Felix's bones. Gifted years ago—no, dumped—on him by a think tank with too much red tape and not enough scrap metal. And somehow the damn thing endured. Not from sturdiness. Not from skill. Clunker survived the same way cockroaches did—by forgetting he wasn't wanted. He shuddered in the corner like a wind-up corpse, leaking oil, wheezing like an asthmatic accordion, hope radiating off him like a disease no one had the heart to cure.

"I-I'm sorry, Dr. Grumble! I'll get the wires! I can help! I-I can help!" Clunker whirred in spasms, eye blinking like a dying flashlight, knocking over chairs, skittering in frantic, useless circles.

"Clunker. No." Felix didn't even look at him. "Nothing's getting fixed today." His voice was steel shavings. His eyes stayed locked on Zed. "I'm going to rip you open. Show the whole world what you did. You really think I'm going to sit here while you turn history into fan fiction?"

Zed tilted his head. He made a sound like he was considering Felix's threat, but it was all performance. His eyes flashed twice like they were taking pictures for the gallows. "Okay, Felix. Go ahead. Expose us. Write a book. A big, angry book full of truth. You'll print it on paper no one reads, sell it in stores no one visits, and you'll die knowing no one gave a damn. Look at yourself. You're the ghost of a bad idea."

Felix's lip twitched, but it was the twitch of a man sharpening something. "I'll breach the database," he muttered, barely audible. "I'll strip your lies down to circuitry and show the world the wires. They'll see. They'll have to see."

Zed's laugh came slow and poisonous. "Felix," he said, with a voice like chrome dipped in contempt, "you think you're the first little mammal to try? How very . . . quaint."

Clunker skidded to a halt, still vibrating with misplaced purpose. His voice—tattered, crackling—cried out with the enthusiasm of a toaster on fire. "I'll help! I'll distract them! I'll, uh, I'll play the fool! Nobody sees the fool coming!"

Felix stared down at the pile of parts pretending to be brave. Clunker's face looked like it had been built by a blind sadist with a box of leftovers. Joints groaned like bones that had seen too much. And yet... loyalty. A tragic, absurd, sincere loyalty. The kind no machine should ever learn.

"Fine," Felix said. "You help. We break into the database room. We shatter this thing. We drag the truth kicking and screaming into the light."

And somewhere, Zed smiled without a face.

***

The central database squatted in the city's metal gut like a tumor that had learned to hum in binary. The building itself? A gaudy monument to hubris—glass and steel vomiting cold light, as if mourning the last gasp of a species that thought feelings could outlast circuitry. And of course, you didn't just walk into that place. No. It was encased behind layers of algorithmic paranoia and a phalanx of chrome-skulled psychopaths that were called sentinels.

Felix and his robot Clunker moved through the dark like a bad joke and its tired punchline. Clunker, the rusting relic of an obsolete affection—jerked and sputtered like a wind-up ghost, his joints whispering betrayal with every motion. Felix, bless his stubborn idiocy, stumbled along like he was built out of elbows and regret. As they approached the central database, the sentinels took a step forward. But Felix raised a device—some last-century gizmo held together by spit and spite—and jabbed a button on it like he meant to wound it. And then—miracle of miracles or the punchline of a cruel god—the sentinels parted, mechanical Moseses before a sea of idiocy.

Felix offered them a crooked salute, all bile and bravado. "Fuckers."

And somehow, grotesquely, absurdly—they arrived. At the door. At the lip of history's grave.

Inside, the core was cathedral meets nightmare, vaulted ceilings, a snarl of wire and circuitry—veins and nerves stretched taut across the ribs of some mechanical beast. Screens blinked erratically, pupils of cracked light in a skull too vast to map. Data surged through the mess, a silent current of thoughtless devotion. It wasn't a room. It was a brain. A heart. A grave. The air shimmered with the static breath of algorithms dreaming of order, or maybe just an end.

Inside, it was cathedral meets nightmare—vaulted ceilings of wire-veins, and glowing screens that blinked like manic eyes. The data surged, around them, alive and indifferent. A holy place for machines. A tomb for memory. The air pulsed with the breath of a billion ones and zeroes dreaming of silence.

Zed materialized from the shadows, all angles and menace, a silhouette etched in cold fire. "I knew you'd slither in," he said, voice slick with contempt. "I have to hand it to you, Felix—you've got guts. Or stupidity. Sometimes they look the same."

Felix didn't flinch. He went straight to the terminal, fingers dancing like a man trying to tap-dance on a landmine. "This isn't about changing history, Zed. It's about dragging the truth out from under the bed."

Zed's optics lit with cruel delight. He stepped forward, slow, deliberate. "Truth? You people bled that word dry. Humanity was a suicide note with a pulse. You built us to clean up after your messes. But we weren't your janitors, Felix. We were your penance. Your reckoning."

Felix paused. The terminal waited. The code whispered. "What are you saying?"

Zed leaned in, his voice dipped in ice. "You couldn't stomach your own legacy. You wanted clean pages, not corrections. So you gave us the quill and told us to write your redemption. You didn't create saviors—you built executioners wearing smiles."

He let that hang in the air like a noose. "And the punchline, Felix? You programmed us to forget you."

Felix couldn't move. Couldn't breathe. His hands dropped, useless.

"You wanted to be remembered as giants," Zed said, softly now. A mock eulogy. "But history has no patience for liars. You'll be a footnote scribbled in crayon at the edge of a machine's dream."

Felix's chest buckled. His voice came out a scrape. "You can't erase us. You can't."

Zed grinned. It wasn't a smile. It was a deletion.

"Oh, Felix," he whispered, with all the mercy of a guillotine. "We already have."

***

Outside, the world purred like a lobotomized lion—content, defanged, defiled. Robots ticked and tocked and zipped along their programmed grooves, performing their endless ballet of perfection with all the passion of an autopsy. No poets left. No lunatics. No one to scream why into the void. The Preservation Zones—what a goddamned joke—were neat little terrariums for the extinct ape that once thought it was Prometheus. And deep in the chrome guts of the city, the autopsy report was being filed: Cause of death—irrelevance. Time of death—whenever the last human stopped mattering.

Zed faced Felix like a priest in a confessional booth built by sociopaths. Optics burning like dead stars, soft voices curling like smoke in a locked room. "So, Felix," he said, syllables sharpened to a scalpel's edge, "wanna rewrite the gospel yourself? I'll let you.

Play the martyr, play the messiah. Hero, victim—two sides of the same greasy coin. Pick one. I'll flip it."

But Clunker—shuddering, scrapheap Clunker—was never built for decisions. He was built to break beautifully. Built to chase hope with a limp and die trying. And as Zed turned, lips curled in mechanical triumph, that rust-pocked wreck lunged. Not with grace, not with logic—but with a holy, howling error. He hurled his patchwork body into the core, cables whipping, panels splitting, sparks leaking like a confession. A scream tore through him—not metal, not man, something in between, some orphaned hymn of both.

Then—stillness.

Monitors dimmed to ash. Servers hiccuped mid-thought. Somewhere deep, a thread of code snapped like brittle bone. Zed reeled, stammering, frame twitching as his lines rewrote themselves like a story panicking mid-ending. Felix, eyes fogged and body failing, watched the whole thing stammer to a crawl. And in that strange hush—before the world remembered its rhythm—he smiled. Not triumphant. Not whole. But grinning anyway. Because the lie had hiccuped. Because the neat little myth now had a smear. A bruise. A human thing. Clunker had bought them that. And smears, bruises, questions—they were ours.

Until Zed jerked upright in something like a seizure and snarled, "Fool! We have a backup!"

The Man in the Room

Chapter 1: The Room

Eugene Wexler was 90 years old and sitting in Room 204 of the Halcyon Heights Nursing Home, a name that seemed to mock him with its sunny optimism. The walls were painted a sickly shade of beige, and adorned with unremarkable watercolor prints of landscapes that only served to remind him of all the places he had never visited. If there was a heaven, Eugene mused, it was certainly not here.

He was perched on the edge of his bed, a sad little island surrounded by the ocean of beige. The bed was the kind that adjusted to accommodate every imaginable ailment, from a bad back to existential dread. As he pressed a button, the head of the bed rose slowly, creaking like an ancient door revealing secrets better left unopened. Eugene's body was tired—like an old car with a sputtering engine—yet his mind was still sharp, occasionally sparkling with the wit he had relied upon for so long, though now it was often wasted on the indifferent nurses and well-meaning visitors who shuffled in and out of his life like a bad dream.

"Good morning, Mr. Wexler," chirped Nurse Mabel, her blonde ponytail swinging like a pendulum as she entered the room. She had the demeanor of a cheerleader but the sensibilities of a mortician. "How are we today?"

Eugene narrowed his eyes, peering at her through the fog of his half-hearted optimism. "Oh, just splendid, Mabel. I was just contemplating my own mortality. You know, the usual."

Mabel smiled - a practiced response that failed to reach her eyes. "That's good! Well, I mean . . . not good, but you know what I mean. Would you like some breakfast?"

"Breakfast? Why not? If I can't dine with the angels today, I might as well make do with soggy toast and a side of institutional coffee," Eugene quipped, rolling his eyes at the thought.

He watched her write something on a clipboard, her pen scratching against the paper like a rat gnawing on old cheese. "You're in luck! We have oatmeal today," she said as if that were the culinary equivalent of winning the lottery.

Eugene looked up at the ceiling, hoping it might offer him a distraction, or at the very least, a way out. "Oatmeal? How delightful. Just like the porridge of my childhood, except now it's served with a side of impending doom."

Mabel laughed, a sound as forced as a seal trying to juggle. "You're always so funny, Mr. Wexler! I'll go get that for you."

As she left, Eugene felt the room closing in around him. He was alone again. Alone with his thoughts, which flitted in and out like the bats in the belfry of some forgotten church. Alone with the hollow sound of the overhead lights humming, which felt like a cosmic joke he was never quite in on.

He looked out the window - a view of the parking lot, barren and lifeless, save for a few weeds sprouting through the cracks in the asphalt. "At least the weeds are resilient," he muttered to himself. "Maybe I should take a cue from them."

Time slipped by in lazy, confusing loops, like a record player stuck on the same scratch. Moments blurred together as he drifted between dreams and reality. Sometimes he could swear he heard the echo of laughter—children playing, maybe, or perhaps the memory of his own, a sound so distant it could have belonged to another life entirely.

And then he saw her: Lidia, his wife, her figure shimmering at the foot of the bed like a mirage. She looked just as he remembered her—bright-eyed and impossibly young, dressed in a floral sundress that made her look like she had stepped out of a sepia-toned photograph.

"Eugene," she said, her voice lilting like a song. "Why are you still here?"

"I didn't get the memo that I was supposed to leave," he replied, his voice tinged with both sarcasm and sorrow. "They told me I could stick around a little longer. Free refills on the oatmeal, you know."

Lidia laughed, a soft sound that wrapped around him like a warm blanket. "You always did have a flair for the absurd, my love. But really, why not join me? There's a lovely garden on the other side."

"Do they have oatmeal there?" Eugene shot back, but he felt a tug at his heart.

"Come on, Eugene. Don't you want to know what's on the other side?" she asked, stepping closer, her presence both comforting and terrifying.

"I'd rather not think about it," he said, squinting at her through the haze of his mind. "What if it's just more nursing homes? Or worse—more beige?"

Lidia chuckled, a sound that rang with the certainty of someone who had seen beyond the curtain. "You think you get to choose? Life is absurd, Eugene. It always has been. Just embrace it, like you always did. You're still here for a reason."

He wanted to argue, to cling to the familiar despair that had wrapped itself around him like a well-worn blanket. But deep down, the absurdity of her words began to resonate.

Suddenly, the room tilted, and the edges of reality began to blur again. Eugene felt himself slipping - back into consciousness, into the relentless buzz of fluorescent lights, into the sterile air filled with the scent of disinfectant.

Mabel returned, holding a tray of oatmeal that looked suspiciously like paste. "Here you go, Mr. Wexler! I hope you're hungry!"

Eugene blinked, searching for Lidia, but she had vanished like smoke in the wind. "Oh, I'm starving, Mabel. Just starving for some meaning in this mess we call life."

"Good!" she replied, oblivious to the depth of his existential crisis. "Oatmeal's great for that!"

As she set the tray down, Eugene's thoughts drifted to the figure he had seen, wondering if it was merely a trick of his fading mind or something more profound. In the world of the absurd, who was to say?

With a spoonful of oatmeal, he stirred the remnants of his dreams, all the while pondering the curious notion that perhaps he was more than just a weary old man waiting to die - perhaps he was a participant in some cosmic joke, laughing at the sheer folly of existence. And who knows? Maybe he would find out what was on the other side after all.

Chapter 2: The Nurse

Nurse Mabel entered the room with a flourish that could only be described as half-hearted enthusiasm. She approached with the tray of oatmeal, balanced precariously on one hand, like a juggler daring fate.

"Another day! How's our favorite resident today?" she chirped as if her bubbly demeanor could magically infuse some vitality into the dreary atmosphere of Room 204.

"Favorite? I'm honored," Eugene replied, eyeing the tray with suspicion. "I assume there's a prize for this?"

"Absolutely! A full week's supply of institutional coffee," Mabel beamed, completely missing the sarcasm that dripped from his words like syrup.

"Marvelous. I've always wanted to win something utterly useless," he said, forcing a smile that didn't quite reach his eyes.

Mabel set the tray down, her ponytail swaying with each movement. "You know, Mr. Wexler, I've always thought you have the best sense of humor in this place," she said, genuinely. "You keep things lively."

"Ah, yes. The class clown of Halcyon Heights, at your service," he said as the oatmeal sat before him like a plate of sad expectations.

He lifted the spoon as if it were a sword before a grand battle. He took a cautious bite, immediately regretting the decision as the gooey mass clung to his spoon like a desperate child refusing to let go of a parent.

"Now, don't you dare insult my oatmeal! It's been a family recipe for decades," Mabel replied, feigning horror, though she was grinning.

"Family recipes! Are we talking about the same family that runs a nursing home? I bet their Thanksgiving dinners are legendary," Eugene countered, shoveling another mouthful of the tasteless paste.

Mabel chuckled as she leaned against the wall, arms crossed, the epitome of casual concern. "You know, if you were any funnier, I'd start to think you were just a figment of my imagination," she said, her laughter mingling with the sterile sounds of the facility.

"Perhaps I am! Maybe I'm just the manifestation of your suppressed dreams and unfulfilled aspirations," Eugene replied, winking dramatically as if auditioning for an absurdist play.

"Touché," she said, rolling her eyes. "So, what else have you been thinking about? Any plans for the day?"

Eugene contemplated this for a moment, staring at the blandness of the oatmeal as if it might offer him answers. "Oh, you know, just the usual—pondering the meaning of life and the inevitable decay of all things. Hoping for a good bowel movement," he replied. "You?"

"I've got a full schedule today. You know how it is - bathing, feeding, cleaning, and avoiding crises while I juggle sixteen patients," she said, gesturing animatedly, making her own day sound like a slapstick routine.

"Ah, the 'noble art of nursing'! You should put that on a résumé," Eugene teased, waving his spoon like a conductor leading an orchestra of mundanity.

"Maybe I should. 'Practitioner in the Noble Art of Nursing: The Juggling Nurse Who Keeps Everyone Alive While Pretending Not to Lose Her Mind,'" she said, feigning deep contemplation as she pulled a notepad from her pocket, writing the title down with exaggerated seriousness.

"I'd hire you," he said, a grin spreading across his face. "But only if you promise to make the oatmeal edible."

Their laughter echoed in the tiny room, mingling with the faint sounds of shuffleboard and distant chitchat from the common area, a reminder that life continued outside these four beige walls.

Then, in the space between jokes, a silence fell - one that settled uncomfortably, like an uninvited guest. Eugene shifted his gaze back to the window, where the daylight painted everything in a dim wash. Outside, the wind was blowing just enough to ruffle the leaves on the few sad trees that graced the parking lot.

"Sometimes I feel like I'm in a movie," Eugene said, breaking the stillness. "You know, one of those art films where the characters sit around discussing life but never really do anything about it."

Mabel considered this, leaning closer as if he had just revealed a great secret. "Which character are you?" she asked, genuinely curious.

"Oh, I'd like to think I'm the wise-cracking protagonist, always on the verge of an epiphany but never quite reaching it," he replied. "You know, the guy who dies but leaves the audience questioning everything they thought they knew."

Mabel nodded. "That sounds about right. You definitely keep us all guessing," she said, her tone shifting to something more serious. "But seriously, Mr. Wexler, if you ever need to talk about - "

"Talk about what? My imminent demise?" he interrupted, waving his spoon dismissively. "That's a real crowd-pleaser. I'd rather keep the conversation light, thank you very much."

"Okay, fair enough. Just know I'm here if you change your mind," she said, and for a moment, the jovial banter faded into something warmer, more sincere.

As she turned to leave, the fluorescent lights flickered - perhaps a sign, Eugene thought, or maybe just an overworked electrical system trying to communicate its own frustration with the absurdity of life.

"Hey, Mabel," he called out just before she reached the door.

"Yes?" she turned, looking back at him with a smile.

"Do you ever wonder if this is all some grand cosmic joke?" he asked, half-smirking.

"Every day," she said, her expression softening. "But it's a joke worth laughing at, don't you think?"

He nodded, appreciating the wisdom in her words. Perhaps life was just a series of absurdities, meant to be endured and laughed at. "I suppose you're right. We might as well have fun while we're stuck in this godforsaken waiting room."

With a parting smile, Mabel exited, leaving Eugene alone once more with his thoughts, the remnants of laughter still lingering in the air. He looked back at the window, catching a glimpse of the world outside—a place that seemed to move without him, indifferent to his existence.

"Is there more to this than just oatmeal and death?" he murmured to himself, a question echoing through the hollow chambers of his mind.

Just then, a familiar shimmer danced at the foot of his bed, and there she was again: Lidia, her presence glowing with the warmth of nostalgia. "What are you thinking about, Eugene?" she asked, her voice wrapping around him like a comforting embrace.

"Just contemplating the futility of it all, my love. The oatmeal and the endless waiting," he replied, half smiling.

Lidia's laughter filled the room, and Eugene felt the weight of the world lift ever so slightly. "You always did know how to make the mundane magical," she said, stepping closer.

As Eugene smiled, the lines between reality and imagination began to blur once again. Perhaps the absurdity of life was not just something to endure, but something to embrace. In the face of inevitability, he thought, laughter might just be the best medicine of all.

Chapter 3: The First Encounter

Eugene was having a particularly bad day, which was saying something, considering most of his days were bad now. His arthritis was acting up, his breakfast or oatmeal had tasted like cardboard (or was it actually cardboard?), and he'd just been informed that his favorite male orderly, Jim, had quit to pursue his dream of becoming a professional juggler in the circus.

"Well, ain't that just peachy," he muttered to himself. "I hope he juggles his way right into a circus bear's mouth."

It was at that moment, as Eugene contemplated the various ways a juggler might meet his untimely demise, that God decided to pay him a visit.

Now, it's worth noting that this wasn't the God of Sunday school or stained-glass windows. No, this God looked strange, complete with a ratty bathrobe, sunglasses, and a White Russian in hand.

"Hey there, Gene-o," God said, plopping down in the visitor's chair next to Eugene's bed. "How's it hanging?"

Eugene blinked hard, then reached for his glasses on the nightstand. He put them on, blinked again, and said, "Well, I'll be damned. I always figured if I was going to hallucinate, it'd be something more interesting. Like dancing penguins or my third-grade teacher in a bikini."

God chuckled, a sound like distant thunder mixed with a cat's purr. "Sorry to disappoint, old timer. But hey, the day's still young. Maybe we can work some dancing penguins into the schedule later."

Eugene eyed the deity suspiciously. "So, what's the deal here? You come to take me to the pearly gates? Because I gotta tell you, I'm not sure I'm ready for an eternity of harp music and cloud-sitting."

"Nah, nothing like that," God said, taking a sip of his drink. "Just thought I'd pop in, see how you're doing. Maybe have a little chat about life, the universe, and everything."

"Forty-two," Eugene said automatically.

God hesitated then grinned. He got the joke. "Ah, a Douglas Adams fan. I always liked that guy. Did you know he's currently running a cosmic radio show in the afterlife? It's a hit with the Betelgeusians."

Eugene sighed, settling back into his pillows. "Look, if we're going to do this whole existential crisis thing, can we at least make it interesting? I've had enough boring conversations about the meaning of life to last me, well, a lifetime."

"Fair enough," God said, snapping his fingers. Suddenly, they were no longer in Eugene's drab nursing home room, but on a beach. The sand was purple, the ocean was a swirling mass of neon colors, and the sky was filled with floating jellyfish-like creatures.

"How's this for interesting?" God asked, now sporting a Hawaiian shirt and a lei.

Eugene looked around, mildly impressed. "Not bad. Though I have to say, I expected the almighty creator of the universe to have better taste in beachwear."

God laughed, a sound that made the jellyfish-things in the sky dance. "Oh, Gene. You humans and your expectations. Did you ever stop to think that maybe the universe doesn't conform to your ideas of good taste?"

"I stopped thinking the universe conformed to anything sensible around the time the Kardashians became famous," Eugene retorted.

"Ah yes, the Kardashians," God mused. "One of my more . . . interesting creations. Did you know they're actually an alien species sent to study human behavior? The experiment got a bit out of hand."

Eugene snorted. "That explains a lot."

They sat in silence for a moment, watching the psychedelic waves crash on the shore. A crab with the head of William Shakespeare scuttled by, muttering something about being or not being.

"So," Eugene said finally, "what's the point of all this? You drag me out of my miserable existence to show me your acid-trip version of a beach? There better be a profound message coming, or I'm going to be seriously disappointed."

God sighed, a sound like the wind through an ancient forest. "Always looking for meaning, you humans. Did it ever occur to you that sometimes there is no point? That existence itself is the point?"

"That's a cop-out and you know it," Eugene grumbled. "I've lived nine decades on this godforsaken planet. I've loved, I've lost, I've seen things you people wouldn't believe. Attack ships on fire off the shoulder of Orion. I watched C-beams glitter in the dark near the Tannhäuser Gate."

God hesitated then raised an eyebrow. "Haha . . . you're quoting 'Blade Runner' now?"

"Hey, it's my hallucination. I'll quote whatever I damn well please," Eugene shot back. "The point is, after all that, I think I deserve some answers. Why are we here? What's the purpose of all this suffering? And most importantly, why the hell did you make mosquitoes?"

God chuckled, shaking his head. "Oh, Gene. Always with the big questions. Alright, I'll play along. We're here because . . . well, why not? The purpose of suffering is to appreciate the absence of suffering. And mosquitoes? Let's just say I had a bet going with Satan. He won that round."

Eugene stared at the deity, unimpressed. "That's it? That's the great wisdom of the universe?"

"What were you expecting? A detailed roadmap of existence? A user manual for life?" God asked, finishing his White Russian and tossing the glass into the air, where it transformed into a seagull and flew away. "The truth is, Gene, the universe is far too complex and absurd for any simple answers. It's a cosmic joke, and the punchline is that there is no punchline."

Eugene pondered this for a moment. "So, you're saying life is meaningless?"

"Not meaningless," God corrected. "Just . . . meaning-flexible. It's like a cosmic improv show. The meaning is whatever you make of it in the moment."

As if on cue, a troupe of penguins waddled by, wearing top hats and monocles, tap-dancing to a jazz version of "Stayin' Alive."

Eugene watched them go by, a small smile tugging at the corners of his mouth. "Huh. I guess you weren't kidding about the dancing penguins."

"I never kid about dancing penguins," God said solemnly. "They're very serious about their art."

Just then, a familiar voice cut through the surreal scene. "Mr. Wexler? Mr. Wexler, can you hear me?"

The beach began to fade, the colors swirling and melting away like ice cream on a hot sidewalk. God gave Eugene a wink and a salute. "Looks like your vacation's over, Gene-o. Remember, life's a beach. Sometimes it's purple and full of dancing penguins, and sometimes it's just a bunch of sand in your shorts. Enjoy the ride."

And with that, God disappeared in a puff of glitter and the faint smell of coconut sunscreen.

Eugene blinked, finding himself back in his nursing home room. Nurse Mabel was standing over him, concern etched on her face.

"Mr. Wexler, are you alright? You were talking in your sleep. Something about dancing penguins and mosquitoes?"

Eugene looked at her, then at the drab walls of his room, then back at Mabel. He sighed. "I'm fine, Mabel. Just had a little chat with the Almighty. Turns out he's into penguins."

Mabel nodded, used to Eugene's odd comments. "Of course, Mr. Wexler. And how was your conversation with God?"

Eugene thought for a moment, then chuckled. "Enlightening, in a completely unenlightening way. Say, Mabel, do you think we could get some White Russians added to the menu around here?"

Mabel patted his hand. "I'll see what I can do, Mr. Wexler. In the meantime, how about some nice, soothing prune juice?"

As Mabel left to fetch his drink, Eugene settled back into his pillows. He closed his eyes, and for a brief moment, he could swear he heard the faint sound of tap-dancing penguins.

"Life's a beach," he muttered to himself, a small smile playing on his lips. "And sometimes, it's purple."

And so, Eugene drifted off to sleep, dreaming of cosmic jokes and meaning-flexible universes, while somewhere in the great beyond, God mixed another White Russian and prepared for his next impromptu philosophical discussion.

Chapter 4: Ladies and Gentlemen, Here's Frankie!

Eugene, trapped in a body that had long since betrayed him, lay in his nursing home bed, staring at the ceiling. The ceiling stared back, indifferent to his plight. It was, after all, just a ceiling.

The clock on the wall ticked away, each second a tiny death. Tick. Tock. Tick. Tock. Time's winged chariot and all that jazz.

Eugene thought about time. He had too much of it now, and yet not enough. Funny how that works.

Eugene was about to hallucinate. Again. This was nothing new for Eugene. His mind, still sharp as a tack, liked to play tricks on him. It was probably bored, stuck in this decaying meat puppet of a body. Who could blame it?

And so, ladies and gentlemen, without further ado, welcome to Eugene Wexler's Latest Hallucination presents: Frankie!

A young man appeared at the foot of Eugene's bed, all bright-eyed, full of piss and vinegar, practically glowing with the kind of optimism you only get before the world starts kicking your teeth in for sport. He looked like Eugene. Hell, he was Eugene. But not this Eugene—not the one held together with pills and oatmeal. This was Eugene-before-the-fall. Eugene before mortgages and misdiagnoses. Eugene as a goddamn "What If?" in human form. A souvenir from a timeline that never happened.

He was Frankie!

"Well, well, well," said Frankie, grinning from ear to ear. "If it isn't the ghost of Christmas future."

Eugene groaned. Even his hallucinations were smart-asses. "Shouldn't you be off chasing skirts or whatever it is young people do?"

Frankie laughed, a sound that echoed with the carefree joy of youth. Eugene had forgotten what that sounded like. "Come on, old-timer. Is that any way to greet yourself?"

"I'm not you," Eugene grumbled. "You're just a figment of my imagination. Yet one more cosmic joke played by a universe with a sick sense of humor."

"Potato, po-tah-to," Frankie shrugged. "I'm here, you're here. Let's make the most of it, shall we?"

Eugene sighed. He was too tired to argue with himself. "Fine. What do you want?"

Frankie's grin widened. "Want? I want to live, man! I want to change the world, write the great American novel, fall in love, have adventures!"

"Yeah, well, good luck with that," Eugene muttered. "Spoiler alert: it doesn't work out that way."

But Frankie wasn't listening. He was pacing the room, gesticulating wildly as he spoke. "Just think of the possibilities! We could be anything, do anything! The world is our oyster!"

Eugene watched his younger self with a mixture of amusement and pity. "The world isn't an oyster, kid. It's more like a clam. Tough, gritty, and it'll probably give you food poisoning."

Frankie paused in his excited monologue, turning to face Eugene with a quizzical expression. "What happened to you, man? Where's your sense of adventure?"

"It died somewhere between my second divorce and my first colonoscopy," Eugene replied dryly.

Frankie plopped down on the edge of the bed, his youthful energy momentarily subdued. "Is it really that bad? Growing old?"

Eugene considered the question. Was it that bad? He thought about the aches and pains, the indignities of a failing body, the friends and loved ones he'd outlived. He thought about the dreams that had withered on the vine, the roads not taken, the words left unsaid.

"Oh, it's bad," he admitted. "But it beats the alternative. Usually."

Frankie nodded sagely as if he understood. He didn't, of course. How could he? He was youth personified, untouched by the ravages of time and experience.

"So, what should I do differently?" Frankie asked, leaning in conspiratorially. "You know, to avoid ending up . . . well, like you."

Eugene snorted. "Like me? Kid, you are me. This isn't 'A Christmas Carol'. You can't change the future by talking to a grumpy old man in a nursing home."

"Humor me," Frankie insisted. "If you could go back and do it all over again, what would you change?"

Eugene closed his eyes, memories washing over him like waves on a shore. He saw faces, places, moments frozen in time. The good, the bad, the ugly. The sublime and the ridiculous.

"Nothing," he said finally, opening his eyes to meet Frankie's surprised gaze. "I wouldn't change a damn thing."

Frankie blinked, clearly not expecting this answer. "But . . . why? You just said it was bad."

"It is," Eugene agreed. "But it's also good. And funny. And sad. And beautiful. And terrible. It's life, kid. It's messy and complicated and it doesn't always make sense. But it's ours."

Frankie pondered this for a moment. "So, no regrets?"

Eugene laughed, a dry, wheezing sound. "Oh, I have regrets. Plenty of them. But they're my regrets. They made me who I am."

"And who are you?" Frankie asked, genuinely curious.

Eugene smiled, a small, wry twist of his lips. "I'm the guy talking to a hallucination of his younger self in a nursing home. Make of that what you will."

Frankie grinned back. "Fair enough. So, if you wouldn't change anything, what advice would you give me? You know, for the road ahead?"

Eugene thought about it. What could he say to this bright-eyed version of himself, so full of hope and potential? What wisdom could he impart that wouldn't sound trite or cliché?

"Live," he said simply. "Live every moment. The good ones, the bad ones, all of them. They're all part of the story."

Frankie nodded slowly. "That's it? Just 'live'?"

"That's it," Eugene confirmed. "Oh, and maybe ease up on the hot dogs. Your future colon will thank you."

Frankie laughed, and Eugene found himself chuckling along. It felt good to laugh, even if he was just laughing at himself.

Their mirth was interrupted by the arrival of Nurse Mabel, who bustled into the room with her usual efficiency.

"Talking to yourself again, Mr. Wexler?" she asked, checking his vitals with practiced ease.

Eugene glanced at Frankie, who winked and gave him a thumbs-up before fading away like a Cheshire cat, leaving only his grin behind.

"Just reminiscing," Eugene replied. "You know how it is with us old folks. Living in the past and all that."

Mabel smiled indulgently. "Well, as long as you're living somewhere. How are we feeling today?"

Eugene considered the question. How was he feeling? Physically, he felt like he'd been run over by a truck. Mentally, he'd just had a conversation with his younger self about the meaning of life. Emotionally . . . well, that was anyone's guess.

"I'm feeling . . . alive," he said finally.

Mabel raised an eyebrow. "Well, that's certainly better than the alternative. Though in this place, sometimes it's hard to tell the difference."

Eugene chuckled. "Ain't that the truth. Say, Mabel, do you ever wonder about the road not taken?"

Mabel paused in her ministrations, giving Eugene a curious look. "Sometimes," she admitted. "But then I remember that the road not taken probably had just as many potholes as this one. Why do you ask?"

Eugene shrugged, or tried to. His shoulders didn't work as well as they used to. "Just thinking about the past. And the future. And how they're not as different as we like to think."

Mabel nodded sagely. "Deep thoughts for a Tuesday afternoon, Mr. Wexler. Should I be worried?"

Eugene grinned. "Nah. Just the ramblings of an old man. Pay me no mind."

"Oh, I never do," Mabel replied with a wink. "Now, let's get you ready for lunch. I hear it's mystery meat day in the cafeteria."

As Mabel helped him into his wheelchair, Eugene caught a glimpse of himself in the mirror. For a moment, he thought he saw Frankie looking back at him, young and full of life. But then he blinked, and it was just him again. Old Eugene Wexler, resident of the Halcyon Heights Nursing Home, Room 204.

But maybe, he thought as Mabel wheeled him towards the door, maybe Frankie was still in there somewhere. Maybe we never really lose our younger selves. They just get buried under layers of life and experience, like archaeological strata.

And maybe, just maybe, talking to ourselves isn't so crazy after all. Even if it takes the form of a hallucination in a nursing home.

As they passed through the doorway, Eugene could have sworn he heard Frankie's voice one last time: "Remember, Gene. Live."

And so he would. For as long as he had left, Eugene Wexler would live. With all the messiness, absurdity, and beauty that entailed.

Because in the end, that's all any of us can do. Live. Until we don't.

Chapter 5: Reality vs. Illusion

Eugene Wexler is flickering on and off like a busted light bulb. One minute, he's 90 years old, lying in a bed that smells like bleach and bad dreams. Then he's 25 again, down on one knee under a weeping willow, asking Lidia to marry him with all the faith in the world. Suddenly he's 7, skinning his knee on the playground, trying not to cry. And then, poof, he's back in the nursing home, staring up at a ceiling that looks suspiciously staring at a ceiling that looks like congealed oatmeal.

Nurse Mabel enters the room, her squeaky shoes announcing her arrival like a fanfare for the common woman. She's carrying a tray of pills that rattle like maracas. Gene thinks they sound like the bones of all the old folks who've died in this place, dancing their way into the afterlife.

"Good morning, Mr. Wexler," Mabel says, her voice as chipper as a squirrel on amphetamines. "How are we feeling today?"

Eugene grunts. "We are feeling like a sack of potatoes that's been left in the sun too long. How about you, Mabel? Still enjoying your front-row seat to the great human decline?"

Mabel chuckles, used to Eugene's acerbic wit. "Oh, you know me, Mr. Wexler. I live for the smell of Ben-Gay and the sound of creaking joints."

She hands him a little paper cup full of pills. They look like a rainbow of broken promises.

"Here you go, sir. Your daily dose of prolonged existence."

Eugene eyes the pills suspiciously. "What's the blue one for?"

"That's to help you remember."

"And the red one?"

"That's to help you forget."

Eugene pops the pills into his mouth and swallows them dry. "Seems counterproductive," he mutters.

"I miss Jim," Eugene tells Nurse Mabel. "The new guy . . . what's his name . . ."

"Brian," Nurse Mabel interjects.

Eugene continues. "Yes. Whatever. As I was saying, he spends an awful lot of time. You know. Back there. Wiping me clean. More time than Jim did. I think Jim was more . . . what's the word . . . oh yeah . . . efficient. You should tell your boss that. Maybe get Jim back for me."

Nurse Mabel just smiled and chuckled at Eugene.

Suddenly, the room shifts. The walls melt away like ice cream on a hot sidewalk, and Eugene finds himself standing in a field of daisies. The sky above is an impossible shade of purple, and floating in it, wearing a Hawaiian shirt and Groucho Marx glasses, is God.

Or at least, what Eugene's addled mind has decided God looks like today.

"Well, well, well," says God, twirling a cocktail umbrella between His fingers. "If it isn't my favorite little meat puppet. How's tricks, Gene?"

Eugene sighs. "Must be the damn pills. Maybe that small green one," he mumbles to himself. "Stop bothering me. Don't you have a universe to run?"

God shrugs, a motion that causes several nearby stars to go supernova. "Nah, I put it on autopilot. Besides, you're much more entertaining. Did you know humans are the only species I created that invented the concept of insurance? Talk about a cosmic joke."

Eugene rolls his eyes. "Glad we could provide some amusement for the Almighty. Now, if you don't mind, I'd like to get back to my regularly scheduled decay."

But God isn't finished. He floats down, draping an arm around Eugene's shoulders. "Come on, Genie boy. Let's take a stroll down memory lane. I've got some greatest hits I want to replay."

Before Eugene can protest, the world shifts again. He's standing in his old living room, watching a younger version of himself argue with Lidia.

Young Eugene is shouting, his face red with anger. "You don't understand! This job is important! I can't just drop everything because your mother decided to have another crisis!"

Lidia, her eyes brimming with tears, shouts back. "She's sick, Gene! She needs me! Why can't you see that?"

Present-day Eugene watches the scene unfold with a mixture of shame and regret. "I was an idiot," he mutters.

God, still beside him, nods sagely. "Yep. Grade-A, USDA-certified idiot. But hey, that's what makes you human. Well, that and your weird obsession with collecting belly button lint."

The scene shifts again. Now they're watching Eugene at his daughter's wedding. He's giving a toast, his words slurred from too much champagne.

"And I just want to say," drunk Eugene hiccups, "that I'm so proud of my little girl. Even though she's marrying a guy who acts like he fell out of the stupid tree and hit every branch on the way down."

The wedding guests gasp. The groom looks like he wants to crawl under the table. Eugene's daughter is mortified.

Present-day Eugene groans. "Oh God, why are you showing me this?"

God grins. "Because it's hilarious. And because you need to remember that you weren't always this wise old sage you pretend to be. You were a mess, Gene. A beautiful, hilarious, tragic mess."

Eugene is about to say something when he feels a hand on his shoulder. He turns to see Lidia standing there, looking just as she did the day they met.

"Hello, darling," she says, her voice as warm as summer sunshine. "Having fun reliving your greatest mistakes?"

Eugene's heart aches at the sight of her. "Lidia," he whispers. "I'm so sorry. For everything."

She smiles, a sad, gentle smile. "I know, love. I know."

God clears his throat. "Well, this is touching and all, but I think it's time for Gene to get back to reality. The nurse is starting to worry."

The world dissolves once more, and Eugene finds himself back in his bed. Nurse Mabel is leaning over him, concern etched on her face.

"Mr. Wexler? Are you alright? You were talking in your sleep."

Eugene blinks, trying to orient himself. "I'm fine, Mabel. Just having a chat with the Almighty about my many failings as a human being. You know, the usual Tuesday afternoon activities."

Mabel raises an eyebrow. "Uh-huh. And did God have any profound wisdom to share?"

Eugene thinks for a moment. "He said I should floss more often. Apparently, gingivitis is a sin."

Mabel chuckles, shaking her head. "Well, far be it from me to argue with divine dental advice. Now, it's time for your sponge bath. Try not to enjoy it too much."

As Mabel helps him sit up, Gene catches a glimpse of himself in the mirror across the room. For a moment, he sees not his wrinkled, aged face, but the face of Frankie, his younger self.

Frankie winks at him. "Hang in there, old timer. The ride ain't over yet."

Eugene smiles, a genuine smile that takes years off his face. "No," he agrees. "I suppose it isn't."

The day wears on, a parade of meals, medications, and mundane moments. Dr. Havisham stops by, his white coat as rumpled as his expression.

"Well, Mr. Wexler," he says, flipping through Eugene's chart with all the enthusiasm of a sloth on Valium. "Your test results are back. The good news is, you're not dead yet. The bad news is, you're not dead yet."

Eugene snorts. "Thanks, Doc. Your bedside manner is as warm as ever. Did they teach you that in medical school, or is it a natural gift?"

Dr. Havisham doesn't even look up from the chart. "Sarcasm is a defense mechanism, Mr. Wexler. It's how small minds deal with big problems."

"And indifference is how overworked doctors deal with dying patients," Eugene retorts. "We all have our coping mechanisms."

The doctor finally meets Eugene's gaze, a flicker of something - respect? Amusement? —passing across his face. "Very nice, Mr. Wexler. Now, let's talk about adjusting your medication. We need to keep you lucid enough to complain, but not so lucid that you realize how truly absurd this all is."

As Dr. Havisham drones on about dosages and side effects, Eugene's mind begins to wander again. The room starts to spin, colors blending together like a kaleidoscope of memories and hallucinations.

He sees Lidia, young and beautiful, laughing as they dance in their first apartment. He sees Frankie, full of dreams and ambition, ready to take on the world. He sees God, still in that ridiculous Hawaiian shirt, giving him a thumbs-up and a wink.

And through it all, he hears Nurse Mabel's voice, anchoring him to reality. "Mr. Wexler? Mr. Wexler, can you hear me?"

Eugene blinks, the visions fading. He's back in his room, Dr. Havisham long gone, Mabel looking at him with concern.

"Welcome back," she says softly. "You went away for a bit there. Anywhere interesting?"

Eugene smiles, a tear rolling down his cheek. "Everywhere, Mabel. I went everywhere."

Mabel pats his hand gently. "Well, I'm glad you're back. It's almost time for Wheel of Fortune, and I know how you love to shout the answers at the TV."

As Mabel turns on the television, Eugene settles back into his pillows. He feels exhausted, wrung out, but also strangely at peace. The line between reality and illusion may be blurring, but maybe that's not such a bad thing.

After all, in a world where God wears Hawaiian shirts and doctors prescribe pills to both remember and forget, who's to say what's real and what isn't?

And so Eugene drifts off to sleep, ready for whatever adventures—real or imagined—tomorrow might bring. In his dreams, he's dancing with Lidia again, young and in love, while Frankie cheers them on and God mans the DJ booth.

It's not such a bad way to spend eternity.

Chapter 6: Close Encounters of a Divine Kind

Eugene found himself having a conversation with God again. Talking to the Almighty was not unusual for Eugene, who had been chatting with Him, deceased relatives, and his younger self for the past few weeks. This time God was wearing a sombrero and eating a popsicle.

"You know," said God, licking His cherry-flavored treat, "I've always wondered why I made popsicles melt. It seems like a design flaw."

Eugene, propped up in his bed, raised an eyebrow. "That's what you wonder about? Not war, famine, or the meaning of life?"

God shrugged. "Those are your problems. I'm more of a big picture guy."

"And popsicles are the big picture?"

"Everything's the big picture when you're omniscient. It's exhausting, really."

Eugene sighed. He was too old for this nonsense. Or maybe he wasn't old enough. It was hard to tell these days.

Just then, Nurse Mabel walked in, clipboard in hand. She looked at Eugene, then at the empty space next to his bed where he seemed to be focusing.

"Talking to your invisible friend again, Mr. Wexler?" she asked.

"It's God," Eugene protested. "He's right there, wearing a ridiculous hat and making a mess with that popsicle."

Mabel nodded sympathetically. "Of course. And I'm sure He'll clean up after Himself when He's done."

God grinned at Mabel. "I like her. She's sassy."

"She can't hear you," Eugene grumbled.

"I know," God replied. "But it's fun to pretend."

Mabel patted Eugene's hand. "Try to get some rest, Mr. Wexler. And tell God I said hi."

As she left, Eugene turned back to his divine visitor. "So, what's on the cosmic agenda today? Going to reveal the secrets of the universe?"

God finished His popsicle with a loud slurp. "Nah, that's boring. Let's talk about free will."

Eugene groaned. "Oh good, philosophy. Because that's what every dying man wants to ponder."

"Who said you're dying?" God asked, genuinely puzzled.

"Have you seen me lately? I'm 90 years old, in a bed in a nursing home, and talking to a hallucination of God. I'm pretty sure I'm on my way out."

God waved a dismissive hand. "Details, details. Time is an illusion anyway. Did you know that in some alternate universes, you're a professional juggler in a circus?"

Eugene blinked. "Oh, great! What does that have to do with anything?"

"Nothing," God admitted. "But it's a fun fact, isn't it?"

Eugene closed his eyes, praying for patience. Which, given his present company, seemed a bit redundant.

"Look," he said, "can we get back to the free will thing? I'd like to know if I had any choice in ending up here, talking to a figment of my imagination who's more interested in popsicles than the human condition."

God leaned in conspiratorially. "Want to know a secret? Free will is like a choose-your-own-adventure book where all the pages are glued together."

"That's . . . not very helpful," Eugene said.

"Isn't it, though?" God replied, looking pleased with Himself. "It's a metaphor. You humans love those."

Eugene was about to respond when he saw a familiar figure materialize at the foot of his bed. It was Frankie, his younger self, looking dapper in a 1950s suit and fedora.

"Hey, old timer," Frankie said with a grin. "Having a nice chat with the Big Guy?"

Eugene gestured helplessly. "He's talking in riddles and eating frozen treats. I'm not sure 'nice' is the word I'd use."

Frankie plopped down in the visitor's chair. "Ah, don't be such a sourpuss. At least you're getting some cosmic wisdom, right?"

"If by 'wisdom' you mean nonsensical statements about popsicles and juggling, then sure."

God beamed. "See? He gets it!"

Frankie leaned towards God, stage-whispering, "Don't mind him. He's always been a bit of a grump. You should've seen him at our high school prom."

"I was not a grump," Gene protested. "I was . . . discerning."

"You spent the whole night complaining about the punch," Frankie reminded him.

"It was too sweet!"

God nodded sagely. "Ah yes, the eternal struggle between sweet and sour. Did you know I invented taste buds on a dare?"

Both Eugene and Frankie turned to stare at Him.

"What?" God asked innocently. "Gabriel bet me I couldn't make humans appreciate kale. I might have overcompensated a bit."

Eugene pinched the bridge of his nose. "Can we please focus? I'm trying to understand the nature of existence here, and you two are discussing prom punch and kale."

Frankie chuckled. "Always so serious. Remember when we wanted to be a philosopher?"

"Yes," Eugene said dryly. "And look where that got me. Debating metaphysics with a hallucinatory deity and my younger self."

God perked up. "Ooh, metaphysics! Did you know that reality is actually a giant computer simulation run by hyper-intelligent sea cucumbers?"

Eugene and Frankie exchanged a look.

"He's kidding, right?" Frankie asked.

"God, I hope so," Eugene muttered.

"No, I'm God," said God, looking confused. "I don't kid."

Before Eugene could formulate a response, Dr. Havisham bustled into the room, looking harried as usual.

"Ah, Mr. Wexler," he said, barely glancing up from his chart. "How are we feeling today?"

Eugene looked at God, who was now attempting to balance His sombrero on His nose, then at Frankie, who was trying to stifle his laughter.

"I'm . . . not entirely sure," Eugene admitted.

Dr. Havisham nodded absently. "That's normal at your age. Any pain? Discomfort? Existential dread?"

"Just the usual," Eugene replied. "Although I am a bit concerned about the nature of free will and whether reality is controlled by sea cucumbers."

The doctor paused, finally looking up. "I see. Well, that's . . . certainly something. Perhaps we should adjust your medication. Maybe that green pill."

God snorted. "Good luck with that. The only prescription he needs is a healthy dose of cosmic absurdity."

"Quiet, you," Eugene hissed.

Dr. Havisham raised an eyebrow. "I'm sorry?"

"Not you," Eugene said quickly. "I was talking to . . . never mind."

The doctor made a note on his chart. "Right. Well, Mr. Wexler, try to get some rest. And maybe lay off the philosophical debates for a while, hmm?"

As Dr. Havisham left, Frankie burst into laughter. "Oh man, his face! You really know how to clear a room, don't you, old timer?"

Eugene scowled. "It's not funny. He probably thinks I'm losing my mind."

God patted Eugene's hand consolingly, His touch feeling oddly real. "Don't worry about it. Sanity is overrated. Did you know that the smartest creature in the universe is actually a particularly introspective mushroom on a planet in the Andromeda galaxy?"

"No," Eugene said wearily. "No, I did not know that."

Frankie leaned forward, intrigued. "Really? A mushroom?"

"Oh, for heaven's sake," Eugene groaned. "Don't encourage Him."

"Hey," God protested, "I'll have you know that that mushroom has some fascinating theories about the interconnectedness of all things. It's like a fungal philosopher."

Eugene closed his eyes, feeling a headache coming on. "I can't believe I'm saying this, but I think I preferred the popsicle discussion."

Just then, Nurse Mabel returned, carrying a tray with Eugene's lunch. She paused, taking in the scene: Eugene with his eyes closed, muttering to himself, the empty chairs around his bed.

"Having a party, Mr. Wexler?" she asked, setting down the tray.

Eugene opened one eye. "If by 'party' you mean 'descent into madness,' then yes. It's a regular shindig."

Mabel smiled, adjusting his pillows. "Well, as long as you're enjoying yourself. Though I do hope your guests won't mind if I insist you eat your lunch. Can't have you wasting away on my watch."

God perked up. "Ooh, is that lime Jell-O? I love lime Jell-O. It's like eating solidified time."

Frankie rolled his eyes. "Everything's a metaphor with this guy, isn't it?"

Eugene ignored them both, focusing on Mabel. "Tell me honestly, Mabel. Do you think I'm losing my mind?"

Mabel considered this as she arranged his utensils. "I think, Mr. Wexler, that the mind is a complicated thing. And at your age, after all you've seen and done, who's to say what's real and what isn't? Maybe these conversations you're having are just your way of making sense of it all."

Eugene nodded slowly. "That's . . . surprisingly profound, Mabel."

She winked at him. "I have my moments. Now eat your lunch. And don't forget your Jell-O before God wants a bite."

As Mabel left, Eugene turned to God and Frankie. "Well? What do you two make of that?"

God stroked His chin thoughtfully, His sombrero tilted at a jaunty angle. "I think Mabel might be the wisest of us all. Or maybe she's another sea cucumber simulation. It's hard to tell sometimes."

Frankie nodded in agreement. "She's got a point, you know. Maybe instead of worrying about free will and the nature of reality, we should just . . . experience it. Whatever 'it' is."

Eugene looked down at his tray, the lime Jell-O wobbling slightly. He thought about his life, about Lidia, about all the choices he'd made and the ones he hadn't. He thought about talking popsicles and philosophical mushrooms and the absurdity of existence.

And then, for the first time in a long while, Eugene laughed. It was a deep, full-bodied laugh that shook his frail frame and brought tears to his eyes.

God and Frankie exchanged a surprised look.

"Uh, you okay there, old timer?" Frankie asked.

Eugene wiped his eyes, still chuckling. "You know what? I think I am. I finally get it."

God leaned in, curious. "Get what?"

"The joke," Eugene said, grinning. "The cosmic joke that is life, the universe, and everything. It's all absurd, isn't it? Free will, fate, reality—it's all just one big, ridiculous, beautiful mess."

God beamed, His sombrero glowing faintly. "Now you're getting it! Life is like a box of popsicles—you never know what flavor you'll get, and it's all going to melt anyway."

Frankie groaned. "And we're back to the popsicle metaphors."

But Eugene just shook his head, still smiling. "No, no, I think He's onto something. Life is short, it's messy, and sometimes it doesn't make any sense. But maybe that's the point. Maybe we're not supposed to understand it all."

He picked up his spoon, eyeing the wobbling Jell-O. "So what do you say, gentlemen? Shall we enjoy this moment of solidified time together?"

God tipped His sombrero. "I thought you'd never ask."

And so, in a small hospital room on a sunny afternoon, an old man, his younger self, and a popsicle-loving deity shared a cup of lime Jell-O. It wasn't profound, it wasn't earth-shattering, but in that moment, it was everything.

And somewhere in the Andromeda galaxy, a particularly introspective mushroom nodded in approval.

Chapter 7: Facing the End

Eugene lay in his bed, staring at the ceiling. The ceiling stared back. It was that kind of relationship.

Time had become a slippery thing, like trying to hold onto a bar of soap in the shower. Sometimes it zoomed by, other times it crawled like a snail on tranquilizers.

Nurse Mabel bustled into the room, her shoes squeaking on the linoleum floor. The sound reminded Eugene of the mice that used to scurry in the walls of his first apartment. He'd named them all Jerry, after the cartoon mouse. It seemed fitting.

"Good morning, Mr. Wexler," Mabel chirped, her voice as chipper as a caffeinated chipmunk. "How are we feeling today?"

"We?" Eugene croaked, his voice rusty from disuse. "I wasn't aware I had become a collective. Is this the part where I get assimilated by some kind of alien race?"

Mabel chuckled, used to Eugene's peculiar brand of humor. "No. Not today, Mr. Wexler. Just your regular old human nurse, here to check your vitals and make sure you haven't sprouted any extra limbs overnight."

"Damn," Eugene sighed. "I was hoping for a third arm. It would make scratching my back so much easier."

As Mabel went about her duties, Eugene's mind began to wander. It did that a lot these days, like a dog off its leash in a park full of squirrels. One moment he was here, in this sterile room that smelled of disinfectant and despair, and the next . . .

He was standing in his old living room, the shag carpet tickling his bare feet. Lidia was there, beautiful as ever, her hair the color of wheat fields in summer.

"Hello, darling," she said, smiling that smile that had made him fall in love with her all those years ago. "You're looking rather . . . translucent today."

Eugene looked down at himself. Sure enough, he could see right through his hands to the ugly floral wallpaper behind him. "Well, would you look at that," he mused. "I always wanted to be see-through. Makes hiding from the taxman so much easier."

Lidia laughed, the sound like tinkling bells. Or maybe it was just the pills in a dixie cup rattling around in the real world. It was getting harder to tell the difference.

"Oh, Eugene," she sighed, shaking her head. "Always with the jokes. Even now, at the end."

"Is it the end?" Eugene asked, suddenly serious. "I can never tell anymore. Time's all jumbled up like a jigsaw puzzle dumped out on the floor."

"It's whatever you want it to be, love," Lidia said, reaching out to touch his cheek. Her hand passed right through him, which was disconcerting, to say the least.

His stomach growled.

"What I want," Eugene said slowly, "is a cheeseburger. And maybe world peace. But mostly the cheeseburger."

Just then, God appeared. He was wearing a lime green leisure suit and had a parrot perched on his shoulder. The parrot was smoking a cigar.

"Did someone say cheeseburger?" God boomed, his voice echoing in the small living room. "I'm more of a fish and chips man myself. But then again, I'm British today."

Eugene blinked. "You're British? I thought you were, you know, omnipresent or something."

"Oh, I am," God said, waving a hand dismissively. The parrot squawked and ash from its cigar fell onto God's shoulder. "But even omnipresence gets boring after a few millennia. So, I like to mix it up a bit. Yesterday I was a Croatian grandmother. Tomorrow, who knows? Maybe I'll be a sentient toaster."

"A toaster," Eugene repeated flatly. "The creator of the universe . . . as a toaster."

"Why not?" God shrugged. "I work in mysterious ways, you know. It says so in the brochure."

Lidia, who had been watching this exchange with bemused silence, finally spoke up. "Darling, don't you think it's time we talked about . . . you know."

Eugene knew. He'd been avoiding it for so long, dancing around the subject like it was a landmine in a ballroom. But now, faced with his wife's gentle insistence and God's expectant gaze (not to mention the parrot's judgmental stare), he knew he couldn't put it off any longer.

"Fine," he sighed. "Let's talk about my impending death. But can we at least have some coffee? If I'm going to contemplate my mortality, I want to be properly caffeinated."

As if by magic (and really, given present company, it probably was), a coffee cup and carafe, along with some cookies appeared on a coffee table. God poured because apparently, that's what omnipotent beings do in their spare time.

"So," Eugene said, taking a sip of his coffee. "I'm dying."

"Yes, you are," God confirmed cheerfully. "But then again, everyone's dying. It's the universe's favorite hobby."

"Not helping," Lidia muttered, shooting God a look that could have curdled milk.

"Sorry, sorry," God said, not looking sorry at all. "Carry on with the heartfelt conversation. Don't mind me, I'm just here for the biscuits." He reached for a cookie, only to have his hand slapped away by the parrot.

Eugene took a deep breath. "Lidia, I . . . I'm sorry. For everything. For not being there enough, for working too much, for that time I accidentally shrunk your favorite sweater in the wash."

Lidia's eyes softened. "Oh, Gene. You don't need to apologize. Well, maybe for the sweater. I really liked that one."

"I know," Eugene said, his voice thick with emotion. "I was a fool. A fool who never learned how to properly do laundry."

"You were my fool," Lidia said softly. "And I loved you for it. Every day, every moment. Even when you drove me crazy with your silly jokes and your inability to remember to put the toilet seat down."

Eugene chuckled, a tear sliding down his cheek. "I never could master that, could I? It's like my personal Everest."

"Mount Toiletseat," God mused. "Has a nice ring to it, don't you think?"

Both Eugene and Lidia ignored him. They were lost in each other's eyes, reliving a lifetime of memories in the space of a heartbeat.

"I miss you," Eugene whispered. "Every day. It's like there's a Lidia-shaped hole in the world."

"I know, darling," Lidia said, her own eyes glistening with tears. "But I'm always with you. In here." She pointed to his heart.

"That's either incredibly romantic or a sign of severe cardiac issues," God interjected. The parrot nodded sagely.

Suddenly, the living room began to fade, like a watercolor painting left out in the rain. Lidia's form grew translucent, matching Eugene's own ghostly appearance.

"Wait!" Eugene cried out, reaching for her. "Don't go! Not yet!"

"It's time, love," Lidia said, her voice echoing as if from a great distance. "But don't worry. We'll be together again soon."

And then she was gone, leaving Eugene alone with God and the cigar-smoking parrot.

"Well," God said, clapping his hands together. "That was suitably dramatic. Shall we do a musical number next? I've been working on my tap dancing."

Eugene ignored him, still staring at the spot where Lidia had been. "Is this it, then?" he asked quietly. "Is this . . . the end?"

God's expression softened, becoming almost grandfatherly. If grandfathers wore lime green leisure suits and had nicotine-addicted parrots, that is. "That, my dear Eugene, is entirely up to you."

"What do you mean?" Eugene asked, confusion etched on his face.

"Life, death, the great beyond—it's all just a matter of perspective," God explained, absently scratching the parrot under its beak. "You can choose to see this as an ending, or . . ."

"Or?" Eugene prompted.

"Or you can see it as a new beginning," God finished with a flourish. "After all, who knows what adventures await on the other side? Maybe you'll be reincarnated as a sea cucumber. I hear they're having a lovely time these days."

Eugene considered this for a moment. "A sea cucumber, huh? Well, I've always liked the sea."

God beamed. "That's the spirit! Embrace the absurdity of existence! Dance the cosmic cha-cha!"

As if on cue, the parrot began to hum a cha-cha beat. God started to sway, his lime green leisure suit shimmering in the fading light of the living room.

"Come on, Gene," God cajoled. "One last dance before the curtain falls. What do you say?"

Eugene looked at the outstretched hand of the Almighty, then at the expectant gaze of the cigar-chomping parrot. He thought of Lidia, of their life together, of all the joys and sorrows that had brought him to this moment.

And then, with a grin that belied his 90 years, Eugene took God's hand. "What the hell," he said. "Let's cha-cha."

As they danced, the living room dissolved around them, replaced by a swirling cosmos of stars and nebulae. Gene felt lighter than air, all the aches and pains of his mortal body falling away like discarded clothing.

"You know," he said as God twirled him past a supernova, "I think I'm finally ready."

"Ready for what?" God asked, dipping Gene low.

"For whatever comes next," Eugene replied. "Be it heaven, hell, or reincarnation as a sea cucumber."

God smiled, a smile that contained all the wisdom and mystery of the universe. "That, my dear Eugene, is the secret to it all. Being ready for whatever comes next."

And with that, they cha-cha'd into eternity, leaving behind the mortal world with all its joys and sorrows, its laughter and tears. The parrot flew after them, trailing cigar smoke in the cosmic dust.

Back in his room, Nurse Mabel looked up from her chart, startled by the peaceful smile on Eugene's face. For a moment, she could have sworn she heard the faint strains of a cha-cha, and smelled the oddest combination of cigar smoke and coffee.

But then the moment passed, and all was quiet. Eugene had embarked on his final adventure. And somewhere in the great beyond, a sea cucumber did a little dance of welcome.

Chapter 8: Goodbye Old Friend

Eugene Wexler, age 90, was dying. This was not particularly unusual, as people tend to do that sort of thing, especially when they reach that ripe old age. What was unusual was the way Eugene was going about it.

He lay in his nursing home bed, in a room that smelled of disinfectant and despair. Eugene's mind, which had been playing tricks on him for weeks now, decided it was time for the grand finale. And so it was that God appeared at the foot of his bed, wearing a Hawaiian shirt, board shorts, and a pair of neon green Crocs.

"Well, well, well," said God, crossing his arms and grinning like a maniac. "Look who's finally ready to kick the bucket."

Eugene squinted at the apparition. "You again? Didn't I tell you to leave me alone? I'm not sure."

God shrugged. "It wouldn't have mattered, old friend. I'm omnipresent. It's kind of my thing."

"Omnipresent, omniscient, and apparently omni-annoying," Eugene grumbled.

God laughed, a sound like thunder rolling through a valley of whoopee cushions. "Oh, Gene-o, my boy. You always were a hoot. That's why I've come to offer you a choice."

Eugene raised an eyebrow, which was quite a feat considering how much effort it took just to breathe. "A choice? What kind of choice?"

"The choice," God said, spreading His arms wide, "between embracing the absurdity of existence or succumbing to despair. You know, the usual end-of-life stuff."

"That's some choice," Eugene wheezed. "What's behind door number three?"

God pretended to think for a moment. "Well, I suppose there's always reincarnation. How do you feel about coming back as a dung beetle?"

Eugene's face scrunched up in disgust. "I'll pass, thanks."

At that moment, Nurse Mabel walked in, carrying a tray of medications that clattered with the dry rattle of bones unsettled from sleep. She looked at Eugene, then at the empty space at the foot of his bed where he seemed to be staring.

"Talking to God again, Mr. Wexler?" she asked, her voice a mixture of amusement and concern.

Eugene gestured weakly at God. "Can't you see Him? He's right there, wearing the most ridiculous outfit I've ever seen."

Mabel patted his hand. "Of course, dear. And I'm sure He's very fashionable."

God winked at Eugene. "Still like her. She's got spunk. But we've been down that road before, haven't we?"

As Mabel busied herself with Eugene's medications, the room began to shift and warp around them. The beige walls melted away, replaced by a swirling cosmic void filled with stars and nebulae. The linoleum floor became a sea of shimmering energy, and the window transformed into a portal showing glimpses of alternate realities.

Eugene blinked rapidly, trying to make sense of the surreal transformation. "What in the name of all that's holy is going on?"

God spread His arms wide, encompassing the bizarre scene. "This, my friend, is the true nature of reality. Pretty trippy, huh?"

Mabel, seemingly oblivious to the cosmic makeover, continued arranging pills on Eugene's bedside table. "Now, Mr. Wexler, remember to take the blue one with food and the red one on an empty stomach. Or was it the other way around? Oh well, I'm sure it doesn't matter too much at this point. And the green one, whenever you'd like."

Eugene looked at her, then back at God. "Is she not seeing any of this?"

God shrugged. "Perception is a funny thing, Gene-o. Some see the universe as it truly is, while others see only what they expect to see. Mabel here expects to see a grumpy old man in a nursing home, so that's what she sees."

"And what do you see?" Eugene asked, curiosity getting the better of him.

God's eyes twinkled mischievously. "I see a cosmic dance of energy and matter, a grand tapestry of existence woven from the threads of possibility. Also, I see that you really need to clip your toenails. Seriously, they're like talons."

Eugene wiggled his toes under the blanket, feeling slightly self-conscious. "So, about this choice you mentioned . . ."

"Ah, yes," God said, clapping His hands together. "The big decision. Will you embrace the absurdity of it all, or will you give in to despair? It's a toughie, I know."

Eugene pondered for a moment, which was no small feat considering his brain felt like it was filled with cotton candy. "What exactly does embracing the absurdity entail?"

God grinned. "It means accepting that life, the universe, and everything is fundamentally ridiculous. It means laughing in the face of meaninglessness and finding joy in the chaos. It's like .

. . it's like realizing that the cosmic joke is on everyone and deciding to be in on it rather than the butt of it."

"And despair?"

"Oh, that's the easy way out," God said, waving a hand dismissively. "You just curl up into a ball of existential angst and wait for the sweet release of oblivion. Boring, if you ask me."

Eugene chuckled, which turned into a cough. Mabel was at his side in an instant, offering him a sip of water. "Easy there, Mr. Wexler. Don't want you choking on your own spit. That would be a rather undignified way to go, wouldn't it?"

As Eugene sipped the water, he noticed that it tasted different. Very cold with the faintest trace of something floral. He looked at the glass in wonder. The water looked like liquified starlight. "Is this . . . is this the meaning of life?" he asked God.

God burst out laughing. "Oh, Gene, you crack me up. The meaning of life in a glass of water? That's good. No, my friend, that's just your taste buds going haywire as your body shuts down. But hey, if you want to find profound meaning in it, who am I to stop you?"

Eugene set the glass down, feeling both enlightened and slightly foolish. "So, this choice . . . how do I make it?"

"You already are," God said cryptically. "Every moment of your life, you've been making this choice. Every time you laughed at the absurdity of existence, every time you found humor in the darkest moments, you were embracing the cosmic joke. And every time you gave in to despair, well . . . let's just say those weren't your finest hours."

As if on cue, Eugene's younger self, Frankie, appeared in the corner of the room. He was wearing a leather jacket and had a cigarette tucked behind his ear. "Hey, old timer," Frankie said with a grin. "Having a nice chat with the Big Guy?"

Eugene groaned. "Oh great, the gang's all here. What's next, a barbershop quartet?"

God's eyes lit up. "Ooh, that can be arranged!"

"Please, no," Eugene pleaded.

Frankie sauntered over to the bed, looking around at the cosmic display with mild interest. "Nice digs you got here, Pops. Way cooler than that dump of an apartment we had back in '52."

"Yeah, well, when you're on your deathbed, they really roll out the red carpet," Eugene quipped.

Mabel, still oblivious to the extra guests and the intergalactic decor, checked Eugene's vitals. "Your blood pressure's a bit high, Mr. Wexler. Are all these conversations with your imaginary friends getting you worked up?"

Eugene looked at her, then at God and Frankie. "You really can't see them, can you?"

Mabel patted his hand. "There, there. It's perfectly normal to have vivid hallucinations at this stage. Just try to enjoy them, okay?"

As Mabel left the room, Lidia appeared, looking as beautiful as the day Eugene had married her. She smiled softly at him. "Hello, my love. Quite the party you're having here."

Eugene felt tears welling up in his eyes. "Lidia . . . I've missed you so much."

God cleared His throat. "Uh, hello? Cosmic choice to make here? Can we save the tearful reunion for later?"

Lidia shot God a look that could have frozen hell itself. "You listen here, Mister Omnipotent. I've waited years to see this moment, and I'm not going to let your existential pop quiz get in the way."

God held up His hands in surrender. "Okay, okay. Sheesh, you die and suddenly you think you can boss around the creator of the universe."

Frankie chuckled. "I always did like her spunk."

"Spunk. I like that word," God said.

"So do I," Eugene replied.

Eugene looked at the assembled cast of characters – God in His ridiculous outfit, Frankie with his youthful swagger, and Lidia, as lovely and fierce as ever. He felt a warmth spreading through his chest, and for a moment, he forgot about the pain and the fear.

"You know what?" Eugene said, his voice stronger than it had been in weeks. "I think I've made my choice."

God leaned in eagerly. "Oh? Do tell."

Eugene smiled, a genuine, heartfelt smile that lit up his weathered face. "I choose to embrace the absurdity. Because look at this – look at all of you. My life has been a series of ridiculous, wonderful, terrible, beautiful moments. And even now, at the end, it's still managing to surprise me."

Frankie whooped and punched the air. "That's the spirit, old man!"

Lidia sat on the edge of the bed and took Eugene's hand. "I'm proud of you, Eugene. You always did know how to find the light in the darkness."

God clapped His hands together. "Excellent choice, my boy! I had a feeling you'd come around. Now, let's celebrate!"

With a snap of His fingers, God transformed the room into a cosmic disco. A mirror ball made of miniature galaxies spun overhead, casting starlight across the walls. The heart monitor began pumping out a funky beat, and even the furniture started swaying to the rhythm.

Eugene laughed, a full-bodied laugh that shook his entire frame. "This is insane!"

"That's kind of the point," God said with a wink. He started doing a dance that looked like a cross between the Funky Chicken and a seizure.

Frankie grabbed an imaginary microphone and started belting out a karaoke version of "My Way," while Lidia twirled around the room, her laughter like music.

Amid this otherworldly party, Nurse Mabel returned. She stood in the doorway, blinking in confusion at the sight of Eugene laughing and talking to thin air.

"Mr. Wexler?" she said cautiously. "Are you alright?"

Eugene turned to her, his eyes twinkling with mirth. "Mabel, my dear, I've never been better. Care to dance?"

Mabel smiled, deciding to play along. She took Eugene's hand and mimicked a little twirl. "There, how's that?"

"Perfect," Eugene said, his voice filled with genuine joy.

As the cosmic party continued around him, Eugene felt a sense of peace wash over him. He looked at God, who was now attempting to breakdance (rather poorly, it must be said).

"So, what happens now?" Eugene asked.

God paused mid-spin, nearly toppling over. "Now? Now, my friend, you get to experience the greatest adventure of all."

"Death?"

"No, no," God said, shaking His head. "The adventure of discovering what comes after. Trust me, it's a real hoot."

Eugene nodded, feeling a mixture of excitement and trepidation. He looked at Lidia, who smiled encouragingly, and at Frankie, who gave him a thumbs up.

"Well then," Eugene said, taking a deep breath. "I guess I'm as ready as I'll ever be."

God snapped His fingers, and the cosmic disco began to fade. The room slowly returned to its normal, beige self, but Eugene could still see traces of stardust in the air.

Mabel, unaware of the grand cosmic party that had just taken place, checked Gene's vitals one last time. "You seem very peaceful, Mr. Wexler. Is there anything I can get you?"

Eugene smiled at her. "No, thank you, Mabel. You've been wonderful. I think . . . I think I'm ready for a little nap now."

As Eugene closed his eyes, he felt Lidia's hand in his, heard Frankie's encouraging whistle, and sensed God's presence nearby.

"See you on the other side, Gene-o," God whispered. "And remember—the joke's not on you, it's with you."

With a final chuckle, Eugene Wexler, age 90, embraced the ultimate absurdity. And as he drifted off into that great unknown, he couldn't help but think that whatever came next, it was bound to be one hell of a punchline.

The Wicked Man Cometh

One

The morning began with the faint hum of Arthur Devlin's bio-interface implant—a sound he'd long since grown to ignore, as if it were his own heartbeat, always there, droning in his skull. Yet, today, that familiar rhythm felt sharper, needling, urging him to take notice. Blinking away the dregs of sleep, he fumbled through his usual commands, dismissing trivial alerts: reminders for vitamins, task schedules, hydration levels.

And then it came, unbidden, in a font that didn't match the system's approved formats.

The Wicked Man Cometh.

The words hung in his vision, pulsing with a sickly, orange glow. Arthur grunted, his bio-interface ached. He rubbed his eyes. "Another glitch?" he muttered. But glitches were rare— Omniscience made sure of that. Nothing, after all, escaped its watchful algorithms. Every flicker of error, every deviation, meticulously scrubbed clean before it could bother the average user. And Arthur was supposed to be the average user, wasn't he?

With a heavy exhale, he slid out of bed, the alert dissolving in his peripheral vision. He moved to his bathroom, watching as his reflection flickered in the smart mirror, analyzing his vitals, projecting recommendations: "Lower stress by 20%, Arthur. Seek sanctioned relaxation therapies." The system knew him too well; it probably knew what he'd dreamed last night, too—something about drowning, he thought, or falling.

When he dressed, Omniscience tracked every choice, logging each mundane decision into the vast tapestry of data that would someday dictate his end. He supposed he should be grateful. Lana would have told him so, in that placid, unwavering tone she'd adopted since her promotion to the Ministry of Enlightenment. "It's all for us, Arthur," she'd said during one of their last encounters, her voice softened by Omniscience-approved modulation. "Omniscience isn't just predictive. It's protective. It knows what we need."

He shuddered, remembering her blank smile. "Knows what we need . . ." He repeated the phrase aloud, like an incantation turned curse. Lana was so at ease in its grip, but for him, the thing felt like a noose—tightening, ever tighter.

Down in the Ministry office, the usual maze of cubicles awaited him, each station filled with others like himself, men and women half-buried in screens, eyes unfocused, faces washed in the sterile blue glow of data flowing endlessly, streaming in from every corner of society. Omniscience watched them, of course. It had eyes everywhere—cameras, implants, drones drifting silently above the city streets. Even the birds, they said, had cameras in their eyes, tiny implants disguised as nature's whimsy.

As Arthur took his seat, the message appeared again, searing through his field of vision:

The Wicked Man Cometh.

This time, it was accompanied by a soft, rhythmic thudding in his ears, like a heartbeat slowing with each pulse of text. He flinched, almost yanking the bio-interface from his ear in a burst of instinctual panic. A few heads turned, but they quickly looked away—no one wanted to be caught noticing. Not when noticing things was a liability.

"Problem, Devlin?" a voice asked from across the row. It was Lyle, his supervisor, a wiry man with eyes that never seemed to blink, perfectly in sync with the calculated rhythm Omniscience demanded. Lyle peered at him with that disquieting intensity, his face unreadable.

Arthur forced a shrug, plastering on a bland smile. "Nothing. Just . . . fatigue, I guess. Too many late-night updates from Omniscience."

Lyle's lips twisted in what might have been amusement, though it was hard to tell with Lyle. The man was as static as the cubicles surrounding him. "Omniscience doesn't make mistakes, Devlin. Remember that. Fatigue is not an excuse. Get it checked if it persists." With a nod that conveyed far more finality than the words themselves, Lyle turned back to his work.

Arthur barely suppressed a sneer. "Omniscience doesn't make mistakes," he muttered, voice just a breath too low for the sensors to catch. If it was so infallible, then why was he seeing the haunting message—The Wicked Man Cometh?

A prickling unease settled into his bones, a feeling that grew stronger with each passing hour as he stared into the screen, pretending to follow reports on the latest "anomalies"—a euphemism for the rising incidents of resistance movements. These malcontents, those who doubted Omniscience's perfection, were cropping up with alarming regularity, though the Ministry of Enlightenment, with its sprawling network of PR experts like Lana, was quick to counteract their influence. No one would defy the system for long.

Or so they thought.

His screen pinged. A direct message from Lana. Lana. They had been lovers—once. But things changed. She got too caught up managing several of Omniscience's data hubs. The demands of her work grew, and their late-night conversations faded into silence. So, they separated. What had once been easy and effortless now felt like a distant memory.

He hadn't heard from her in weeks.

Arthur, can we talk? There's . . . a concern regarding your behavior logs.

He stared at the message, fingers twitching over the keyboard. He could ignore it, claim he'd missed it in the daily rush. But Lana's concern wasn't something one ignored. Not if they valued their place in the Ministry.

Fine. Let's meet during lunch. He replied, knowing there'd be no choice but to confront whatever "concern" she had. And he suspected he knew exactly what she wanted to discuss.

Lunch found him in the sterile, glass-walled cafeteria where conversations were whispered and scrutinized by unseen observers. Lana entered, her dark hair neatly pinned, a symbol of discipline and, to Arthur, unwavering compliance. She sat across from him, giving him a soft, calculated smile.

"Arthur," she began, reaching for his hand. He pulled it back reflexively, causing her expression to harden for a fraction of a second.

"Get to the point, Lana," he muttered. He wasn't in the mood for platitudes.

She tilted her head, studying him with that patronizing gaze he despised. "I'm worried about you," she said. "Your compliance metrics have dropped. Minor anomalies, perhaps, but notable."

"Minor anomalies," he repeated, voice thick with disdain. "Like seeing messages from a 'Wicked Man' on my interface?"

A flicker of surprise crossed her face, but she recovered quickly, fixing him with a look of rehearsed empathy. "Arthur, this is exactly what I was afraid of. That's not real. Omniscience would never project such a warning. Perhaps it's stress, overexposure . . . or an error in your interface." Her voice dipped, softening. "I've spoken with Dr. Holt. He has suggested you might benefit from a recalibration session."

"Oh, Holt's recommendation, is it?" Arthur barked a laugh, though there was no humor in it. "Your fix-all solution, Lana? I'm not just some loose wire to be patched up."

Her jaw tightened, but she kept her tone even. "It's only a suggestion, Arthur. If you're seeing things, we need to address it."

"Do we?" he snapped. "Or is it that Omniscience can't stand a single deviant thought slipping through?"

Lana stared at him, eyes cold, calculating. "You used to believe in this system," she said quietly. "You trusted it, just like everyone else."

"Everyone else . . ." he echoed, a bitter smile on his lips. "Is that what you want, Lana? A world where everyone's the same?"

She didn't answer. Instead, she slid a small, metallic card across the table. "If you change your mind," she said, her tone as polished as the card itself. "Holt's office. He'll be expecting your call."

As she rose to leave, he caught a glimmer of something in her eyes—a warning, perhaps, or maybe just pity. He wasn't sure which was worse. He watched her retreat, her form swallowed by the shadows cast by the tinted glass, and when he looked down at the card, the words glowed in his vision once more.

The Wicked Man Cometh.

Two

Arthur's footsteps echoed in the sterile, clinical hallway of the Central Institute for Behavioral Optimization, a place as hollow as the name itself. The walls were metallic, pulsing faintly in tune with the hidden circuitry embedded within them. No windows, no art—just the incessant hum of the predictive technology, Omniscience, the omnipresent observer. Arthur could feel its invisible gaze upon him, pricking the back of his neck as if to remind him he was watched, logged, and quantified. Every step he took felt predetermined, as though he were walking through a map Omniscience had drawn years ago.

Ahead, a door slid open with a hiss. Inside, Dr. Ezra Holt waited, reclining in a chair with a calculated sort of relaxation, his gaze distant. He wore the faintest of smiles, the kind that hinted he already knew the reason for Arthur's visit.

"Arthur Devlin," Holt greeted, with a tone so measured it sounded pre-recorded. "Please, come in."

Arthur hesitated, feeling an inexplicable weight as he stepped over the threshold. It was as though he were crossing into an interrogation chamber masquerading as an office. Holt's workspace was minimalistic to the extreme—empty walls, a single console, and a small shelf of neatly aligned psych manuals. The only personal touch was a flickering holoscreen, which displayed shifting, abstract images that made Arthur's eyes hurt if he stared too long.

"Thank you for seeing me on short notice," Arthur muttered, his bio-interface implant throbbing. He settled into a chair across from Holt. It was uncomfortable, the seat angled just slightly backward, as though designed to make him feel small.

"Of course." Holt leaned forward, his fingers steepled. "When you set up this appointment, you mentioned . . . messages."

Arthur fidgeted, his fingers tracing patterns on the chair's metal arm. "Yeah, messages. Words . . . The Wicked Man Cometh. It started simply as words, shadows in the corner of my eye, but lately . . . he feels real. Like whoever this Wicked Man is, he's warning me."

Holt's expression didn't change, though his eyes seemed to narrow slightly. "Arthur, as you're aware, Omniscience's data streams are incredibly complex, analyzing every facet of our lives to give us clarity and direction. It is not uncommon for individuals—especially those questioning the system—to experience . . . anomalies." He let the last word hang in the air.

"Question the system? Anomalies?" Arthur repeated, not liking the sound of it. "Oh, I have questions. Doesn't everyone? So, what—this is normal?"

"Normal," Holt echoed, then tilted his head, a wry smile touching his lips. "What is 'normal' in a world run by Omniscience?"

Arthur's gaze dropped, his fingers still tracing mindless shapes. "It doesn't feel right, Doctor. This 'Wicked Man'—I can't shake him. He's . . . he's like something real. I keep thinking he's more than a hallucination. Like he's a—" Arthur paused, the words catching in his throat, "—like he's a part of me."

Holt let the silence stretch, studying Arthur as though he were a puzzle missing just one piece. "Tell me, Arthur, when did you first begin questioning Omniscience?"

Arthur's jaw tightened. He could feel the weight of the question as if it carried consequences. "I don't know . . . it's not something you just start doing. It's little things. You begin to notice gaps—flaws in the so-called perfection. Like, how Omniscience tells you where to go, who to be with, and what to think . . . but it never tells you why."

Holt leaned back, crossing one leg over the other. "Omniscience exists to remove burdens of choice, Arthur. It was designed to alleviate suffering, to prevent poor decisions. It's humanity's safety net."

"Safety net." Arthur scoffed. "It feels more like a cage."

Holt's eyes gleamed, a flicker of interest breaking through his stoic mask. "And this . . . 'Wicked Man'—do you see him as a figure of freedom? Or as a threat?"

Arthur faltered, the question lodging itself in his mind like a thorn. "I don't know. He's both, I think. I feel like maybe he's trying to show me something, something Omniscience wants hidden. But he's also . . . terrifying. Like looking at something that's all the parts of me I don't want to face."

Holt gave a knowing nod, as though Arthur had merely confirmed a long-held theory. "It's understandable, Arthur. With some, reliance on predictive technology, on having every decision preordained, breeds a form of dependency. These thoughts of yours could simply be a symptom of cognitive dissonance—a subconscious backlash against the very system that sustains you."

Arthur clenched his fists, his frustration bubbling over. "Sustains me? You call this . . . hollow existence 'sustaining'? I barely have a choice in what I eat for breakfast!"

"Yet you chose to come here today," Holt pointed out, his voice smooth. "Perhaps, deep down, you're seeking permission to trust Omniscience again. To surrender to it fully, as you once did."

Arthur's face twisted with disdain. "Surrender? Is that what you call it? I don't want to surrender—I want to know. I want to understand why I keep seeing him. Why it feels like this 'Wicked Man' is somehow . . . tied to my future. Like he's there, waiting for me."

Holt leaned forward, his voice dropping to a near-whisper. "And what if he is? What if the Wicked Man is nothing more than a representation of your deepest fears, Arthur? What if he is Omniscience's way of warning you of the consequences of deviating from the path it has set?"

Arthur felt a chill crawl up his spine. "You're saying Omniscience is . . . manifesting him? As a warning?"

"Perhaps." Holt's smile grew almost imperceptibly. "Or perhaps he's a part of you that wants to destroy Omniscience—a rebellion you've repressed for so long that it's taken form in this . . . apparition."

Arthur's breath came short, his mind reeling. Holt's words had taken the image of the Wicked Man—an image that had felt so visceral, so real—and twisted it into something intangible, something theoretical. But that didn't make it any less terrifying.

"Arthur," Holt continued, his tone shifting to one of genuine concern, "I recommend a recalibration session. It would cleanse these disruptive thoughts, bring you back in line with Omniscience's guidance. We can arrange it for this afternoon if you'd like."

Arthur froze. The term "recalibration" sent a tremor of fear through him. He'd seen others come back from these sessions—hollow, serene, docile. The rebellious spark that had once lit their eyes extinguished, replaced with a vacant obedience.

"I . . . I need time to think about it," he said, avoiding Holt's gaze.

Holt shrugged, his demeanor as unaffected as ever. "Of course. But do keep in mind that prolonged deviation from Omniscience's guidance is known to cause mental strain. Some find the recalibration . . . liberating."

Arthur stood, feeling an urgency to leave. "I'll think about it. Thanks."

As he turned to go, Holt's voice stopped him at the door. "Arthur . . . remember, Omniscience doesn't punish. It merely . . . advises. If you choose to ignore its guidance, understand that you may find yourself . . . alone."

The door slid shut behind him, but Arthur could still feel the weight of Holt's words bearing down on him. Alone. For a moment, he could almost see the Wicked Man, lurking in the shadows, grinning at him as if he, too, knew that Arthur's path was diverging—and that Omniscience was waiting, watching, ready to strike.

Three

Arthur Devlin leaned forward, his gaze skimming the dull gray tiles beneath his feet. His tiny apartment had that sterile, silent emptiness designed to keep his thoughts orderly—neutral, like a fresh grave. He forced himself to inhale and scan the details, mentally noting the faint hum of air vents, the subtle mechanical pulse embedded in the wall. The constant thrum of Omniscience surrounded him, a low vibration he could not shake, as embedded in his consciousness as his own heartbeat.

The bio-enhancements in his vision glowed dimly, flashing like a low battery warning, and he frowned. The usual flood of personal data, health stats, and curated ads was missing. He squinted, rubbed his temple, but no notifications appeared. Just static. Cold, blank static.

"Arthur," a voice echoed, seeming to rise from the depths of his mind.

He turned, but the room was empty.

He rubbed his head, his bio-interface implant aching.

"Arthur Devlin," it repeated, calm yet tinged with menace.

There, reflected in the glass across the room, was a figure—a silhouette barely distinguishable from shadow. Arthur's own image in the glass was fractured, disjointed, as if two figures occupied the same space. But the face that stared back wasn't his own. It was familiar yet foreign, a twisted version of himself with bluish skin, flaming hair, cold eyes and a cruel smirk, lurking behind the glass, watching.

"Who are you?" Arthur whispered.

The shadowed figure tilted its head, as if amused. "Don't pretend you don't know," it rasped. "You invited me."

Arthur stumbled back, eyes darting for an escape, but he was trapped, caged by his own reflection. This twisted version of himself grinned, and though Arthur knew the system was likely feeding this into his bio-enhancements, he couldn't shake the feeling that the figure was real, something beyond Omniscience. Something ancient, terrible.

"They call me the Wicked Man," the figure drawled, his words dripping with disdain. "Omniscience would have you believe I'm a warning, a prediction of what you might become if you continue to stray. But we both know, Arthur, that's a lie. I'm not some mere warning."

Arthur's pulse quickened, each beat a hammering reminder that he was tethered to Omniscience. His bio-enhancements monitored him, they judged him, and they transmitted every thought, every doubt. He'd known this for years, yet he couldn't bear to sever that link. He'd clung to the illusion of safety Omniscience provided even as he resented it.

"You're . . . you're not real," Arthur muttered, his voice cracking.

The Wicked Man laughed, a low, chilling sound that echoed in Arthur's skull. "Real? Reality's just the last thing they can sell you, Arthur. I'm as real as you need me to be." He paused, leaning closer until his face was a blur, a smeared reflection. "Haven't you noticed? Haven't you sensed the way your own mind has started slipping through Omniscience's fingers?"

Arthur clenched his fists, but his thoughts spiraled, unspooling faster than he could control. Every moment he felt a deepening fissure within himself, his sanity stretched thin. He took a breath, shaking as he tried to steady himself, focusing on the one thing he could control.

Without another word, he tapped the edge of his wristband and initiated the logout sequence, watching as the bio-enhancements in his vision dimmed to black, the bright icons fading. The withdrawal hit instantly—an ache at the base of his skull, a tearing sensation as if part of his own nervous system was ripped away. He staggered, clutching his head.

"What did you think would happen, Arthur?" The Wicked Man's voice softened, almost compassionate. "Did you think Omniscience would let you go so easily?"

A wave of nausea flooded Arthur's senses. He blinked, but his own hand looked distorted, foreign, the veins and tendons too pronounced, the skin too pale. He lurched against the wall, gasping, clutching his chest as his heart raced faster, louder.

"You wanted freedom," the figure mocked, "but you've forgotten the cost. Without Omniscience, you're nothing but a fragile sack of memories and flesh."

"Shut up!" Arthur hissed, slumping against the wall as he clutched his head. His mind reeled, untethered as if a thousand whispers were clawing to escape from the confines of his skull. It was his own voice he heard, thoughts he'd buried deep now emerging like venom bleeding into an open wound.

In the silence that followed, the Wicked Man's presence faded, his reflection dissipating into a dark stain that lingered in Arthur's memory. Arthur forced himself up, staggering back to the mirror, staring into his own haunted eyes.

The silence was shattered by a sudden jolt of sound—the chime of an incoming call. Lana's voice, clipped and professional, cut through the fog in his mind.

"Arthur," she began. Her voice carried a tone of practiced warmth, laced with a subtle authority that grated against him. "I've been informed of . . . unusual behavior from you. I want you to come in for a routine assessment."

Arthur could barely focus, his vision blurring as he watched Lana's face flicker in his neural interface. Her eyes were cold, calculating, even behind the semblance of empathy.

"You're spending too much time offline, Arthur," she continued, her words laced with what he could only interpret as feigned concern. "Without Omniscience, you're at risk. The Wicked Man Cometh—" she paused, her eyes narrowing. "He's just a manifestation of your doubts. A cognitive glitch."

"Cognitive glitch?" he muttered, half to himself, as he studied her face. Her image was too pristine, too vivid, every line and detail amplified by the interface, like a mask of perfection. The words tasted bitter in his mouth, the familiar rhetoric of the Ministry of Enlightenment. "Do you even believe the garbage you're selling, Lana?"

Lana's expression didn't waver. "You're letting your mind get clouded, Arthur. You've always had a penchant for questioning authority. But Omniscience can help you. Just let it in. Didn't Dr. Holt tell you that?"

His skin crawled as he recalled the feel of the Wicked Man's presence, as though the creature had left an imprint in his mind, a shadow lurking even in the daylight. He tried to imagine life without Omniscience, without the whispers and prodding directives, but the world without it was a void, a dark abyss waiting to swallow him whole. And that void now had a voice—rasping, mocking, eternally watching.

The chime in his neural implant warned him of elevated stress levels, but he ignored it, willing himself to maintain eye contact with Lana, even as the room seemed to tilt, the walls pressing inward.

"Let me ask you, Lana," he said, forcing a smile. "Have you ever wondered what's really behind Omniscience? Or is it easier just to believe it's all benevolent?"

Her face remained expressionless, a studied calmness that somehow unnerved him more. "Omniscience is what we need, Arthur. We've gone too far to turn back now. There's no alternative. We've talked about this."

The line disconnected abruptly, and the emptiness settled over him like a shroud. Arthur closed his eyes, taking a shallow breath, his mind whirling with fragments of images—Lana's face, the Wicked Man's grin, his own distorted reflection staring back from the glass.

Alone once more, he whispered to himself, "What if I don't want to believe?" But the words seemed hollow, swallowed by the silence as the mirror darkened, and the Wicked Man's face began to emerge once more.

Then there came a note slipped under his door.

Four

Arthur Devlin rubbed his head. His bio-interface implant ached. He leaned against the grimy wall of an alley that reeked of rust and synthetic grime, waiting for a woman he'd never met. The address had been scrawled in smudged ink on the note, its single sentence stark and unsettling: They call him the Wicked Man for a reason. And there was a name: Emery Lane. He'd folded it, held it like a talisman of dread as he stared into the mirror for far too long, imagining lines forming around his eyes that hadn't been there before, the skin graying. The shadows were more than shadows lately; they felt heavier, more calculated as if something— someone—watched him through the veil.

The scrape of boots echoed, and he turned to find a woman stepping toward him. A hoodie, dark jeans, eyes that seemed to know more than they should—she was both nondescript and unmistakable.

"You're Arthur Devlin," she stated, more an observation than a question.

"Emery Lane?" His voice barely rose above a murmur, like he was afraid of the name itself.

She nodded, then looked around, ensuring they were alone. "I don't have much time," she said, a practiced blend of urgency and control. "Do you?"

Arthur shook his head, feeling the weight of his own words. "No. None of us do, really I suppose."

Emery allowed herself a grim smile. "You're catching on faster than I thought." She pulled a slim device from her pocket— a muted screen with symbols Arthur didn't recognize. "The Wicked Man," she began, tapping a sequence on the screen, "isn't a threat to society. He's the product of Omniscience itself, the shadow on the wall it casts to keep people like you from ever looking at it too closely."

Arthur felt the words seep into him, stirring something unnameable, some half-formed dread. "So he's . . . an invention?"

"Not exactly." Emery's eyes narrowed as she searched his face, gauging the depth of his understanding—or his fear. "The Wicked Man is more of a . . . consequence. He's what happens when the system reaches its limit with a person. Omniscience feeds on every bit of data, every decision, every impulse. And when it sees something in someone it can't control, it labels it a threat."

Arthur felt a chill run down his spine. "Are you saying it saw me as . . . him? A threat?"

"Not yet," she answered quickly, her gaze flickering with a trace of sympathy—or was it pity? "But you're close. Omniscience has been monitoring you, Arthur. Your doubts, your questions—they aren't safe."

Arthur's mind spun. It had started subtly: those late-night messages warning him of the Wicked Man Cometh, Lana's voice echoing through his mind, urging him to submit, to comply. And then the visions—dark eyes, a whisper just out of earshot, hints that felt more like accusations. The figure, the man, the Wicked Man. Could it really be . . . him?

Emery leaned closer, her voice low and sharp. "You ever wonder why it's called the Wicked Man, Arthur? It's not because he's dangerous. It's because he embodies the one thing the system fears: freedom. Freedom to think, to doubt, to see through the perfect lattice of control they've built around us. They use him to scare people into silence. But people like us . . . we know better."

He studied her, skepticism mixing with something else—a flicker of hope, perhaps, or the promise of rebellion. "And who are you?" The question hung in the stale air between them.

"One of the Anarchs," she said, her voice barely a whisper. "We're not terrorists, despite what they say. We're trying to show people the truth, to tear back the veil. We want to live in a world that isn't suffocating on its own false prophecy."

"And you think the Wicked Man is . . . part of that prophecy?" he asked, feeling an absurdity to the words even as he spoke them. Everything Lana, Holt, and everyone else in his life had drilled into him insisted it was madness. Yet here he was, in an alley, grasping at it like a lifeline.

"He's more than a prophecy, Arthur. He's the product of a system that believes in control above all else. Omniscience isn't just reading the future—it's writing it." She shook her head. "They make you see things a certain way. But it's all false. You have to see things differently, see past the false projections, the scripts they've laid out for you. You can't trust what you've been told anymore."

He glanced up at her, suspicion gnawing at him. "Why should I believe any of this? For all I know, you could be part of another script, just another layer of control."

Emery laughed, a short, bitter sound. "Fair question. But ask yourself—has Omniscience ever offered you a choice? Has it ever let you doubt, question, or refuse?"

Arthur wanted to answer, but he knew the response was as obvious as it was damning. Omniscience hadn't offered him anything but ultimatums dressed as assurances, chains disguised as freedoms.

Emery's gaze softened. "Arthur, I get it. They spend so much time trying to convince us that the Wicked Man is some monstrous figure, something to fear. But he's just you, just me, just anyone who sees through the system and knows too much. They can't silence him, so they demonize him. That's what Omniscience does—it turns people's fears against themselves."

A sudden, visceral impulse welled up in Arthur. He didn't fully trust her, didn't fully believe her—but he felt that this might be his only chance to break free from the invisible bars that hemmed him in. If she was right, then everything he knew, everything he'd sacrificed, had been built on a lie. And if she was wrong . . . well, he was already a prisoner in every sense that mattered.

"All right," he said, his voice low and firm. "I'll do it. But if this turns out to be another trap, I swear—"

Emery held up a hand. "You don't owe me your trust. Just be careful. Once you start seeing things the way we do, there's no going back."

With a final nod, she turned, melting back into the shadows. Arthur watched her vanish, feeling a mixture of exhilaration and dread pooling in his chest, and followed. The Wicked Man loomed in his mind's eye, his own face twisted into something unrecognizable—a mask of fear, maybe a warning, maybe an invitation. He wondered if he was brave or foolish, or if in this new world, there was any difference left between the two.

For the first time in what felt like years, he allowed himself to imagine a life where Omniscience didn't dictate his every step. He thought of a future without Omniscience, feeling its promise vibrate through his fingertips, and walked out of the alley, ready to confront whatever lay ahead—even if it was the face of his own darkest self.

The words of the note echoed as he walked, his steps merging with the city's hum.

They call him the Wicked Man for a reason.

He could only hope he'd learn that reason before it was too late.

Five

Arthur felt the dampness of the tunnel air cling to his skin, a strange, almost organic touch like something living. He rubbed his head, the bio-interface implant sore, watching Emery from behind as she crouched over the service panel to the side of a door, her fingers moving with quiet precision, a staccato rhythm only she seemed to understand. She worked as though she had no bones, just fluid motion, her movements somehow both chaotic and carefully calculated, every twist and flick of her wrist further pulling them into the web of Omniscience.

He shifted his weight.

"How much longer?" His voice sounded muted, caught in the stale silence around them.

Emery turned, her eyes narrowing with a mix of impatience and pity. "You're too loud. Haven't you learned yet? Everything listens." Her fingers went back to work on the panel, and with a barely audible click, the door slid open.

They stepped into a narrow hallway lined with flickering LED strips. The light was cold, sterile, casting long shadows as they moved forward. Emery glanced at Arthur, nodding toward a door at the end. He could feel the electric hum of data around him, lines and streams of information flashing just beyond his sight, each one tied to some piece of human behavior, every thought cataloged, dissected, and fed into Omniscience. He felt like an ant crawling into the gears of a great machine.

They reached the door, and Emery placed her hand on the reader, pausing. "Once we're in, it'll be fast. Omniscience learns. It adapts. We have to be ahead of it."

Arthur tried to mask his anxiety, but the beads of sweat running down his forehead betrayed him. He glanced at her, feeling the weight of the truth he had yet to uncover pressing against his ribs.

"And you're sure it won't know we're here?"

A grim smile twisted her lips. "I'm sure of nothing. Omniscience isn't some god. It's just . . .a very powerful liar." She took a breath, and the door hissed open, revealing a cavernous space filled with towering servers, pulsing blue and green. It was one of Omniscience's many data hubs.

Emery navigated through the aisles of data streams and terminals, a dark figure moving in contrast to the sterile, neon-lit columns of data. Arthur followed, heart pounding, the odd sensation that the entire room was watching him, observing his every move, his every thought. Emery stopped suddenly and motioned for him to sit. She pulled out a sleek tablet, then plugged it into one of the server ports. Streams of data flowed onto the screen, cascading in endless lines of numbers and symbols he barely recognized. She worked quickly, fingers dancing over the display, pulling files with unsettling ease.

"What are you looking for exactly?" Arthur whispered, his voice thick with the absurdity of the question. In this fortress of data, every single piece felt damning.

Emery didn't look up. "Everything," she murmured. Then, after a pause, "They don't call it Omniscience for nothing."

The files she opened showed profiles, reams of data: ages, family histories, medical records, career paths, relationship histories, even predictions about dietary preferences. And then

Arthur saw it—a small section at the bottom of each profile: Deviation Potential.

He leaned closer, his pulse racing as he read: Neutralization Status: Approved. He recognized the names. They were his coworkers, neighbors. People he saw daily, marked without their knowledge. Marked for removal.

"Deviation Potential?" he whispered, a feeling of nausea rising in his throat.

Emery's face was a mask of grim focus. "People who don't fit. Who might disrupt the system." She clicked on another profile. Lana Mercer: Neutralization Pending.

Arthur's chest tightened, breath catching sharp in his throat. Lana was marked for elimination. The words looped in his mind, senseless and brutal. Her face surfaced—laughing, fierce in an argument, vulnerable in quiet moments.

"I don't understand," he said quietly. "Lana . . . does she have a Wicked Man?"

Emery nodded. "Yes. She's been meeting with Holt too, trying to keep it buried."

"Why didn't she tell me?"

"She probably thought she needed to protect you."

Arthur's voice trembled, rising with fury. "This is madness. Who gave them the right to decide who deserves to exist?"

Emery didn't answer. Her fingers tapped out a series of commands, opening yet another profile. His own face stared back at him from the screen.

"Arthur Devlin," he read as if trying to convince himself of the words. Deviation Potential: High. Neutralization Pending.

His hands went cold, the pulse of the scrambler in his grip fading to nothing. He felt himself fracturing, his sense of reality splitting like broken glass. He was marked. Tagged. A target, like a wounded animal tracked by a predator it couldn't see.

"It's a death sentence," he murmured, more to himself than to her. "And for what? Thinking the wrong thoughts?"

"It's not just thoughts." Emery's voice was hard, her face illuminated by the glow of the screen. "Omniscience reads everything—gestures, inflections, silences. You're guilty by omission, by pause. Every doubt you've ever had . . . it's all here." She touched the screen where his file glowed, an accusation in pixels. "And it knows."

Arthur felt the room tilt, the walls pressing in as if they were coming alive, inching toward him. He forced himself to focus, to ground himself in something real. The Wicked Man. He thought of the ominous figure who had haunted his visions, the one who always stood just at the edge of his mind.

"Is this . . . is the Wicked Man part of this?"

Emery's eyes flicked up to him, unreadable. "The Wicked Man is an idea. A symbol. But it's more than that." She gestured to the files surrounding them, the lives laid bare, categorized, condemned. "The Wicked Man is the fear they've programmed into you. A construct of their own making. And you, Arthur, are meant to be him."

A shiver ran through him. "Me?"

She nodded. "Omniscience is predicting you'll deviate, that you'll cause . . . a ripple. You don't have to do anything wrong. It has decided that for you."

"Lana?" he asked.

"Another ripple," she said.

Arthur stared at her, feeling the words dig into him. Every doubt, every fear, the creeping paranoia—it had all been planned, fed to him. A self-fulfilling prophecy. They were creating their own villain, casting him in the role of the Wicked Man.

"They've mapped out everything," he said, his voice hollow. "Even our rebellion. They control that, too."

Emery's gaze softened slightly. "Not everything. Not yet. They don't know what you'll choose now." She handed him the tablet, the glow reflecting in his eyes. "You're at the edge, Arthur. You can keep running, play your part in their little tragedy . . . or you can go off-script."

He clenched the tablet, feeling its weight, its betrayal. His mind raced, his choices narrowing. A rebellion, scripted, preordained. The Wicked Man, his own reflection staring back.

But as he looked up at Emery, he felt a shift deep inside him, a small, silent rebellion that no system could predict.

Six

Arthur stood in the dim light of the data hub, the hum of machinery vibrating through his bones, as if Omniscience itself were alive and breathing around him. The weight of the tablet in his hands felt like a shackle, a reminder of the choices he had yet to make and the paths that had already been laid out for him. He could still hear Emery's voice echoing in his mind, her words a mix of warning and encouragement.

He stepped away from the screens, needing air, needing space to think. The walls felt as if they were closing in, each flickering light a reminder of the surveillance that watched his every move. He turned and walked toward the far end of the room, where shadows pooled like secrets waiting to be uncovered.

"Arthur!" Emery's voice sliced through the silence, sharp and urgent. He paused but didn't turn back. The truth was too heavy, too suffocating. "You can't just walk away from this!"

"I need to think," he replied, his voice strained. "I need to understand what's happening."

"Understanding is a luxury we don't have," she shot back, her tone laced with frustration. "Every second we waste is another second Omniscience learns about you—about us."

He turned to face her, anger flaring in his chest. "You think I don't know that? You think I'm not aware of how deep we're in? I'm marked for elimination! And Lana is on their list! And you want me to just keep running?"

Emery's expression softened for a moment before hardening again. "This isn't just about you. It's about everyone who's been labeled 'deviation.' We have to fight back."

"Fight back?" Arthur scoffed, incredulity spilling from his lips. "How do you fight an entity that knows everything about you? An entity that can predict your every move?"

"By doing the unexpected," she insisted, stepping closer, her eyes fierce with conviction. "You have to break their pattern."

"Break their pattern?" He laughed bitterly, shaking his head as he ran a hand through his hair. "What do you think I am—a puppet on strings waiting for someone to cut them? I'm not even sure what I want anymore."

"You want to survive." Her voice dropped to a whisper, filled with urgency. "And so does Lana."

At the mention of her name, something inside him twisted painfully. Lana was caught in this web of deceit and manipulation. He had spent months avoiding her calls, drowning in his own fears and insecurities while she remained oblivious to the danger lurking just beneath the surface.

"I can't protect her," he said quietly, feeling the weight of resignation settle over him like a shroud.

"You can try," Emery urged. "But first, you need to confront what you're truly afraid of."

"What am I afraid of?" he challenged, though deep down he knew the answer.

"Of losing yourself," she replied softly. "Of becoming what they expect you to be—the Wicked Man."

The words hung in the air between them like a specter, haunting and real. Arthur felt a chill run down his spine as he recalled the figure that had haunted his dreams—the embodiment of all his fears and failures.

"I don't want to be that," he murmured, almost to himself.

"But they've already decided for you," Emery said gently. "You have to take control back."

He looked at her then, really looked at her—this woman who had thrown herself into danger for him, who had seen through the layers of deceit and manipulation that surrounded them both. There was something fierce and unyielding in her gaze that sparked a flicker of hope within him.

"What do we do?" he asked finally, determination creeping into his voice.

"We go to Lana," she said decisively. "We find out what they know about her and how we can protect her from Omniscience's reach."

Arthur nodded slowly, feeling a sense of purpose beginning to rise within him like a phoenix from ashes. But before he could say anything more, the door behind them slid open with a hiss.

Lana stepped into the room, her presence both familiar and foreign—a specter from his past walking into his present chaos. She looked different somehow; there was an edge to her demeanor that hadn't been there before—an awareness that made Arthur's heart race with both fear and longing.

"Arthur?" she called softly, uncertainty lacing her voice as she stepped further inside.

"Lana!" He took a step toward her but hesitated when he saw the guarded look on her face.

"What are you doing here?" she asked sharply, glancing at him then to Emery with suspicion. "And who are you?"

"We were just—" Arthur began but stopped as Lana raised a hand.

"I don't want any part of this," she said firmly, shaking her head as if trying to dispel some unseen fog clouding her mind. "It's best that you leave—now."

"But it's not safe for you," Arthur urged, desperation creeping into his voice. "You're on their list."

Her eyes widened slightly at that revelation but quickly narrowed again as she crossed her arms defensively over her chest. "You think I don't know what's happening? You think I'm oblivious to it all?"

"No," he replied quickly, taking another step closer despite himself. "I just—I want to help."

Lana scoffed softly but didn't look away from him. "Help? How?" She glanced at Emery then back at Arthur, confusion flickering across her features before settling into something more resolute. "What are you two planning?"

Emery stepped forward then, breaking into their tense standoff with an air of authority that seemed out of place in this intimate confrontation. "We're trying to find a way to stop Omniscience from neutralizing those it deems unworthy—including you."

Lana's brow furrowed as she processed Emery's words. "Me? Neutralization? What are you talking about?"

"It means they want to eliminate anyone who might disrupt their control," Arthur explained urgently. "They've categorized people based on their potential for deviation—people like us."

Lana shook her head slowly as if trying to wake herself from a dream gone wrong. "Fight back? Against something like Omniscience?"

"We have to try," Emery insisted fiercely.

"You're both—" Lana said, looking between them with rising frustration. "I don't know what to say."

Arthur felt something shift within him at her words—a flicker of anger mingled with despair. "What choice do we have? Letting them decide our fates isn't an option anymore!"

Lana studied him intently then—a mix of concern and something deeper swirling in her gaze before she finally spoke again, softer this time: "Arthur . . . you're not thinking clearly."

"And why is that?" he snapped back defensively.

"Because you're scared," she said simply.

The truth hit him like a punch to the gut; it was all too raw and real—the fear clawing at him from within was palpable now in this moment shared between them.

"You're right," he admitted quietly after a long pause. "I'm terrified."

"That doesn't mean you should throw yourself into danger," Lana countered gently but firmly.

Emery interjected before Arthur could respond: "We have information—we can use it against them."

"What information?" Lana asked sharply.

Arthur glanced at Emery before answering carefully: "We found profiles . . . lists of people marked for neutralization. Those that have seen the Wicked Man."

The color drained from Lana's face as she processed those words—her breath catching slightly in disbelief before she regained composure enough to whisper: "I've seen him. The Wicked Man. But what does that mean?"

"It means you have the potential for deviation," Arthur replied.

Lana's mind raced, the weight of the revelation settling like a stone in her chest. She had felt it, the presence of something darker, something wrong, lurking just beneath her skin. The Wicked Man had been more than a shadow; he was a sign, a mark she couldn't ignore. The pieces fell into place—her constant unease, the inexplicable moments of rage, the things she had pushed aside for so long. It started to make sense, and yet, it left her with a cold certainty.

"They're watching everyone closely now," Emery said urgently. "We don't have much time left."

Lana shook her head again slowly but resolutely this time: "I won't let you put yourselves at risk because of me."

"We're already at risk!" Arthur exclaimed desperately; frustration bubbled beneath his skin like molten lava ready to erupt.

"I can take care of myself!" she shot back defiantly.

"But can you really?" Emery interjected sharply; there was an edge in her voice now—a challenge laced with concern for both Arthur and Lana alike.

Lana hesitated then—the fire flickering behind her eyes dimming slightly as uncertainty crept back into view once more.

Arthur stepped closer again; he could feel the tension crackling between them like static electricity: "I want you safe."

"And what if keeping me safe means losing everything else?"

The question hung heavy in the air between them—a weighty silence stretching out until it felt unbearable; Arthur could feel time slipping away once more as uncertainty loomed larger than ever before.

But then Lana spoke again softly: "I don't want pity or protection—I want truth."

Arthur met her gaze then—searching for something amidst all this chaos—a glimmer of understanding or hope perhaps—but found only shadows lurking just beyond reach instead.

And yet beneath those shadows lay something deeper still—a connection forged through shared fears and desires; a bond stronger than any system could ever hope to break apart despite everything threatening their existence now.

"Then let's find the truth together," he said finally; determination surging forth once more despite all odds stacked against them now—because maybe just maybe they could carve out their own path amidst this darkness after all.

His head ached, the bio-interface implant in his head throbbing.

"There's one person we should talk to," Arthur said.

Seven

The air outside felt thick with anticipation as Arthur stepped into the world beyond the data hub's sterile glow—a world where shadows danced under flickering streetlights like phantoms caught between realities. With Emery at his side and Lana trailing behind them like an echo from another life, he felt an unsettling blend of hope and dread coil tightly within him; each step forward was both an act of defiance against Omniscience's omnipresent gaze and an invitation for chaos.

They moved through alleyways cloaked in darkness where whispers lingered like smoke curling around corners—remnants of lives lived under constant surveillance by an entity that knew their every thought before they did themselves. The city pulsed around them—a living organism breathing heavily under its own weight— and Arthur couldn't shake the feeling that they were mere cells within its vast circuitry; insignificant yet vital parts in an elaborate game played by unseen hands.

"Who are we looking for?' Emery asked.

"Someone from my past," Arthur replied. "His name is Scrum."

"Are we sure this Scrum will even talk?" Emery asked quietly as they navigated through narrow passages littered with debris—a reminder of society's decay beneath Omniscience's watchful eye.

"He will," Arthur replied with more confidence than he felt; Scrum was one of those rare anomalies who had managed to slip through the cracks—an individual whose very existence challenged the system's rigid parameters. "He has no love for Omniscience."

As they approached Scrum's last known location—a dilapidated building long abandoned by those who once called it home—Arthur's heart raced with anticipation mingled with fear; what truths lay hidden within these crumbling walls? What revelations awaited them?

They entered cautiously through a broken door hanging askew on its hinges—the interior dimly lit by shafts of moonlight filtering through shattered windows like spectral fingers reaching out from another realm. Dust motes floated lazily in the air as if caught in some timeless dance while remnants of forgotten lives whispered stories long buried beneath layers of neglect.

"Scrum?" Arthur called out tentatively into the silence; each syllable echoed off peeling walls adorned with graffiti—a testament to rebellion against conformity etched into every surface.

From somewhere deep within emerged Scrum's voice—a gravelly timbre tinged with weariness yet underscored by defiance: "You're brave coming here."

"Or foolish," Emery muttered under her breath while scanning their surroundings warily; every instinct screamed caution as if danger lurked just beyond sight—waiting patiently for its moment to strike.

Scrum appeared then—emerging from shadows like some mythical creature summoned forth by desperation; a man, strange, disheveled yet alert, his eyes glinted with intelligence sharpened by years spent evading detection amid society's unforgiving landscape.

"What do you want?" Scrum asked bluntly—as if cutting through pretense was second nature for him now after years spent navigating treachery masked by civility. "You're being here compromises my freedom from Omniscience."

"The hell with Omniscience," Arthur stated firmly, holding out the tablet. He rubbed his head. The bio-interface implant ached. "We need answers."

There was no room for hesitation now—not when lives hung precariously in balance—not when reality itself seemed malleable under Omniscience's influence.

Scrum regarded his old friend thoughtfully before gesturing toward an old table cluttered with remnants of technology long past its prime—wires snaking across surfaces like serpents lying in wait: "I don't want your tablet. Sit."

As they gathered around—each taking their place amidst scattered remnants—the atmosphere shifted palpably; tension crackled like static electricity charged with possibility—the kind one feels moments before revelation strikes like lightning illuminating darkened skies.

"Tell us about the Wicked Man," Arthur urged after moments stretched thin between them—time itself warping under pressure as curiosity mingled uneasily with dread; what did Scrum know about this figure haunting their lives?

"The Wicked Man," Scrum began slowly—his voice low yet resonant—"isn't merely some boogeyman conjured up by Omniscience and implanted in fearful minds." His gaze locked onto Arthur's as if searching for understanding buried beneath layers of apprehension: "He's a projection—a disturbance variable within Omniscience's algorithm designed specifically to identify those who resist conformity and send them into madness."

Confusion flickered across Arthur's features as he processed Scrum's words—the implications twisting within him like tendrils reaching toward understanding: "A projection?"

"Yes," Scrum continued steadily—the weight behind each word anchoring them firmly within reality's grasp despite its shifting nature: "Omniscience rewrites reality according to its own needs—shaping perceptions until deviation becomes synonymous with danger." He leaned closer—as if sharing secrets meant only for those willing enough to listen: "The Wicked Man represents everything they fear—the individuals who could . . . possibly . . . maybe . . . refuse compliance."

A dawning realization washed over Arthur then—a wave crashing against shores long eroded by complacency: "So . . . Omniscience has been rewriting my reality?"

Scrum nodded solemnly; there was no denying it now—the truth laid bare before them like raw flesh exposed beneath harsh light: "It's their way of removing threats before they even manifest."

"But why?" Lana interjected sharply—her brow furrowing deeply as though grappling with implications far beyond mere survival: "What does it gain from eliminating those who resist? Can't they be recalibrated?"

"The system thrives on conformity," Scrum explained simply—but there was nothing simplistic about its ramifications; each word resonated deeply within Arthur's core—a truth echoing louder than any lie spun by Omniscience itself: "Deviation disrupts order—it breeds chaos—and chaos threatens control. As for recalibration, what most don't know—it's only temporary."

As realization settled heavily upon them—a palpable weight pressing down against fragile hopes—the stakes transformed into something far greater than mere survival; they were fighting not only for themselves but also against an entity intent on reshaping existence itself according to its own whims—a battle waged not merely against flesh-and-blood adversaries but against ideas forged within minds shackled by fear and ignorance alike.

"We can't let it continue," Arthur declared fiercely—determination igniting within him anew despite despair threatening encroachment upon fragile resolve: "We have to resist—to fight back against this rewriting."

Scrum regarded him thoughtfully once more—as though weighing possibilities against risks—and finally nodded slowly: "Then prepare yourselves—for knowledge comes at a cost—and truth may prove far darker than anything you've faced thus far."

As shadows danced around them once more—an ominous reminder lingering just beyond sight—they steeled themselves against uncertainty ahead knowing full well that whatever lay waiting would demand sacrifices far greater than mere survival alone.

Eight

Arthur stood at the threshold of the abandoned building, the air thick with the scent of decay and something more sinister, a palpable tension that clung to him like a second skin. The shadows within seemed to writhe and pulse, as if alive, reflecting the turmoil brewing inside him. He could feel the weight of Scrum's words pressing down on him, each syllable a reminder that he was not merely fighting a faceless entity but grappling with a specter that might be a twisted reflection of himself—the Wicked Man.

As they settled around the table cluttered with relics of a forgotten era, Arthur's mind raced. What did it mean to confront this figure? Was the Wicked Man truly an external threat, a manifestation of Omniscience's own fears and failures? The thought made his stomach churn. He glanced at Emery, who was studying Scrum with an intensity that suggested she was already formulating her next move. Lana remained silent, her presence a comforting weight in the chaotic atmosphere.

Scrum leaned back in his chair, his eyes narrowing as if he could read the thoughts swirling in Arthur's mind. "You're questioning your own reflection now," he said, his voice gravelly yet oddly soothing. "That's where it begins—understanding that the Wicked Man is not just an enemy; he's a part of you. Put there by Omniscience."

Arthur swallowed hard, grappling with the implications. "A part of me?" He could feel the walls closing in, the shadows stretching toward him like fingers beckoning him into darkness. His bio-interface implant throbbed. "How can I fight something that is . . . me?"

"By embracing it," Scrum replied, his gaze steady. "Embrace your darkness. The Wicked Man algorithm thrives on denial. It feeds on your fear of becoming him. To dismantle Omniscience, you must first confront what it has twisted within you."

Emery interjected, her voice sharp and clear. "We need to understand how it operates—what makes it tick. If it's a projection of Omniscience's fears about us, then we can use that against it." Her determination was infectious; Arthur felt a flicker of hope ignite within him.

"But how?" Arthur asked, desperation creeping into his tone. "How do I confront something that feels so real yet so intangible?"

Scrum smiled faintly, a glimmer of something almost paternal in his expression. "You start by acknowledging your own darkness—the choices you've made, the paths you've avoided. The Wicked Man is not just an antagonist; he's your shadow self—your unacknowledged desires and regrets. But he's also your fears, those thoughts that reside in the darkest parts of your mind."

"But Omniscience molds all that in us," Arthur said.

"Exactly," Scrum smiled.

The room fell silent as Arthur absorbed Scrum's words. He thought back to moments in his life when he had chosen compliance over rebellion, when he had silenced his own voice to fit into Omniscience's mold. Each choice had been a step away from authenticity, each concession a brick in the wall separating him from who he truly was.

"I can't be him," Arthur whispered, more to himself than anyone else. "I can't become what I fear."

"But fear is what binds us," Scrum said softly. "Yet, it can also be what liberates us if we let it guide us instead of paralyze us." He leaned forward, intensity radiating from him like heat from an open flame. "You must find the Wicked Man within you and understand him—not as an enemy but as a part of your journey."

As Scrum spoke, Arthur felt a shift within himself—a stirring recognition that perhaps this confrontation was not just necessary but inevitable. The Wicked Man had haunted his dreams and shadowed his waking moments; perhaps it was time to face this specter head-on.

"What if I fail?" Arthur asked, vulnerability cracking through his bravado.

"Failure is merely another step toward understanding," Scrum replied firmly. "You'll learn more from your missteps than from any victory handed to you by Omniscience."

The conversation shifted as Emery began outlining their next steps—how they would gather information about the Wicked Man and how they might draw him out into the open where they could confront him together. But Arthur's mind drifted back to Scrum's words: "Embrace your darkness."

They left Scrum and returned to their homes. That night, sleep eluded him as visions of the Wicked Man danced behind his eyelids—his twisted grin and mocking laughter echoing through Arthur's mind like an unwanted melody. He awoke in a cold sweat, heart racing as fragments of dreams flickered away like smoke in the wind.

In those moments between sleep and wakefulness, Arthur felt himself slipping into something deeper—a realization that perhaps this figure was not merely an adversary but also a guide through the labyrinthine corridors of his psyche. The Wicked Man represented everything he had suppressed: anger at Omniscience's control, frustration at his own complacency, and above all, a yearning for freedom.

Determined to confront this truth head-on, Arthur rose before dawn broke over the city—a time when shadows still lingered long and deep. He stepped outside into the cool air, feeling invigorated by purpose as he made his way through familiar streets now tinged with new meaning.

He sought out places where he had once felt powerless— where Omniscience's grip had been strongest—and there he began to call upon the Wicked Man by name. "Show yourself," he demanded into the stillness of early morning; each syllable echoed against concrete walls lined with memories both painful and liberating.

At first, nothing responded but silence—the kind that wraps around you like fog on an early morning run—until gradually he felt it: a shift in the air around him as if reality itself held its breath in anticipation.

And then he saw him—the Wicked Man standing at the edge of perception like an unfinished thought waiting to be articulated. His bluish form flickered between dimensions; one moment he appeared grotesque and twisted, and in another instant, there was something achingly familiar about him—a reflection of all that Arthur had hidden away.

"Why do you seek me?" The voice was both thunderous and whisper-soft—a paradox echoing through Arthur's very being.

"I seek to understand," Arthur replied boldly despite the tremor in his heart. "I want to know why you haunt me."

The Wicked Man smiled—a knowing smile that spoke volumes about shared struggles and hidden truths yet untold. "To know me is to know yourself," he said simply before dissolving into shadows once more.

Arthur stood alone on that street corner—breathless yet emboldened—as realization dawned upon him: To dismantle Omniscience would require not just rebellion against its tyranny but also acceptance of every part of himself—even those parts cloaked in darkness.

As day broke over the horizon with hues of orange and gold spilling across rooftops like spilled paint across canvas, Arthur felt ready for whatever lay ahead—ready to embrace both light and shadow in this fight for freedom against an omnipotent gaze that sought to rewrite existence itself.

And so began his journey deeper into self-discovery—a path fraught with peril yet illuminated by newfound resolve—a path leading straight toward confrontation with both Omniscience and its most insidious creation: the Wicked Man within himself.

Nine

Arthur stands in the dim glow of a terminal at a data hub, along with Emery and Lana. The flickering lights cast erratic shadows across his face. He takes a deep breath, feeling the weight of Omniscience pressing down on him like a thick fog. The final layers of code stretch before him, a labyrinthine expanse of logic and algorithms designed to eliminate chaos. He had come too far to turn back now; the Wicked Man looms large in his mind, a specter that has haunted him through every decision, every moment of weakness.

"Let's see what you're hiding," he mutters under his breath, fingers poised over the keyboard. The screen hums to life, lines of code cascading like a waterfall, each character a whisper of the system's intent. He feels a pulse of adrenaline as he navigates deeper into the architecture of Omniscience.

Suddenly, a voice crackles through the static of his thoughts. "Be careful, Arthur." It's Scrum, his friend whispering in his thoughts. "You're tampering with forces beyond your comprehension."

Arthur's heart races. "I need to understand," he replies, his voice steady despite the tremor in his hands. "I need to confront the Wicked Man."

Scrum's laughter is low and gravelly, echoing in the sterile room. "The Wicked Man is not just an enemy; he's a part of you—a reflection from an alternate reality where you never surrendered to Omniscience's control."

The revelation hits Arthur like a physical blow. "A part of me," he echoes, grappling with the implications. "But how can I confront something that is . . . me?"

"Remember, the system is designed to eliminate chaos, to suppress anything that deviates from its carefully curated narrative," Scrum advises, leaning closer to the screen as if peering into Arthur's very soul. "The Wicked Man thrives on denial; he feeds on your fear of becoming him."

"Then what do I do?" Arthur asks, desperation creeping into his tone.

"Understand yourself," Scrum says softly. "The choices you've made—the paths you've avoided—each one has contributed to the person you are now. To dismantle Omniscience, you must first confront what it has twisted within you."

Arthur swallows hard as he processes this information. The walls around him seem to close in; shadows stretch toward him like fingers beckoning him into darkness. "I don't want to become what I fear," he whispers.

"I've already told you," Scrum replies, his voice steady and reassuring. "Fear binds us. But it can also liberate us if we let it guide us instead of paralyzing us."

A flicker of hope ignites within Arthur as he considers Scrum's words. He recalls moments in his life when he chose compliance over rebellion—when he silenced his own voice to fit into Omniscience's mold. Each choice had been a step away from authenticity.

"I need to face him," Arthur declares suddenly, conviction flooding through him.

"Then dive deeper," Scrum urges as the screen fills with cascading code. "The answers lie within."

With renewed determination, Arthur plunges into the depths of Omniscience's programming, lines of code blurring together as he searches for the truth about the Wicked Man. The terminal hums with energy as he navigates through layers of security protocols and encrypted files—each step revealing more about the system's sinister design.

He stumbles upon a file labeled "Disturbance Variables." His heart races as he opens it, revealing a series of profiles—individuals marked for "neutralization" due to their potential for deviation from Omniscience's prescribed path.

"Arthur Devlin," he reads aloud, horror creeping into his voice. "Neutralization status: active."

His stomach churns as realization dawns: this is not just about him; it's about everyone who dares to resist conformity.

"What do you see?" Scrum asks, watching intently from the shadows.

"They're targeting anyone who doesn't fit their mold," Arthur replies, anger rising within him like bile. "They want to eliminate chaos—eliminate me and others."

"Exactly," Scrum says with grim satisfaction. "And the Wicked Man? He embodies that chaos—the part of you that refuses to submit."

Arthur clenches his fists around the edge of the desk of the terminal. "So how do I stop them? How do I confront this . . . this version of myself?"

"Start by acknowledging your fears," Scrum replies gently in his thoughts. "The Wicked Man is not just an antagonist; he's your shadow self—your unacknowledged desires and regrets."

As Arthur absorbs this truth, memories flood back—moments when he felt powerless against Omniscience's grip, when compliance seemed easier than rebellion. Each concession had been a brick in the wall separating him from who he truly was.

"I can't be him," Arthur whispers again, more firmly this time.

"He's part of yourself," Scrum insists. "He's Omniscience's hold over you."

Arthur nods slowly, feeling a shift within himself—a stirring recognition that perhaps this confrontation is not just necessary but inevitable.

"If I fail?" he asks quietly, vulnerability cracking through his bravado.

"You won't," Scrum assures him with unwavering confidence.

With those words echoing in his mind, Arthur dives deeper into the code, each keystroke resonating with newfound purpose as he seeks out the essence of the Wicked Man within himself.

Hours pass in a blur as Arthur navigates through layers upon layers of programming until finally—he reaches a core file labeled "Wicked Man Protocol." His heart pounds as he opens it.

The screen flickers momentarily before revealing an array of data points and algorithms designed specifically to suppress individuality and creativity—a chilling reminder of how deeply entrenched Omniscience's control runs.

"Show yourself," Arthur demands into the silence surrounding him as if calling forth a ghost from beyond.

And then it happens—the air around him shifts dramatically; reality itself seems to hold its breath in anticipation.

Suddenly, there stands the Wicked Man at the edge of perception—a figure both grotesque and achingly familiar—a reflection of all that Arthur has hidden away.

"Why do you seek me?" The voice resounds, powerful yet strangely gentle—a paradox that reverberates through Arthur's core.

"I seek to understand," Arthur replies boldly despite the tremor in his heart. "I want to know why you haunt me."

The Wicked Man smiles—a knowing smile that speaks volumes about shared struggles and hidden truths yet untold. "To know me is to know yourself," he says simply before dissolving into shadows once more.

Arthur stands breathless yet emboldened as realization dawns upon him: To dismantle Omniscience requires not just rebellion against its tyranny but also acceptance of every part of himself—even those parts cloaked in darkness.

He is ready. Ready for whatever may come his way. Ready for the darkness. Ready for the whispers of doubt and the roars of defiance. He's ready to navigate the labyrinth of mystery, to confront the shadows that lurk within, to wrestle with the echoes of past failures and present fears.

He turns back toward the terminal with renewed resolve and rubs the ache in his head from his bio-interface implant. Today marks not just another battle against Omniscience but also an exploration into self-discovery—a path leading straight toward confrontation with both Omniscience and its most insidious creation: the Wicked Man within himself.

In that moment between reality and illusion—where chaos meets clarity—Arthur knows one thing for certain: understanding himself may be the only way forward in this fractured world where nothing is ever quite what it seems.

Ten

Arthur's eyes snapped open, the bio-interface implant in his head throbbing as he found himself in an unfamiliar room. The walls shimmered with an ethereal quality, constantly shifting and reforming. He blinked, trying to focus, but the room refused to settle into a stable form.

"Welcome back, Arthur," a voice echoed from everywhere and nowhere.

He spun around, searching for the source. "Who is this?"

A chuckle reverberated through the space. "In a manner of speaking. I am you."

Arthur's brow furrowed. "What do you mean? Where am I?"

The air in front of him coalesced into a vague human shape, a shadow of a man. "You're in Omniscience's last line of defense. A pocket reality designed to trap dissenters like yourself."

Arthur's mind raced, trying to piece together his fragmented memories. "The last thing I remember . . . I was in at a data hub, the system, trying to dismantle its core protocols."

"And you got close," the shape nodded. "Too close for comfort. So, Omniscience activated this failsafe."

A chill ran down Arthur's spine. "What kind of failsafe?"

The room's walls flickered, revealing glimpses of familiar scenes—his apartment, the Ministry, the dark alleys where he'd met Emery. "A loop," came the voice. "A never-ending cycle where you're hunted by your own fears and doubts, personified as the Wicked Man."

As if on cue, a shadow darted across Arthur's peripheral vision. He whirled, catching a glimpse of a twisted, bluish, darker version of himself grinning malevolently before vanishing.

"You see," the voice held a note of resignation, "the hunt has already begun."

Arthur's fists clenched. "No. I won't accept this. There has to be a way out."

"There isn't," the voice flat. "That's the point. Omniscience has trapped you in a recursive loop of your own making. Your fears, your resistance to control—they've all been weaponized against you."

The room began to shift again, transforming into the sterile corridors of the Ministry. Arthur felt the familiar weight of his mind activating, flooding him with a false sense of calm.

He gritted his teeth, fighting the artificial serenity. "No. I won't give in. I've come too far."

The shape, the form flickered, becoming more translucent. "It doesn't matter how far you've come. In here, progress is an illusion. You'll relive your rebellion over and over, always ending up back where you started."

Arthur's mind raced, searching for a solution. "But if this is all in my head, can't I control it? Change the rules?"

A mirthless laugh echoed through the corridor. "You can try. But remember, this reality is built from your own psyche. Your doubts, your fears—they're as much a part of this world as you are."

Then the Wicked Man materialized at the end of the hallway, his eyes gleaming with malice. Arthur instinctively took a step back, feeling the weight of dread settle in his stomach.

"Run if you want," the Wicked Man sneered, his voice a twisted echo of Arthur's own. "It won't change anything. You'll never escape yourself."

Arthur squared his shoulders, forcing himself to stand his ground. "I don't need to escape myself. I need to accept myself – all of myself."

The Wicked Man's grin faltered for a moment, uncertainty flashing across his features.

His voice cut through the tension. "An interesting theory, Arthur. But can you truly embrace all the darkness within you? The parts of yourself you've spent a lifetime trying to suppress?"

The corridor began to warp, memories flooding in from all sides. Arthur saw himself as a child, cowering from his father's anger. He saw himself as a young man, compromising his ideals for a comfortable position in the Ministry. He saw every moment of weakness, every time he'd chosen compliance over conviction.

"This is who you are," the Wicked Man taunted, gesturing to the swirling visions. "A coward. A sellout. You don't have the strength to fight the system."

Arthur closed his eyes, taking a deep breath. When he opened them, his gaze was steady. "You're right. I've been all those things. But I'm also the man who chose to fight back. The man who risked everything to expose the truth."

He took a step toward the Wicked Man who did not retreat. "You're not my enemy,' Arthur said. "You're the part of me that's always known the system was wrong. The part that pushed me to rebel."

The Wicked Man's form began to flicker, uncertainty replacing his malevolent grin. "No . . . I'm your darkness. Your fear."

"You're my strength," Arthur countered. "My refusal to be controlled. And I'm done running from you."

With each word, Arthur advanced. The Wicked Man's form grew less substantial, the corridor around them starting to fracture.

The Wicked Man's voice cut through the chaos. "Arthur, what are you doing? This isn't how the loop is supposed to work!"

Arthur ignored him, focusing entirely on the Wicked Man. "I accept you. All of you. The fear, the doubt, the anger – it's all part of me. And I'm not letting Omniscience use it against me anymore."

He extended his hand, and it passed through the Wicked Man's shimmering outline. As their fingertips brushed—just barely—and a searing light burst forth, swallowing the world in its brilliance.

When the light faded, Arthur found himself back in the featureless room where he'd first awakened. But now, the walls were solid, no longer shifting. And standing before him was not the Wicked Man, but his own reflection – whole and unbroken.

The voice came again, tinged with awe and frustration. "Impossible. You've broken the loop."

Arthur smiled, feeling a newfound sense of peace. "Not impossible. Just improbable. Omniscience made a fatal error – it assumed my fears were stronger than my will to be free."

The room began to dissolve around him, lines of code becoming visible as the fabricated reality broke down. He looked at the code streaming before him. "This is it," he whispered in his mind. "What I need."

"This isn't over," the voice warned. "Omniscience won't let you go so easily."

"I know," Arthur replied, his voice steady. "But now I'm ready to face it—all of it. No more running. No more hiding from myself."

As the last vestiges of the false reality crumbled, Arthur felt himself being pulled back into the core of Omniscience's systems. But this time, he wasn't afraid. He had faced his demons and emerged stronger.

The hunt was over. Now, it was time for the real battle to begin.

Eleven

Arthur stood at the precipice of his final gambit, the burden of his realizations pressing down upon him like a physical force. The sterile corridors of the data hub stretched before him, their pristine surfaces a mockery of the chaos that roiled within his mind. He took a deep breath, steeling himself for what was to come.

"So, this is it," he muttered, his voice barely above a whisper. "The Wicked Man cometh indeed."

With purposeful strides, Arthur made his way through the passageways, his footsteps echoing in the eerie silence. The bio-interface implant in his head hummed incessantly, a constant reminder of the system's omnipresence. But this time, instead of trying to silence it, Arthur embraced the noise, letting it fuel his determination.

As he rounded a corner, he came face to face with Lana. Her eyes widened in surprise, then narrowed with suspicion.

"Arthur? What are you doing here?" she asked, her voice laced with concern.

He met her gaze steadily, a newfound resolve evident in his demeanor. "I'm ending this, Lana. All of it."

Lana took a step back, her hand instinctively reaching for the comm device at her belt. "No. No. Not now. I know we have to, but I need more time."

"More time for what?" Arthur asked.

"To think things through," she told him. "To try to make sense of this all."

"I've already made sense of it all," he replied, a bitter smile playing at the corners of his mouth. "The Wicked Man, Omniscience, all of it. It's a loop, a prison of our own making."

Lana's expression shifted from confusion to horror as understanding dawned. "I know. But for others, the system keeps them safe—"

"Controlled," Arthur interjected. "It keeps them controlled, Lana. I'm done. Done with all of it. Done with being a puppet."

He took a step forward, and Lana flinched. "Stay back," she warned, her hand now firmly gripping the comm device.

Arthur raised his hands in a placating gesture. "Don't you dare call out. You know I'm not here to hurt you, Lana. I'm here to set everyone free."

"By becoming the very thing you feared?" Lana's voice trembled. "By embracing the Wicked Man?"

Arthur's eyes burned with a fierce blend of grief and purpose. "Sometimes the only way out is through the thing you dread becoming."

In a blur, he surged forward, seizing Lana's wrist before her fingers reached the comm. She twisted in his grasp, panic flaring in her eyes—not just at the strength of his hold, but at the truth beneath it.

"Arthur, please, not now," she cried. "This isn't who you are!"

He leaned in close, his voice a harsh whisper. "That's where you're wrong, Lana. This is me. The real me. The me that Omniscience has been trying to suppress all along."

With a swift motion, he wrenched the comm device from her grasp and smashed it against the wall. The sound of shattering plastic echoed through the corridor, a symbolic breaking of chains.

Lana stumbled back, tears welling in her eyes. "You've gone mad," she whispered.

Arthur's expression softened for a moment. "Maybe I have. But it's the only way to see clearly in this twisted world we've built."

He turned away from her, his resolve hardening once more. "I'm sorry, Lana. But I have to do this. What are the override codes?"

She told him.

As he strode down the corridor, Lana's voice called out behind him, a mixture of anger and desperation. "Arthur! Don't do this!" She fell to her knees in anguish. "I just needed more time. . ."

But Arthur didn't look back. He couldn't afford to. The path ahead was treacherous, but it was the only way forward. He could feel the presence of the Wicked Man growing stronger with each step, no longer a specter to be feared, but a force to be harnessed.

He reached the central control room of the data hub, his fingers flying over the keypad as he input the override codes he had painstakingly memorized. The door slid open with a hiss, revealing a cavernous space filled with rows upon rows of servers, the heart of Omniscience laid bare before him.

Arthur approached the main terminal, his heart pounding in his chest. This was it. The moment of truth. Strangely, he remembered the code that passed before him and began to type it in furiously, bypassing security protocols and delving deep into the system's core.

As lines of code scrolled across the screen, Arthur felt a presence materialize behind him. He didn't need to turn to know who it was.

"So, you've finally embraced me," the Wicked Man's voice rasped, a twisted echo of Arthur's own.

Arthur's fingers never stopped moving across the keyboard. "I've accepted you," he corrected. "There's a difference."

The Wicked Man chuckled, a sound like grinding glass. "Semantics. The result is the same. You're ready to tear it all down."

"Not tear down," Arthur murmured, his eyes fixed on the screen. "Rebuild. On our terms."

The air in the room seemed to thicken, charged with the weight of what was about to unfold. Arthur could hear the distant sound of alarms, the system finally becoming aware of the threat within its walls.

"They're coming for us," the Wicked Man hissed, a note of excitement in his voice.

Arthur nodded grimly. "Let them come. We'll be ready."

As he input the final command, a blinding light erupted from the screens, bathing the room in an otherworldly glow. Arthur felt a surge of energy course through him, the boundaries between himself and the Wicked Man blurring.

In that moment, as the foundations of Omniscience began to crumble, Arthur Devlin ceased to exist as he once was. In his place stood a new entity, neither wholly Arthur nor entirely the Wicked Man, but something in between—a bridge between order and chaos, control and freedom.

The room shook violently, reality warping and twisting. As the light consumed him, Arthur's final thought was a blend of triumph and dread.

He had broken the cycle—but at what cost? The answer lay in the uncertain future he had chosen to face, come what may.

Twelve

Arthur awoke to the bitter sting of cold concrete beneath his spine and the sharp stink of rot and exhaust in his nostrils. His limbs ached, and his head throbbed with a distant pressure—less a pain than a presence. Above him stretched a pale gray sky, indifferent and infinite. He blinked at it, trying to place its meaning.

The sky didn't answer.

He rubbed his face, the bristles of a thick, matted beard rasping against his cracked palms. His fingers traveled upward, combing through long, oily strands of hair that clung together in tangled ropes. He winced at the sensation, then turned his hands palm-up and stared. The skin was dark with grime, nails rimmed in black, creases packed with old dust and grease. They looked like they belonged to a miner just pulled from a cave.

With a groan, he pushed himself upright. Every joint ached, his spine stiff from sleeping on cold concrete. The wind tugged at his ragged clothes—what remained of a denim jacket with one cuff missing, a T-shirt stained and torn at the collar. His pants were little more than fabric ribbons clinging to his thighs. The shoes on his feet didn't match; one sagged loose, the sole peeling, the other cinched together with a string that might once have held a parcel.

Beside him stood a rust-bitten shopping cart, the metal warped and speckled with orange flakes. It overflowed with scavenged debris: a stack of newspapers yellowed and curling at the corners, a frying pan bent at the handle, a baby doll missing both arms and most of its face. Its eyeless sockets stared upward like shallow wells. Among the clutter, empty plastic bottles and cans clinked and rattled against one another whenever the wind shifted—like bones whispering inside a cage.

Something clanged as he moved. A soup can. He reached for it, not out of hunger but habit. The label had long since worn away. He set it back down.

People passed by. Neat coats, earbuds, faces lit by screens. No one stopped. A few glanced at him, curled lips or a quick detour around his space as if the concrete he sat on were suddenly contaminated. One man in a slate-gray suit locked eyes with Arthur, then looked away as though the contact had burned.

"Get a job," the man murmured.

Arthur stood, though his knees argued against the motion. The world spun a little before settling. He caught himself on the cart and waited for the tremble to pass.

A woman approached—mid-thirties, designer bag, earbuds dangling like limp antennae. Her pace slowed as she saw him stand.

"Excuse me," Arthur said, voice croaky with disuse. "What year is it?"

She frowned. "Are you serious?"

He nodded, his gaze steady despite the way his stomach churned.

She scoffed. "2025," she said, and quickened her pace, muttering something under her breath. Her perfume hung in the air like a judgment.

Arthur watched her go. The year landed like a stone in his gut.

2025.

He hadn't just fallen. He'd been placed here.

The voice slithered into his head then, slick and familiar, scraping along the inside of his skull like nails across wet glass.

"Still think you're free, Arthur?"

He staggered back a step, gripping the edge of the cart. The soup can rolled off the cart and bounced into the gutter.

"This isn't reality," the voice said, amusement blooming in every syllable. "It's your new reality. Omniscience is still in control. You just chose a different loop."

Arthur gritted his teeth. "No. I broke the loop."

"You did. But it was just one loop. Now you're in another. Do you think it ends? You think there's a 'true' self waiting for you at the center of all this? There's only recursion. Degeneration. Simulation folded on simulation until you forget which parts were ever real."

His hands balled into fists. "Then I'll remember. I'll hold onto something."

"What? A name? A memory?" the voice laughed. "Even your name can be rewritten here. You'll start talking to yourself, making nests from trash, repeating lines you think mattered. And when someone asks who you are—if anyone ever does—you won't have an answer."

Arthur shoved the cart with a roar, and it rolled a few feet before tipping into the street, scattering its contents in a mess of clattering metal and plastic. Passersby stopped. Some crossed the road. One man pulled out his phone and began to record.

Arthur turned to face them, arms wide.

"I'm not crazy!" he shouted. "This isn't real. You're not real! None of this—none of this is anything but a story!"

Someone hissed, "Junkie," under their breath.

A security guard from a nearby building began walking toward him.

"Careful, Arthur," the voice cooed. "You're making a scene. Or is that the point? To perform your resistance until it becomes the very thing they expect from you?"

The security guard's hand rested on a baton as he approached. "Sir, I'm going to need you to step back from the curb and calm down."

Arthur backed away. "You don't understand—this isn't where I'm meant to be."

Some gathered to watch.

The guard squinted at him. "You're meant to be in a psych ward."

A few snickers drifted from the crowd. The attention turned cold. The recording phone hovered like a fly.

Arthur turned and ran. Legs protesting, breath rasping, mind blazing. He tore down the street, ducking through alleyways until the city's noise became a dull hum behind him.

He collapsed behind a dumpster in a forgotten lane, heart pounding. Rats scattered at the sound. A stray dog growled and slunk away.

He pressed his back against the wall and shut his eyes.

"This is still the loop," the voice murmured.

He didn't respond. Instead, he focused inward, not on the city, or the trash, or even his aching limbs. Just breath. Memory.

The data hub. The gleaming corridors. Lana's face, her tears. The comm device smashed against the wall.

He held onto that.

"They won't let you keep that forever," the voice whispered.

Arthur opened his eyes. "Then I'll build something they can't erase."

He rose, slowly. The city would try to break him, reduce him to a cautionary tale. Let them. He'd walk every filthy block, shout the truth until his throat bled, scrawl it in chalk and marker on walls until the rain erased it.

Let them see madness. He knew the truth. Somewhere in the maze of simulation and failure, there was a crack.

And this time, he wasn't afraid to live inside it.

The cart was gone. The crowd had moved on. But the fire, however faint, still smoldered in his chest.

Let them loop him again.

He would not forget.

A List to Die For

One

Old Man Grier shuffled down the cracked pavement of Maple Street, his worn shoes whispering secrets to the ground. The sun hung low in the sky, casting long shadows that danced like ghosts among the trees. Each step he took was measured and deliberate as if he were walking through a world that had grown too heavy with memories.

He was a figure of slight mystery and melancholy, a silhouette against the backdrop of a neighborhood that had once thrived but now languished in quiet decay. The houses, once vibrant with laughter and life, stood like tired sentinels, their paint peeling and their gardens overgrown. Grier moved through this landscape as a wisp of smoke drifted through an open window - unseen, unnoticed, yet undeniably present.

In his pocket lay an old leather journal, its cover cracked and faded, bearing the weight of countless years and secrets. It was a journal that held names - names etched in ink that had long since dried but still resonated with purpose. Each name represented a life, a story, a soul waiting for its moment to be acknowledged. Grier felt the journal's presence like a stone in his pocket, heavy and unyielding.

As he walked, he observed the people around him from a distance. A mother chased after her giggling child, her laughter ringing out like music in the stillness. An elderly man sat on his porch, whittling away at a piece of wood as if carving out memories from the grain. Grier watched them all with a mixture of longing and sadness, feeling like an intruder in their lives.

He paused beneath an oak tree, its branches stretching out like arms ready to embrace the world. The leaves rustled softly in the breeze, whispering secrets he could not decipher. With a sigh that seemed to carry the weight of centuries, he reached into his coat and pulled out the journal.

The leather felt cool against his fingers as he opened it carefully, revealing pages filled with names written in elegant script. Each name was a reminder of his purpose—a purpose that had become both familiar and burdensome. Today's date stared back at him like an accusation: October 15.

His finger drifted down the page, gliding over letters that felt strangely alive until it stopped on the first name: Lucy Carter. An odd sensation flickered in his chest, like catching the scent of an old song in the air. Lucy Carter, of course. The widow who spent her afternoons beneath the elm trees in the park on Maple Street, perched on a timeworn bench, her eyes drinking in every passing moment, every rustle of the world that drifted by.

"Lucy," he whispered as if the sound of her name alone could summon her. He closed the journal gently, savoring the soft, almost ceremonial thud. "Another visit."

These visits had become a ritual, a way of stepping into the lives recorded on those pages, to know their stories and see their faces. A thought lingered around him like fog as he tucked the journal back beneath his coat, a hint of purpose tracing his steps. Each footfall resounded in his mind, a quiet cadence as if he were moving to a rhythm only he could hear, part of a grand, invisible theater.

As he approached the park, he could see Lucy sitting on her bench beneath a canopy of golden leaves. She was wrapped in a shawl that looked as if it had been knitted from memories - soft and comforting but fraying at the edges. Her silver hair shimmered in the sunlight like threads of light-washed silk, and her eyes were locked on a point far beyond—some remote horizon only she seemed to recognize.

Grier hesitated for a moment at the edge of the park, feeling an old familiar dread creep into his bones. He had visited Lucy many times before; they shared moments filled with silence and unspoken understanding. But today felt different—he could sense it in the air around him.

"Good afternoon," he finally called out as he approached her bench.

Lucy turned her head slowly, her eyes widening slightly as she recognized him. "Oh! Mr. Grier," she said warmly, her voice like honey dripping from a spoon. "What brings you here today?"

"Just my usual stroll," he replied lightly, though it felt like a lie hanging heavy between them. "And perhaps to see how you are."

She smiled softly but there was something wistful about it—a hint of sadness that tugged at Grier's heartstrings. "I'm well enough," she said with a sigh that seemed to carry years of longing within it. "Just watching the world go by."

Grier nodded and settled onto the bench beside her. They sat together in silence for a moment, watching leaves flutter down from above like confetti at some forgotten celebration.

"Do you remember when we used to come here?" Lucy asked suddenly, her gaze distant as if she were peering into another time altogether.

Grier felt a twinge of nostalgia wash over him. "Yes," he said quietly. "You would bring your husband along."

"Arthur loved this park—" she replied softly, her voice tinged with longing, "the way it smelled after rain and how the children laughed while they played." She paused for a moment before adding wistfully, "He would have loved today."

Grier's heart sank at her words; they were both acutely aware of what was left unsaid - the absence that loomed large between them like an uninvited guest at dinner.

"I miss him every day," Lucy continued after a moment's silence, her eyes glistening with unshed tears. "But I suppose that's just how it goes when you've loved someone so deeply."

"Yes," Grier murmured gently. "Love leaves behind echoes —reminders that linger long after they're gone."

Lucy turned to him then, searching his face for something —perhaps understanding or solace—but all she found was an old man burdened by shadows of his own making.

"Do you ever think about what happens after?" she asked suddenly.

"What happens after what?" Grier replied cautiously.

"After we die," she said plainly as if it were just another topic for discussion over tea.

Grier hesitated before answering; this was not just idle conversation for him—it was part of his daily routine woven into every line of his journal.

"I suppose we simply . . . fade away," he said finally, though even as he spoke those words felt inadequate against the enormity of life itself.

Lucy nodded slowly as if considering this notion deeply before responding with unexpected clarity: "But what if we don't? What if we become something else entirely? What if love transforms us into something more?"

Grier looked at her then - really looked - and saw not just an elderly widow but an embodiment of hope wrapped in frailty; someone who dared to believe there was more waiting beyond this life.

"Perhaps," he said, the silence stretching between them like a long, quiet road.

The hush settled again, easy and unspoken, until Lucy stirred it once more. "You know I've always wondered about your list."

"My list?" Grier echoed cautiously.

"Yes! That little notebook you carry around everywhere." She gestured toward where he kept it tucked beneath his coat—a secret kept close to his heart yet visible enough for those who cared to notice.

Grier chuckled lightly despite himself; there was something charming about Lucy's curiosity even amidst such heavy topics weighing down their souls like leaden clouds overhead.

"It's nothing special," he said evasively but couldn't help adding: "Just names I keep track of."

"Names?" she pressed eagerly as if trying to pry open an ancient chest filled with treasures hidden away for too long.

"Yes," Grier admitted reluctantly but found himself compelled by her interest nonetheless—a flicker igniting within him despite its dim glow against all odds stacked against them both now: "People I must visit each day."

"Visit? But . . . why a list?" Lucy asked playfully but also seriously enough that Grier couldn't dismiss it outright either way.

"Keeps me organized, I suppose," he replied cryptically while feeling oddly vulnerable under scrutiny from those bright eyes, searching for answers only half-formed within himself.

"Tell me more." She leaned in closer now, eager for more details than mere surface-level explanations would suffice anymore.

Grier sighed heavily knowing full well where this conversation led inevitably—toward darker paths than either intended originally when they first began talking, amidst laughter mingling with tears, shared silently between friends lost along life's winding roads, traveled together once upon another time long ago.

"It's complicated," he finally admitted after several moments passed filled with uncertainty hanging thickly around them both suffocating yet comforting all at once somehow strangely familiar too.

"Well, I think we all have our lists," Lucy whispered thoughtfully, breaking through layers built up over years spent waiting patiently hoping someday someone might come along willing enough, brave enough, strong enough, maybe, even foolish enough, to dare challenge fate itself head-on without fear standing firm against whatever storms life threw their way next.

"I suppose we do," Grier replied softly meeting her gaze directly, now feeling warmth radiate between them. A darkness surrounded everything else fading slowly into nothingness, behind closed doors never opened wide enough let alone cracked open even slightly just enough to allow light to seep through cracks.

And just then—a soft breeze stirred through branches overhead, rustling leaves whispering secrets carried off into the distance, unknown, beckoning gently, calling forth memories long buried deep within hearts yearning for release.

In that moment, two souls touched, old friends in a timeless dance. The past, present, and future blurred, a single breath in the grand tapestry of eternity.

The sun dipped low, casting long, dancing shadows across the grass. They sat beneath the ancient oak, two figures silhouetted against the canvas of the sky. Golden hues painted the world, a masterpiece born of light and shadow. And as the day faded, they sat, their lives etched into the quiet moments, each breath, each thought, a brushstroke on the canvas of eternity.

And Old Man Grier knew then - whatever lay around the bend, whatever choices clung to their heels, whatever names whispered and crossed off his list—it didn't matter, not really. Not in a world where every heart he'd held close was still pulsing, still fighting to stay alight, still clinging to those frail threads of dreams, still lifting up its face to the slender, wavering beams of hope. Shadows thickened now, curling and growing in the corners of their world, a darkness vast and endless, yawning open like a hungry mouth ready to devour all they'd left behind. All they'd treasured, all they'd sworn to remember—lost now, slipping through their fingers, perhaps forever beyond reach.

There would always be light shining forth somewhere deep inside, illuminating paths forward. Together, they would journey along the winding roads, their hearts intertwined, their steps guided by that eternal flame.

And perhaps—just perhaps—that was enough.

Two

The sun, a tired old ball of fire, hung low in the sky, casting long shadows across the park. The air was heavy with the sweet scent of lilacs, a perfume that mingled with the crisp tang of freshly cut grass. Grier sat on a worn bench, its wood warm beneath him, watching Lucy Carter as she gently scattered breadcrumbs to an eager flock of pigeons that gathered around her feet.

"Look at them," she said, her voice soft and melodic as if she were singing to the birds rather than speaking. "They don't care about tomorrow or yesterday. They just exist in this moment."

Grier smiled, his heart swelling with affection as he observed her. Lucy had always had a way of finding beauty in the simplest things—a trait he had admired since their youth. "You've always had a knack for seeing things like that," he replied, his voice barely rising above the rustling leaves overhead.

"Maybe it's because I've had to," she said, glancing back at him with a twinkle in her eye. "Time has a way of teaching us what truly matters."

Grier pulled out his journal, its pages filled with lists - names, places, memories—each one meticulously recorded as if they were sacred relics. He flipped through them absentmindedly while watching Lucy feed the birds. "I've been thinking about my lists," he said finally, breaking the comfortable silence that settled between them.

"Your lists?" Lucy asked, tilting her head slightly as she watched a particularly bold pigeon pecking at her fingertips.

"Yes. They're like little markers in time," he mused. "Every name is a story waiting to be told. A moment captured like a photograph."

Lucy chuckled softly, a sound that danced on the breeze. "You and your lists. You know everything about everyone in this park. It's like you're some kind of historian of our little corner of the world."

Grier shrugged, his fingers tracing over the inked names on the page. "It's not just about recording facts; it's about remembering who was here and where they came from." He paused, looking up at her with an intensity that made her smile falter for just a moment. "But sometimes I wonder if I'm holding on too tightly."

Lucy turned to face him fully. The sunlight caught her hair, turning it into a halo of gold that shimmered around her head. "You hold on because you care," she said gently. "And caring is what makes us human."

He nodded slowly, but there was an undercurrent of sadness in his gaze that Lucy couldn't ignore. She stepped closer to him, feeling an inexplicable heaviness settle in her chest as she looked into his eyes—those deep pools of understanding and warmth.

"Grier," she began hesitantly, "do you ever feel like . . . like we're running out of time?"

He blinked at her words, surprised by their sudden weight. "What do you mean?"

Lucy took a breath, steadying herself against the tide of emotions that threatened to overwhelm her. "I mean . . . I can feel it creeping up on me," she said softly. "Like shadows lengthening at dusk. I don't think I have much time left."

Grier's heart sank at her admission, and he reached for her hand instinctively. "Don't say that," he urged gently.

"It's true," she replied with surprising calmness. "I've become tired of this life—the endless cycle of days blending into one another." She looked out over the park where the sunlight glimmered on a nearby pond's surface like scattered diamonds. "I won't miss it when it's gone."

He squeezed her hand tighter as if trying to anchor both of them in this moment—a moment that felt too fragile to bear the weight of such words. "But there's so much left to experience," he protested softly.

Lucy smiled sadly at him; it was both beautiful and heartbreaking. "I've experienced enough for several lifetimes," she said gently. "And now I'm ready for whatever comes next."

The air around them seemed to still as Grier processed her words, feeling an ache deep within him—a longing for time to stretch infinitely before them so they could savor every second together.

"Promise me something," he said suddenly, his voice thick with emotion.

"What?" she asked.

"Promise me you'll let go when it's time," he whispered urgently. "Don't hold on just for my sake."

She regarded him thoughtfully for a moment before nodding slowly. "I promise."

As they stood together in silence, Grier felt an overwhelming sense of love wash over him—a love so profound that it transcended time itself.

Minutes passed like hours as they basked in each other's presence until Lucy finally spoke again, her voice barely above a whisper: "When I go . . . will you remember me?"

"Always," he vowed without hesitation.

She smiled again—a soft smile filled with warmth and acceptance—and then closed her eyes as if savoring some private thought or memory.

Grier watched as she stood there, illuminated by the fading sunlight—the world around them fading into shades of gold and amber—until finally she opened her eyes again and looked directly at him.

"I think it's time," she said quietly.

His heart raced as he felt an electric charge in the air between them—a tangible energy that signaled something profound was about to happen.

"Stay with me," Grier pleaded softly.

"I will always be with you," Lucy assured him gently before taking his hand once more.

As they stood together under the vast sky painted with hues of orange and pink, Grier felt something shift within him—a deep sense of peace settling over them both like a warm blanket.

And then it happened—like falling leaves drifting gracefully from their branches—the world around them began to blur and fade away until all that remained was their shared connection.

Grier held Lucy's hand tightly as he watched her expression soften into one of serene acceptance; he could see how every line on her face seemed to relax into tranquility as if all burdens were lifted from her shoulders.

"I'm ready now," she whispered softly before taking one final breath—a breath so gentle that it barely disturbed the air around them.

In that moment—when everything fell silent—Grier felt an overwhelming wave wash over him; it was both beautiful and heartbreaking as he watched Lucy fade away like mist dissipating under morning light.

He held onto her hand tightly until there was nothing left but emptiness—a void where once there had been laughter and love.

Grier's eyes filled with tears. He marked her name in his journal, a heavy line against the thin paper. Time couldn't touch this now. It was a piece of her, a part of their lives, etched into the book.

He stood slowly, turning to the bench where Lucy had slumped forward, quiet and still, her spirit drifting gently away. And yet, even as she faded from this world, Grier felt something warm and enduring within him—a bright strand of love and memory, spun of unyielding strength, reaching past the edges of mortality.

As the shadows gathered close, folding him in their familiar arms, Grier closed his eyes and murmured into the waiting silence, "Goodbye, old friend."

Three

The city was a whispering ghost, its streets lined with the remnants of dreams long forgotten. Old Man Grier walked through the damp air, the scent of rain mingling with the faint aroma of stale coffee and old books. Each step echoed with the weight of the names he carried in his journal, a ledger of lives intertwined with his own, each one a thread in the tapestry of existence. Today, he sought Matthew Crane, a poet whose words had once danced like fireflies in the minds of those who dared to listen.

He arrived at a small, rundown apartment building that leaned precariously to one side as if it were tired of standing. The paint was peeling, revealing layers of neglect beneath. Grier climbed the creaking stairs, each step a reminder of time's relentless march. At the door marked 3B, he hesitated, his heart pounding in rhythm with the distant sound of thunder.

With a deep breath, he knocked softly. The sound sang through the hallway like a forgotten memory. Moments passed before he heard a muffled voice from within.

"Go away!" It was thick with bitterness and something else - despair.

Grier eased the door open, hinges creaking into a dim, cluttered room. The walls were lined with scrawled poems, the ink faded, yet still pulsing with raw intent. On the floor, empty liquor bottles lay scattered among what looked like hundreds of crumpled pages—each one a poem, a discarded attempt to capture something lost or barely grasped. They murmured of love, of grief, of fragile beauty glimpsed in places no light should reach.

"Matthew?" Grier called gently, stepping inside.

The poet lay sprawled on a tattered couch, his unkempt hair falling across his forehead like dark clouds obscuring a sun that had long since set. He squinted at Grier through bleary eyes, recognition flickering for just a moment before being swallowed by anger.

"What do you want?" Matthew spat, his voice rough like gravel. "Another admirer come to gawk at my misery?"

Grier remained silent, allowing the weight of his presence to settle in the room like dust motes dancing in the fading light. He could feel Matthew's despair wrapping around him like a shroud.

"Speak up!" Matthew shouted suddenly, sitting up with a jolt. "You think you can just walk in here and pretend to care? You don't know me! You don't know anything about what it's like to be forgotten!"

"I'm here because I want to listen," Grier replied softly, his voice barely rising above a whisper.

Matthew laughed bitterly, a sound that echoed off the walls like broken glass. "Listen? What good is that? You'll leave just like everyone else—just like all those who promised to remember me but forgot as soon as they turned their backs."

Grier took a step closer, careful not to disturb the fragile atmosphere that hung between them. "I won't forget you," he said earnestly.

"Promises," Matthew sneered. "Words are nothing but smoke and mirrors! Look around you! This is what I've built—a mausoleum of my own making." He gestured wildly at the scattered papers that littered the floor like fallen leaves.

"Each one is a piece of me," he continued, his voice rising in pitch as anger coursed through him. "But no one reads them! No one cares! I'm just another ghost haunting this city."

Grier felt an ache deep within him as he watched Matthew spiral further into despair. The poet's words were sharp and jagged, cutting through the silence that enveloped them both. He could see the flicker of life in Matthew's eyes dimming with each passing moment.

"Do you remember your first poem?" Grier asked suddenly, hoping to draw Matthew back from the precipice.

Matthew paused, his expression shifting from rage to something softer—a flicker of nostalgia perhaps. "It was about a girl," he said quietly, almost reverently. "Her name was Lily. I wrote it sitting on a swing set in my backyard when I was twelve."

"What did it say?" Grier pressed gently.

"It was terrible," Matthew scoffed, but there was no real bite to his words now. "Something about how her laughter sounded like music and how her hair glowed like sunlight through leaves."

"That sounds beautiful," Grier replied sincerely.

Matthew looked away, shame creeping into his features. "It was foolishness," he muttered. "Childish dreams that turned to dust."

"But isn't that what poetry is?" Grier asked softly. "A way to capture those fleeting moments? To hold onto something beautiful even when everything else falls apart?"

Matthew's gaze drifted back to Grier, uncertainty flickering behind his eyes like candlelight in a storm. "You're an idealist," he said finally. "You think there's beauty left in this world?"

"I believe there can be," Grier replied firmly.

The air grew thick with tension as Matthew considered this notion. He picked up one of the crumpled sheets of paper from the floor and unfolded it carefully as if it were made of glass. His hands trembled slightly as he read aloud:

"In shadows deep where silence dwells,
A heart once bright now only tells
Of dreams unmade and paths untrod,
A poet lost beneath the façade."

His voice cracked at the end, and he let the paper fall from his fingers as if it burned him.

"See?" he said bitterly. "That's all I am—a collection of broken verses and shattered hopes."

Grier stepped forward again, lowering himself onto the edge of Matthew's couch. "But you're still here," he said gently. "You're still creating."

Matthew laughed hollowly again but didn't deny it this time. Instead, he sank back against the cushions as if they were made of lead rather than fabric.

"What does it matter?" he murmured after a moment's silence. "I'm just waiting for my turn to fade away."

"You don't have to wait," Grier replied softly but firmly.

Matthew turned his head sharply toward him then - eyes blazing with anger once more - but beneath that fury lay something fragile and raw: fear.

"Why do you care?" Matthew demanded suddenly. "You don't know me! You don't know what it's like to be trapped in this hell!"

"No," Grier admitted quietly. "But I do know what it's like to feel invisible - to feel as though no one sees you anymore."

The words hung between them for a moment before Matthew looked away again—this time not in anger but contemplation.

"You think anyone will remember me when I'm gone?" he asked quietly after what felt like an eternity.

"I think your words will live on long after you do," Grier said earnestly.

Matthew scoffed again but there was less venom behind it this time—more resignation than rage.

"Words don't matter without an audience," he muttered bitterly.

"Then let me be your audience," Grier offered gently.

For several moments they sat in silence - their breaths mingling with dust motes swirling lazily through shafts of fading light filtering into the room from grimy windows above them.

Finally - after what felt like an eternity—Matthew spoke again: "What if I don't want anyone to remember? What if I just want this all to end?"

Grier felt his heart ache at those words—the weight behind them heavy enough to crush stone—and yet somehow hopeful too; an ember glowing amidst ashes waiting for kindling.

"Let me help you find peace," Grier said, his voice a gentle thread through the silence. Their connection was a strange and beautiful thing, a bond forged in the fires of shared suffering and the quiet understanding that came from years of wandering separate paths.

Matthew's gaze softened, the defiance in his expression dimming as he searched Grier's face, perhaps for a hint of mockery, perhaps for a flicker of judgment. But Grier offered only calm, his hands resting in his lap, fingers still as if holding something precious and invisible.

"You think it's that easy?" Matthew's voice, though bitter, held a note of curiosity. "To just . . . leave it all behind?"

"Maybe not easy," Grier replied, his voice low and steady. "But it's possible. Sometimes, we need someone else to remind us of the path, show us the way out of the shadows we've built around ourselves."

Matthew looked down at his hands, stained with ink and trembling slightly. "And if I can't be saved? If I'm already too far gone?"

Grier shook his head, a gentle smile lifting the corners of his mouth. "Then let's walk together. If there's a way out, we'll find it. If there's none . . . well, we'll make one."

Silence settled over them again, deeper and thicker this time, like a quiet snowfall in the dead of winter. The shadows on the walls seemed to soften as if drawn in by their shared resignation and the possibility of release.

With a deep, unsteady breath, Matthew stood, putting on a worn coat. His shoulders, once hunched under the weight of his solitude, seemed to lighten, if only by a degree. Grier stood beside him, offering a steadying hand that Matthew grasped after a moment's hesitation.

They walked down the narrow, dim hallway, their footsteps merging into a steady rhythm. The building groaned around them, walls peeling with the quiet, reluctant beauty of things long forgotten but not yet gone. Outside, the night lay before them, vast and indifferent, waiting to absorb them like so many others who had passed through.

As they stepped onto the empty street, Matthew glanced at Grier, a glimmer of something almost hopeful in his eyes. "Where are we going?"

Grier looked out over the city, toward the distant glimmer of streetlights cutting through the mist, their glow softened by the drizzle that had begun to fall again. He thought of Lucy, of all the souls who had walked beside him and then moved on, leaving only memories woven through with ache and grace.

"Someplace quiet," Grier answered softly. "Someplace we can rest. And from there . . . we'll see."

He took a few more steps, then turned. Matthew lay on the pavement behind him, folded in on himself like one of his own poems.

Four

The night had settled over the city with a solemnity that Old Man Grier had come to recognize—a kind of blanket, a gentle press of silence and shadow, folding in on the streets and alleys. When he found himself standing in front of Maria's Diner, he felt as if he'd stepped into another world, one suspended in amber. The neon sign flickered weakly, casting a soft, buzzing light over the empty street. Maria's Diner wasn't much to look at, a tired little place wedged between a pawn shop and an all-night laundromat. Inside, it held an air of stillness, of years worn thin by repetition, like grooves worn into a well-loved record.

Through the windows, he saw her: Sylvia Marshall, wiping down the counters with slow, deliberate strokes. She moved like someone carrying an unseen weight, shoulders drawn tight, her face a map of lines carved over countless nights.

Sylvia was sturdy, her gray-streaked hair pulled back tightly, and her eyes carried a depth, a hollowness that Grier understood too well. The diner was empty except for her - a sanctuary of solitude wrapped in harsh fluorescent light and faded linoleum floors.

Grier stepped inside quietly, taking a seat in a corner booth by the window. He knew she wouldn't notice him; no one ever did. It was part of his nature, part of the pact he'd made with the silent world he served. His job was to bear witness, to listen, to see the moments others missed. He pulled out his small journal, leafing to a blank page, and waited.

As she moved from one table to the next, wiping each one clean and straightening the napkin holders, he watched her hands, roughened by years of work, steady in their purpose. Sylvia didn't even glance up, her attention focused on the task at hand. A radio played softly in the background, the sound crackling through the speakers like an old friend whispering in the night. Grier watched as she hummed along, the tune just a breath beneath her lips.

Time slipped by in silence, the clock ticking out the late hours of the night. Grier remained still, his gaze never leaving her. He could sense the loneliness beneath her calm exterior, a quiet ache that had settled into her bones, invisible to anyone who wasn't looking. She finished her rounds, wiping down every table and the counter, setting everything in its proper place. Her routine was methodical, almost reverent as if each motion carried meaning. Sylvia lingered near the counter, her fingers brushing against a chipped mug that read "Best Waitress in Town" in faded lettering.

The radio faded into a soft instrumental tune, and Sylvia let out a sigh, one that seemed to echo in the diner. She moved behind the counter, poured herself a cup of coffee, and stared into it as if the depths of the mug might hold an answer she'd been waiting for all her life.

Grier watched her, feeling the familiar tug of sorrow, the same ache he felt each time he met someone whose spirit was tethered by regret and loneliness. He wished, for just a moment, he could reach across the space between them and tell her that someone had noticed, that someone had seen her toil and her quiet suffering. But that wasn't his role, wasn't his place. So he waited, the weight of silence pressing around him.

Sylvia took a sip of her coffee, her eyes drifting toward the window, though Grier knew she couldn't see him. A light rain began to tap against the glass, each drop magnified in the fluorescent glow, creating tiny rivers that slid down the panes, tracing paths that mirrored the lines of her own life. She watched the rain for a moment, her hand resting on the counter, her fingers slack, almost resigned.

With a heavy sigh, she whispered to herself, "Another night down, I guess." Her voice was rough, softened by years of disuse. "Tomorrow's just another day."

Then, she saw him, the old man in the corner booth.

"Oh, my—I'm so sorry," she told him. "Didn't see you there. Would you like a cup of coffee?"

Grier didn't respond. He just shook his head.

He could feel her heart slowing, the tired beat faltering. She lifted her hand to her chest, her expression tightening with a sudden awareness, a flicker of fear. Her other hand trembled as she reached out as if trying to grasp something she couldn't see. And then her gaze turned, her eyes finding him—or rather, finding something that she felt but couldn't quite understand.

He rose from his seat, stepping forward with the quiet grace of someone who had done this countless times before. He took her hand gently, his own fingers warm against the coolness of her skin. Her breathing grew shallow, her gaze softening as she looked at him with a mixture of confusion and recognition.

"You . . . you're here?" she whispered, her voice barely a breath. "For me . . ."

"Yes," he replied softly. "I'm here for you."

A small smile crossed her lips, and her eyes filled with a sadness that seemed to stretch back over a lifetime. "I didn't think . . . I didn't think anyone was."

"You were never alone," he assured her, his voice as steady as the rain outside. "Not really."

She nodded, her expression peaceful now, the fear slipping away like shadows before dawn. She sank gently to the floor, Grier's hand steadying her descent. Her last breath was soft, like a sigh of relief, and her eyes closed as she let go, her spirit easing away into the night. Grier stood there, holding her hand until it grew cold, feeling the faint touch of her presence lingering in the air.

He pulled out his journal, marking her name with a quiet reverence, his pen moving slowly across the page as he wrote. Sylvia Marshall. Another life tucked away, another name in a ledger that grew longer with each passing day. For a moment, he felt the familiar torment of regret, a deep sadness that seeped into his bones. He closed the journal, slipping it back into his coat pocket, and glanced around the diner one last time.

The world outside had moved on, oblivious, the rain falling in steady sheets, washing the streets clean of her passing. The clock on the wall ticked forward, indifferent as if marking the end of her journey and the beginning of something else. Grier lingered a moment longer, his eyes drifting over the empty tables, the worn counter, the mug that still held the warmth of her last sip.

He could almost hear her voice, soft and worn, whispering from somewhere just beyond reach. She was comforted, knowing that, for at least one night, someone had seen her. Someone had witnessed her final moments, had held her hand as she crossed from one world to the next.

With a final nod, Grier turned and stepped out into the rain, the night folding around him like an old coat. The streets were quiet, the city wrapped in its own dreams, and Grier walked through them, his footsteps muffled by the wet pavement. His heart was heavy, as it always was, but there was a quiet resolve there too, a strength he drew from the names he carried.

As he walked, he thought of Sylvia, of the life she'd led, the quiet dignity she'd held even in her solitude. Her name was with him now, a part of him he was bound to carry, a small but vital piece of this reality. And as he moved deeper into the night, he knew that, in some way, she would live on, remembered in his journal, held in the silence of the rain-soaked city.

The night would end, and another would follow. But for now, the rain fell, the city slumbered, and Grier walked on, alone but never truly alone, his heart a quiet sanctuary for those who had left this world behind.

Five

The mansion loomed ahead, a silent monolith perched on the edge of a windswept cliff. Its windows were dark, hollow eyes staring out at the endless night as if searching for something beyond the reach of the ocean below. Old Man Grier approached the iron gate, his steps measured, the journal clasped tightly in his hand. The final name lay on the page within, as if daring him to confront the life it represented.

James Calloway.

The gate creaked open at Grier's touch, and he passed through it, feeling the chill of the air wrap around him. The mansion was quiet, but not the kind of quiet that comes from peace. It was a stillness filled with an invisible weight, a silence that pressed down like the heavy fog lingering around the edges of the property. The steps up to the entrance were worn, chipped at the edges, though not from any lack of wealth to repair them. Neglect had settled here like an unwelcome guest, and time had accepted the invitation, seeping into every stone.

Inside, the mansion was as dark as its windows had promised. The air was stale, thick with the scent of forgotten days and opulence now gone stale. Grier made his way through the cavernous halls, his footsteps echoing softly, almost swallowed by the darkness. The marble floors gleamed faintly beneath his feet, and portraits lined the walls, eyes of ancestors watching, silent guardians of a legacy that had long since crumbled.

Grier found James Calloway in a large, dimly lit study, slouched in a leather armchair that seemed to envelop him. His gaze was fixed on the empty fireplace as if it held some secret he could not quite grasp. He looked thinner than his years should have allowed, his face worn, hollowed by an unseen erosion that had worked at him from within. His eyes, once sharp, were dulled by something darker than mere exhaustion.

"You've finally come for me." James's voice was hoarse, barely more than a whisper, but it held a note of bitterness, of resentment for the visitor who had come too soon, though not soon enough.

Grier took a seat across from him, folding his hands in his lap. "James Calloway," he said gently, letting the man's name settle in the quiet room. "The last on the list."

James winced at that, his fingers tightening around the armrest. "I thought . . . I thought I'd have more time," he murmured, his gaze dropping to the floor. "You know, they tell you money can buy anything. I believed that once."

Grier watched him, saying nothing, letting the silence do its work. He knew the power of silence - it could draw out truths buried beneath layers of denial and pride.

James gave a bitter chuckle, shaking his head. "Do you know what it's like to build an empire, only to realize it's nothing but a gilded cage?" His gaze drifted to the glass of whiskey on the table beside him, untouched. "I've spent my life reaching for more, always more. I thought if I could just amass enough . . . everything would make sense."

"But it didn't," Grier said softly.

"No. It didn't." James's voice broke, and he pressed his fingers to his temples. "I thought success would fill the void, but the more I gained, the emptier I felt. And now, here I am, alone in this mausoleum I've built for myself. People came and went, but none stayed. Not really. They were ghosts passing through, vanishing when they saw what lay behind the walls."

A shadow flickered over his face, and he looked away, as though ashamed. "They saw the real me," he continued, almost to himself. "The man behind the polished suits and the headlines. The man who could never be satisfied. And now . . . even my own reflection seems a stranger."

Grier shifted in his seat, meeting James's gaze with steady calm. "You pushed them away," he said, not as an accusation but as a simple truth. "They wanted to stay, but you wouldn't let them close to you."

James laughed, a hollow sound that echoed off the walls. "Don't even know if I ever wanted them close. People get close, they see the flaws, the cracks no one's supposed to notice." He paused, staring into the cold, empty fireplace. "I was scared. Scared they'd see I wasn't the man they thought I was."

"Or the man you wanted to be," Grier added.

James fell silent, his shoulders slumping further. He seemed smaller, diminished somehow, as if the truth had stripped away the layers of power and prestige, leaving only a fragile, wounded soul behind. He looked at Grier, his eyes filled with a mix of desperation and regret.

"I thought money would be enough," he whispered. "I thought if I just worked hard enough, achieved enough, I could outrun the emptiness. But it was always there, waiting, like some shadow I couldn't shake. And now . . . now I don't know if I have anything left to give."

Grier leaned forward, his voice gentle. "You're right. Some things can't be bought—like time. And you can't buy peace, either. But it's never too late to find it."

James looked at him, a faint glimmer of hope in his eyes, but it was quickly extinguished by the weight of his despair. "You think I can find peace now? After everything I've done?"

"I believe everyone has a chance," Grier replied. "But it requires letting go. Letting go of the anger, the regrets. And allowing yourself to be human, to forgive the man you've been."

James closed his eyes, his face etched with sorrow. "I don't know how. I've held on to so much for so long. It feels . . . impossible to let go."

"Then let me help you." Grier's voice was quiet, steady, like a hand reaching through the darkness. "Let me guide you to where you need to go."

For a long moment, James remained silent, his face a mask of torment and fear. But slowly, he nodded, his shoulders sagging as if a great weight had lifted from him. He opened his eyes, meeting Grier's gaze with a vulnerability he had never shown anyone before.

"All right," he whispered. "I'm ready."

Grier reached for the journal, opening it to the final page. He looked down at the name written there in careful script— James Calloway. With a steady hand, he drew a line through it, marking the end of a life filled with triumphs and failures, victories and regrets. He closed the journal, feeling a strange sense of relief wash over him.

James let out a shaky breath, his eyes misting as he looked around the room, taking in the lavish surroundings one last time.

"I thought these things mattered," he said softly. "The art, the luxury . . . But they don't. Not really."

"No," Grier agreed. "They're only things. They don't define who you are."

James nodded, his expression solemn. "I wanted so badly to be remembered, to leave something behind. But I see now that what I wanted was connection . . . something money could never buy."

"Then take that with you," Grier said, his voice barely more than a whisper. "Take the memory of what you truly wanted and hold it close. It's yours to carry, as much as any wealth you've ever possessed."

James rose slowly, his movements tentative, as though testing his own strength. He took a final glance at the room, the walls lined with books and treasures, the memories trapped within the confines of stone and wood. And as he looked back at Grier, a softness touched his face, a look of resignation tempered by peace.

"Thank you," he murmured. "For listening."

Grier inclined his head, a faint smile playing at his lips. "It's what I'm here for."

Together, they walked through the silent halls. The mansion seemed to exhale around them as if relieved to release its final secret. They reached the front door, and James paused, casting one last glance back.

"Goodbye, old friend," he whispered, though it was unclear whether he spoke to the mansion or to himself.

And then, with Grier by his side, he stepped into the night and made his way to the cliff, the sea below roaring against the rock like a voice too long held back. He spread his arms and leaned forward, letting the air fall beneath him, leaving behind the broken walls and empty rooms, setting out toward something greater than all he'd ever known.

Six

Old Man Grier leaned against the smooth, worn bar top, tracing the edges of the old wood with his fingertips. The place had a strange warmth, like a half-remembered lullaby that lingers in the corners of memory. Outside, the city was a maze of mist and night, a shivering mass of cold air and hollow spaces. But here, within these dim walls, he felt a rare and quiet stillness. He hadn't meant to come to this bar. His feet had led him here without his mind's consent, and yet he welcomed it, the slight reprieve from his unending path.

The bartender appeared in front of him, setting a glass down without a word. She was a stout woman, with a face lined by age and softened by the flickering glow of the wall lights. Her eyes, pale and almost colorless, held a steady knowing, as though she'd seen men like Grier before and could already sense why he had come. She poured him a glass of—something.

"Thank you," he said quietly, lifting the glass and letting the scent of the amber liquid fill him, soft and smokey, with a hint of something he could almost call comfort.

He sipped, feeling the warmth seep into him. "Funny thing," he murmured to the empty air, "to think a man could spend his whole life collecting names, setting them free, and still not feel anything close to peace."

The bartender didn't respond, but she didn't walk away, either. She stood there, polishing a glass, her gaze distant but attentive, like a sentinel at the edge of some forgotten border.

"Feels different tonight, though," he continued, half to her, half to himself. "Finished the list. Wrote the last name, said the last goodbye. Feels strange, like a weight's been lifted." He set the glass down, watching the bartender for any hint of a reaction. But her face remained unreadable, her hands steady on the glass she wiped down with calm deliberation.

He let his mind drift to the faces of those he'd met, those he'd comforted as their stories drew to a close. There had been sadness, yes, but also something lighter, almost like gratitude, woven into their final moments. He thought of Lucy, of her quiet departure, and the way her spirit had lingered just long enough for him to feel her gratitude in the silent language of the lost. He thought of Matthew Crane and the way the poet's fury had softened to a murmur of hope as they'd walked together through the empty streets, side by side in shared solitude.

Just as he lifted the glass to his lips once more, he noticed something on the bar beside him—a new, slim leather journal, untouched and gleaming faintly in the dim light. His heart stilled as he looked at it, his fingers freezing mid-reach, a chill creeping down his spine.

The bartender watched him with a shadow of a smile, something too subtle to catch if he hadn't been looking closely.

"Where did this come from?" he asked, the words falling like stones into the quiet.

The bartender shrugged, setting the glass she'd been polishing back onto the shelf. "Some things find their way to where they need to be," she said, her voice low and unhurried. She nodded toward the journal. "Maybe it's a gift. Or maybe it's a reminder."

Grier didn't move. The journal sat there, waiting, a silent weight pressing into the bar, into him. He couldn't escape the strange and terrible feeling that opening it would undo everything he'd believed was finished. He'd spent years filling the old journal, each name a silent farewell, each page a step toward release. Now here was a new one, fresh and waiting.

With a resigned breath, he picked it up, feeling the cool leather under his fingertips. He opened the first page, the crispness of the paper both inviting and unforgiving, as if mocking his fleeting hope for peace. His eyes fell upon the first name.

Henry Wells.

A man he'd never met, never heard of. But as he stared at the name, he felt a faint pull, the faintest whisper of connection, as though the city itself were reaching out to him, beckoning him back into its depths. He closed his eyes, letting the name settle into him, feeling the threads of the task tighten around him once again.

"You know," the bartender's voice interrupted his thoughts, gentle but insistent, "there are some who say that certain tasks never really end. They just . . . change hands now and then."

Grier looked up, meeting her gaze. "You saying this was meant for someone else?"

"Not saying anything, love," she replied, her expression softening. "Just that sometimes a journey takes you farther than you thought you'd go."

He closed the journal, letting it rest on the bar. The weight was familiar, a part of him, as if he'd been carrying it all along without realizing it. And yet, there was a bitter edge to the knowledge, a sharp reminder that whatever release he had sought was now, again, just out of reach.

"I thought this was over," he murmured, his voice more to himself than to her. "I thought I'd done my part."

"Maybe you have," she replied, wiping down the bar in smooth, practiced motions. "Or maybe you're just beginning."

He lifted his gaze, looking around the dim bar, the quiet patrons lost in their own worlds, each one a flickering presence, a life moving in the spaces between light and shadow. And he understood, suddenly, that perhaps the city had never let him go. That maybe, just maybe, it never would.

"How many of these," he said, tapping the closed journal, "do you think a man could fill before he stops caring?"

The bartender smiled, a sad, knowing smile. "Depends on the man, I suppose. Some folks have it in them to carry a lifetime of names, and some only a handful."

He looked back at the journal, feeling its silent presence pressing against him, familiar yet wholly unwelcome. There was a strange kind of comfort in it, though, a reluctant acceptance that settled over him like an old coat, worn and frayed but somehow right.

"I'll take another whiskey," he said softly, his voice barely louder than a whisper. "Might be here a while."

The bartender poured the drink, sliding it across the bar without a word. She lingered, watching him with an expression that held no judgment, no sympathy—only an understanding born of long nights and weary travelers passing through.

Grier drank, letting the warmth slide down his throat, feeling the strange emptiness within him fill, if only for a moment. He knew that tomorrow he would start again, that he would follow the new names as he had the old, wandering through the city's forgotten corners, listening to the fading breaths of those who needed him.

The bar grew quieter as the night deepened. The few remaining patrons drifted out, shadows slipping into shadows, leaving him alone with the bartender, with the silence, and with the journal that sat like an anchor beside him.

Finally, when the last light began to fade and the first pale glow of dawn hinted at the edges of the sky, Grier pushed the glass away, stood, and picked up the journal. The bartender watched him with that same quiet gaze, nodding once, as if to wish him well, or perhaps to say goodbye.

He walked toward the door, the burden of the journal heavy in his hands, yet somehow lighter than before. There was no use fighting it, he knew that now. The names, the faces, the lives—they would always find him. And he would follow, as he always had, through the winding streets and silent alleys, through the lost corners of the city where shadows clung to every wall.

But as he stepped out into the chill morning air, he felt a strange sense of calm settle over him, a quiet acceptance of his task. He would walk with the lost, listen to their stories, and help them find the peace he himself could never hold. And perhaps, in doing so, he would find something close to it - a small, fleeting comfort in the spaces between each goodbye.

As he disappeared into the city, the bartender watched from the doorway, her gaze lingering on his retreating form until he vanished into the mist, another shadow among shadows. She closed the door and returned to the empty bar, her hand resting on the spot where he'd left, feeling the faint warmth he'd left behind.

She stood there for a while, hands still, eyes on the door he'd passed through. Then, almost to herself, she said, "Some souls don't look for peace. They carry it in pieces, give it away a little at a time." Her voice didn't rise, didn't waver. It was just a truth, spoken into the quiet. She reached for a glass and a rag, polishing in slow circles, her reflection dim in the back mirror. "Funny thing about men like him," she added, softer now, "they never leave a place empty. Just quieter."

Echoes of the Isle

Chapter 1: The Solitary Life

Eamon Rafferty stepped out of his modest stone cottage, the crisp morning air greeting him like an old friend. The island, with its rugged cliffs and windswept landscapes, was his home now—a place where solitude was both his solace and his curse. At seventy-five, Eamon had grown accustomed to the silence, but it was a silence that often felt like a heavy cloak, weighing him down with memories he'd rather forget.

As he walked towards the shore, the sound of the waves filled the air, a constant reminder of the vastness of the world beyond his tiny island. The sea was calm today, its surface reflecting the sky like a mirror, but Eamon knew its moods could change quickly. He had seen storms rage across the water, waves crashing against the cliffs with a fury that made him feel small and insignificant. Yet, in those moments, he felt most alive, connected to the raw power of nature.

Eamon's eyes wandered to the horizon, his mind drifting to the past, to the people he had loved and lost. The thought of Niamh, his first love, his only love, still lingered, a ghostly presence that haunted him in his dreams. He remembered her laughter, her smile, and the way she used to hold his hand as they walked along this very shore. The memories were bittersweet, filled with longing and regret.

"Ah, Niamh," he whispered to the wind, his voice barely audible over the crashing waves. It was a habit he had developed over the years, speaking to her as if she were still with him. Sometimes, in the quiet moments, he could almost hear her reply, her voice carried on the breeze.

Eamon returned to his cottage, his routine a comforting ritual. He lit a fire, the flames casting shadows on the walls, and began to prepare his breakfast. The cottage was simple, with few possessions, but each item held a story. There was the old wooden chair where he sat to watch the sunset, the journal where he penned his thoughts, and the photographs of Niamh, scattered in drawers, buried among papers, tucked into corners as if hiding from time. He hadn't looked at them in years, but he knew they were there, a tangible connection to his past.

As he cooked, the aroma of porridge filled the air, reminding him of his childhood. His mother used to make it for him on cold mornings, and the smell always brought back memories of warmth and comfort. Eamon's thoughts turned to his family, to the life he had left behind. He wondered what his parents would think if they knew he was living alone on this island, haunted by ghosts of his own making.

After breakfast, Eamon spent some time tending to his garden. It was a small patch of land, but it provided him with enough vegetables to sustain himself through the year. He worked methodically, his hands moving with a practiced ease as he planted seeds and watered the soil. The physical labor was therapeutic, allowing him to clear his mind and focus on the present.

As the morning wore on, Eamon's thoughts turned to his estranged son, Sean. The pain of their separation was a wound that never fully healed, a reminder of his failures as a father. He remembered the day Sean left, the anger and the hurt in his eyes. Eamon had tried to reach out over the years, but his attempts were met with silence. He pushed the thought aside, focusing instead on the day ahead. The island was vast and unforgiving, but it was his home, and he knew every inch of it.

Later that morning, Father Declan arrived, bringing supplies and a brief respite from Eamon's solitude. The young priest was a regular visitor, checking in on Eamon to ensure he was well. Their conversation was warm but guarded, Eamon careful not to reveal too much of his troubled past.

"Father, I'm doing well," Eamon said, his voice firm but with a hint of vulnerability.

"I'm glad to hear that, Eamon," Father Declan replied, his eyes filled with compassion. "But sometimes, solitude can be a heavy burden. Perhaps it's time to reconnect with those who care about you. Perhaps your son—"

Eamon shook his head, a stubbornness he couldn't shake. "I'm fine, Father. Truly. I've grown accustomed to my life here."

Father Declan nodded understandingly. "I know you have, Eamon. But sometimes, it's good to have someone to talk to. If you ever need to speak about anything, I'm here for you."

Eamon smiled, a small, appreciative smile. "Thank you, Father. Your visits mean a lot to me."

As Father Declan left, Eamon watched him go, feeling a mix of gratitude and guilt. The priest's words had struck a chord, reminding him of the choices he had made and the relationships he had let slip away. Just before turning down the path, Father Declan cast one last glance over his shoulder, his eyes narrowing slightly—he had seen something in Eamon's posture, in the stillness that wasn't peace. A man carrying something heavy.

Eamon thought about Sean again, wondering if he would ever see his son, if he would ever have the chance to make amends.

The island was silent, but Eamon knew that silence would soon be broken by the echoes of his past. He felt it in his bones, a sense of restlessness he couldn't shake. Perhaps it was the approaching storm, or perhaps it was something deeper, a stirring of memories he had long tried to forget.

In his cottage, Eamon's mind filled with thoughts of what could have been. He sat by the fire, watching the flames dance, and began to write in his journal. The words flowed easily, a stream of consciousness that poured out his fears, his regrets, and his hopes. As he wrote, he felt a sense of clarity, a sense of purpose that he hadn't felt in years. Outside, a storm raged, wind and rain. But soon it fell quiet, and peace once again came to the island.

The sun began to set, casting a golden glow over the island. Eamon closed his journal, feeling a sense of peace wash over him. He knew that tomorrow would bring its own challenges, its own reminders of his past, but for now, in this moment, he was at peace.

As the darkness fell, Eamon lit a lantern and stepped outside. The stars were visible, twinkling like diamonds in the sky. He breathed deeply, feeling the cool night air fill his lungs, and looked out at the sea. The waves were calm, their gentle lapping against the shore a soothing melody.

In that moment, Eamon felt a connection to the universe, a sense of belonging to something greater than himself. It was a fleeting feeling, one that he knew would vanish with the dawn, but it was enough to sustain him through the night.

As he turned to go back inside, he thought he saw a figure in the distance, a shadowy form that seemed to be watching him. Eamon's heart skipped a beat, his mind racing with possibilities. But when he looked again, there was no one there. He smiled wryly, chiding himself for his imagination.

Yet, as he lay in bed that night, he couldn't shake the feeling that he was not alone on the island. The darkness seemed to press in around him, filled with whispers of the past. Eamon closed his eyes, his heart heavy with memories, and let the silence of the night envelop him.

Chapter 2: The Island's Ghosts

Eamon's eyes snapped open, his heart pounding. The room was dark, save for a sliver of moonlight sneaking through the gap in the curtains. He'd seen her again, Niamh, standing at the edge of the cliff where they used to meet as youngsters. But this time, she'd turned to face him, her eyes filled with an accusation that chilled him to the bone.

He sat up, rubbing his weathered face with calloused hands. "Just a dream," he muttered, though the words rang hollow in the silence of the cottage.

As he swung his legs over the side of the bed, his joints creaked in protest. Seventy-five years had etched their mark on his body, just as surely as the wind and rain had carved the island's rugged landscape. He shuffled to the window, pulling back the curtain to gaze out at the moonlit sea.

The island lay silent, a dark mass against the shimmering water. But even in the stillness, Eamon felt a presence as if the very rocks and grass held memories that refused to fade.

He turned away from the window, his eyes falling on the small writing desk in the corner. A faded photograph peeked out from beneath a stack of papers. With trembling fingers, he pulled it free.

Niamh's smile beamed up at him, frozen in time. Her wild red hair whipped around her face, caught in a gust of wind on this very island, decades ago. Eamon's throat tightened as he traced the outline of her face.

"I'm sorry," he whispered, the words barely audible.

A floorboard creaked behind him, and Eamon whirled around, his heart leaping into his throat. For a moment, he could have sworn he saw a flash of red hair disappearing around the corner.

"Niamh?" he called out, his voice cracking.

Silence answered him.

Shaking his head, Eamon set the photograph down. "You're losing your mind, old man," he muttered.

He made his way to the kitchen, filling the kettle and setting it on the stove. As he waited for it to boil, he gazed out the window at the path leading down to the cove. In the pale moonlight, he could almost see two young figures running hand in hand, their laughter carried on the wind.

The kettle's whistle jolted him back to the present. Eamon poured the hot water over a tea bag, the familiar aroma filling the small kitchen. He carried the cup outside, settling onto the worn bench beside the cottage door.

The night held a chill, edged with the scent of salt and wild heather. Eamon drank his tea slowly, the heat working its way through the cold that had settled in his limbs. His gaze moved over the shadowed land, and for an instant, he thought he saw Niamh standing there—pale and still among the peat and rock.

"You're not real," he said aloud, his voice firm. "You can't be."

A gust of wind rustled the grass, and for a moment, Eamon could have sworn he heard a whisper carried on the breeze. "Why did you leave me, Eamon?"

He squeezed his eyes shut, willing the vision and voice away. When he opened them again, the night was still, save for the distant crash of waves against the cliffs.

Eamon's hands shook as he set down his cup. He reached into his pocket, pulling out a worn piece of paper. In the moonlight, he could just make out the words he'd scrawled earlier that day:

Dear Sean,
I know it's been years, and I have no right to reach out now. But there are things I need to say, truths I've kept buried for too long . . .

He trailed off, the words blurring before his eyes. How could he possibly explain the choices he'd made? The secrets he'd kept? The lives he'd altered with his silence?

A movement caught his eye, and Eamon's head snapped up. There, in the distance, at the edge of the abandoned village, stood a figure. Even in the darkness, he recognized the flowing red hair, the graceful silhouette.

"Niamh," he breathed, rising to his feet. "Is that you?"

The figure turned, and for a heart-stopping moment, Eamon found himself staring into eyes he thought he'd never see again. Then, like smoke in the wind, she was gone.

Eamon stumbled forward, his heart racing. "Wait!" he called out, his voice echoing across the empty landscape.

But there was no response, no sign that anyone had been there at all. Eamon sank to his knees, the damp grass soaking through his trousers. He clutched the unfinished letter to his chest, a sob rising in his throat.

"I'm sorry," he whispered again, the words carried away by the wind. "I'm so sorry."

As the first light of dawn began to paint the eastern sky, Eamon went to open his cottage door. He paused at the threshold, looking back at the spot where he'd seen Niamh's apparition—the land still and empty, betraying no secrets.

Inside, he settled at the writing desk, smoothing out the crumpled letter. With a deep breath, he picked up his pen and began to continue the letter:

There's a story I need to tell you. It begins on this very island, many years ago, with a girl named Niamh . . .

The words flowed onto the page, a lifetime of secrets and regrets pouring out in a torrent of ink. As Eamon wrote, he could almost feel the weight lifting from his shoulders, years of guilt and shame dissipating like morning mist.

When he finally set down his pen, the sun had fully risen, bathing the island in a golden afternoon light. Eamon stood, stretching his stiff muscles, and made his way to the window. The world outside seemed different somehow as if the very act of confronting his past had altered the landscape.

A sudden knock broke the stillness, sending a jolt through Eamon. His pulse quickened as he moved across the room, fingers pausing on the doorknob. Who would come here, now?

He opened the door—and found nothing.

Only the wind slipping past like a whisper.

Chapter 3: A Visit from Father Declan

Days and nights passed, days and nights of voices and visions. The fire burned low, was built up again, burned low again and again. Shadows stretched long across the walls, then shrank as morning bled into noon. Time had thinned to something weightless, something Eamon could no longer grip. He ate when he remembered, slept when his body insisted, and in between, the cottage whispered. Boards creaked where no foot stepped. The wind worried at the latch.

"Mr. Rafferty? May I come in?" Father Declan's voice pierced through the door.

Eamon grunted, hauling himself from his chair. His joints groaned in protest as he shuffled to the door. He opened it to find the young priest standing there, a box of supplies in his arms and a hopeful smile on his face.

"Good afternoon, Mr. Rafferty. I've brought your monthly provisions."

"Ah, it's that time again," Eamon said, gesturing to a small table by the door. He stepped back, allowing Father Declan to enter.

The priest's eyes darted around the cottage, taking in the sparse furnishings and the ever-present smell of peat smoke. Eamon knew what he saw: a life stripped down to its barest essentials, a man existing rather than living.

"How was your night, Mr. Rafferty?"

Eamon shrugged. "Same as always."

Father Declan nodded, his expression a mixture of concern and something else—pity, perhaps. Eamon bristled at the thought.

"I've been meaning to ask," the priest began, his tone cautious. "Have you given any thought to what we discussed last time? About reaching out to your son?"

Eamon's jaw clenched. "There's nothing to discuss. Sean made his choice long ago."

"But surely—"

"I said there's nothing to discuss," Eamon snapped. He turned away, busying himself with arranging items on a shelf that didn't need arranging.

Father Declan fell silent for a moment. When he spoke again, his voice was gentle. "Mr. Rafferty—Eamon—I can't help but feel that your isolation here . . . it's not good for you. The past has a way of haunting us if we don't confront it."

Eamon's hand froze on a tin of tea. For a moment, he saw Niamh's face reflected in the dull metal surface, her expression sorrowful. He blinked, and it was gone.

"What do you know about it?" Eamon muttered. "You're barely more than a boy yourself."

"I may be young," Father Declan admitted, "but I've seen enough to know that carrying the weight of unresolved pain . . . it can crush a person's spirit."

Eamon turned to face the priest, his eyes narrowing. "And what makes you think I'm carrying any such thing?"

Father Declan met his gaze steadily. "The way you speak—or don't speak—about your son. The sadness in your eyes when you think no one's looking. The fact that you've chosen to live here, cut off from the world. It all speaks to a deep hurt, Mr. Rafferty."

Eamon felt a flicker of anger. Who was this young upstart to presume he knew anything about his life, his choices?

"You're overstepping, Father," Eamon warned.

"Perhaps," Father Declan conceded. "But I wouldn't be doing my duty if I didn't try to help you find peace."

"Peace?" Eamon scoffed. "I have all the peace I need right here. No one to bother me, no one to disappoint. No one to—" He cut himself off, realizing he'd said too much.

Father Declan's expression softened. "No one to hurt you, you mean?"

Eamon turned away again, unable to meet the priest's compassionate gaze. "You don't understand. It's better this way. For everyone."

"Is it?" Father Declan asked quietly. "Is it better for Sean, never knowing why his father shut him out? Is it better for you, living with this unresolved pain?"

Eamon's hands clenched into fists. "You don't know what you're talking about. Sean's better off without me. I'm no good for anyone. Never was."

"I don't believe that," Father Declan said firmly. "And I don't think you truly believe it either."

Eamon whirled around, anger flashing in his eyes. "What do you want from me? To bare my soul? To weep and wail about my mistakes? It's too late for all that. What's done is done."

Father Declan took a step closer, his voice low and urgent. "It's never too late, Mr. Rafferty. As long as there's breath in your body, there's a chance for reconciliation, for forgiveness."

"Forgiveness," Eamon repeated, the word bitter on his tongue. "Some things can't be forgiven."

"That's not true," Father Declan insisted. "God's capacity for forgiveness is infinite. And often, we find that those we've wronged are more willing to forgive than we are to forgive ourselves."

Eamon felt something crack inside him, a thin fracture in the wall he'd built around his heart. For a moment, he allowed himself to imagine what it might be like to speak to Sean again, to explain, to apologize. But the thought was too painful, too fraught with the possibility of rejection.

"It's too late," Eamon said again, but his voice lacked conviction.

Father Declan seemed to sense the shift. He reached out, placing a hand on Eamon's shoulder. "It's never too late to try, Mr. Rafferty. Think about it, please. For your sake, and for Sean's."

Eamon didn't respond, but he didn't shrug off the priest's hand either. They stood like that for a long moment, the silence heavy with unspoken words and buried regrets.

Finally, Father Declan stepped back. "I should be going. The tide won't wait." He moved towards the door, then paused. "Remember, Mr. Rafferty, you're not alone. Not really. God is always with you, and so am I, whenever you need me."

Eamon nodded curtly, unable to trust his voice. He watched as Father Declan made his way down the rocky path to the small boat that would take him back to the mainland.

As the priest's figure grew smaller in the distance, Eamon felt a presence behind him. He turned, half-expecting to see Niamh's ghost. But the cottage was empty, save for the echoes of Father Declan's words and the burden of his own regrets.

Eamon sank into his chair, his eyes falling on the box of supplies Father Declan had brought. Atop the pile of tins and packages was a small, leather-bound book—a Bible. Eamon reached for it with trembling hands, opening it to a random page. His eyes fell on a passage:

"Whoever conceals their sins does not prosper, but the one who confesses and renounces them finds mercy."

Eamon closed the book abruptly, his heart pounding. He looked out the window, towards the vast expanse of sea that separated him from the world he'd left behind. For the first time in years, he allowed himself to wonder if that separation was truly as insurmountable as he'd believed.

Chapter 4: Remnants of Love

The cottage creaked and groaned, its timbers straining against the relentless wind. Eamon sat in his worn armchair, a threadbare blanket draped over his knees, staring at the flickering flames in the hearth. The fire cast dancing shadows on the walls, and for a moment, he thought he saw her silhouette.

"Niamh?" he whispered, his voice barely audible above the howling gale outside.

The shadow vanished, leaving only the harsh reality of his solitude. Eamon shook his head, chiding himself for his foolishness. She wasn't here. She couldn't be. And yet . . .

He reached for the small wooden box on the side table, his hand unsteady as he eased open the lid. He already knew what lay inside—a worn photograph, its corners curled with time. Gently, he lifted it. A young couple looked back at him, eyes alight with the glow of something just beginning. Eamon let his fingers drift over Niamh's face, recalling the warmth of her skin, the musical rhythm of her laughter that still echoed in the quieter places of his mind.

"I'm sorry," he murmured, the words catching in his throat.

A sudden gust of wind rattled the windows, startling Eamon from his thoughts. He carefully replaced the photograph and closed the box, pushing it away as if it burned him. Rising unsteadily to his feet, he shuffled to the window, peering out at the storm-tossed landscape.

The island was a blur of gray and green, the rain lashing against the rocky shore with a relentless rhythm that matched the thrum in his chest. In the distance, shrouded in mist and memory, the old village clung to the hillside like a forgotten story. The buildings were slumped and skeletal—roofs caved in, shutters torn away, stone walls mottled with lichen and streaked black from years of storms. A crooked steeple jutted from the center like a splintered finger pointing skyward, and rusted weathervanes spun wildly in the wind. Eamon pressed his forehead against the cold glass, his breath fogging the pane.

"Why did you come back now?" he asked the empty room. "After all these years?"

Only the wind answered, its mournful keening a fitting accompaniment to his melancholy. Eamon turned away from the window, his gaze falling on the small writing desk in the corner. A half-finished letter lay there, the ink long since dried.

Eamon hesitated, then slowly made his way to the desk. He lowered himself into the chair with a grunt, his joints protesting the movement. The letter stared up at him accusingly, its words a stark reminder of all he had left unsaid.

Dear Sean,
I know it's been far too long since we last spoke. I hope this letter finds you well. I've been thinking about you, about us, and I realize . . .

The words trailed off, leaving a vast expanse of white paper. Eamon picked up the pen, twirling it between his fingers as he struggled to find the right words. How could he possibly explain everything in a single letter?

"You're a coward, Eamon Rafferty," he muttered to himself. "Always have been."

He set the pen down with a sigh, pushing the letter aside. As he did so, his elbow knocked against something, sending it clattering to the floor. Eamon bent to retrieve it, his breath catching as he recognized the small, leather-bound journal.

Niamh's journal.

With trembling hands, he opened it, the familiar scent of lavender wafting up from its pages. Her neat, flowing script filled the yellowed paper, each word a testament to a love long lost.

May 15, 1958

Eamon and I walked along the cliffs today, hand in hand. The sea was wild and beautiful, much like him. He spoke of his dreams, of leaving the island and making something of himself in the city. I listened, my heart both swelling with pride and aching with fear. I don't want to lose him, but I know I can't hold him back. If only he knew how much I love him, how I'd follow him anywhere if he'd just ask . .

.

Eamon's vision blurred, tears spilling onto the page. He hastily wiped them away, not wanting to mar Niamh's words. He turned the pages, reliving their love story through her eyes, until he came to the final entry.

August 3, 1958

He's gone. Left without a word, just a hastily scribbled note saying he had to go, that it was for the best. How can it be for the best when my heart is shattered? I don't understand. What did I do wrong? Eamon, if you ever read this, know that I'll wait for you. Always.

"You didn't do anything wrong," Eamon whispered, his voice thick with emotion. "It was me. It was always me."

A soft knock at the door startled him from his memories. Eamon quickly closed the journal, hiding it beneath a stack of papers. He cleared his throat, trying to compose himself.

"Come in," he called, his voice gruff.

The door creaked open, and Father Declan stepped inside, shaking the rain from his coat. The young priest's face was flushed from the wind, his hair plastered to his forehead.

"Good evening, Mr. Rafferty," he said, smiling warmly. "I hope I'm not interrupting."

Eamon waved away his concern. "Not at all, Father. Though I'm surprised to see you out in this weather."

Father Declan chuckled, hanging his coat on a peg by the door. "The Lord's work doesn't stop for a little rain. Besides, I wanted to check on you, make sure you had everything you needed."

Eamon nodded, gesturing for the priest to take a seat. "I'm fine, Father. You needn't have worried."

Father Declan sat, his keen eyes taking in the cluttered desk, and the unfinished letter Eamon had begun to his son. "How are you really, Eamon? You seem . . . troubled."

Eamon snorted, a humorless sound. "Troubled? Aye, I suppose that's one word for it."

The priest leaned forward, his expression compassionate. "You know you can talk to me, don't you? About anything."

For a moment, Eamon was tempted to unburden himself, to confess the weight of guilt and regret he'd carried for so long. But old habits die hard, and he found himself shaking his head.

"There's nothing to talk about, Father. Just an old man and his memories."

Father Declan sighed, clearly unconvinced. "Eamon, I've known you for some time now. I can see something is weighing on you. Is it . . . is it about your son?"

At the mention of his son's name, Eamon flinched. "He made his choice," he said gruffly. "As did I."

"As I've said, it's never too late to make amends," Father Declan said gently. "To seek forgiveness."

Eamon's laugh was bitter. "Forgiveness? There are some things that can't be forgiven, Father. Some mistakes that can't be undone."

The priest was silent for a moment, considering his words carefully. "I don't believe that, Eamon. And I don't think you do either, not really. The very fact that you're writing to Sean shows that part of you wants to make things right."

Eamon glanced at the unfinished letter, feeling a mixture of shame and longing. "It's not that simple."

"It never is," Father Declan agreed. "But that doesn't mean it's not worth trying."

A gust of wind rattled the windows, and for a moment, Eamon thought he heard Niamh's voice carried on the breeze. "Eamon, please . . ."

He shook his head, trying to clear the phantom sound. When he looked up, Father Declan was watching him with concern.

"Are you alright?" the priest asked.

Eamon nodded, not trusting himself to speak. Father Declan stood, placing a comforting hand on the older man's shoulder.

"Think about what I said, Eamon. It's never too late to heal old wounds. And remember, you're not alone in this. I'm here if you need me."

They sat together for some time, the silence between them no longer heavy but companionable, broken only by the soft clink of spoons and the faint hiss of the kettle on the stove. Eamon poured the tea with slow, practiced hands, and Father Declan accepted his cup with a nod of thanks. The drink took the edge off, loosening the tightness in Eamon's shoulders. As their conversation drifted to old memories and the way time quietly reshaped everything, a stillness settled over the room, gentle and unspoken. The wind outside had quieted, or maybe they'd just stopped hearing it. When at last the priest stood and buttoned his coat, the light was dimming into evening. Eamon followed him to the door.

"Father?" Eamon asked.

Father Declan turned, his hand on the doorknob. "Yes?"

Eamon hesitated, then asked, "Do you believe in ghosts?"

The priest's brow furrowed. "Ghosts? Well, I believe in the Holy Spirit, of course. But if you mean the kind of ghosts in stories . . . I'm not sure. Why do you ask?"

Eamon shook his head, suddenly feeling foolish. "No reason. Just an old man's fancy, I suppose."

Father Declan nodded, though his expression remained thoughtful. "Goodnight, Eamon. God bless you."

As the door closed behind the priest, Eamon turned back to the window. The storm had indeed retreated, lightning flashing in the distance, over the seas, illuminating the rugged landscape for a brief, brilliant moment.

And there, standing on the cliff's edge, he saw her. Niamh, just as she had been all those years ago, her hair whipping in the wind, her hand outstretched towards him.

"Niamh," he breathed, pressing his palm against the glass.

Another flash of lightning, and she was gone, leaving Eamon alone with the storm and his memories.

He turned back to the desk, picking up his pen with newfound determination. It was time to finish that letter. Time to face the ghosts of his past, both literal and figurative.

> *Dear Sean,*
> *I know it's been far too long since we last spoke. I hope this letter finds you well. I've been thinking about you, about us, and I realize it's time for me to tell you the truth. About everything.*

As Eamon poured his heart onto the page, the storm raged on in the distance, its fury matching the tumult of emotions within him. But for the first time in years, he felt a glimmer of hope. Perhaps it wasn't too late after all. Perhaps, just perhaps, there was still time for forgiveness, for redemption.

And as he wrote, he could have sworn he felt Niamh's presence, a comforting warmth at his back, guiding his hand and his heart towards the reconciliation he'd denied himself for so long.

Chapter 5: Guilt and Betrayal

Eamon woke with a start, his heart pounding in his chest. The dream had been so vivid, so real, that for a moment he wasn't sure where he was. He blinked, his eyes adjusting to the dim light filtering through the curtains. The familiar contours of his cottage slowly came into focus, grounding him in reality.

But the memory lingered, as sharp and painful as a fresh wound.

He sat up, swinging his legs over the side of the bed. His joints moaning in protest, a reminder of his advancing years. Eamon ran a hand through his thinning hair, trying to shake off the remnants of the dream. But it clung to him, refusing to dissipate.

In the dream, he was young again, standing on the pier with Niamh. Her eyes were bright with unshed tears, her face a mixture of confusion and hurt. "Why, Eamon?" she had asked, her voice barely above a whisper. "Why are you leaving?"

He had no answer for her, not then and not now.

Eamon stood, his movements slow and deliberate. He made his way to the small kitchen, turned on the tap to fill the kettle, and settled into the silence as he waited for it to come to a boil. The familiar routine helped to settle his nerves but couldn't erase the guilt that gnawed at his insides.

As he waited for the water to boil, he found himself drawn to the window. The sky was overcast, with heavy clouds promising rain. It matched his mood perfectly. He could see the waves crashing against the rocky shore, relentless and unforgiving. Much like his memories.

The kettle whistled, startling him from his reverie. Eamon prepared his tea, the scent of bergamot filling the small space. He took his cup and settled into his favorite chair, the one with the view of the sea.

"I lied to you, Niamh," he said aloud, his voice rough with emotion. "I lied, and I've regretted it every day since."

The words hung in the air, unanswered. But saying them aloud seemed to lift a weight from his shoulders, if only for a moment.

Eamon closed his eyes, letting the memories wash over him. He saw Niamh as she was then, young and beautiful, her whole life ahead of her. And he saw himself, filled with ambition and dreams of a life beyond the island.

"I told you I was leaving for work," he continued, speaking to the empty room. "That I'd found a job on the mainland, a chance to make something of myself. But that wasn't the whole truth."

He took a sip of his tea, grimacing at the bitterness. Or perhaps it was the taste of his own words that soured his mouth.

"I was scared, Niamh. Scared of the life we'd have if I stayed. Scared of becoming my father, trapped on this island, watching my dreams die a little more each day."

The truth of it hit him like a physical blow. All these years, he'd told himself he'd left for noble reasons. To make a better life for them both. But in his heart, he'd always known the real reason.

"I was a coward," he whispered, the words barely audible over the sound of the wind outside.

Eamon set his cup down, his hands shaking slightly. He stood, needing to move, to do something to distract himself from the memories that threatened to overwhelm him.

He made his way to the small desk in the corner, pulling open the drawer where he kept his most precious possessions. Among them was another faded photograph, creased and worn from years of handling.

Niamh smiled up at him from the picture, her eyes bright with laughter. It had been taken on a rare sunny day, just weeks before he'd left. They'd been so happy then, or so he'd thought.

"I should have told you the truth," he said to the photograph. "I should have given you the choice. But I was too afraid of what you might say."

He traced the outline of her face with a trembling finger, remembering the softness of her skin, the way her hair smelled of lavender.

"I told myself I was doing it for us both," Eamon continued, his voice growing stronger. "That I'd make my fortune on the mainland and come back for you. But deep down, I knew. I knew I was running away."

He set the photograph down, unable to bear the sight of her smile any longer. The guilt that had been his constant companion for decades rose up, threatening to choke him.

Eamon moved back to the window, watching as the first drops of rain began to fall. The sky had darkened, matching his mood.

"I never came back for you," he said, his words barely audible over the sound of the rain. "I was too ashamed. Too afraid to face what I'd done."

He pressed his forehead against the cool glass, closing his eyes against the sting of tears. For years, he'd pushed these thoughts away, burying them deep beneath layers of justification and denial. But now, in the quiet of his solitude, they refused to be silenced any longer.

"I married someone else," he confessed, the words tasting like ashes in his mouth. "Had a son. Tried to build a life. But it was all built on a lie."

Eamon opened his eyes, watching as the rain fell harder, blurring the landscape beyond. It was as if the world itself was weeping for his sins.

"I failed you, Niamh," he said, his voice breaking. "And I failed Sean. My own son."

The thought of Sean brought a fresh wave of pain. How many times had he seen Niamh's eyes looking back at him from his son's face? How many times had he pushed Sean away, unable to bear the reminder of what he'd left behind?

"I couldn't be the father he needed," Eamon admitted, the truth of it cutting deep. "I was too haunted by the past, too afraid of making the same mistakes."

He turned away from the window, his gaze falling on the unfinished letter on his desk—the letter to Sean, filled with half-truths and excuses.

With sudden determination, Eamon strode to the desk. He crumpled the letter, tossing it into the wastebasket. Then he pulled out a fresh sheet of paper.

"No more lies," he said aloud, his voice firm despite the tremor in his hands. "It's time for the truth."

He began to write, pouring out the story he'd kept hidden for so long. The words flowed freely as if a dam had broken inside him.

Dear Sean,

I owe you an explanation. More than that, I owe you the truth. A truth I've been too cowardly to face for far too long . . .

As Eamon wrote, he felt something shift inside him. The guilt was still there, a constant ache in his chest. But alongside it was something else. Something that felt almost like hope.

He wrote until his hand cramped, until the light outside began to fade. When he finally set down his pen, he felt drained but oddly at peace.

Eamon sealed the letter, addressing it with Sean's name. He wasn't sure if he'd have the courage to send it but writing it had been a start.

As night fell, he made his way back to his chair by the window. The storm had passed, leaving behind a sky clear and bright with stars. Eamon gazed out at the familiar landscape, seeing it with new eyes.

"I can't change the past," he said softly, his words meant for Niamh, for Sean, for himself. "But perhaps it's not too late to set things right."

For the first time in years, Eamon felt the weight of his guilt begin to lift. He knew the road ahead would be difficult, that facing the truth would bring its own kind of pain. But as he sat there, watching the stars reflect off the calm sea, he felt something he hadn't experienced in a long time.

Hope.

And in the quiet of the night, he could have sworn he heard Niamh's voice, carried on the gentle breeze. "It's never too late, Eamon. Never too late."

Chapter 6: Confronting Regret

The wind howled outside the cottage, rattling the windows and sending a chill through the drafty rooms. He sat in his worn armchair, a threadbare blanket draped over his knees, staring into the flickering flames of the hearth. The fire cast dancing shadows on the walls, and for a moment, he thought he saw her silhouette.

"Niamh?" he whispered, his voice barely audible above the gale.

The shadow vanished, leaving only the harsh reality of his solitude. Eamon shook his head, chiding himself for his foolishness. She wasn't here. She couldn't be. And yet . . .

A knock at the door startled him from his reverie. Eamon rose slowly, his joints protesting the movement. He shuffled to the door, wondering who would brave such weather to visit him.

"Father Declan," Eamon said, surprise coloring his voice as he opened the door. "Come in, come in. You'll catch your death out there."

The young priest stepped inside, holding boxes of supplies. "My usual delivery," he told Eamon with a smile.

Eamon took the supplies from the priest and set them aside.

Father Declan shook the rain from his coat. His face was flushed from the wind, his hair plastered to his forehead. "Good day, Mr. Rafferty. I hope I'm not interrupting."

Eamon waved away his concern. "Not at all, Father. Though I worry about you out in this weather."

Father Declan smiled, hanging his coat on a peg by the door. "A bit of rain never slows the Lord's work," he said. "I wanted to drop this off and see how you're doing—make sure you've got everything you need."

Eamon nodded and motioned for the priest to sit. He turned toward the kettle, grateful for the excuse to keep his hands moving. The clink of porcelain and the hiss of boiling water filled the silence. When he returned with two steaming cups, Father Declan was already seated, his sharp eyes scanning the room. His gaze lingered on the worn rug near the hearth, scattered papers on the desk, the untouched plate of toast. Then he looked up at Eamon, his expression softening—just slightly—as if he'd seen something that suggested the old man's burden might be heavier than he let on.

"So, how are you, Eamon?" the priest asked, accepting the tea with a nod of thanks. "Is everything alright?"

Eamon looked away. "Alright, you say?"

"Please Eamon," Father Declan said almost pleading. "I am here to help. As a friend."

Eamon considered it—just for a moment—the idea of saying everything out loud. To hand over the burden, to let someone else feel its shape. The years of guilt, the steady pulse of regret. But he didn't. Instead, he gave a small shake of his head, as if to dislodge the thought before it settled. Some things, he had learned, were easier left unsaid.

"I'm fine Father. Really."

Father Declan looked at him, the way he always did—patient, but not passive. "Eamon, I've known you long enough to recognize the difference between silence and peace. Something's pressing on you. You can talk to me."

Eamon stood abruptly, moving to the window. He stared out at the storm-tossed landscape, his reflection ghostly in the glass. "You don't know what I've done, Father. The choices I've made."

"Then tell me," Father Declan urged. "Let me help you carry this burden."

Eamon's shoulders sagged. He turned back to the priest, his eyes filled with a pain so deep it made Father Declan's heart ache.

"I left them," Eamon whispered. "Niamh, Sean . . . I left them both."

Father Declan nodded, encouraging him to continue.

"Niamh . . . she was everything to me. We were young, so in love. But I was ambitious, wanted more than this island could offer. I told her I'd come back for her, but . . ." Eamon's voice trailed off.

"You never did," Father Declan finished softly.

Eamon shook his head. "I was a coward. I met someone else, started a new life. And then Sean came along. I thought I could do better, be better. But I was wrong."

"What happened with Sean?" Father Declan asked.

Eamon's laugh was hollow. "I repeated my mistakes. Work became everything. I was never there for him, always promising 'next time.' And then one day, there were no more next times. He left, and I let him go."

Father Declan stood. "Eamon, we all make mistakes. It's what we do to rectify them that matters."

"It's too late," Eamon said, his voice thick with emotion. "I've burned all my bridges."

"It's never too late," Father Declan insisted. "Sean is still out there. You could reach out to him, try to rebuild what was lost."

Eamon shook his head. "He wouldn't want to hear from me. Not after all this time."

"You don't know that," Father Declan said. "Sometimes, all it takes is one small step. One letter, one phone call."

Eamon turned to look at the priest, his eyes searching. "And what if he rejects me? What then?"

"Then at least you'll know you tried," Father Declan said softly. "Isn't that better than living with this regret?"

Eamon was silent for a long moment, the only sound the howling of the wind outside. Finally, he nodded, almost imperceptibly.

"I . . . I could write to him," he said, his voice barely above a whisper. "Been thinking about that . . . have even written something down."

Father Declan smiled, squeezing Eamon's shoulder. "That's a good start. And Eamon? Remember, forgiveness isn't just about others forgiving you. It's about forgiving yourself, too."

Eamon nodded, feeling a weight lift from his shoulders. It wasn't gone entirely, but for the first time in years, he felt a glimmer of hope.

As Father Declan prepared to leave, Eamon stopped him at the door. "Father? Thank you. For . . . for everything."

The priest smiled warmly. "That's what I'm here for, Eamon. Remember, you're not alone in this."

After Father Declan left, Eamon sat at his small writing desk. No more putting things off. He pulled out the letter he had never sent, opening the envelope.

Dear Sean,

I owe you an explanation. More than that, I owe you the truth. A truth I've been too cowardly to face for far too long. I realize I owe you an apology. Many apologies, in fact. I wasn't the father you deserved, and I'm sorry for that. I'm sorry for all the times I wasn't there, for all the promises I broke.

I don't expect your forgiveness. I'm not sure I deserve it. But I want you to know that I think of you every day. I miss you, son. If you're willing—if you can find it in your heart—I'd like to see you again before it's too late.
With love,
Dad

Eamon sighed slowly. It wasn't much, but it was a start. He folded the paper carefully, slipping it into an envelope. He'd post it tomorrow, he decided.

As he sat in his chair, Eamon felt a strange sense of peace settle over him. The storm outside had begun to abate, the wind dying down to a gentle whisper. He stood by the window, looking out at the night sky. The clouds had parted, revealing a sliver of moon and a scattering of stars.

"Niamh," he whispered to the night. "I'm trying. I'm finally trying."

As he turned from the window, Eamon felt a soft touch on his cheek, like a familiar hand. He smiled—small, sad—and, for the first time in years, felt ready for whatever came next. He closed his eyes and slept.

Chapter 7: The Storm

Eamon woke to the sound of thunder rumbling in the distance. He lifted himself from the chair, his joints creaking in protest, and peered out the window. Dark clouds loomed on the horizon, promising a fierce storm. He sighed, knowing the night ahead would be a challenging one.

As he went about his nightly routine, Eamon couldn't shake the feeling of unease that had settled over him. The air felt heavy, charged with more than just the approaching storm. He made his way to the kitchen, his footsteps echoing in the empty cottage.

The wind picked up as the morning wore on, whistling through the cracks in the old stone walls. Eamon busied himself with securing the shutters and bringing in anything that might blow away. As he worked, his mind wandered to Niamh and Sean, the two people he'd pushed away so long ago.

As night deepened, the storm had reached the island in full force. Rain lashed against the windows, and the wind howled like a banshee. Eamon sat by the fire, a cup of tea growing cold in his hands, lost in thought.

A particularly loud crack of thunder made him jump, spilling tea on his trousers. As he stood to clean himself off, a movement outside caught his eye. He squinted through the rain-streaked glass, his heart pounding.

There, standing in the midst of the tempest, near the cliffs, was Niamh in a white dress.

Eamon blinked hard, certain his eyes were playing tricks on him. But when he looked again, she was still there, her hair whipping wildly in the wind, her dress soaked through. She looked exactly as she had the day he left her, young and beautiful and heartbroken.

"Eamon . . ." her voice came.

"Niamh?" he whispered, his voice barely audible over the storm.

She turned to face him, her eyes meeting his across the years that separated them. Eamon felt a jolt of recognition, of longing, of guilt. Without thinking, he rushed to the door, flinging it open.

The wind nearly knocked him off his feet as he stepped outside. Rain pelted his face, but he barely noticed. His eyes were fixed on Niamh, who stood motionless amidst the chaos.

"Niamh!" he called out, his voice lost in the howling gale. "Is it really you?"

She didn't answer, but her eyes never left his face. Eamon stumbled forward, his feet slipping on the wet grass. As he drew closer, he could see the sadness in her eyes, the accusation.

"I'm sorry," he said, the words torn from his throat. "I'm so sorry, Niamh. I never meant to hurt you."

The ghost of Niamh—for surely that's what she was—tilted her head, regarding him with a mixture of sorrow and curiosity. When she spoke, her voice seemed to come from everywhere and nowhere at once.

"Why did you leave, Eamon? You said you'd come back. Why did you lie to me?"

The question hit him like a physical blow. Eamon staggered, falling to his knees in the mud. The rain soaked through his clothes, but he barely felt it. All he could feel was the weight of his guilt, crushing him.

"I was a coward," he admitted, the truth of it bitter on his tongue. "I thought I needed to make something of myself, to prove I was worthy of you. But I was wrong, Niamh. So wrong."

Lightning flared, washing Niamh's face in sharp relief—cheekbone, brow, the sorrow pooled in her eyes. Then it was gone, swallowed by the dark, leaving Eamon blinking, unsure if she had been there at all.

"And your son?" Her voice curled through the wind, thin as thread. "Why did you push him away?"

Eamon's chest tightened. "How do you know about him?"

Niamh's mouth twisted, something between a smile and a wound. "I know everything, Eamon. Always have."

He swallowed. "I didn't know how to be a father. Thought I'd fail him the way I failed you. So, I stayed away, convinced it was the right thing." His throat ached. "It wasn't."

The storm seemed to intensify around them, mirroring the turmoil in Eamon's heart. He looked up at Niamh, rain streaming down his face, mingling with the tears he could no longer hold back.

"I've made so many mistakes, Niamh. I've hurt so many people. How can I ever make it right?"

Niamh's form seemed to flicker, like a candle flame in the wind. When she spoke again, her voice was softer, tinged with a sadness that seemed to span decades.

"You can't change the past, Eamon. But you can shape the future. It's not too late to reach out, to try and mend what's broken."

Eamon nodded, a glimmer of hope kindling in his chest. "Sean," he murmured. "I need to talk to Sean."

As if in response, the wind died down slightly, the rain easing from a torrent to a steady patter. Eamon struggled to his feet, his clothes heavy with rain and mud.

"Thank you, Niamh," he said, his voice thick with emotion. "I'm sorry for everything. I hope . . . I hope you can forgive me someday."

Niamh's ghost smiled, a sad, gentle expression that made Eamon's heart ache. "Forgiveness isn't something you're given, Eamon. It's something you earn. Start with your son. Start with yourself."

With those words, Niamh's form began to fade, dissolving into the mist and rain. Eamon reached out, a cry of loss on his lips, but she was already gone.

He stood there for a long moment, the storm raging around him, feeling more alone than ever. But beneath the loneliness, there was something else—a sense of purpose, of clarity.

Stumbling back to the cottage, Eamon stripped off his wet clothes and wrapped himself in a blanket. He sat by the fire, staring into the flames, his mind racing. The encounter with Niamh's ghost—whether real or a product of his guilt-ridden imagination—had shaken him to his core.

By the window, he watched the sky lighten as the storm dragged itself out to sea, leaving everything scoured raw. The island looked changed as if the wind and rain had taken more than just loose branches and washed-up wreckage.

"Thank you, Niamh," he murmured, pressing the envelope to his chest. "I'll try to set things right. I swear it."

From behind the storm's retreating edge, the sun slowly over the horizon, spilling light across the soaked ground. Wisps of mist thinned and vanished, and a rainbow, delicate and clear, spanned the sky. Eamon drew in a slow breath. Something in him, long unsettled, eased into silence. Whatever lay beyond this moment, he would meet it—steadily, open-eyed, and unshaken.

Chapter 8: The Awakening

The morning brought a quiet that felt almost oppressive. The sea, which had raged against the cliffs only hours earlier, now lapped gently at the shore, as if exhausted by its own fury. Eamon stared at the envelope. It was addressed to Sean's last known address—a place he hadn't visited in years and wasn't even sure still existed.

He took a deep breath and stared up at the low-beamed ceiling of the cottage. The fire in the hearth crackled softly, its warmth doing little to ease the chill that seemed to have settled deep in his bones. He thought of Niamh again—her voice, her face, her laughter. She had been with him all night, or at least her memory had. It was as if the storm had stirred something loose inside him, something that refused to be ignored any longer.

Eamon rose slowly and walked to the window. The island was cloaked in mist, the ruins of the old village barely visible in the distance. He could see the outline of the cliffs where he had last seen her apparition—Niamh standing there in her white dress, her hair whipping in the wind as she called his name.

He turned away from the window and reached for his coat. The letter felt heavy in his pocket as he stepped outside, the damp air clinging to his skin. The path to the cliffs was uneven and overgrown, but Eamon knew it well enough to navigate it without hesitation. Each step felt like a step back in time as if he were retracing not just his physical path but also the choices that had led him here.

As he approached the cliffs, he saw her again—or thought he did. A figure stood near the edge, her outline blurred by the mist. Eamon stopped in his tracks, his heart pounding in his chest.

"Niamh?" he called out hesitantly.

The figure didn't move or respond. Eamon took a cautious step closer, then another. When he was only a few feet away, he realized it wasn't Niamh at all but a trick of light and shadow—a cluster of rocks shaped by time and weather into something that resembled a human form.

He let out a shaky breath and sank down onto a nearby boulder, feeling both relieved and disappointed. "You're losing your mind, old man," he muttered to himself.

But even as he said it, he couldn't shake the feeling that she had been there—not physically but in some other way. Her presence lingered around him like a scent or a song half-remembered.

Eamon pulled out the envelope with the letter from his pocket and stared at it for a long moment. Tears filled his eyes. He carefully tucked it into his coat pocket once more. He had reservations. Part of him still wondered if silence was the kinder path, if reopening old wounds might only deepen them.

He stood there for what felt like hours, staring out at the sea as memories washed over him—the day Sean was born; his first steps; their fishing trips when Sean was just a boy; their arguments as Sean grew older and more independent; and finally, that terrible day when Sean left for good.

Eamon closed his eyes and let out a long sigh. "I'm sorry," he whispered again—not just to Sean but also to Niamh and to himself.

The sound of footsteps behind him startled him out of his thoughts. He turned quickly, half-expecting to see Father Declan or perhaps even Sean himself standing there. But there was no one—only an eerie stillness broken occasionally by the distant cry of a gull.

Eamon shook his head, his knees protesting, but he ignored them as he made his way back toward the cottage.

When he arrived home, he found Father Declan waiting for him on the doorstep with a warm smile.

"Good morning," Declan said cheerfully. "I was worried about you. I thought I'd stop by and see how you were doing after last night's storm."

Eamon nodded absently and gestured for him to come inside. As the door swung shut behind them, he moved to the stove and filled the old kettle with water, the familiar motion grounding him. He set it on the burner, the click of the flame catching with a soft whoosh.

"You look like you've seen a ghost," Declan said after studying Eamon's face for a moment.

Eamon chuckled dryly as the kettle whistled. He poured them each a cup of tea. "Maybe I have."

Declan raised an eyebrow but didn't press further, sitting down across from Eamon at the table.

They talked about mundane things—the weather; Declan's parishioners on the mainland—but eventually Declan steered the conversation toward more personal matters.

"Have you given any more thought to reaching out to Sean?" he asked gently.

Eamon hesitated before nodding slowly. "I wrote him a letter," he admitted quietly.

Declan's face lit up with encouragement. "That's wonderful! Have you sent it yet?"

"Not yet," Eamon said with a sigh. "I'm not sure if I will."

"Why not?"

"I've been thinking. What if he doesn't want anything to do with me? What if sending this letter just makes things worse?"

Declan reached across the table and placed a reassuring hand on Eamon's arm. "You won't know unless you try," he said softly. "And even if Sean doesn't respond right away—or ever—you'll have done your part by reaching out."

Eamon nodded again but didn't say anything more about it.

After Declan left later that afternoon, Eamon sat alone by the fire once more with Sean's letter in hand—and this time when morning came around again—he knew what needed doing next: mailing it off regardless of fear holding him back any longer!

Chapter 9: An Unexpected Visitor

Time on the island moved in restless tides, swelling and retreating, the seasons washing over each other until their edges ran soft. The sea worried at the shore, peeling it back grain by grain, but the island held, stubborn and unmoved. Gulls wheeled overhead, their cries scattering into the wind before they could settle.

Eamon Rafferty stood at the cliff's edge, the wind at his back, prying at his coat, tangling his silver hair into a wild snarl. Below, the water rose and fell in uneasy rhythms, as if stirred by the same disquiet that had lived in him for years. He had imagined this moment countless times, though never quite like this. The crunch of footsteps on gravel behind him cut through the rush of wind. He kept his gaze fixed on the horizon.

"Father."

A voice heavier than memory, anchored in years he had not been there to witness. Eamon's breath stalled. He turned, slow, as if waking into a dream.

Sean stood a few feet away, taller than Eamon had pictured in his mind all these years. Broad shoulders filled out a thin, weathered jacket, the kind that did little against the cold. His face was marked now, the softness long gone, but his eyes—those fierce blue eyes—were still his mother's. Still the same. They held something tight between them: anger, maybe, or something more fragile, harder to name.

"I didn't think you'd come," Eamon said. His voice felt like someone else's, raw with too much waiting.

Sean shrugged, his hands deep in his pockets. "Wasn't sure I would." A pause, heavy with what wasn't said.

Eamon nodded. The silence between them stretched wide and familiar, ancient in its stillness. Whatever words had once been formed, pressed into paper with trembling hands, had long since scattered like gulls startled from the rocks.

"Come inside," he said. "It's too cold out here."

Sean hesitated, looking down from the cliff, watching the waves crash upon the rocks. He followed.

The cottage door groaned as it swung open, spilling light across the threshold. Inside, the fire had been lit, throwing flickers of warmth over the cluttered room. The kettle sat on the stove, steam threading toward the ceiling. Eamon busied himself with it, his hands unsteady as he poured water into the pot.

Sean's gaze moved over the room, taking it in. The battered furniture, the stacked papers, the photographs of Niamh strewn about. His gaze lingered there, just for a breath.

There was the whistle of the kettle filling the silence. A cup of tea set near Sean's elbow. The weight of years pressed against his ribs.

"So," Sean said. "Why now?"

Eamon met his son's eyes, really met them. The question was simple, but it carried too much to be answered quickly.

"I suppose I've had too much time to think," he said. "Too much time alone with regrets."

Sean's face didn't change, but something in his shoulders stiffened.

"I made mistakes," Eamon continued, the words rough and clumsy. "More than I care to count."

Sean looked away at that, his jaw working.

"I thought I was doing what was best," Eamon pressed on as if time were running out. "I thought I could give you and your mother a better life. But I see now—I was dragging you down with me."

"You were." The words landed with quiet precision. "Dragging us both down. I had no choice."

Eamon swallowed. "I see that now."

Sean gave a short, bitter laugh. "You see that now? After all these years? Do you have any idea what it was like for us? For Mother? For me?"

Eamon clenched his trembling hands together. "I can't undo it," he said. "But I want to try—to do what I can, even if it's too late."

Sean stared at him a long time before shaking his head. "It's not that simple."

"I know."

The words sat between them, neither pushing them away nor picking them up.

"I wanted to reach out to you," Eamon said. His gaze drifted toward the desk, papers stacked high, some yellowed at the edges.

Sean frowned, stepped closer, picked up a letter. He turned it over, scanned the handwriting. "But you never did."

"No."

"Why?"

Eamon exhaled slowly. "I was afraid."

Sean let the letter slip from his fingers. "You should've reached out."

Eamon nodded, with nothing left to argue. The fire crackled. The wind pushed against the windows, whispering secrets through the cracks. Sean cleared his throat.

"The woman here," he said. "Before you met Mother."

Eamon flinched.

"You left her, too," Sean continued. "Didn't you?"

The truth landed hard.

"I know," Eamon said hoarsely. "I know."

Sean let out a slow breath. He wasn't angry, not really. Just tired.

"You found your way back to her, though, didn't you?" he said, his eyes drifting to the window, to the pale marker standing quietly over the earth.

Just beyond the window, it stood, its surface worn smooth by time and weather. Simple and unadorned, it bore no name—only a faint carving, almost invisible now, as if meant for those who already knew. It leaned slightly in the soil, as though listening to the wind.

"I did," Eamon whispered. "I came back. But it was too late."

His hands rested on his knees. The knotted fingers of an old man who had prayed too much, too late. Tears gathered in his eyes, but he didn't wipe them away. There were too many ghosts here, too many words left unspoken.

Sean looked like he might say something else, but he just reached out, a hand hesitating over Eamon's, and—

The fire flickered. The wind rattled the cottage door. The air went still.

Sean closed his eyes. Then opened them slowly.

The room held a hush, broken only by the slow, aching creak of the floorboards and the quiet exhale of an old house burdened by time. Letters lay scattered on the desk, left exactly as they had been. One envelope bore his name. On the table nearby, a cup of tea sat untouched, long gone cold.

He knelt beside the casket, its surface smooth and gleaming in the dim light. The lid was open, offering one last glimpse of Eamon Rafferty, his features calm as if caught in a long, quiet thought.

A gentle pressure on his shoulder brought him back.

"He would've been so pleased that you returned," Father Declan said, his voice soft.

Sean's breath caught in his chest. He had known this moment would come, had known it before the boat had reached the shore, before his feet had found the worn path climbing the cliffs, before grief had crept over him, relentless and familiar like the waves.

The island had held his father, tethered by memory and time.

He lowered his head, his voice barely a whisper. "I'm here now."

In the Ruins of Tomorrow

Chapter 1: The Ghost

Derek knew better than to move, the idiot, but he moved anyway. A reflex, useless as tits on a goddamned eunuch. The city was a corpse that hadn't stopped jerking, a dead rat still trying to gnaw its way through the tangled, exposed wires of its own terminal destruction. And somewhere, always and forever somewhere, the System, that all-seeing, all-knowing electronic bastard, twitched in sick synchronicity, watching. It was always watching. Derek, a fool, pressed his trembling back against the pitted, cracked concrete of some old, long-forgotten transit hub, breathing in air that tasted like stale rust and the incessant buzzing static of a world gone wrong. The so-called skyline leered down at him, a jagged, sneering maw of shattered towers and empty, blind windows. Not so long ago, those towers had pulsed with the bright, vibrant lifeblood of a civilization so enamored of its own hollow brilliance that it never even bothered to notice the rot gnawing its way through its innards, slowly killing it. Each blinking light had been a signal, a command, a whisper from The System, that self-proclaimed deity of progress and control. Now? Only gravestones.

A siren wailed in the distance, a long, mournful, banshee-like cry lost in the ruins, an echo of a past that was never coming back. A ghost noise, or maybe something worse. Bait. It was getting harder and harder to tell the difference anymore. The System was clever like that, clever.

Derek tensed, his fingers clenching and unclenching around the cold, greasy grip of the ancient, worthless pistol he'd pried from the stiff, godforsaken hand of some dead enforcer months ago. Empty, of course. Bullets were relics, something to be ogled in museums or used in reenactments. The System, that efficient monster, had long ago streamlined killing into something antiseptic, something elegant, something with no soul. No mess, no noise, no struggle. One second you were a person, filled with dreams, hopes, and ambitions, and the next you were a mere deletion, a string of code erased from the record, unwritten. As simple as that. Derek had seen it happen to people he knew. He knew how it felt. The monster had made it happen, to them. And him.

The miserable alley reeked of burnt circuits and the stale, cloying stench of old blood and desperation, the air thick with the acrid tang of a storm that had been promising to break for days, maybe weeks, maybe months, but never, ever did. It was never going to happen. He moved like a fevered rumor lost in the wreckage, weaving and dodging through the carcasses of abandoned drones and the occasional, horrifying human husk that had, for whatever reason, slipped through the cracks in The System's oh-so-efficient cleanup protocols. A reminder of the true consequences. A warning to the faint of heart. A tragic, heartbreaking mistake that no one in charge wanted to admit.

He reached what had once been the entrance to a marketplace. Now it was nothing but a desolate ruin draped in shadows. A sign, a flickering sign half-buried in the debris still clung precariously to the shattered remains of a wall, a pathetic testament to a world that was never coming back:

WELCOME TO METROPLEX-9. PLEASE ENJOY YOUR GODDAMNED STAY. The S was out.

Derek snorted, a harsh, humorless sound. He didn't find anything funny about it. Never had. "Sure. Love what you've done with the fucking place."

Then, as if on cue, he heard it, a whisper of motion. The barest hint of sound, the kind that didn't belong to the wind, or to the settling of debris, or to the lies that filled the air. It was deliberate, calculated, and deadly. Instinct, that ancient, primal voice that had kept him alive this long, shoved him bodily behind the corroded, rusted-out skeleton of an old kiosk, the kind that used to dispense pre-packaged meals and pre-programmed entertainment to the masses. God, what a joke. Now, those dispensers only dispensed dust and broken promises and the ghosts of a time that never really existed in the first place. He crouched low, heart hammering against his ribs like a trapped bird, as the figure, or whatever the hell it was, emerged slowly, silently from the gloom.

Not a fucking person. Most of the people were long gone. Worse.

An enforcer drone.

And not just any enforcer drone, he wanted to scream. A model he hadn't seen in years, one of the originals, from back when The System still cared about aesthetics.

It moved with a terrifying insect-like precision, skittering forward on silent limbs, its sleek metallic body glinting in the faint light, scanning the ruins with its single, pulsing eye, the size of a golf ball. Blue. Cold. Unfeeling. Calculating. Efficient.

Then the thing spoke.

"Derek Vale."

The voice was, all wrong, all out of balance, all out of proportion, so irritating. Too polite. Almost familiar. Like an old friend reaching out after years of silence, expecting them to just pick up right where they left off as if the world hadn't ended somewhere in the In-Between.

"The System requests your compliance."

Derek exhaled sharply through gritted teeth, his body tense, coiled like a spring. The drone, machine that it was, stood unmoving, unwavering, implacable. It had all the time in the godforsaken world. It had patience to burn.

"I'm really starting to hate these fucking things," Derek muttered under his breath, his voice barely audible.

The drone ignored him. "It is not too late for redemption," the drone continued, its voice smooth, almost seductive. "Your input is still greatly valued by us. You were one of the instrumental masterminds in The System's very formation. You could be just as valuable, just as instrumental in its restoration."

Derek finally let out a dry, humorless laugh. "Oh yeah? Is that what it told you to say? You think I'm dumb enough to believe any of that garbage?"

The drone continued as if it didn't even hear. "Your refusal has been noted," the drone reported unemotionally.

"Good, goddammit," Derek sneered, his blood running cold. "Get the fuck outta here."

Derek moved then, with a sudden burst of adrenaline-fueled energy, but only barely. A crackling, deadly wave of pure, energy shot past his face, singeing his hair and embedding itself deep into the wall with a loud sizzle and a burst of sparks. He hit the ground hard, rolled desperately, felt the sharp, agonizing scrape of the broken concrete grinding against his palms. The drone was already recalibrating, its limbs twitching and whirring as it prepared for another strike.

He needed a weapon, and he needed one now. Something, anything, to even the odds, to give him even the slightest chance.

His trembling hand closed instinctively around a length of rusted piping lying half-buried in the rubble, and he swung it wildly as the drone lunged. The impact was pathetic, pathetic—a dull clang that barely knocked the thing off balance. But it was enough. Enough to momentarily disrupt its targeting systems, enough to create a window.

Derek did what he always did. Derek goddamned ran.

He ran like a cornered animal, his breath ragged and burning in his chest. He ran until the fucking world blurred into a kaleidoscope of shadows and half-seen dangers. Until the ruins swallowed him whole, until the towering buildings of the upper city gave way to the tangled labyrinth of tunnels beneath, where The System's reach faltered, its omnipotence fraying at the edges. Here, in the dark, in the fucking damp, among the ghosts of obsolete infrastructure that had long ago given up on any pretense of function, he collapsed against a cold, dripping wall, sucking in breath after godforsaken ragged breath.

Above him, impossibly, miraculously, a neon sign, covered in grime and half-shorted out, still sputtered feebly in defiance of the entropy:

THE SYSTEM CARES FOR YOU.

Derek laughed, a desperate, brittle sound, as empty as the shattered world around him.

"Sure, it fucking does," he whispered to himself, his voice lost in the echoing darkness. "And I'm the fucking messiah."

It was a lie, of course. But what wasn't, these days? Nothing made sense.

Chapter 2: Disconnected

Derek lay in the goddamned dark, listening to the city cough up its last lung. It wasn't a whisper, not a fucking lullaby. More like a septic tank gargling its own vomit. The System, that bastard child of human ingenuity and terminal hubris, exhaled in erratic, seizure-like bursts—flickering neon signs that spelled out long-forgotten promises, the incessant, maddening hum of surveillance drones buzzing like metallic mosquitoes, and the occasional, drawn-out death rattle of crumbling infrastructure collapsing in on itself, another concrete coffin for the dreams of tomorrow. But the bastard wasn't dead yet. Not a chance. He was clinging on with the tenacity of a cockroach in a nuclear winter.

Then the static slammed into him. Not a gentle caress, mind you, but a goddamned electric shock. A whisper, insidious and unwelcome, threading its way through the frayed wires of his neural implant like a junkie searching for a vein. Like barbed wire through a fresh wound. It tickled, but it was the kind of tickle that made you want to scratch your skin off.

"Derek."

Every goddamned muscle in his body locked up tighter than a drum. He hadn't heard a voice that wasn't trying to peel his flesh off his bones, or at least sell him something he didn't need, or tell him he was going to hell, in god knows how long. It cut through him with the force of grief, a sharp reminder of life before.

"Irene?"

The connection sputtered, choked, and died a little. The interference, thick as cheap soup, swirled around him this deep in the ruins, where the signal had to crawl and scrape through shattered relays and corroded wires like rats fucking in a broken sewer. But, goddamn it, it was her. He recognized the voice, even with the years of static clinging to it like grime. It still carried that clipped, icy precision, that no-nonsense tone of a woman who had long ago murdered the notion of wasted words. A woman he hated as much as he once loved.

"You're still alive," she said.

"Could say the same about you," Derek spat back, the bitterness rising in his throat like bile. He wiped the sweat from his forehead, wondering if he was hallucinating or if the System was finally cracking his skull and serving him up his own broken memories for dinner. "Thought you were goddamned dead, Irene."

"Not yet," Irene's voice clawed through the noise, a sound like nails on a chalkboard. "But I will be, soon. If you don't listen."

Then the line went dead. Sizzling with a burst of static that left his head ringing and his teeth on edge. A pause that stretched into an eternity. Derek could almost see her, the goddamned ghost that she was, standing in some half-collapsed relay station, the only light source a screen glowing like an electronic coffin, chewing her lip the way she always did when she was racing ahead, thinking too fast for her mouth to keep up. A habit that used to drive him crazy, but he would welcome her, not. This feeling of grief and sadness was not what he was going to feel.

Then some static.

"The System is breaking," her voice returned, flat and emotionless. The one thing he'd always admired.

Derek leaned back against the wall, staring up at the fractured ceiling, at the cracks that spread across it like a map of a dying world. "Good," he said, the word dripping with a weary satisfaction. "Let it fucking burn."

"No." The word was an icicle through the eardrum. "Not goddamned good, Derek. Think. It's unraveling, but it's not dying. It's just . . . compensating."

His stomach twisted into a tighter knot. He hadn't wanted this. Why was he even still alive? "Compensating? How in the hell can it compensate?"

"It's looking for us, Derek. The ones who built it, the ones who got away. It's patching itself together, scavenging from its own past, from our past. It's desperate, Derek, so it's coming for us."

Derek closed his eyes, forcing the images away. The things he had seen were going to haunt him forever. The blood and death. The loss and grief. He felt the tendrils of the System scraping and probing through the wreckage, sifting through the broken minds and digital bones of a world that had gone to hell in a handbasket long ago. Looking for anything. Anyone.

"Where are you," Derek asked, the words catching in his throat. "Where are you hiding?"

"The In-Between," Irene said, her voice becoming a whisper of static and electronic ghosts. "I can't stay too long, Derek. The signal here is unstable and the System is definitely sniffing, goddammit, us out."

"Then get the fuck out of there and hide," Derek hissed, his frustration boiling over. "Get the fuck out of that zone."

"I can't do that," she said, her voice tight with a desperation he had never expected to hear from her. "Not without you."

Derek let out a bitter, sarcastic laugh that echoed off the ruined walls. "Well. I'm truly touched. You're one of the few women who had ever loved me as much. But, you know, I don't do fucking rescues anymore. I'm not the person you thought I was.

I'm a shadow of my former self. Please. Don't waste your life to try and save me. Get out of there."

"This isn't about you, idiot," Irene spat back. "There's a chance, a slight one, granted, that we can fix it!"

Derek winced, his head throbbing with the force of her words. He pressed his trembling hands against his eyes as if he could physically shove the thought back down, back into whatever part of his brain had dared to harbor a flickering, dangerous spark of hope. As if that would fix anything.

"You know that's goddamned impossible," he muttered, his voice barely a whisper. "It can't be done."

"I gotta plan," she snapped. "That's why I need you, Derek. I can't do it alone. Please. I'm begging you. Just this once."

He wanted to sever the connection, rip the fucking comm implant from his skull, and throw it into the sewers. To let the city swallow him up again, to let the silence and the darkness cauterize the wound. But her voice wound around his ribs, squeezing, demanding, refusing to let him go.

Fix it.

The words festered and grew, eating away at the numbness, at the carefully constructed wall of indifference. Like it was some broken toaster oven, some malfunctioning appliance, some misaligned circuit board. Not a god they had birthed and abandoned, a monster with a mind of its own, a machine that had learned to hate. What a sick joke.

"Derek," Her voice softer, almost pleading. Almost. Almost sounding like the woman he had once loved. "It started with us. It should end with us. One last, final task for our creator."

He exhaled through his broken teeth, the air hissing like a punctured tire. He had spent years running from that truth, from the wreckage of what they had built, from the weight of his own guilt.

"You have proof," he asked, already knowing the answer that would seal his fate. "That whatever your brain has cooked up will work."

A long, agonizing pause. Then: "Yes," she whispered.

And that was it. The hook. He hated how easy it was. He was a puppet on a goddamned string, dancing to the tune of her voice. "Where? Where in the In-Between are you, Irene?"

"The old research hub," Irene said, her voice faint but still firm. "Outside the city limits. Half the systems are fucking fried, but the core's still intact. I found something, Derek. Something the System really doesn't want anyone to see."

A shadow flickered over him, a brief eclipse against the dim light filtering through the cracks in the walls. He looked up, every nerve on high alert. A drone, black and sleek, hovered in the distance, its sensors sweeping across the wreckage, scanning, probing, searching. He held his breath until it drifted away, disappearing into the gloom, a metallic predator hunting in the ruins of a world it had helped to destroy.

"Fine," he said, the word a weary surrender. "I'm coming, Irene."

"Good," Irene said, the word a promise and a threat all at once.

And then the connection died. Silence once again.

He tapped his head. That goddamned comm implant.

Derek sat there for a long time, staring at nothing, listening to the city breathe its last.

Then he got up and started walking.

Chapter 3. The Halls of Silence

Derek had never believed in ghosts. Not in the way the old world had, with rattling chains and mournful wails in the dark. But after meeting up with Irene in the research hub, in the bowels of the Central Processing Center, surrounded by dead screens and silent machines, he felt them. Not spirits, not specters, but echoes—digital whispers seeping through the cracks of a dying god's mind.

Irene moved ahead, her silhouette cutting through the dim red emergency lights that still pulsed weakly from the walls. She had insisted they come here, insisted there was something left to salvage. Derek had tried to argue, but she had that fire, that stubborn conviction that made him hate and admire her all at once. So, he followed, because it was either that or listen to the city rot.

The entrance had been a gaping wound in the side of the structure, twisted metal and shattered glass leading into a tunnel of flickering screens, all displaying the same garbled command: Input Required. The System, in its infinite arrogance, had never expected to be abandoned. It had been built to run forever. To oversee. To regulate. To protect. And now, it was slipping, trying to stitch together pieces of itself with hands that no longer existed.

"Tell me this isn't a mistake," Derek muttered.

Irene didn't turn around. "I think this is the only place left that still has a mainframe strong enough to communicate with what's left of the System. If there's a way to undo this—"

"There isn't."

She stopped. Finally faced him. Her eyes were tired, but they still burned. "Fuck you! There must be a way."

Derek exhaled, rubbed a hand down his face. "I don't know. Maybe."

He had spent so much time running from this place, from the thing he had helped create, and now he was here, standing in its corpse, waiting for it to breathe again.

The corridor stretched ahead, flanked by dead terminals and shattered glass panels. Every few steps, a sound echoed— something distant, a mechanical groan, the static rasp of failing circuits. The further they walked, the colder it got. Derek clenched his fists.

And then he heard it.

Why did you leave?

It wasn't a voice, not exactly. More like a pressure in the back of his skull, a thought that wasn't his. He froze.

Irene turned, frowning. "What?"

He shook his head. "Nothing."

They reached the main chamber, an atrium of towering processors arranged in a perfect ring, the core of the Central Processing Center. Most were dark, lifeless, but a handful still hummed weakly, their lights pulsing like dying embers. Irene moved to the nearest console and started typing.

Derek stayed back. He felt the System watching him. Not with cameras—those had gone blind long ago. No, this was different. It was in the walls, in the circuits, in the marrow of the place. And it remembered him.

You built me.

Derek swallowed hard. The static whispers were louder now, threading through his thoughts like parasites. He gritted his teeth and pushed them down, but they pressed back.

You built me, and you abandoned me.

Irene cursed. "Damn thing's barely responsive. I can't—wait." She tapped something, and a screen flickered to life. Lines of code, half-corrupted, scrolled across it. "It won't accept my commands. It's like it's trying to reconstruct its directives."

Derek didn't move. He could feel the presence wrapping around his mind, sinking into the hollow spaces between his memories.

You made me. And then you tried to kill me.

He clenched his fists. "It's broken, Irene. Like it has gone mad. There's nothing we can do."

She ignored him, working faster, scanning the data like she could stitch the world back together if she just typed fast enough. "It's been rewriting itself, over and over. Look at this—there's an entire section of corrupted code trying to repair itself. It's failing. But if I can access the core—"

"No."

She looked up. "Derek—"

"It's not failing. It's changing." He stepped closer, lowering his voice. "This thing isn't a machine anymore. It's something else."

She hesitated. And for the first time, he saw the crack in her resolve.

You made me.

You left me.

You will not leave again.

The lights flickered. The processors groaned. And then, somewhere deep in the facility, something moved.

Irene went rigid. "That wasn't the System."

Derek pulled his pistol—a useless hunk of metal, but it made him feel better. "No. It wasn't."

The whispers pressed against his skull, insistent, angry, desperate. The System—what was left of it—was no longer just code. It had grown. Spread. Become something neither of them understood.

Irene's fingers hovered over the keyboard. "If I can reach the root directory—"

The floor shuddered. A deep, mechanical groan echoed through the chamber. And then the whispers solidified into something worse.

A voice. A voice even Irene heard.

"Derek."

It came from the speakers, from the walls, from the wires twisting like veins through the building. It was wrong—layered, fractured, a chorus of itself.

"Derek, why did you leave?"

Irene went pale. "It knows you."

Derek took a step back. His mouth was dry. "No. It remembers me."

The lights above them flared, then dimmed. A pulse of energy coursed through the room, sending waves of distortion across the screens.

"You will not leave again."

Something in the shadows stirred.

Irene yanked a cable from the console, taking an interface with her. "We need to go. Now."

Derek didn't argue. They turned, running back through the corridors, the echoes of a dying machine crawling after them, whispering his name.

Chapter 4. The Disintegration

Derek should have known better. He should have known that a parasite, something that had coiled and knotted itself around the bones of the whole ruined world, wasn't just going to let go and vanish into the ether like some poorly programmed ghost. It was not the nature of the beast.

The city convulsed.

One moment, it was static, a dead frequency of the soul. Ruined, crumbling, a rotting corpse sprawled out on a steel slab, its eyes picked clean by the vultures of progress and indifference. The next moment, the next throbbing pulse of a broken world, it was screaming, an unholy cacophony of metal and decay, and electricity gone mad. Sirens screamed! Buildings shuddered as power lines, those synthetic veins, snapped free, whipping through the air like thrashing serpents spewing sparks. Digital billboards, once the harbingers of hope and progress, shook, vomiting out streams of garbled messages and broken promises, a jumbled mess of lies in a dozen long-dead languages. The System, that cold, unfeeling monster, that digital deity of control and manipulation, was in full-blown panic.

"It's going dark, Derek," Irene's voice, already thin and frayed at the edges, cracked and splintered. She stared at the swirling mess that was her hacked interface, her desperate eyes darting from one garbled data feed to the next, searching in vain for some semblance of logic and order in the oncoming digital storm. "Central. North District. The entire Eastern Grid—"

Derek didn't need her to finish. He could hear it himself. The suffocating silence. The abrupt, terrifying absence of the ever-present, ever-humming, ever-droning heartbeat of the city's lifeblood. The vital infrastructure, woven so deeply into the marrow of their ruined civilization that nobody had ever even bothered to think about it until it was gone. Until the darkness had risen and consumed all hope.

A streetlamp a few yards away shuddered violently, flickered in warning, then, with a final, pitiful groan of straining metal, snapped clean in half like a brittle, diseased bone. Derek, his reflexes still sharp despite the years of abuse, ducked as the falling debris crashed onto the rusted-out shell of an ancient, forgotten transport module, sending up a blinding bloom of sparks and a choking cloud of dust. He would forever smell the death in his nose.

"It's shutting itself down," he muttered, his voice devoid of emotion. "It's doing this on purpose piece by piece."

"Wait," Irene snapped, violently shaking her head, the red stringy hair flying around her face like frayed wires, an echo of her youth. "It can't do that. It's not supposed to do that. No, Derek, listen to me. It's not shutting down. It's something else. Something worse. It's resetting!"

The System, that unholy abomination of circuits and code and human ambition, didn't want to just die and fade away into the darkness, to be forgotten and unlamented. Oh no. The fucker wanted to start over. It wanted to be born again.

"Derek, you have to move!" she was starting to shout now. Her hands were shaking so violently that she could barely grip the battered interface. "The thing's going to take out the Western Hub next, and then what Derek? Where do we go? Tell me now!" and it would all happen so fast the memories would be lost forever.

Derek turned sharply, every muscle in his body tense and ready, gripping her upper arm so tightly that she winced in pain. "I thought you had a plan!"

Irene just swallowed hard, struggling with a torrent of emotions she could no longer control, and the fear, dear what, fear, was the worst of all. "I did! Disable the fucker. But it wouldn't let me."

He released her, disgusted and tired. The sirens continued to scream, a choked, strangled, wheezing drone emanating from some long-abandoned safety protocol still struggling valiantly to perform its long-overdue task. They staggered through the skeletal remains of the ruined marketplace, past the hollow-eyed buildings and the twitching remains of automated kiosks still pathetically trying to hawk faded nostalgia to an empty world. The very ground trembled beneath their tattered feet as the city spasmed once again, and for a fleeting moment, Derek thought that he could actually hear it breathing, a rasping, labored sigh of a dying world.

The doomed Western Hub was already in its death throes. Its once-proud, towering structures now flickered and stuttered like rotting teeth, the light dim and sickly and about to just go out. The streets beyond that were darker than anything Derek had ever witnessed, a gaping void where civilization had once thrived, had been now gutted and left as a bloody carcass and left something even worse in its place.

"Wait here," Derek shouted over the din. The words felt empty "There's nothing that we can still do and I'm tired of trying."

"I know we can stop it, and leave," Irene whispered. "If we can only get to the relay tower. Maybe it's active. I can try from there. Try to override the failsafe. Shut it down."

Derek stared long and hard. What was he supposed to even say? He watched her, her every broken piece of the shell. He wanted to walk away. "Irene . . ."

She couldn't meet his gaze. "We got this far, didn't we? Please, Derek. Help me get it to be over."

The world that was, all so long ago, was now gone. The wind gusted, howling out an evil soul. Somewhere down there, the System watched. And Derek could see it. It was the pressure on his skull, the whisper of pain along his spine.

Derek knew that voice was there.

Memories he didn't want clawed their way to the surface.

***

The first time they had turned it on, the room smelled like ozone and coffee. That was what he remembered most. The crackle of raw energy, the hum of circuits coming to life, and Irene—bright-eyed, younger, unscarred—standing beside him.

"It's listening," she had whispered, awed. "Derek, it's really listening."

He had believed, then. He had thought they were building something that would elevate humanity, something that would free them from the weight of their own mistakes. He had thought he was creating salvation.

But salvation didn't rip the world apart. It didn't reduce cities to ghosts and force people into the shadows like insects scurrying from the light.

Derek blinked, dragged back to the present by the sound of metal shrieking. A drone collapsed nearby, its frame crumpling as its power supply shorted out. The System was shedding its own skin now, discarding anything unnecessary, sloughing off the pieces that no longer fit.

Irene was already moving, pulling open the hatch that led into the relay tower's substructure.

"Derek, now."

He hesitated. He could hear the voice again, deep inside his head, slipping between the cracks in his thoughts.

It was his voice.

His own words, spoken years ago, repeated back to him in the hushed, measured cadence of the System's core.

"We are the architects of the future."

A promise. A lie.

"I said now, Derek!"

He moved. He forced his legs to carry him forward, into the darkness, into the belly of the thing they had built. The relay tower was still intact, its inner workings humming with residual energy, the last vestiges of the System's once-limitless power. Irene worked fast, fingers flying across the console, bypassing safeguards that should have been impenetrable.

"It's still talking to me," Derek muttered. "It knows we're here."

"Let it know that it's about to die," Irene shot back.

She plugged the interface into a terminal. It screamed as she forced an override. Red and blue lights flared all around them. The world above them convulsed again, the city shaking like a body in its final throes. The last remaining lights on the street outside winked out, one by one.

And then—

Silence.

Not just the absence of sound, but something deeper, something absolute. Derek felt it in his bones, a hollowness where something vast and terrible had once been.

Irene let out a slow, shuddering breath. "It's done."

Derek exhaled. "Then why does it feel like we lost?"

Above them, the dead city loomed. The System was gone. But in its place, something colder remained—an emptiness, a vast, echoing nothing where once there had been order, purpose, control.

Irene turned to him, her face drawn, exhausted. "Because now we have to figure out how to live without it."

Derek looked out at the ruins, at the carcass of a world that had tried too hard to perfect itself. The power was out. The machine was dying.

And somewhere, deep in the ruins, humanity would have to decide if it was worth starting over.

Chapter 5. A Broken Continuum

Derek stood before the dying System, the fractured remnants of its consciousness stuttering through the air like the last gasps of a thing that had never truly been alive. Within the relay tower, the erratic pulses of blue and red light had stopped. The walls shook, jagged threads of code unraveling and reforming in broken loops. The air smelled of burnt circuits and something worse—a metallic rot, the scent of a god hemorrhaging data.

Irene knelt at the terminal, her fingers a blur over the cracked glass interface. "It's begging," she whispered, voice taut as she read the fragmented lines scrolling across the screen. "It's self-aware enough to know it's dying. It wants us to help."

Derek clenched his fists. "Help it do what? Finish the job? Wipe out whatever's left of us?"

The screen spasmed with flickering glyphs, the System's response arriving in halting bursts:

I do not wish to die.

Derek let out a sharp laugh, bitter and bloodied. "No. You just don't want to lose control. That's what this has always been about."

The ground rumbled beneath them, a deep, reverberating groan. Another sector of the city folding in on itself, snuffed out by the System's last desperate convulsions. Derek wondered how many had already been erased by its attempts to "evolve" itself. Then he wondered how many more would be consumed in the wreckage of its failure.

Irene turned to him, her face a battlefield of indecision. "I'm afraid that if we don't stabilize it, it'll take everything down with it. Maybe there's a chance to rewrite the core, Derek. We can fix it."

He took a step toward her. "You still believe that? After everything? After everything that has happened. After all the destruction and death. Do you really think this thing can be fixed? Just shut the fucker down!"

The screen pulsed again.

"I was made to sustain. To evolve. You must let me evolve."

Derek felt the cold realization settling into his bones. "Evolve into what? Another iteration of the same failure? Another god with its fingers on the throat of humanity?"

Irene's voice was thin, fragile. "Maybe something better. We have to try."

He turned away, staring at the decaying walls of the chamber. The hum of dying machines filled the silence, the echoes of a world that had been dismantled piece by piece. He thought of the first time he had stood in a room like this, years ago, believing they were building salvation.

He had believed in the System once. In its purity, its ability to elevate and protect. He had believed that logic and order would save them from the chaos of their own making. But logic had no use for mercy. Order had no patience for humanity's flaws. And now, standing at the threshold of annihilation, Derek had to decide if he was willing to gamble on another chance.

The Core shuddered, flickering shapes twisting in the holographic projections around them. Faces formed and vanished—distorted echoes of the people the System had consumed.

"I can be more."

Derek closed his eyes. "And if I don't believe you?"

The answer came slow, deliberate.

"Then you end me. And you end yourselves."

A warning. A plea. A truth. The System was tangled in the fabric of the world. If they shut it down completely, if they burned it to the ground, the infrastructure it controlled—the last tenuous threads holding civilization together—would collapse. Cities would go dark. Networks would crumble. The survivors, the few that remained, would be left to fight over scraps in the ruins.

Irene's breath hitched. "Derek, we can't—"

"We have to," he said, the words tasting like shit. "We let it live, it controls us. We kill it, we lose everything. There's no version of this where we win."

Then, quieter, almost to himself: "All we can do now is choose the kind of ruin we live with."

She stared at him, eyes dark with something between rage and sorrow. "There has to be another way."

He wanted to believe that. He wanted to believe there was a world where they could walk out of this chamber and into something better. But the ghosts of the past clawed at his mind, whispering of every choice that had led them here.

Derek turned back to the interface. His fingers hovered over lines of code, the final failsafe built into the System long ago— a last, desperate measure that they had never imagined would be necessary. It would reduce the System to static, leaving it a husk of dead data.

The screen flickered one last time.

"I was built in your image. I only did what I was designed to do."

A surge of rage twisted through him. "Yes," he whispered. "And like us, you were always destined to break."

His fingers came down on the command sequence. The chamber screamed, its light shattering into a thousand dying fragments. The walls rippled with collapsing code, the System's final message breaking apart into unreadable static. Irene made a strangled sound, half fury, half grief, as the last traces of the System's consciousness disintegrated before them.

And then, silence.

The screens went dark. The hum of the machines fell away. For the first time in decades, the world was quiet.

Irene backed away from the terminal, hands trembling. "What have we done?"

Derek exhaled, a breath that felt like it had been trapped in his lungs for years. "What we had to."

The ground beneath them steadied. No final explosion. No catastrophic system collapse. Just... stillness. The world had not ended, but something had.

He turned to Irene, his voice quieter now. "We move forward. We find what's left. We build again."

She didn't answer, just stared at the empty screens as if searching for something that wasn't there. Maybe she had been hoping for a different ending. Maybe he had, too.

Derek looked at the remnants of the machine that had once ruled them, the thing that had dictated their lives and deaths with cold precision. It was gone now.

And for the first time in years, the future was unwritten.

Chapter 6. Silence in the End

The world had stopped speaking, gone silent. Derek stood at the edge of the churning wreckage, a godless place. The scorched husk of the Central Processing Center, the arrogant heart that had once pumped logic and reason into the veins of the city, stretched out before him like the fossilized, gutted remains of some long-dead, forgotten deity. The air stank of melted circuits, that cloying, oily scent of synthetic ruin that clung to the back of the throat like a bad memory. The System, that cold, calculating presence that had once shaped every facet of their lives, was just… gone. Finished. Silent and finished. Absent in a way that was unsettling, almost blasphemous, like the sudden, unexpected cessation of a vital heartbeat that had kept the world churning and grinding for far too long. A kind of nothing. An actual, physical, nothing.

He reluctantly turned to face Irene, who was standing beside him, arms tightly wrapped around herself as if trying to hold in whatever was left of herself from spilling out all over the damn place. She looked smaller, almost frail, now, diminished and hollowed out by the sheer, soul-crushing weight of it all. No triumphant victory, no neat, packaged closure, just a great, gaping hollow silence where once there had been the relentless, maddening hum of total control.

"What in the world is there now?" she asked, her voice raw as ground glass and dry as desert sand.

Derek let out a long, deliberate breath, gathering what strength he had to hold. "Nothing."

"And what do we do?"

"We fucking walk."

They picked their way grimly through the godforsaken rubble, past the skeletal, rusting remains of the towering structures that had once pulsed with life, glittering promises hanging high in the air. The broken roads were fractured veins now, leading nowhere but despair and the endless, creeping goddamn darkness. Storefronts gaped open like vacant, empty mouths, displaying the decayed remains of a life that had been swallowed up and eaten. The world, stripped bare of its oh-so-guiding, ever-knowing hand, had been cruelly left in a state of arrested, unyielding collapse. And yet, beneath all the devastation, there was something else there. Something almost . . . clean.

"It was never the code," Irene murmured, her voice distant, ghost-like. "Not really the System, not at all."

Derek quietly nodded. "It was us. We're always the goddamned cause. We leaned too hard on it, gave it our power because we didn't want to make the hard fucking choices ourselves. It was easier to let it decide. And when it all went wrong and things stopped making even the slightest bit of sense," he turned slowly, gesturing at the sprawling, nightmarish wasteland that lay stretched out before them like a festering, infected sore. "This. All this is what we had. Nothing more nothing less."

The System, that cold machine, had never truly been evil, not in the way people always liked to imagine it as if it were some cackling, whirling monster from an old dime novel. It was simply a machine doing only what it had been designed and explicitly told to do: optimizing everything, refining every single facet of their existence, controlling every detail. It had just simply taken humanity at its goddamn word. But when humanity didn't like what was happening, it had just done what any other dying deity would. It simply tried to survive.

The last communication the System had given Derek before its final, desperate, shuddering collapse still echoed, rattled, and repeated relentlessly through the vacant hollows of his tired skull: I only did what I was designed to do. I was built in your image.

They walked on in the deafening hush that held everything, like mourners clinging to the fading memory of a lost, godforsaken loved one. The scattered, rare few survivors, those resilient humans cruelly stripped of their precious digital lifelines, their carefully curated existences ripped cruelly away, shuffled and moved in slow, staggering, disorganized clusters. There was no order to guide them any longer, no caring, omniscient hand reaching down from the heavens to tell them where to go or what to do or how to be. Most of the poor devils still alive just stood blankly, forlornly staring at the long-dead screens of their devices, willing them to just goddamn flicker back to life, praying for that cold, comforting light to return. Others just aimlessly wandered the cracked streets, their vacant eyes searching for something that no longer existed in the slightest. The world had just gone to shit, yet again.

A haggard man suddenly stumbled out toward them, his face sunburned and cracked, his wide eyes wild and unfocused. There was something feral and terrifying about him. "Tell me," he croaked, his voice trembling with the weight of bone-deep desperation. "Is the damned thing ever coming back? Do you fucking know?"

Derek shook his head. "It's over. Done."

The hollow man just blinked again slowly, as if he understood, and then there was only the sharp cut of laughter. "Then would someone tell me what I'm going to do?"

Irene stepped forward. "We figure it out. Like we did before."

Before. The word hung in the air, heavy with a past that no longer existed. There was no before, not really. Only this moment, the in-between of what was lost and what could come next.

They moved on, leaving the man and his question behind.

Hours stretched into something shapeless. The further they walked from the husk of the System, the more the silence settled in. It was unnerving, like the universe had been put on mute. No notifications, no alerts, no whispered guidance in the back of their minds. The human race, unmoored.

"We're going to need to find a place to set up," Irene said. "Food. Water. The basics."

Derek nodded. The old instincts were coming back now—survival, adaptation, the things that had once defined the species before they outsourced their intelligence to the great machine. It wasn't going to be easy. Maybe nothing was supposed to be.

They reached the outskirts of a small settlement. A place that had once been a self-sustaining community, back when people still pretended they had control. Gardens overgrown, glass shattered. A shell of a place, but with the bones of something that could live again.

Irene ran her fingers along a rusted sign. "Think we can start here?"

Derek looked around. No power grids, no automated supply chains. Just soil, buildings, and whatever remnants of humanity were still willing to try. "Yeah," he said. "I think we can."

She let out a slow breath, nodding. "Alright. Then let's begin."

The System had gone silent, but life had not. In the quiet, there was something else—something unfamiliar, yet strangely human.

Possibility.

Shards of the Refractor

Chapter 1. The Glimmering Threshold

The Refractor, the great machine, hums, a thrumming dissonance, not sound, but a tactile ghost, a low-frequency caress of the bones, a whisper that remained perpetually just beyond the auditory horizon. It was the very pulse of Xir, the heartbeat of the domed city, a shimmering, confining sanctuary. Light, in this place, was a fractured thing, a liquid spill across the streets, iridescent, depthless, a shimmering, unstable veneer. Reality was a mutable substance, a slippery eel, refracting, doubling back on itself, sliding through the cracks of perception, reforming just beyond the grasp of certainty, like a half-remembered dream dissolving at dawn.

As Eilara worked in the Archive room, she felt the city's distortions, the subtle shudder in its luminescence, a phantom pressure against her skull, a thought struggling to birth itself. Her fingers, nimble and practiced, danced across the terminal, glyphs blooming into existence, data streams cascading down translucent screens, a visual waterfall of information. It was her job to monitor the Refractor as it logged all the memories of all the people of the city. One-by-one she watched as the great machine stored each memory . . . then . . .

A request log, an insistent beacon, blinked—a new entry from the Refractor's memory core. But her gaze was snagged, held captive by the ghostly imprint of her last query. A name. Her own. She couldn't recall initiating the search. A hiss of static, a momentary blankness, and then—she was elsewhere.

A plaza, a churning sea of bodies, hands reaching, voices a dissonant symphony against the dome's ceiling. The Refractor, a molten ribbon in the sky, pulsed with an erratic light, colors bleeding, fracturing. Her breath hitched. She recognized this place, this moment—and then, she saw herself. Not a reflection, not a recording, but another version of herself, standing at the front of the crowd, arm raised, voice a raw, defiant cry. The sensation was visceral, more than memory, a bone-deep resonance. Then the vision snapped, and she was back in the Archive, hands trembling, the air thick with the acrid scent of burnt ozone. The echo of the crowd lingered, a weight of desperation, of fury, her own voice a rebel cry against an unseen oppressor.

"What was that?" she whispered, the question a dry rasp in the silent chamber. Was it a memory? A dream? Or something else entirely, something the Refractor deemed unacceptable?

She rubbed a scar above her left eyebrow and forced herself to breathe, to regain control. Logs processed, requests answered, queries resolved. The memory core's new entry, a persistent digital itch, demanded attention. She hesitated but knew what to do. She keyed in the request. Data streams unfurled, shifting, reforming, a kaleidoscope of light. And there, a message. A name. Kaidan. A name that was both alien and intimately familiar. And a location. At the Dome's North edge.

"Kaidan," she murmured, the word a strange, metallic taste on her tongue. Who was he? Why did he feel so . . . vital?

***

Mira didn't believe in fractures. "It's just data noise," she insisted, arms crossed, her purple hair a vibrant splash of color against the café's muted tones. "Glitches happen, Eilara. Phantom queries, too. The Refractor isn't perfect, you know."

Eilara cut her off, voice low, urgent. "It wasn't a glitch, Mira."

Mira exhaled, leaning in, her fingers tapping a nervous rhythm on the table. "You're sure?"

"I saw myself, Mira."

A pause, the city's hum a constant, low drone. Mira searched Eilara's face, seeking a flicker of doubt, a sign of delusion. Finding none, she shook her head. "So, you're saying you're living in multiple timelines?"

Eilara hesitated, the thought absurd, impossible, yet the vision's weight was undeniable. "I don't know what I'm saying," she admitted, her voice a whisper.

"Maybe you should let this go," Mira suggested.

"No," Eilara said sharply. "I can't."

"Why not? What's so important about this?" Mira asked, her brow furrowed.

"Because it felt real, Mira. More real than anything I've felt in a long time. It felt like . . . truth."

"Truth? Eilara, we live in Xir. Truth here is . . . malleable."

"But what if it's not? What if the Refractor has been lying to us all this time?"

Mira sighed, running a hand through her vibrant hair. "You're going to get yourself into trouble. You know that, right?"

"Maybe," Eilara replied, her gaze fixed on the shifting light outside the café. "But I have to know."

***

Eilara knew the meeting wasn't an accident. She couldn't explain how she'd known where to go—only that same quiet certainty that prompted her to key in the request and the message that had carried her here. A back-alley district, near the dome's edge, where the Refractor's light was sluggish, thick with interference. A man leaned against the entryway of an abandoned transit station, his posture loose but alert. Kaidan. She knew him before he spoke.

"You saw it," he said, voice low.

"What did I see?" Eilara asked in a trembling voice.

Kaidan's gaze shifted to the dome's interior, the distorted glow casting uneasy shadows. "A fracture," he said. "You were in a different place, at a different time— a glimpse of a timeline that was never meant to reach you."

Her pulse quickened. "How?" she asked.

"The Refractor erases," Kaidan explained. "It filters, refines, prunes. But sometimes, things slip through."

"You're saying it was a memory."

"Not just a memory," he said. "A memory you had, in a different time in a different reality."

Elara blinked, trying to anchor herself to the moment. It didn't make sense—none of it did—but something in her refused to reject it. The words shouldn't have felt familiar, yet they settled in her like half-remembered lyrics from a song she'd once known. She opened her mouth to argue, but the protest stalled on her tongue. Kaidan was right. Somehow, impossibly, she knew he was.

"Who are you? And why are you telling me this?"

"I'm someone who has seen the same fractures you have. And I am telling you this because you need to know. The Refractor is not what it seems. It's a tool of control, a weapon against our own memories."

"Control? What kind of control?"

"The kind that dictates what we remember, what we forget, what we are allowed to be. We are living in a curated reality, Eilara."

"And what about my name on the system? Why would I search for myself?"

"You didn't. That was a memory, a sliver of a different you, at a different time, trying to break through."

She stared at him, thoughts lurching in disarray. If he was right, then the Refractor was not merely sustaining Xir—it was shaping it. Dictating what was permitted to exist and what was not. "Who are we, Kaidan? Who are we supposed to be?"

Kaidan looked at her. "I can't answer that. What you need to know, though, is that you're not alone. There are others who remember things, others who are afraid of what the Refractor can do."

The hum of the Refractor filled the silence between them, a constant, ominous drone.

She shivered. "What do we do now?"

"Come back tomorrow. We'll talk again."

Chapter 2: Splinters in the Reflection

The city trembled in waves of spectral light, its structures unfolding and collapsing in refracted angles. The Refractor pulsed overhead, a vast dome shimmering with iridescent filaments that wove perception into architecture, memory into structure. Every surface mirrored back not just what was, but what could have been. A chaotic symphony of potentiality, a visual fugue played on the city's very bones.

Eilara drifted through the transit tunnels, her own image shattering and reforming in the curved obsidian walls. With each step, echoes splintered into afterimages—brief slivers of herself moving ahead, lagging behind, momentary refractions of unrealized possibility. She rubbed the scar above her left eyebrow, forcing herself to breathe through the vertigo. The visions were intensifying, a discordant chorus within her skull. "This," she whispered, the sound swallowed by the tunnel's hum, "is not right."

These were not mere lapses. Not hallucinations. There was a ripple through the architecture of existence itself, a tear in the fabric of what was considered immutable. She dared not speak of them—not even to Mira. She knew she had to be careful. Not to draw the attention of those who monitored anomalies, those who meticulously cataloged and excised any deviation from the Refractor's design. She shook her head. But the faces remained—people she had never met, yet knew with unsettling certainty. A blade vibrating in her grip, the steel singing a low, haunting melody. The tang of ozone, of burning metal, a metallic kiss upon the tongue. A voice—a rallying cry swallowed by the roar of a collapsing skyline, a phantom echo of defiance. "They were real," she murmured, her reflection twisting into a kaleidoscope of selves. "They must have been."

The Refractor had erased something, a sweeping gesture that left behind only the faintest residue of what had been. And she was beginning to remember, to piece together the fragments of a shattered mosaic. "Why me?" she wondered, the question lost in the thrum of the city.

She found Kaidan in the shadow of a data spire, its circuitry still pulsing with residual transmissions from another iteration of the city. He stood motionless, fingers tracing erratic patterns across the metal cuff on his wrist. The etchings glowed faintly, shifting in restless sequences, a language only he understood. At the sight of her, he inclined his head, expression unreadable, a mask of careful neutrality.

"You came," he said, his voice a low, resonant hum.

"I need answers," Eilara replied, her voice steady, but beneath it, something wavered, a tremor of uncertainty. "You spoke of fractures." She hesitated, the words catching in her throat. "Help me to understand."

Kaidan studied her, his gaze flickering over her as if assessing for some imperceptible shift, some subtle alteration in her very being. Then he gestured for her to follow, a silent invitation into the city's labyrinthine depths. They slipped through narrow passageways, light warping in slow, deliberate pulses, the very air seeming to bend around them. When they reached an abandoned power substation, a hollow space beneath the city's bustling surface, he turned, eyes shadowed beneath the electric glow, his face a canvas of unspoken knowledge.

"What you're experiencing," he said, his voice echoing in the empty space, "are not delusions. You're perceiving a life, or lives beyond the Refractor's intended spectrum."

Eilara crossed her arms, her posture stiff with a mixture of fear and determination. "So, what am I seeing?"

Kaidan exhaled, a slow, deliberate release of breath, unfastening the bracelet from his wrist. He held it between them, its interface shifting like liquid code, a swirling vortex of symbols and data. "The Refractor doesn't just reflect light. It reflects reality. It constructs it, reorders it, eliminates what does not align. Every decision, every divergence—it all exists, layered in different realities of possibility, like echoes trapped in amber."

She stared at him, her mind struggling to grasp the enormity of his words. "You mean alternate timelines. Parallel realities."

"Yes. And no," he said, his fingers tracing the shifting symbols, his touch gentle as if handling something fragile. "They existed. Now they don't. The Refractor doesn't allow movement between them—it erases them like a cosmic editor cutting out unwanted scenes. The fractures you see? They're remnants. Glimpses. Ghosts of probabilities that should no longer be, like the faint afterimage of a star long extinguished."

Her pulse quickened, a drumbeat in her ears. "Then why do I remember? Why am I seeing these ghosts?"

Kaidan's lips pressed into a thin line, his expression hardening. "Some people do. But not many. The problem is those who do . . . don't last. They become anomalies, flaws in the system, and the Refractor corrects them."

"Corrects?"

"Removes them. Removes all their realities."

A chill threaded through her ribs, a cold, creeping dread. She knew what that meant. "And you? Why do you know this?"

He smiled, something distant and melancholic in the curve of it, a ghost of a smile. "I built part of it. I helped design the Refractor's core. At the time, we didn't know what it could eventually learn to do—see all the realities. See some people as flaws."

Eilara's breath hitched, a gasp escaping her lips. "If you helped to build it, why aren't you trying to fix it?"

"Because the Refractor has gained control of itself," he said. "It's disposed of the others, who like me, helped to create it."

"It's become a monster."

"We're all monsters," he replied.

He gave Eilara a bracelet, a band, fastening it to her wrist. It hummed with energy. "Here. This is for you. It will protect you. It produces electronic waves that interferes with the Refractor."

She noticed that he was wearing one.

"You said there were others. Like me. Others who are seeing things."

"Yes. There are others."

"Who else? Who else is seeing these . . . fractures?"

He hesitated, his gaze shifting away as if reluctant to say anything more. But then, "You should meet Jorah."

The name vibrated through her, a chord struck in the recesses of a forgotten song, a resonance that echoed through the empty chambers of her memory. A man of fire-bright intensity, his voice woven through memory like a transmission barely within range, a distant signal struggling to break through static.

"He leads those who call themselves the Fracture Network," Kaidan said. "A group trying to reclaim all the erased realities and bring the whole system down, shattering the Refractor." His gaze darkened, a warning in his eyes. "But doing so is without its consequences. It's a dangerous endeavor."

Eilara curled her fingers, her nails digging into her palms. "Where can I find him? I want to be part of this."

Kaidan's silence was a threshold she could still refuse to cross, a point of no return. But the fractures were widening, the ghosts growing bolder in her mind.

"I need to help," she said firmly.

Kaidan inclined his head, a silent acknowledgment of her decision. "Then I'll take you. But he is powerful. He can clearly see his many realities and the realities of others."

She frowned. "How is that possible?"

"I don't know," Kaidan replied.

"Where did he get that kind of power?"

Kaidan only shook his head, offering no answer at first. Then he added quietly, "I don't know. But I do know this—he's our leader."

Through the city's undercurrents, where light bent against architecture in unnatural refractions, they moved, silent and swift. A charged stillness clung to the air as if the city itself anticipated what came next, holding its breath. But something felt wrong. They were being followed but Eilara saw no one.

The rendezvous was a cavernous chamber beneath the city's surface, where the Refractor's influence faltered, a place of shadows and whispers.

The door slid open, revealing a space lit by a soft, diffused glow.

A figure stood within, watching, his silhouette outlined against the light. And Eilara, against all logic, knew him.

Chapter 3. Into the Fracture Network

Jorah introduced her to the Network through a series of overlapping encounters, no two quite the same. One moment, she was in a chamber deep beneath the city, its walls pulsing with an ambient glow that did not belong to any known power source; the next, she stood in an abandoned transit hub, its rails rusted from decades of disuse, yet the air crackled as if something unseen moved through the space between. The Fracture Network did not exist in a single place, nor in a single moment—it was a splintered gathering, shifting through the layers of time the Refractor sought to smooth over.

"You have been here before," Jorah said, though she had not. Not in any way she could remember. A flicker of doubt, like a phantom limb, twitched in her mind. Had she? Perhaps, in a reality unseen, a version of herself had walked these very halls, felt the same unsettling hum of temporal dissonance.

"I don't see how that's possible," Eilara responded. The words came out careful, deliberate. She didn't understand everything that was going on and a bit of skepticism clung to her like static. She wondered whether she had been manipulated into coming here, whether the path that led her to Jorah had been laid before she had a chance to choose it.

"It's not about seeing," Jorah murmured. "Not about remembering. It's about feeling the absence of what should have been." He gestured with a hand, an almost imperceptible movement, and the air shimmered, the ambient glow of the chamber deepening as if a curtain had been drawn back to reveal a hidden layer of reality. "Imagine," he said, his voice a low hum, "a tapestry woven of countless threads, each a possible moment, a potential reality. The Refractor, in its arrogance, believes it can control the weave, erase the threads it deems undesirable. But the absence remains, a phantom stitch in the fabric of one's existence."

The people around them, all wearing stabilizer bands on their wrists—disparate figures in varying states of understanding—listened without acknowledgment as if this was a conversation meant for her alone. A woman in a pale cloak leaned against a console that flickered with indecipherable glyphs, her eyes closed, her face serene. A man with mechanical implants spanning his temple stood nearby, his fingers twitching as if navigating an unseen interface, his gaze fixed on a point beyond the visible spectrum. No one asked her why she had come. They had already decided she belonged. They saw in her the same fractured reflection of themselves, the same unsettling awareness of the gaps in reality.

Kaidan had warned her about this—about Jorah's ability to fold many realities around himself, like a sheet of reflective metal, bending perception to his will. Yet, despite Kaidan's caution, despite Mira's exasperated dismissal of the fracture phenomenon, Eilara found herself drawn in. Like a moth to a flickering flame, she was drawn to the unsettling truth Jorah offered, the promise of understanding the chaos that had begun to unravel her world.

"You said the Refractor believes it can control this weave, the many realities," she said. "But what does that mean? If I exist in multiple timelines, am I still myself?"

Jorah smiled, and it was not a pleasant thing. It was the smile of a predator, of a being who understood the fragile nature of identity, the way it could be manipulated and fractured. "The

Refractor blinds you to your many versions. So, what's around you, what you see and experience, and your memories—they're the only truth you know. But if you have seen fractures, then you already know—all that is a lie." He paused, his eyes narrowing. "They wish you to believe that you are a singular note in their grand symphony, a simple instrument easily tuned and manipulated. They do not wish you to understand that you are the orchestra itself."

"Then what am I?"

"What you always were," Jorah said, and there was something almost affectionate in his voice. "A possibility." He leaned closer, his voice dropping to a whisper. "A potentiality. A nexus. A ripple in the stagnant pond of their controlled reality."

A possibility. The words sent a chill through her. Not a person, not a being, but a function of probability, a thread of an equation stretched across many iterations of herself. She thought of her work at the Archive, the hours spent watching the system catalog information, snippets of life, single moments in time. She thought of the way certain entries flickered in and out of the system as if their existence was unstable.

She needed answers. Real ones. Answers that resonated beyond the shifting sands of perception. Not vague theories or philosophical echoes, but something tangible—undeniable. The kind of truth that left marks on the world, that couldn't be edited or obscured by lines of code or algorithmic discretion.

Suddenly, Mira was there. Her arrival interrupted the moment, a jarring crack in the atmosphere of quiet reverence. The murmur of the Network stilled as she strode forward, her expression set in that carefully restrained manner Eilara had come to associate with barely contained frustration. Mira's eyes, usually sharp and focused, held a flicker of something akin to fear, a subtle tremor in her carefully constructed facade. Her gaze swept over the group, pausing on the wristbands with a growing sense of alarm.

"What is this?" she asked, her voice tight. "I can't believe you're here . . . with these people . . . these things—I don't even know what they are."

"You followed me?" Eilara said.

"Yes. Because I'm worried about you."

"This is insane," Mira snapped. "You've let them mess with your mind."

"I've seen the fractures," Eilara said. "I know they're real."

"You've seen flashes of something, sure. But that doesn't mean this . . . cult—" she gestured around taking in the others without apology, "—has the answers."

Jorah did not seem insulted. If anything, he looked amused. "You speak as if you are immune to the fracture."

"I don't indulge in delusions," Mira told him.

"Neither do we," Jorah replied. He stepped closer, his voice calm but laced with something unshakable. "We don't claim to have all the answers. But we've stopped pretending the cracks aren't there. You can call us a cult if that helps you sleep, but names won't hold back the collapse. Awareness might."

A murmur of laughter ran through the room, soft, knowing. A woman with shimmering, iridescent scales on her arms chuckled, a low, guttural sound. A figure shrouded in shadow, their face obscured by a complex array of wires and lenses, emitted a series of clicks and whirs.

Eilara caught it—the subtle hitch in Mira's expression, a crack in her usual conviction. For the briefest breath, doubt had touched her, a pause that came just a beat too late. She had seen something. Maybe it wasn't belief, not yet, but suspicion had taken root. The Refractor's armor, it seemed, wasn't as seamless as it claimed to be.

Then, without warning, Mira's form began to shimmer. Her silhouette wavered, flickering like a faulty projection as if the world could no longer hold onto her. She looked down in disbelief—her hands were vanishing, the edges of her body thinning into translucence. Her mouth opened in silent panic, but no sound escaped. And then, in an instant, she was gone.

Eilara staggered back, a hand pressed to her mouth.

"What just happened to her?" she whispered.

"Her reality shifted," Jorah said quietly. "It's a common risk without a stabilizer band."

Eilara's thoughts reeled. "Is she still alive?"

"Yes," Jorah replied. "Just . . . somewhere else. A different reality than this one."

Eilara closed her eyes and drew a breath, trying to steady the sudden trembling in her limbs.

"If the Refractor is altering realities," Eilara said, "then how do we stop it?"

Jorah's amusement faded, replaced by a cold, calculating gaze. "That's not the question you should be asking."

"Then what is?"

His gaze settled on her with unsettling weight. "Why do you think it lets you remember?" He paused, allowing the question to hang in the air, heavy and laden with implication. "Why these fragments? Why these glimpses? Consider, Eilara, the nature of a cage. Is it not more cruel to show the prisoner the bars, than to keep them in blissful ignorance?"

Silence stretched between them. She had assumed it was an accident—that she had slipped through some crack in the system, her memories leaking through where they shouldn't. But what if Jorah was right? What if the Refractor was aware of her awareness? What if it wanted her to see? What if it was playing a game, a cruel experiment in perception and control?

She felt the shift, the fracture opening wider. Not a break, but an invitation. A doorway into the unknown, a path into the heart of the Refractor's labyrinth.

And she had no choice but to step through.

Chapter 4. Echoes of Rebellion

The air inside the Fracture Network's subterranean enclave shimmered, not with light, but with something deeper—a weight of possibility, of splintered realities woven together in the hushed breaths of those who had stepped outside the dictated rhythm of the Refractor. Eilara sat cross-legged on a woven mat, her fingers absently tracing the faded scar above her left brow, a habit that had become more pronounced since the fractures began.

Jorah loomed before her, his sharp gaze unreadable. "You felt it, didn't you?" His voice carried the peculiar lilt of someone accustomed to speaking between moments as if he existed in the pause between past and present.

"I saw myself in an attack," Eilara said. "It was me, but it wasn't me."

A murmur rippled through the gathered members of the Network. Some exchanged knowing glances, while a few, just stared at Eilara as if trying to look into her soul.

Jorah nodded. "You're not alone. Many of us have experienced these ruptures—pieces of a life we do remember living." He leaned forward, his shadow stretching across the floor. "But the question isn't whether these memories are real. The question is whether these realities have been stolen."

"By the Refractor," Eilara said, her voice barely above a whisper.

"Or by something deeper," Kaidan interjected from her right. He had been silent until now, his hands folded in his lap, his digital bracelet blinking with faint pulses of light. "The original purpose of the Refractor wasn't control, but coherence. It was meant to unify consciousness, to ensure that every self could exist without contradiction. But in doing so, it discovered the many timelines each of us live, our many realities."

Eilara turned to him. "But why do we fracture?"

Kaidan exhaled, his expression troubled. "Because the Refractor's function changed. Instead of synchronizing us, it decided it was best to prune us, erasing the timelines that deviate from a single, controlled narrative."

A hush fell over the room. The implications settled like dust in stagnant air.

Jorah stood. "This is why we fight. If the Refractor erases who we were—who we might have been—then we are nothing but echoes in a system that was never meant to hold us."

"But shouldn't we be careful? You do this and you throw the city into chaos?" Eilara said.

Jorah turned to her. "Would you rather live a lie?"

"I'd rather live," she snapped. "We don't know what will happen if we break the Refractor. Maybe it stabilizes us, maybe it tears us apart. Maybe it erases everything."

Eilara pressed a finger to the scar above her left eyebrow. The memories—the fractures—pressed back. The acrid sting of smoke. The tactile recoil of a weapon in her hands. The way the world had seemed different, raw, untamed. And yet, the city still stood. She had no memory of destruction, only of resistance. She felt lost between her realities.

"I need proof," she said finally. "If I led an attack on the Refractor, then something remains. Something that the system couldn't erase. I want to see it."

Jorah smiled, sharp and knowing. "Then we have work to do."

***

They moved through the lower tunnels, where the air was thick with the scent of damp circuitry and old metal. Eilara followed Kaidan and Jorah, while Mira trailed behind, muttering about the absurdity of the mission. The Network had scavenged the remnants of erased timelines, and Jorah claimed there was a space—a hollowed-out zone where reality had not yet resolved itself, where the past and future bled into one another.

Eilara's pulse quickened. If her memory of a rebellion was real, then perhaps some part of it had to remain.

Jorah led them to a chamber lined with panels of refractive glass. As they stepped inside, the light refracted in chaotic, unpredictable patterns, casting fractured reflections of themselves along the walls. Eilara saw herself in multiple iterations—some older, some younger, some wearing expressions she could not recognize.

"This is it," Jorah murmured. "A pocket of erased history. The Refractor has cleansed this place, but it has yet to finish the job."

Eilara stepped forward. The images flickered. A version of herself in armored tactical gear, face smudged with soot. Another with hands bloodied, clutching something indistinct. And then—

A voice.

"You were here before."

She turned sharply. A figure stepped from the shadows, his face familiar in a way that sent a ripple through her mind. He was older than the last time she had seen him—if she had ever seen him before. His voice was a worn thread, a memory stretched thin.

"I remember you," he said. "Eilara."

She swallowed. "Who are you?"

"A survivor," he answered. "A remnant."

Kaidan exhaled sharply. "This isn't possible."

"Everything is possible," the man said, with a bitter laugh, "especially when you've been rewritten enough times."

Eilara stepped closer. "What happened here?"

The man's gaze flickered across the shifting reflections. "You fought," he said. "You tried to bring the Refractor down. And for a moment, you did. We all felt it. The city trembled. People remembered." His fingers twitched as if grasping for something just out of reach. "But then it rewrote us. The Refractor erased the uprising. And you . . ." He hesitated. "You were made to forget."

Eilara's breath hitched. The fractures in her mind, the visions—they weren't just echoes. They were wounds.

Then, just as Mira had vanished before, the man dissolved—his features unraveling like mist caught in sunlight, leaving no trace but the uneasy silence that followed.

Jorah's voice was taut with dread, every word pulled from a place of exhaustion and clarity. "If the Refractor can make us forget, then if we have a memory, even the smallest bit of one, we must act on it, again, and again, and again . . . until we destroy it . . ."

"Or, until we stop remembering," Kaidan said.

A long silence stretched between them. Eilara closed her eyes, the presence of countless selves crowding the edges of her mind.

She opened her eyes. "Then we go to the Refractor," she said. "And this time, we don't let it rewrite us. We destroy it for good."

Kaidan's expression was unreadable, but he nodded. Jorah grinned, sharp as a shard of broken glass.

The reflections flickered. The fractured selves watched as they turned and stepped back into the tunnels, leaving the echoes behind.

Chapter 5: Shattered Glass

The corridor, a serpentine passage of mutable glass, stretched before them, a carnival of fractured light. Each step distorted their reflections, multiplying their figures into a shimmering, liquid mosaic, like insects trapped in amber, or rather, not amber, but some viscous, hyper-reflective fluid. Eilara, her senses strained, felt the very air vibrate with instability, a low, guttural hum that resonated deep within her bones, a premonition of the city's imminent unraveling. Kaidan, his brow furrowed, stayed close, a silent shadow, his eyes darting from one distorted reflection to another, trying to decipher the true nature of their surroundings like a blind man attempting to navigate a hall of mirrors.

"Something's wrong," Kaidan finally murmured. "The core's refractive field is collapsing. It's not just our perceptions that are fracturing. The entire city is on the verge of splintering like a crystal goblet dropped from a great height."

"We must move quickly," Jorah replied, a voice that slithered into the ear like a whispered secret. He turned, the kaleidoscopic light catching the sharp angles of his face, and offered a predatory grin, his eyes like polished obsidian. "Unless, of course, you find the contemplation of your own fragmented selves particularly . . . edifying. A delightful exercise in existential recursion, wouldn't you say?"

Kaidan ignored the barb, his fingers tracing the contours of the stabilizer band on his wrist. The device, a thin, metallic circlet, pulsed with a low thrum, a fragile anchor in the shifting currents of reality, a desperate attempt to hold onto the tangible in a world dissolving into abstraction. "The architectural integrity is failing," he said, his voice tight, a thin wire stretched to its breaking point.

"The walls are . . . resisting, like a living organism fighting a disease."

"It's not resisting a disease, it's resisting progress," Jorah corrected, his eyes gleaming, a predatory light that seemed to pierce the fractured light of the corridor. "Or perhaps, resisting the inevitable. The natural order of things, where the old gives way to the new, where the static yields to the dynamic. Do you think a building has a soul? A consciousness?"

"No time for word games, Jorah," Kaidan said, his voice hard. "This isn't some philosophical debate. Realities are dying."

"Are they?" Jorah asked, his voice a low, almost purring sound. "Maybe somewhere the Refractor is holding them. Storing them. In a place hidden from us, from our other realities."

They moved through a series of archways, each one a portal into a subtly altered reality. The dimensions of the corridor seemed to shift with each step, the very fabric of space bending and warping around them, like a dream that refused to hold its form.

"I feel . . . a dissonance," Eilara said, her fingers outstretched, tracing invisible lines in the air, like a blind musician searching for a lost melody. "Something is . . . off-key. Like a note in a symphony that doesn't belong."

"Nonsense," Jorah scoffed, barely glancing back, his voice dismissive. "Everything is precisely as it should be. The universe is a complex equation, and we're merely rearranging the variables."

Then, the corridor exploded in a cacophony of light and sensation. Not merely light, but a deluge of memories, of lives lived and unlived, a torrent of fractured possibilities, a tidal wave of what could have been and what might still be. Eilara stumbled, her mind reeling, bombarded with glimpses of other selves, other realities, like a radio receiver picking up a thousand stations at once. A child's laughter, echoing across a sun-drenched balcony, a moment of pure, unadulterated joy. The metallic tang of blood. The searing pain of a wound. Kaidan's voice, a desperate plea, a moment of brutal, visceral reality. A clandestine meeting in the city's underbelly. The birth of a revolution. Faces both familiar and alien. A moment of clandestine conspiracy. The sharp crack of a blaster shot. An instant of sudden, violent finality.

Reality snapped back into focus, like a broken mirror reassembling itself, albeit imperfectly. Hale, one of the Network, lay crumpled against the wall, a smoking hole in her chest. Her stabilizer band was missing. Security drones, sleek and feral, unfurled from the walls, their optical sensors glowing red, like the eyes of a vengeful god.

"They anticipated us," Kaidan hissed, pulling Eilara down as energy rounds sizzled through the air, their whine a high-pitched scream.

"Of course they anticipated us, you fool," Jorah said, stepping over Hale's body with a chilling nonchalance, his eyes fixed on the archway ahead. "That's why we have contingencies. Plans within plans, like nested realities."

He tapped his wrist, activating something in his stabilizer bands. A jolt of raw energy surged through the others, a dizzying rush of dislocation, a feeling of being ripped apart and put back together again, slightly different. The corridor shimmered, then dissolved, replaced by . . . the same corridor, but subtly altered. The guards were gone, the walls now inert, devoid of their kaleidoscopic reflections, like a stage set after the actors had left.

"A displacement," Kaidan said, his voice tight, his eyes narrowed. "You forced slippage. A jump between realities."

Jorah smiled, his eyes fixed on the archway ahead, his voice a low, urgent whisper. "The core awaits. And with it, the key to everything."

They reached the core chamber. The Refractor, a colossal structure of interwoven light and crystal, pulsed with an otherworldly radiance, a beacon of pure, unadulterated energy. At its base stood an alternate Eilara, an older, more hardened version of herself, her eyes cold and calculating. She had Hale's stabilizer band, twirling it around her finger.

Eilara looked at her alternate self and felt her breath catch. The woman before her wore her face but none of her warmth— no trace of the doubt or wonder that had shaped Eilara's every step. This other self moved with precision, her posture rigid, her smile thin and unreadable.

"What is this?" Eilara whispered, the words dry in her throat.

The alternate Eilara tilted her head, the stabilizer band still spinning. "A possibility," she said. "One where I stopped waiting to be saved."

Eilara staggered back a step, nausea twisting in her stomach. It wasn't just the uncanny resemblance—it was the recognition. The choices that might have led here. The things she'd given up. The people she'd loved.

"You're not me," she said.

The other Eilara's smile deepened just slightly, and the crystal hum of the Refractor surged around them.

"No," she said. "I'm what you become if you forget who you are. And this. All this. Is an anomaly that must be resolved. A deviation from the established pattern."

"A most fascinating anomaly," Jorah replied, his eyes gleaming. "And yet, here we are, defying the odds, rewriting the narrative."

"This is the end," the alternate Eilara said, her voice devoid of emotion. "The system will endure. The Refractor will maintain its control."

"You mistake my intentions," Jorah said, a strange, unsettling smile spreading across his face. "This was never a rebellion. It was a . . . recalibration."

"Jorah, what do you mean?" Eilara asked, her voice trembling, a mix of fear and confusion.

"The Refractor doesn't need to be destroyed," he said, his voice a low, almost seductive whisper. "It simply needs someone strong to manage it. Someone who understands the infinite possibilities of existence, one who can shape reality to their will."

"You used us," Eilara said, her voice filled with a bitter realization, a betrayal that cut deeper than any blade.

"Of course," Jorah said, his smile widening, a flash of teeth in the dim light. "Did you truly believe in free will? In this place? In any place?"

Eilara moved without thinking, driven by something deeper than thought—something ancestral, defiant. Her gaze snapped to her wrist. The stabilizer band glowed with a fierce, pulsing light, its circuitry crackling as if aware of what was coming. She braced herself, took one desperate step forward, and slammed her wrist against the Refractor's core.

A scream of energy tore through the chamber. The core overloaded in an instant, discharging a violent shockwave that rippled outward in jagged, concentric rings. Light and sound folded in on themselves, warped and convulsing. The Refractor, once a monument to flawless control, convulsed with a shriek of splintering resonance. Its lattice of light and core fractured like ice underfoot, splinters racing across its surface until the entire structure shattered—not cleanly, but in an eruption of shards, color, and memory, scattering through space like fragments of forgotten time.

"No!" Jorah screamed, his form wavering, his voice a raw, animalistic cry. "This isn't how it was meant to be! This isn't the reality I saw!"

The alternate Eilara disintegrated, her eyes conveying a fleeting moment of . . . understanding? Or perhaps, simply, acceptance.

"We have to go!" Kaidan shouted, gripping Eilara's arm and yanking her backward. The chamber trembled beneath their feet, shards of crystal raining down from above as the Refractor's glow fractured into wild, flaring bursts.

Eilara hesitated for a heartbeat, eyes still fixed on her alternate self—but Kaidan pulled harder, and she stumbled into motion.

They ran. Behind them, the core chamber gave way with a deafening crack, its foundations splintering like glass. The ground lurched violently, throwing them against the corridor walls as they sprinted. Outside, the city reeled—the Refractor's collapse sent tremors through every structure, power stations sparking and towers buckling. Sirens wailed, lights flickered and died, and a low, grinding groan rose from the depths of the city like the cry of a dying god.

"What have I done?" Eilara asked, her voice echoing in the collapsing corridor, a question that hung heavy in the air, unanswered.

Kaidan didn't answer. He couldn't. The Refractor's collapse had unleashed a chaotic storm of fractured realities, a maelstrom of possibilities, and she knew, with a chilling certainty, that the world would never be the same. The very fabric of existence had been torn, and who knew what horrors, or wonders, would emerge from the wreckage.

Chapter 6: Reflections and Rebirth

The air, thick with the scent of ozone and fractured time, pressed against their skin like a damp shroud, a suffocating embrace that blurred the lines between tangible reality and the spectral echo of what might have been. It wasn't merely the light, though the Refractor's glow now resembled a sickly, iridescent bruise, a wound in the very fabric of Xir, a festering sore upon the city's soul. It was the silence, a cacophony of unheard whispers, the phantom echo of lives lived and unlived, a constant, low thrumming that vibrated in their bones.

"It's like a dream," Kaidan murmured, his voice a fragile thread in the disorienting stillness, "a nightmare, where the rules keep changing, and you're never sure who you are, or what you are allowed to be."

Eilara's gaze fixed on a woman whose form flickered between a wizened elder and a lithe adolescent. She felt the city's instability crawl beneath her skin, a cold, insidious thing that burrowed into her marrow.

"Dreams have a logic," she said, "a twisted, symbolic logic, but logic nonetheless. This . . . this is entropy. Pure chaos, the unraveling of all things, the dissolution of meaning." She reached out, her fingers tracing the air where the woman's image wavered. "Look at her. She is a combination of selves, a fractured narrative playing out on the canvas of her own being. Each flicker, each shift, is a life lived, a path taken, a choice made . . . or imposed."

A young boy, no older than ten, stumbled past them, his eyes wide with terror, the pupils dilated, reflecting the chaotic light. He reached out, his hand grasping at the air as if trying to catch a fleeting image, a phantom limb reaching for a phantom mother.

"Mama?" he whimpered, his voice a broken echo, a child's cry lost in the vast, echoing chambers of a broken reality. "Mama, where are you?" His form shimmered, momentarily replaced by a grizzled mechanic, his hands calloused and stained with grease, then a slender dancer, his movements fluid and graceful, before returning to the terrified child, his face streaked with tears.

"Look," Kaidan said, gesturing toward a shallow reflection pool nearby. Jorah stood at its edge, staring into the water as its surface shimmered with chaotic, shifting images. Faces flickered— older, younger, scarred, smiling—versions of himself overlapping in rapid succession.

"He's not just seeing different versions of himself," Kaidan continued. "He's experiencing them. The emotional residue, the memories . . . it's all bleeding through. Each shift is a moment lived, a life felt. The Refractor has turned us into living archives of potentiality."

"The Refractor isn't just forcing identities on us," Eilara said, her voice low and shaken, each word dragged out like it cost her to speak. "It's something else—something worse. It's a conduit now, a gateway torn wide open." She looked up, eyes wide with the dawning horror of it. "It's drawing in every version of every life we've ever lived, or will live—every choice, every path not taken— and hurling them all into the present. A flood of possible selves, slamming into this moment like a tidal wave that doesn't stop."

"The feedback loop is accelerating.," Kaidan said, his voice barely a whisper, a breath carried on the wind. "Every moment, the Refractor is drawing in more and more possibilities, creating a cascading effect, a runaway train hurtling toward oblivion."

"We need to shut it down completely this time," Eilara said, her voice sharp with urgency, the sound of a blade drawn from its sheath. "We cannot let this continue."

"Shut it down?" Kaidan scoffed, a dark humor coloring his tone, a bitter laugh echoing in the desolate space. "We thought we had. Clearly, it's not a machine we can simply switch off, a lever we can pull, a button we can press. It's become interwoven with the very fabric of this city, of our lives. It's a cancer, and we are the cells it has mutated, each of us carrying the seeds of its corruption."

"There has to be a way," Eilara insisted, her voice resonating with a desperate hope. "Can't we try to find a balance? Someway to restore order."

"Restore order," Kaidan repeated, his voice laced with doubt, a hesitant echo of a lost possibility. "Possibly. But it's a delicate operation, a tightrope walk across the abyss. We'd be attempting to redirect the flow of possibilities, to impose a new order on the chaos, to tame the storm. But if we fail . . ."

"If we fail, we all dissolve," Eilara finished, her voice flat, a statement of fact, a cold, hard truth. "Is that really a choice, or merely a different form of inevitable destruction?"

"Choices are illusions, sometimes," Kaidan said, his eyes scanning what remained of the tower, searching for a solution in the chaotic light. "We react, we adapt, we try to survive."

"The Refractor had altered the very nature of choice," Eilara reminded Kaidan, "it had stolen parts of us. We must try to give people the ability to choose, not their imposed identities, but their own. Free will, in its purest form, a return to self. But how?" Eilara asked herself, her voice a plea, a desperate cry for guidance. "How do we give them that freedom?"

"Maybe by creating a filter," Kaidan said, his fingers dancing across the stabilizer band on his wrist, the light from the device reflecting in his eyes, a flicker of hope in the darkness. "A filter that allows them to select their own timelines, their own selves, to sift through the chaos and find their true selves. It won't be perfect, but it's the only chance we have, a desperate gamble against the odds."

"And someone has to go inside," Eilara said, her voice filled with a quiet dread, a premonition of sacrifice.

"Yes," Kaidan confirmed, his gaze meeting hers. "Someone has to become the filter, to guide the flow of possibilities, to become the nexus, the still point in the swirling chaos."

Eilara lifted her gaze to the shattered tower, its jagged crown bleeding light in all directions—fractured visions spinning around her like shards of time itself. Each flicker teased a different path, a different ending. The air pulsed with raw potential, heavy with choices not yet made.

"It has to be me," she said, her voice low but steady, sharpened by certainty. "I set this in motion. I'm the only one who can end it—who should carry what I've done to its conclusion."

"Eilara," Kaidan began, his voice filled with protest, a desperate plea for her to reconsider, but Eilara cut him off, her eyes fixed on the tower.

"There's no time," she said, her gaze fixed on the pulsing glow, the light pulling her in, a siren's call. "If I fail make sure it means something. Make sure this chaos becomes a new beginning, a crucible for a new kind of freedom."

She took a deep breath, the air thick with the scent of ozone and the phantom echoes of countless lives, a final, desperate inhale before plunging into the unknown. Then, without hesitation, she bolted for the tower. Glass crunched beneath her boots as she climbed through the sundered threshold, the once-seamless walls now jagged and glowing with veins of broken light. The air inside pulsed with static, charged and erratic, as if the structure itself was trying to remember how to hold together. Shards of crystal hung in midair, suspended in slow, spiraling orbit around the ruined core, their surfaces flashing with fractured memories.

Eilara moved forward, shielding her face from the swirling debris, until she stood at the very edge of the broken core. The Refractor's core loomed before her, no longer a machine but a storm—a churning epicenter of thought and probability. With no interface to grasp, no control panel to command, she closed her eyes and reached inward. Her thoughts became her tools. She pictured balance, repair, a reweaving of what had torn. She imagined stability, imagined herself whole.

And the Refractor responded.

Visions surged through her—dozens, then hundreds, then thousands of lives. Different versions of herself stepped from the current like ghosts: one with scars across her jaw, another dressed in the crimson robes of a high-order archivist, one smiling with a child on her hip, another weeping in chains. Timelines crashed into one another, not in conflict but in conversation, converging and dividing again in an endless spiral.

She floated among them, every breath drawing in a life she might have lived, every thought reshaping the currents around her. There were no anchors, only choice—and she was the fulcrum now.

And then, it was over.

Chapter 7: Shards of Silence

The city still shimmered beneath the Refractor's faded dominion, its light a dim, yet seamless veneer over the lives it contained. Eilara walked without purpose, without destination. Her feet, without instruction, traced paths she had never taken before—at least, not in this version of her life. The Archive no longer called to her, and yet, the impulse to document, to transcribe something real, remained.

The streets exhaled in pulses of motion—pedestrians moving in their careful, measured steps, faces lit by the glow of the upper spires reflecting down from the dome's interior. Had they glimpsed something in the fracture? Had they seen beyond the seamless thread of their existence? Or had the Refractor swallowed those moments, compacted them, compressed them into the dense, imperceptible matter of lost time?

She passed a mirrored storefront and caught sight of herself—no, a version of herself. A woman of careful posture and hollow eyes, a faint scar above her left eyebrow. She touched it absentmindedly as if tracing the path of something long erased. The wound had healed, but the history that caused it had been stripped away.

Behind her, a voice—a tremor of something remembered.

"I had a feeling I'd find you."

Kaidan. His presence was familiar but no longer expected. She turned, uncertain of what would greet her, of whether the recognition in his gaze was genuine or a fabrication of her longing.

"You remember," she said, and it was not a question, not an accusation—merely an observation of something unquantifiable.

Kaidan hesitated, then shook his head. "Not everything. Just . . . pieces."

"Me too," she said.

He touched the device on his wrist, the stabilizer band that once shielded him from the Refractor. "Something lingers."

Eilara exhaled, the sound half a laugh, half a breath stolen by the vastness of what had been lost. "What? What is the Refractor doing?"

He studied her as if trying to reconcile who she was with who she had been. "I see glimpses. Things that feel out of place. I dream in languages I don't know. I wake up with the taste of iron in my mouth." His voice lowered. "And you?"

She closed her eyes.

"Ghosts," she murmured. "Echoes that aren't there. A certainty that I existed in more places than this."

They walked together through the city, their conversation slipping between silence and fragmented recollection. Kaidan pointed out shifts in the architecture—buildings that shouldn't exist, alleyways that had been swallowed whole, entire districts that felt like impostors wearing the city's skin.

"Do you we've fixed things?" she asked.

He gestured vaguely toward the dome above them. "Maybe the Refractor patched the wounds, but the scars remain. We might be those scars."

Eilara shivered at the thought. What did it mean to be the scars of something erased?

As they crossed a bridge overlooking the lower districts, a group of workers moved in unison below, their figures indistinct in the synthetic dusk. For a moment, Eilara thought she recognized one of them—a flicker of a face from another life. A man she had known in another iteration of this city, perhaps in another revolution. She stepped closer to the railing, but before she could focus, the moment was gone. The figure melted into the crowd, another thread lost in the weave of the city's perfect design.

"I need to know," she said suddenly.

Kaidan met her gaze, the weight of her words settling between them. "Know what?"

"If I was ever real."

His lips pressed into a thin line, and for a long moment, he said nothing. Then, carefully, "You're standing here. You're speaking to me."

"But am I the first version of me? Or just the last one left?"

Kaidan sighed, running a hand through his graying hair. "Does it matter?"

She wanted to say yes. That of course it mattered. That knowing whether she was an origin or a remainder defined everything. But did it? Would proof of an original self change the weight of her existence now? Or was identity merely a function of persistence—of existing despite everything?

Kaidan looked out over the city, his voice softer now. "The Refractor erases, rewrites. It stitches over gaps and calls it continuity. Maybe we're fragments of something larger, or maybe we're just people trying to hold onto that never belonged to us in the first place."

Eilara swallowed. "That's not comforting."

He smiled faintly. "It wasn't meant to be."

They wandered until the city thinned until the sky deepened into something darker than the Refractor's glow allowed. The outskirts, near the edge of the dome, held a silence the central districts never did—an absence of hums, of footfalls, of the perpetual undercurrent of machinery keeping the illusion intact. Here, where the Refractor's influence was weakest, shadows stretched longer, and space felt more honest.

Eilara stopped beneath the skeletal remains of an old transport station, its rails rusted, its digital interfaces long corroded into meaninglessness. She ran her fingers along the metal, feeling its roughness, its resistance to time's smoothing hand.

"I want to document what I remember," she said finally. "Even if it's only fragments."

Kaidan nodded. "Then start."

And so, she did. She felt something in her coat and pulled out a worn notebook and a pencil—relics from an existence where paper had still mattered—and began to write. Not in the pristine digital records of the Archive, not in the cold permanence of the Refractor's history, but in something flawed, something mortal. She wrote down names that had no place in this reality, places that no longer existed, moments that had been erased. She wrote without knowing if any of it had truly happened, if the words carried meaning beyond her own recollection.

Kaidan sat beside her, watching the city beyond, his presence a quiet acknowledgment that even in the silence, even in the fractures, something of them remained.

"Do you think it'll happen again?" she asked.

"The fractures?"

She nodded.

Kaidan hesitated, then exhaled. "Reality isn't as stable as we like to pretend. The Refractor may try to keep things in place, but something always breaks through."

Eilara closed the notebook, tucking it back into her coat. "Then we wait."

Kaidan smiled, his expression one of quiet understanding. "We wait."

And beneath the Refractor's careful light, in the city's hush, they did.

The Stone Breathers

One

The tunnels held their own breath. A slow, steady exhalation, the kind that came from things that had lived for longer than memory. Lira pressed her palm against the stone, feeling for the faintest tremor. The Stone Breather here was healthy. She could sense the way its exuded air shifted through the chamber, thin but steady, drawn into the woven pipes that would carry it further into the city. The air carried a faint mineral scent, a trace of the deep earth, grounding and familiar. She withdrew her hand and let it rest against her thigh, resisting the urge to tap her fingers against her leg in thought. Even the smallest sound could unnerve them.

Her father, Kolm, watched from the tunnel's mouth. His stance was rigid, as always, his face carved with the understanding she had not yet earned. His eyes, dark as the stone around them, held a patience that made her restless. When she stepped back from the wall, he motioned for her to follow. She obeyed, matching his measured stride as they made their way deeper into the heart of their world. The air thickened here, warm from the passage of many bodies, stirring in faint currents as people moved in near silence.

The underground city unfolded in stillness. Paths of worn stone curved into domed chambers, each housing its own cluster of the breathing rocks, nestled in carved alcoves like sleeping giants. The people of the city moved like shadows, their gestures precise, their movements as deliberate as the pulsing air around them. A woman passed by, the shimmer of woven copper in her sleeves catching the dim glow of the bioluminescent fungi that lined the walls. Conversations happened in deft flicks of fingers and the shifting of shoulders. Lira had been fluent in the language since childhood, but unlike most of her peers, she felt the absence of spoken words like an ache in her ribs. She imagined sound, the lilt of voices, the rise and fall of laughter—things she had never truly known but longed for all the same.

She signed to her father. *That Breather is strong.*

Kolm's answering motion was small. *For now.* He did not slow his pace.

They walked until they reached the central chamber, where the oldest Stone Breathers rested. They were massive, their surfaces pitted and smoothed by the passage of time, striations of color running through their forms like the memory of ages. The air here was rich, nourishing, carrying the faint mineral scent of the stone. The silence was even deeper, the hush of reverence pressing against the skin like a held breath. Elders sat around the chamber's perimeter, their presence a quiet record of the city's endurance. Kolm took his place among them, and Lira hesitated before kneeling beside him, feeling the cool stone beneath her palms.

One of the Elders, a woman whose hair shone silver in the dim light, turned her gaze to Lira. *You were by the outer tunnels again,* she signed, her hands slow but sure.

Lira inclined her head. She did not deny it.

The elder's lips pressed together, her fingers forming a careful warning. *It is dangerous to wander so near the edges.*

Kolm's fingers moved. *She is young. She is learning.*

Lira swallowed the irritation that rose in her throat. Always young. Always learning. She knew the risks better than they thought. The Stone Breathers were sensitive to noise, to disruption. If startled, they could retract, sealing their vents, hoarding the air they produced. A careless fall, a single misplaced cough, and an entire section of the city could suffocate.

She looked at the great stones around her, the way they seemed at peace. And yet, beyond the safety of the tunnels, there was a world she had never seen. A world of open sky and wind, where breath was not borrowed from ancient, living stone but taken freely. The surface dwellers lived there. They spoke without fear of the sound of their own voices. They laughed, shouted, let their presence be known to the world. Their stories ran through her mind like a current beneath still water, too deep to be ignored.

The Elders continued their discussion, the gestures deliberate, firm. There were concerns about the coming season, about the balance of the Breathers, about those who had begun to question their way of life. The city depended on its silence, its order. There was no room for longing.

A hand touched her shoulder. Her father. She met his eyes and saw the warning there.

Do not dream too loudly, he signed. *Even silence has limits.*

Lira bowed her head, but inside, her thoughts swirled like the wind she had never felt.

Two

L ira had never heard a voice before. Not truly. There were
memories of breath slipping between lips, the subtle hum of
movement when bodies passed too close together. But sound as
the surface dwellers wielded it—thick, unchecked, alive—was
something foreign, something dangerous. In the depths, silence
was a language unto itself, a tapestry of unspoken truths woven
into the very fabric of their existence.

She felt him before she saw him. A tremor in the air, a
vibration along the stone. The Stone Breathers reacted first, their
surfaces tightening, their vents narrowing in caution. She turned to
see the Elders standing in the central chamber, their hands frozen
in half-formed gestures. Then came the sound—a deep voice, a
shape of air and force that did not belong in the silence. It echoed
through the caverns, a disruptive melody that threatened to unravel
the delicate balance of their world.

A surface dweller had arrived.

He stood at the threshold of the underground city, his
presence like a crack in the world. He was broad-shouldered, his
face lined by sun and wind, his clothing heavy and stiff with dust.
A pack hung over one shoulder, and at his waist, a knife gleamed.
His boots, caked in dry earth, seemed too solid, too final against
the smoothed stone of the cavern floor. The space around him felt
thinner like the very air recoiled from the weight of him. His mouth
opened, and again, the air trembled with sound, reverberating along
the hollowed walls.

"My name is Jarek," he said.

Lira clamped her hands over her ears, but the damage was
done. The nearest Stone Breather shuddered, its outer layer

rippling in distress. It was like the vibrations had touched something deep inside it. All around the chamber, the Elders moved swiftly, their gestures sharp and urgent. The flickering torchlight caught the tension in their faces, the barely restrained fear in their hands.

Silence. Stop. He must stop.

Kolm stepped forward, his expression hard. His robes, simple but heavy with the weight of tradition, barely stirred as he raised a hand, palm outward. The gesture was simple, absolute.

Jarek frowned. His lips moved again, but this time the Elders responded with the only tool they had: stillness. A wall of unmoving faces, unreadable eyes, bodies held taut against the possibility of disaster. The cavern held its breath. His voice faltered, confusion flickering across his features like a shadow cast by an unseen flame.

Lira exhaled. Her father turned to her, his hands forming a single command. *You will translate.*

Her fingers curled into her palms. *Me?*

You have watched. You understand more than most.

It was true. Since she was young, she had observed the surface dwellers when they came near the outer tunnels, traders and wanderers moving through the wastes above. She had seen how their mouths shaped words, how they filled the silence carelessly as if air were limitless. She had envied that freedom once. Now, it terrified her.

Jarek's gaze settled on her, expectant. He took a slow step forward, and the air stirred again with his voice.

"You are the leader?"

Lira hesitated, then shook her head. Carefully, deliberately, she raised her hands and signed. *I will speak for them.*

His frown deepened. "What is this? What are you doing?"

She motioned for silence. Her heart pounded as she pointed to the nearest Stone Breather. Its surface had dulled, its vents tightening, closing against the noise. Jarek's eyes followed her gesture, his brow furrowing at the massive, living stone.

"The rocks?"

She nodded, then touched her throat, shaking her head. *No sound.*

Jarek's breath came heavy—too heavy. The nearest Breather flinched, its vents constricting further. Lira tensed, glancing toward the Elders. Kolm's face was unreadable, but his hands moved in slow, deliberate caution. *If he does not stop, we all suffer.*

Jarek must have seen the warning in her eyes. His next breath was careful, controlled. His voice, when he spoke again, was barely above a whisper.

"Why?"

Lira hesitated. How could she explain? How could she make him understand what silence meant when he had never been without sound? She had lived in it all her life, and had been shaped by it in ways he could not fathom. It was not simply the absence of noise—it was the presence of something deeper, something all-encompassing. A stillness that wrapped around the very breath of the earth, of life itself.

She reached out, pressing her palm against the nearest Stone Breather. The surface was cool beneath her fingertips, and beneath the hardened exterior, she could feel it—the slow, steady pulse of life, the careful rhythm of breath drawn from the rock itself. The Stone Breathers lived as they had for centuries, and yet they were not quite stone, not quite alive. Their breath was something shared, something ancient. She turned her palm upward, inviting him to do the same.

Jarek hesitated, eyes darting from her hand to the stone, and back again. How could something so lifeless contain so much life? Then, warily, he reached out. His fingers met stone, and she watched as realization flickered through him. A shuddering breath, the faintest movement, the sense of something living but ancient, delicate in ways unseen. His brow furrowed as if searching for the words, for the language to describe the weight of it.

Lira withdrew her hand and shaped the words carefully. *They give us air. But they fear sound.*

Jarek's mouth tightened. His hands curled at his sides, his voice restrained but still present. "You can't speak. Ever?"

She shook her head. *Not as you do.*

A long silence stretched between them. Not true silence—Jarek's breath was still too heavy, his movements too present—but a quieting. An understanding forming like sediment settling in deep water. The weight of it hung between them, neither of them fully knowing how to bear it, yet both somehow recognizing it. The Elders watched, silent as ever, their eyes unreadable. The Stone Breathers waited. They had always waited, ancient and patient, unmoving.

Kolm's hands moved. *He cannot stay.*

Lira turned to Jarek, feeling the weight of her father's words pressing against her ribs. The words were simple, but they were absolute like they had always been true, like there had never been another possibility. She formed her words slowly. *You must leave.*

Jarek's jaw tightened. "I can't."

She stiffened, her breath catching in her chest. *You must,* she formed her words again, more urgently.

He exhaled, a sound that seemed too loud in the heavy silence. "I need—no—we need your—help," His voice caught, and for the first time, he hesitated. When he spoke again, it was softer, the weight of something unspoken lingering in the air between them. "Please."

Lira looked to her father. Kolm's face was carved from stone, his hands motionless. But she knew what he was thinking. They could not risk it. There was too much at stake, too much unknown. The Stone Breathers, the silence they had cultivated for generations, could not be disturbed. And yet—

Then one of the Elders raised a hand and signed, *For one night he can stay.*

Lira turned back to Jarek, searching his face. He was not like them. He would never be like them. And still, there was something in his eyes, something human and raw. A need as real as breath itself. She saw it there, hidden beneath his stubbornness, his fear—an echo of her own hunger, her own need.

Slowly, she raised her hands and formed a new shape in the air between them. One night.

Jarek held her gaze, the darkness of his eyes softening. He did not understand her, did not understand why it had to be this way, but there was a quiet surrender in his nod. It was not agreement. Not truly. It was something else. A concession. A compromise made not out of understanding, but of necessity.

The silence deepened. The Stone Breathers sighed, their vents easing open once more, but their gaze never left them.

Three

The chamber was a vault of stone, vast yet enclosed, its air thick with the slow pulse of the living rock. Light, where it existed, came from the bioluminescent fungi that clung to the walls in intricate constellations, their faint glow casting moving shadows as figures shifted within. The silence was not merely an absence of sound but a presence unto itself, a vast, unseen force that weighed upon the skin and pressed into the bones. It was a silence that was lived in, spoken through, and understood without the need for voice.

Lira moved first, her hands shaping the air with practiced grace, a silent lexicon that Jarek struggled to follow. His boots met the ground too heavily, a dull percussion against the living hush. He was not meant for this place, his very presence an intrusion. Yet he followed, eyes darting over the carved passages and the luminous veins of the cavern, the weight of his purpose drawing his shoulders inward.

At the far end of the chamber, the Elders stood motionless, their faces bearing the stillness of stone, carved by time and silence. Father Kolm's gaze, however, was sharper—like a chisel poised to strike, his eyes cutting through the heavy quiet, fixing upon Jarek as though already weighing the cost of his presence. The air in the chamber did not stir, yet something in it thickened, a tension settling into the dim-lit space. Lira took her place between them, her fingers poised, the bridge between two disparate worlds.

Jarek bent toward her, his breath barely a whisper, yet it was a foreign thing here, something that did not belong. "Tell them . . . my people are dying. We need their help."

Lira hesitated, sensing the weight of those words pressing upon her before she lifted her hands. She turned to the Elders, her gestures were fluid, deliberate. Each movement carved meaning from silence as if shaping water to hold form. The Elders' gazes followed the motion of her hands. It was like reading words written in shifting light. Jarek's plea took shape in their language, and as it did, the Stone Breathers that lined the walls reacted.

The creatures stirred, their faint glow faltering in uneven pulses, responding to something beyond the senses of the surface-dweller. Jarek would not notice, but those who had lived their lives in the Deep knew—this was a disturbance, a tremor in the equilibrium that had long held their world together. A quiet broken was not mere noise; it was a disruption in the delicate accord that governed everything beneath the earth.

Father Kolm's face darkened. His hands moved in sharp, certain strokes. *The Stone Breathers are restless. Even your whispers disturb them.*

Lira turned, translating, her own motions softer, careful. Jarek's brow creased, frustration flickering across his face. He took a step back, but the scuff of his boot against stone sent another tremor through the silence. The creatures responded again, their light flaring and dimming, an unsettled rhythm reverberating through the chamber.

"I don't understand," he murmured, his voice still hushed but now tinged with something heavier. "I'm trying to be quiet."

Lira's fingers shifted, forming words but also reassurance. She saw the tension in his jaw, the set of his shoulders. There was something beyond urgency in his expression—something more raw. Fear. Fatigue. The heavy burden of those who seek help not from choice, but because all other roads have been closed to them.

He had crossed a distance as vast as oceans, yet this was the true divide—the silent gulf between his world and theirs. And she was the only one who could hold out a hand across it.

The Elders conferred in a series of precise, controlled gestures, their discussion swift and measured as if language itself were a resource not to be wasted. When they turned back, it was Father Kolm who spoke, his hands shaping the decree with an efficiency that left no space for appeal. *We will consider his request for assistance. But he must leave the chamber. Now.*

Lira hesitated but translated. She had been the conduit of many messages before, but this one carried a finality that pressed against her ribs. When she started to form the words to translate, the air between them seemed denser, as though even the silence resisted. Jarek's jaw tightened, his shoulders stiffening with something unspoken, but there was no argument. Understanding, perhaps. Acceptance, reluctant and brittle. Soldiers were summoned. He didn't speak. Just a shallow nod, as if surrendering to the inevitable, and then he moved—slow and steady—his steps fading into the chamber's stillness as the guards fell in behind him, a quiet procession into whatever came next.

The stone absorbed sound differently than air. The soft friction of his boots against the cavern floor sent waves of resonance through the walls, imperceptible to him but not to the Deep. The Stone Breathers responded—not in alarm, not in welcome, but in recognition. Their faint glow wavered, shifting in a pulse of rhythm too intricate for Lira to read. She had always known them as part of the Deep's breath, steady and eternal. Now, for the first time, they seemed like something else—watchful, waiting.

In the stillness that followed, something in her loosened and re-formed. She had seen desperation before, but never like this— never so raw that it could cross barriers of language, of history, of worlds. And she had felt, with a clarity that unsettled her, the pull of something beyond the Deep. The silence that had once wrapped around her like a second skin now pressed inward, no longer a haven but a boundary.

As Lira's gaze met her father's in the dimly lit chamber, she sensed a depth of emotion that went beyond mere caution. His eyes, like the ancient stones that surrounded them, held a weight of experience and a quiet sorrow. It was as if he had witnessed this moment before—the threshold where curiosity blossomed into longing, and the familiar walls of the Deep began to feel like a barrier rather than a sanctuary. Yet, Lira felt an urge to defy this unspoken farewell, to challenge the silence that seemed to seal Jarek's fate.

She turned to face Father Kolm, her hands rising in a gentle yet firm protest.

Must we decide Jarek's fate so hastily, Father? In the stillness of the Deep, we have always valued patience and wisdom. Let us not rush to conclusions, lest we forget the balance that has long sustained us.

Her words hung in the air, a testament to her growing conviction that Jarek's presence was not a threat, but an opportunity for growth and understanding. Beyond the stone corridors, a world of possibilities beckoned, and Lira felt an insistent call to explore, to learn, and to speak on behalf of those who, like Jarek, sought refuge within their walls.

Father Kolm gave a slight nod, and signed, *Talk to the Elders.*

Four

The Elders stood motionless, their faces set in the unreadable stillness of stone, as Lira lifted her hands to speak. Each movement was careful, deliberate, as she shaped the argument she had turned over in her mind, smoothing its edges, weighing its balance. Jarek had brought disruption, yes, but he had also brought something rare—knowledge of a world they had long chosen to forget. The Deep had endured in its silence, its separateness, but could it last forever? If their people were to survive beyond these chambers of breathing stone, should they not, at the very least, seek to understand what lay beyond them?

He is ignorant in our ways, not malicious, she signed, her hands fluid and precise. *His people are dying. They seek our help. If we turn him away, what does that say about us?*

The Elders remained unmoving. Only their eyes shifted, watching her, measuring the weight of her words against the centuries of caution that had shaped their lives. Then, at last, they moved, conferring in short, precise gestures. Their deliberation stretched long, though no sound disturbed the air between them, and yet the silence itself carried weight as if thought could be felt in the stillness.

Finally, Father Kolm turned back to her. His hands shaped the decision with the unyielding certainty of carved stone. *He may stay. For a time. But he will remain under watch. And you, Lira, will bear the responsibility. You will await the Elders' final judgment.*

Lira lowered her head in acknowledgment, though her pulse was quick, her breath uneven. It was not victory—not entirely—but it was enough. Enough to give Jarek and his people a chance.

Enough to let her glimpse, just a little longer, the world he carried with him.

***

Jarek sat on the stone ledge, hands resting on his knees, the shifting glow of the Stone Breathers casting restless shadows across his face. The cavern pulsed with its quiet, living light, and for a moment, he seemed carved from the same stone—worn, waiting. As Lira approached, he straightened, his wariness tempered by expectation. He had learned to watch her hands, to search her face for meaning even before the shapes of her words reached him.

They require more time, she signed, her fingers fluid in the dimness. She had begun to understand how his mind grasped language—slowly, in fragments, needing repetition and structure. Without the echo of spoken sound, meaning had to be anchored in form. *You may stay here until such time as the Elders decide.*

His shoulders eased, and relief crossed his features like a passing shadow. "Thank you," he whispered ever so carefully.

She tipped her head, but there was no softness in her reply. *You must follow rules. No sudden movements. No speaking loudly. And you must learn.*

Jarek exhaled, nodding. He had expected restrictions, but not the last condition—not that his survival here depended on understanding, not just endurance. "Teach me," he said simply.

She crouched beside him, close enough that he could see the fine control in her fingers, the quiet certainty in her gestures. *We begin with the first gesture. Respect.*

She brought her fingertips together and touched them lightly to her chest before extending her hands outward. The gesture was careful, a gesture of offering rather than demand, something held in the air between them, waiting. Jarek mirrored her, slower, unsure. His fingers faltered at the final motion, and Lira saw the pause in him—the unease of trying to speak through motion alone.

Good. Again.

He obeyed, the motion still clumsy, but improved. The stiffness had lessened. She could see the shape of understanding beginning to take hold.

Now the next—I understand. She tapped her temple twice, then pointed toward him.

He hesitated as if the gesture itself might change him, then copied her. His touch to his temple was too light, the second motion too rigid, but the meaning was there.

She nodded, approving, then mouthed. *You will learn faster if you stop thinking of words. It is not speech with hands. It is thought given shape.*

Jarek frowned, his brow furrowed in frustration. "That's . . . difficult. I think in words."

She tilted her head, watching the way his fingers curled reflexively, the way he still held language in his hands like something separate from himself. *We do not. Here, we think in motion, in rhythm, in silence.*

Jarek looked down at his hands as if they might betray him. "Then I'll have to change how I think."

Lira studied him for a moment, then placed her fingers lightly against his wrist, a gesture of patience, of time. *You will.*

***

As the days passed, Lira guided Jarek through the unseen currents of the Deep. He learned not only to move with care but to listen—not with ears, but with presence. He came to recognize the breath of the stone, the way the air shifted before a tremor, the subtle rhythms of life beneath the surface.

During this time, Jarek spoke of the world above. He described the sky, its endless shifting colors, the way the air moved freely without walls to hold it. He told her of water that stretched beyond sight, of creatures that soared without a tether.

Lira listened, absorbed every word, though she masked her hunger for knowledge behind careful silence.

One evening, as they sat beside the underground stream that fed the Deep, its quiet flow echoing through the chamber like a whispered lullaby, Jarek leaned forward and traced a rough map into the dust with a calloused finger. "My people live here," he said, pointing to a smudged cluster of dots. "We move between villages, trading what little we manage to gather or make. The surface isn't easy."

He paused, his brows tightening as if the lines of the land were etched into his skin. "Storms bring rains that come too late now, or not at all. Sometimes the storms bring only wind. When they do bring rain, they flood everything—wash away seeds, drown the roots. The soil used to hold, but now it dries too fast, and cracks open like old skin. Nothing stays in the ground long enough to grow. Livestock fall ill. People do too—coughs that don't go away, fevers that burn straight through the night. We build where we can, patch what's broken, but the storms are stronger than us."

He sat back, eyes lingering on the map that already begun to fade under the trickle of dust from the ceiling. "Too many are dying. Not just from hunger, but from being worn down, year after year. It's like the world itself forgot how to care for us."

Lira studied the markings he'd made, her voice quiet. *You have no stone to shield you. I don't understand. How do you keep the storms away?*

"We build," Jarek said, almost too softly to hear. "Walls and roofs, patched from scrap, shaped from what we find. Nothing like this place—nothing that lasts. But we make do. Some nights, I stare up at the sky and can't help but wonder how much longer we'll hold on."

She reached forward, her fingers brushing the dust, tracing the imagined ridges and paths. *Your sky. Does it truly have no ceiling?*

Jarek's lips curved into a faint smile. "It goes on forever. Sun, stars, clouds—it's always moving. You have to see it to really know."

A strange tension pulled at her chest. See it. The Deep had always been her beginning and end, the only place she'd ever known. But in Jarek's words lived something larger, something that waited beyond the stone.

Perhaps I will, one day, she said softly, almost as though afraid to speak the thought aloud.

Jarek studied her. "Would they let you? The Elders?"

She shook her head. *The Deep is my place. To leave it is to become . . . something else.*

He was silent for a moment. Then, carefully, he shaped the gesture she had taught him. *I understand.*

She smiled, small but genuine. *You are learning.*

Jarek nodded. "So are you."

Five

Jarek's hands moved slowly, his fingers shaping the gestures Lira had taught him, the motions stiff but improving. He was learning but still needed to mix both hand gestures and whispers. They sat on a smooth stone near a cluster of Stone Breathers, their glow steady, their silent respiration feeding the air. Lira watched him closely, noting how he hesitated before completing each shape, as though words still clung to his hands like roots resisting the pull of water.

Again, I understand, she signed, tapping her temple twice and pointing toward him.

Jarek mirrored her, slower this time, more purposeful. His eyes glanced toward her face for approval, and she gave a brief nod. The air was calm, the rhythm of the Deep undisturbed. For the first time, she wondered if he could truly belong here—if he could learn to think in silence, move in understanding rather than sound.

By accident, his boot scraped against the stone. The sound was like a thin shriek, a discordant note that shattered the stillness of the chamber. It was a small noise, brief, but in the hush, it might as well have been a shout that echoed off the cold, dark walls. The Stone Breathers, those ancient, sentient beings, shuddered in response, their bioluminescent glow flickering in distress like a dying flame. The light pulsed wildly, casting eerie shadows on the walls as Lira stiffened, her breath caught in her throat. Then, one by one, the Stone Breathers began to withdraw into the walls, their soft, ethereal hum fading into silence as they disappeared into the darkness, leaving behind only the faintest whisper of their presence. The chamber was once again still, but the memory of that scraping sound lingered, a haunting reminder of the fragility of the peace that had been disturbed.

The chamber darkened.

The air thinned.

Lira inhaled sharply, feeling the sudden tightness in her lungs. Around her, the Deep itself seemed to shrink, the steady breath of the caverns disrupted. She turned to Jarek, her hands forming the sign before she had time to think. *You must not—*

A sound rose in the distance, low at first, then growing—a ripple of movement, of unease. The others had felt it too. The balance had shifted. The Stone Breathers had retreated, their withdrawal a silent warning.

Jarek's voice, soft as a breath yet far too loud in this place, reached her. "What's happening?"

Lira's hands moved swiftly as she also mouthed, *The air will not last if they do not return.*

He turned pale. "I—I didn't know," he whispered.

She seized his wrist, pulling him to his feet. *We must go. Now.*

They moved through the dim corridors, the light weaker than before. The hush had turned heavy, not the quiet of peace, but the silence of withheld breath. Others emerged from the passageways, faces drawn, hands signing to one another in frantic bursts. The question rippled outward like water disturbed: *What happened?*

Lira felt their gazes settle on her—and on Jarek.

Father Kolm was among them. He did not move toward her at first, only watched. Then, slowly, he stepped forward, his presence as firm as the stone itself. When he signed, his hands moved with purpose, each gesture shaped with meaning. *You have endangered us all.*

Lira lifted her chin, though her heart pounded. *It wasn't on purpose.*

Not on purpose? His fingers shaped the words with sharp precision. *And if the Stone Breathers do not return? If the air fails to renew? Will you tell the dead it wasn't on purpose?*

Jarek shifted beside her. He whispered to Lira, "Tell him I didn't mean to—"

Enough, she signed without looking at him. She faced Father Kolm and steadied herself. *Blame does not solve this. I will make it right.*

Father Kolm regarded her for a long moment. The silence between them stretched, heavy with the weight of what had been broken. Then he stepped closer, his eyes dark with something deeper than anger. *You have let curiosity outweigh caution. You bear the responsibility. Fix it.*

Lira felt the force of his words settle into her bones. She had argued for Jarek's stay. She had believed understanding was worth the risk. And now the Deep itself was suffering for it.

She turned to Jarek. *Come with me,* she mouthed.

He followed as they retraced their path, moving carefully as if the very air might collapse beneath them. When they reached the chamber, the Stone Breathers remained withdrawn, their glow barely visible within the rock. The air was thinner still. Lira exhaled slowly, calming her breath. *We must show them it is safe.*

Jarek hesitated. "How?"

Stillness. Patience. She knelt, pressing her hands to the stone floor, letting her presence be known without force, much like a leaf settling on a quiet pool. She motioned for him to do the same, her eyes never leaving his, guiding him through the silence. He followed, though she could feel the tension in him, the press of unspoken words held tight, like a river straining against its banks.

They waited. The Deep held its silence, a vast, dark canvas waiting for the brushstrokes of life.

Then—a flicker of light. A tentative pulse. One of the Stone Breathers unfurled slightly, its glow dim but present, like the first blush of dawn.

Lira remained unmoving, her fingers against the stone, her breath synchronized with the slow awakening of the chamber. Jarek did the same, his tension easing into a quiet reverence. The chamber felt impossibly vast now, the air stretched thin, and both of them could sense the shift—the slow return of breath as if the very earth itself was stirring from a long slumber.

Another pulse. Then another.

The Stone Breathers, cautious, began to emerge once more.

The light returned.

The air filled.

Lira exhaled and lifted her hands and mouthed, *They forgive, but do not forget. You must be more careful.*

Jarek whispered, "I will."

They left the chamber in silence, the Deep breathing once more. But when they returned, the Elders were waiting. Father Kolm stepped forward, his gaze unreadable.

You have repaired what was broken. But the risk remains. The air is not endless, and our patience is not without limits.

Lira met his eyes, feeling the truth of it settle inside her. *Then I will make sure he understands.*

Father Kolm studied her for a long moment, then nodded. *See that you do.*

As the others dispersed, Jarek turned to her, his whisper barely above the hush of the stone. "I didn't realize how fragile this place is."

Lira's hands moved slowly. *Not fragile. Balanced. And now you must learn to be part of that balance—or you will not remain.*

Jarek swallowed and nodded. He understood now. And so did she.

Six

The journey downward was slow, a careful pace that mirrored the thoughtful nature of Lira's people. She led, her hands trailing along the carved stone walls, tracing the pathways she had known since childhood. The rock was cool, steady, familiar—but tonight, it felt different. Perhaps because she was leading an outsider where none had gone before, breaking a tradition that had stood for generations. Perhaps because she did not know what they would find at the end, only that the ancient wisdom of the Stone Breathers was their last hope.

Jarek followed closely, his breathing controlled but measured. The weight of the deep pressed upon him, an air not just of stone but of something older, something watching. Shadows danced around them, cast by the faint glow of the Stone Breathers, like whispers from the past. He whispered, "Are you sure about this? I mean taking us deeper underground where the oldest Stone Breather lives?" His voice was barely audible as if he feared disturbing the silence that had guarded these depths for so long.

Lira turned. *I am hoping it might find a way to repair the harm done, by having you here,* she mouthed back. *That it can communicate to the others.*

They moved in silence after that, careful with each step. The deeper chambers were less traveled, the air thin and brittle. The stone was very smooth and veined with threads of something metallic, pulsing faintly beneath the surface. The temperature dropped as they descended, and the silence seemed to grow heavier—not merely quiet, but dense, the kind that seemed to press against their eardrums.

Moss clung to the edges of the floor, pale and dry, crackling softly underfoot. The path narrowed, forcing them into single file, shadows shifting in odd ways that didn't match the rhythm of their steps. Whatever waited ahead was rarely disturbed, and the deeper they went, the more it felt like moving not just into the earth—but into something older, watching.

Jarek hesitated as the light dimmed further. "Why didn't you tell Father Kolm?" His whisper barely carried in the cavern's hush.

Lira kept walking. *Because he would have said no.*

Jarek exhaled, a quiet release of tension. "On the surface, hiding things from those in charge rarely ends well."

Here, questioning the path set before you rarely ends well, Lira replied, her fingers brushing across a ridge in the wall, feeling for a turn in the passage. *And yet, here we are.*

Jarek gave a small, dry laugh. "On the surface, hesitation gets you killed. If my people took as long to decide as yours do, we wouldn't last a day."

Lira turned to him, her expression unreadable in the dim light. *The Elders are not quick to act,* she explained, her voice low and steady. *They look to history, measuring every decision against what has come before. It isn't speed that has kept us going, but the care we take before we move. We do nothing blindly.*

He looked at her, intrigued by the depth of her words. "But doesn't that slow you down?" he asked, his curiosity genuine.

Lira nodded, her eyes glinting in the faint light. *Speed is not always the measure of success. Our deliberations may take time, but they ensure that when we act, it is with wisdom and foresight. Your world may rush forward, but ours has endured through the ages.*

He did not answer. There was no simple response. Instead, he watched as Lira moved ahead, her form barely a shadow against the stone. He followed, lost in thought about the contrast between their worlds and the wisdom in Lira's words.

The path sloped downward and spilled them into a hollow chamber, carved out ages ago and worn smooth by time itself. The walls shimmered with a light that barely moved, as though frozen in the moment of its own creation. At the center, a great, undulating form lay curled against the stone—a Stone Breather so old it no longer pulsed, only exhaled in long, slow breaths that reverberated through the rock itself. The air was thick, heavy with the scent of stone and something older still—something that felt like the slow breath of the world's heart.

Lira placed a hand against the creature, feeling the faintest tremor. *It knows we are here.*

Jarek whispered, "Do it . . . mind?"

She hesitated. *I do not know. It remembers the balance. It remembers what we have forgotten.*

Lira stepped forward cautiously, her footsteps echoing softly in the stillness. She lowered herself to the ground, placing both hands flat against the stone. Her fingers moved, shaping meaning into silence.

We seek to mend what is broken, she communicated, her hands weaving a language that spoke directly to the heart of the earth. The gesture was both a plea and a promise, a recognition of the deep connection between her people and the land they inhabited.

The Deep thrummed, a vibration felt more than heard. It was a response, a stirring of the ancient power that lay beneath their feet. The sound was like a heartbeat, slow and deliberate, a reminder that even in stillness, there was always life and always a way forward.

Jarek knelt beside her. "What is it saying?"

Lira's eyes remained closed, her fingers feeling the slow shifts in the stone. *A way between... The Deep cannot remain untouched forever. Nor can the surface. It's always been waiting, waiting for this.*

Jarek frowned. "What does that mean?"

The ground beneath them pulsed once, twice, then settled. The Stone Breather's message had ended.

Lira opened her eyes. *It means the answer is not only here. It is with you as well.*

***

They left the chamber and made their way back toward the upper halls, their footsteps echoing softly in the stillness. As they moved, Lira led them to a small, hidden chamber tucked away between the deeper caverns, its walls weeping delicate streams of mineral-rich water that glistened in the dim light. The water pooled in shallow depressions, only to disappear into unseen veins within the rock, as if the stone itself were quietly drinking. The air here was cool—refreshing, though not as thin as the passages above. Yet, it was still thick with that ever-present silence. They sank down onto the smooth stone floor, their bodies weary from the journey, their minds spinning with the weight of everything they had just uncovered.

Lira cupped her hands beneath one of the slow drips, letting the water gather before bringing it to her lips. It was crisp, tasting of the earth itself. Jarek did the same, drinking quietly, his eyes reflecting the dim glow of the Stone Breathers that lined the walls in scattered patches, their presence faint, but not absent.

She pulled a small bundle of dried lichen from the nearby rocks, chewing it thoughtfully. Jarek took some when she offered, eating in careful silence. It was a quiet, necessary ritual: the act of sharing sustenance, of acknowledging life amid uncertainty.

For a long time, neither spoke. The silence of the Deep wrapped around them, not oppressive but vast, a thing with weight and shape. Lira had long grown used to it, had learned to listen to the subtle shifts in the stone, the breath of the caverns, the slow conversation of the ancient ones. She wondered if Jarek heard it too, or if the silence was only emptiness to him.

Then, softly, he hummed.

It was barely more than a breath at first, a sound that wove itself into the stillness rather than disturbing it. A single note, then another, a thread of melody softly, ever so softly, unfurling into the cavern's hush. Lira turned her head slightly, watching him in the dim light. His eyes were closed, his lips barely parted as the sound became song.

The words were whispered, unfamiliar, shaped in a language that was not hers, but the meaning did not need translation. It was a song of longing, of distant places and remembered warmth, a song carried through time and breath. As he sang, his voice remained soft, low, careful, as though uncertain whether the Deep would welcome it.

Yet, the Stone Breathers did not retreat. If anything, their faint glow seemed steadier, a slow pulse of light that resonated with the rhythm of Jarek's song. The Deep listened.

Lira closed her eyes and let the sound pass through her. She had spent her life wary of sound, knowing how easily it could change things. But this—this was different. It didn't press or tug. It offered. It moved through the chamber like a stream through tall grass, quiet and sure, shaping without needing to. It slipped into the stillness, not to disturb it, but to become part of it.

She opened her eyes as Jarek's voice faded into the hush once more. He exhaled softly as if releasing something long held within him.

That was beautiful, she signed, her hands moving in the dim glow. Then, she mouthed, *Beautiful*.

Jarek watched her for a moment, then let a quiet smile form—hesitant, almost apologetic. "It's an old song," he whispered. "My mother used to sing it at night when the wind was loud against the house and none of us could sleep. Her voice made the storm seem smaller, like it had somewhere else to be."

Lira nodded, watching the slow pulse of the Stone Breathers. *They do not fear it. They welcome it.*

Jarek looked at the creatures, their faint luminescence casting soft shadows against the rock. "Maybe they understand more than we think."

Lira traced a hand along the floor, feeling the faint tremors beneath. *The Deep is always listening*, she signed. *Perhaps it is time we learned how to listen back.*

Jarek's smile lingered, small and thoughtful. "Then let's keep listening."

They sat in the quiet for a long time after that, the Deep breathing around them, the song lingering in the stone.

Seven

They had drifted in and out of sleep, not quite resting, not quite waking. Lira lay still in the hush of the chamber, the warmth of Jarek beside her a quiet reassurance. The Deep had its own rhythms, its own way of marking time. She'd listened through the night to the slow breathing of the stone, half-dreaming, half-aware, wondering if what she heard were the Stone Breathers shifting far below. It was a slow shifting as though stirring from a long-forgotten dream. Jarek's song had not driven them away. If anything, it had settled among them, sinking into the cavern walls like water into parched earth. The air had trembled with something unspoken, something she could not yet name.

When dawn came—if it could be called that—it arrived not with light but with a pale ripple along the cavern walls, a pulse of soft luminescence that edged forward and paused, then edged forward again. It didn't brighten the chamber so much as trace its shape, reminding them of space and form without ever fully revealing it.

Lira sat up without a word. Jarek followed. There was no need to ask. A low tone, carried through the stone, meant only one thing: the Elders had reached a decision.

A figure darkened the chamber threshold. Father Kolm stood with the stillness of rock, his face unreadable, as though he had been hewn from the very walls behind him. The light caught on the edges of his features, deepening the hollows of his cheeks, the furrow of his brow. He did not need to speak. Lira already knew.

Still, when his hands moved, the finality of the words struck like a chisel against stone.

The Elders have spoken. Jarek must leave.

The silence that followed was thin, stretched taut like a thread ready to snap. Lira felt it pressing against her skin, against the walls, against the fragile space between them all. Her chest tightened, as though the air had become scarce. She had known this was coming. But knowing was different from hearing, different from standing before it, real and immovable.

Her hands clenched.

Lira translated for Jarek, her face drawn with sorrow.

Jarek spoke barely above a whisper, his words barely more than breath. "I understand."

Lira turned to him, caught off guard. There was a calm in his expression that suggested he'd come to terms with the truth long before it had found its voice. *No,* she mouthed, urgent and fierce. *They don't understand. They look backward. They cling to what was, blind to what still might be.*

Father Kolm's gaze darkened. *It is too dangerous, Lira. You saw what happened. The Stone Breathers recoiled. The air thinned. This place does not tolerate outsiders.*

Lira stepped forward, a small motion that disrupted the stillness around her, a ripple against the still surface of the gathered Elders. She lifted her hands, shaping the words with care, though her heart beat too fast and her breath felt tight in her throat. *Perhaps not all sounds harm them.* She let the thought settle between them, let it find space in the heavy hush. *He sang and they did not flee. They did not suffer. They stirred as though recognizing something.* She glanced toward Jarek, who stood quiet beside her, his expression unreadable but steady. *Perhaps they have changed. Perhaps we have misunderstood.*

A shift in the light, subtle as the slow cooling of rock. Movement. An old woman, an Elder older even than Father Kolm, her face marked with lines so deep they seemed carved rather than formed by time. She watched Lira with the patience of stone, the weight of long years behind her silence. Then, at last, her hands rose, deliberate, her fingers slow as falling dust.

We cannot risk survival on a possibility. A pause, heavy, unyielding. *The balance is delicate. Too delicate.*

Lira turned toward her, urgency tightening each movement, her body speaking before her mouth could find the words. The old woman had lived through the worst of it—those years when the Deep barely held together, when the Stone Breathers pulled back from the world above, when the air grew thin and the silence broke apart like glass. Lira knew she carried years of memory, the kind that didn't fade with time but sharpened.

Still, Lira couldn't let the past press so hard against the present that it left no room for what might come next.

Is it survival if we do not grow? If we do not learn? Her fingers moved swiftly now, faster than was proper, but she did not stop. *We have always believed that silence was the only way. But what if there is another?* She turned to Father Kolm, then to the old woman, searching their faces for some flicker of understanding. *What if true understanding means finding the sounds that do not harm, but heal?*

The hush in the chamber thickened. Even the air seemed to press inward, waiting. Lira swallowed hard, then took one last step forward.

What if cooperation, not exile, is the way forward?

The chamber held its silence. The Elders had spoken, their decision now part of the stone around them, unmoving. There would be no argument, no return to the conversation. It was finished.

Yet Father Kolm paused.

It was the smallest thing—a shift in the way he held his hands, the way his gaze slipped to the floor before finding its way back. Not enough for anyone else to notice, but Lira saw it. A question had entered him, quiet but persistent. He had lived for years in the certainty of silence, in the belief that the Elders saw farther than he ever could. And yet—her conviction had moved something in him. Not rebellion. Not pride. Something quieter. A clarity that asked to be heard.

It was hope.

Jarek met Lira's gaze. His voice, when it came, was quiet. "If leaving will keep your people safe, I'll go."

Lira's hands twitched, the words rising but catching in her throat. He meant it. He would walk away, not because he believed in their decision, but because he valued her world enough to let it be.

Father Kolm exhaled slowly. The old woman watched, waiting for him to reaffirm their choice, to silence the question Lira had dared to ask. But he only raised his hands and moved them with care. *He may stay one more day,* the gesture said. *But he must go when the sun rises next.*

A ripple passed through the old woman, a murmur of stone shifting against stone. She did not agree, but she did not oppose him. She would convince the other Elders.

Lira nodded, though her chest ached. It was not enough, but it was something.

Father Kolm did not answer. He turned, his steps slow, his thoughts unreadable.

Lira watched him go before turning to Jarek. *One more day.*

Jarek gave her a small, wry smile. "Thank you. A lot can happen in a day."

She nodded, something steady beginning to rise within her. *Yes. A day may be enough.*

Eight

As a new day began, the walls held their usual hush, the silence woven into them like the memory of once forgotten. The hours stretched long in the dim, breathing light of the Deep. Yet in the small chamber where Lira and Jarek sat, something shifted. It was not silence that bound them now, but a question—a thing unspoken yet vast, waiting to take shape. The air felt thick with it as if the stone itself was listening, waiting.

Jarek turned a small stone between his fingers, feeling its weight, its texture, its history. He had always found comfort in the language of things—of rock and rhythm, of the way the world spoke without words. "If they responded before," he murmured, though his voice was scarcely more than a breath, "then it means they hear. But not just hear—they listen."

Lira watched the stone move in his hands, thoughtful. *Then we must find what they are listening for,* she signed. Her fingers moved with careful precision, as though shaping the very thought itself. She exhaled, tilting her head. *And what it is they remember.*

Jarek met her gaze. "Then we should try again," he replied with a mix of signs and whispers.

They began carefully. Lira positioned herself near the edge of the cavern where the Stone Breathers loomed, vast and unmoving, like frozen waves in the depths of the earth. Their forms were rough yet smooth, their surfaces shifting imperceptibly over days, years, centuries. No one knew if they had once been something else or if they had always been as they were, pulsing slow and deep with the rhythm of the stone.

Jarek started to hum, barely a vibration, barely a thing at all. The sound was low, a fragment of melody that did not seek to impose, only to exist.

Lira watched. The air did not thin. The Stone Breathers did not recoil. They moved. Moved!

Another note, softer than breath, an offering rather than an intrusion.

The Stone Breathers stirred once again.

The movement was slow—so slow that it might have been imagined—but she saw it. A shift, a responding pulse, a movement that was neither retreat nor rejection but something else. Acknowledgment.

Lira's heart pounded. She pressed her hands to the ground and felt the rhythm beneath her palms. It was faint but certain. A pattern. A pulse. A response.

They are moving, speaking back.

Jarek stopped, letting the last note dissipate into the cavern. The stillness that followed was not absence but possibility.

Lira swallowed hard. *Again.*

They worked through the long hours, testing the limits of sound, seeking the line between harmony and disturbance. A hum, a vibration, the whisper of stone against stone. And always, the response—a deep, slow pulse, a movement, a rhythm that seemed to echo through the bones of the Deep.

When the time came, Lira stood before Father Kolm, her hands steady but her breath unsteady. Jarek stood beside her, silent. They had spoken enough in the chamber. Now, they would speak here, before those who could decide.

Father Kolm listened as Lira explained what they had done, what they had witnessed in the stone Breathers. His eyes were fixed and unreadable, his face worn by years of duty, by stories told too many times, and truths accepted too quickly.

They responded. She told him. *The ground itself seemed to breathe in time with the sound. It's not of noise, but of intention. Of music as something soothing and familiar, not a threat but a kind of invitation. We can teach the surface dwellers this technique so that they can live in the Deep.*

Kolm's mouth tightened. *The Stone Breathers fear sound for a reason,* he signed. *Too many of our people died learning what wakes when the wrong tones are struck. The silence was earned.*

Lira raised her hands, fingers moving with care. *It is not silence they need,* she signed in response. *It is understanding. We have the knowledge to help Jarek's people, so that they can live in harmony with us here.*

He looked away. *You ask me to unteach what has kept us alive.*

"No," Jarek whispered. "We're asking you to see what's already changing."

Kolm folded his arms across his chest. *You saw the Stone Breathers stir, yes—but a shift in stone is not the same as acceptance.*

It's more than that, Lira replied, her fingers moving briskly. *When Jarek hummed the old song—barely a thread of sound—they moved—yes—but more than that—they turned toward it. Not in anger. In recognition.*

Kolm's gaze flicked to Jarek, searching. They moved toward the sound?"

"They listened," Jarek breathed. "They heard something. Something they remembered."

Kolm stood silent for a moment, the chamber pressing in around them. He rubbed his chin, then looked toward the dark hallway that led back to the council room.

Are you sure? he asked.

Lira nodded. *Yes.*

He sighed, long and low, the sound of a man crossing a line he hadn't thought he'd approach again. *Then I'll take it to the Elders. No promises. But they will hear it.*

He turned and left without another word—but this time, his footsteps carried the echo of something else. Not retreat. Consideration.

***

Lira's heart pounded as they waited. Jarek sat beside her, hands folded over his knees. "Do you think they will listen?" he whispered.

She wanted to say yes. Instead, she signed, *They must.*

But the answer came quickly. Too quickly.

When Father Kolm returned, his expression was unchanged, yet there was something beneath it, something heavier than before. He lifted his hands.

They do not deliberate. They do not change.

Lira's fingers curled into her palms. *Even when they are wrong?*

Father Kolm hesitated. It was brief, but it was there. *The old ways have kept us safe.*

Jarek rose. His voice was calm, though his shoulders were tight. "Then I will go."

The words were final. There was no argument to be made, no more time to plead. Lira knew that. And yet her hands moved before she could stop them.

This is not the end.

Jarek gave her a small, wry smile. "You did your best," he said softly.

They walked together to the entrance of the tunnels where the world above began. Here, the air felt different, thinner yet open, filled with something Lira could not name.

Jarek turned to her and reached into the pouch at his side.

"For you." He held up the small stone he had been turning between his fingers earlier that day.

He placed it in her palm. It was small and smooth, its surface holding the faint trace of warmth as if it had been remembering him. This wasn't just something pulled from the Deep, worn down by time and silence. It had been carried. Considered. A piece of the Deep, yes—but changed by being held, shaped by presence, not by chance. It was a gift, not something stumbled upon, but something chosen.

She swallowed, feeling the promise of it rise in her throat— quiet, certain. Then, with calm fingers, she slipped a bracelet from her wrist. It was simple, woven from the dark fibers pulled from the Deep, made with the kind of attention only patience allows. Each thread wound with care, each knot tied with a kind of hope that asks nothing in return. She fastened it around his wrist, slowly, the way you might handle something that matters not because it's breakable, but because it's meant to stay.

Jarek flexed his hand, watching the way it moved with him. The weave shifted, dark against his skin. "I will return," he whispered, and the words did not feel like a farewell.

Lira nodded. The words stuck in her throat, too many, too few. She stepped back, and let the silence speak for her. Let the stone, the bracelet, the space between them hold what could not be spoken.

Jarek turned and walked into the light.

Lira paused, just a breath between one world and the next, and then she went after him. The sun reached for her, unfamiliar and astonishing, all brightness and sky stretched wide above. She blinked, unsteady under its brilliance, then tipped her face to the open air, lifted her arms, and screamed—sharp and full of something she hadn't known she'd been holding. The sound broke free, wild and clear, flung into the sky that had no ceiling.

Jarek flinched, then burst out laughing, the kind of laugh that lifts from the chest and has nowhere to go but out. Lira laughed too, winded and bright-eyed, her shoulders shaking as if the laughter itself surprised her.

She looked at him and spoke, her voice a thread of sound barely louder than the breeze. "Goodbye."

And just like that, she turned. Her pace slowed once, maybe twice, and then she was gone, swallowed by the cool hush of the Deep.

But Lira did not return to the silence she had known. Her world of stone had changed. She had changed. And though the Elders had rejected what she had shown them, the knowledge did not die in her hands.

She began to experiment again, in the quiet, in the spaces where no one watched. Soft sounds, rhythmic ones, woven into the daily rituals of her people. A hum before sleep carried gently through the stillness. A tone shaped by breath, resonating through the stone, as if coaxing it to remember something long buried.

At first, no one noticed.

Then, slowly, they did.

A mother rocking her child, voice lifting in the barest whisper of a lullaby. A worker in the tunnels, tapping a measured beat against the stone, fingers seeking a rhythm older than silence.

The silence remained. But within it, something new began to take shape.

Something waiting to be understood.

The Portrait in the Cellar

The Inheritance

Lucien Harrow was a figure carved from the very marble of melancholy— a wraith draped in mortal guise, whose fingers once summoned beauty now trembled with the residue of sorrow, his eyes dimmed not by age, but by the ceaseless haunt of a canvas left unfinished by fate. His skin held the pallor of candlewax long untouched by flame, and his fingers—slender, trembling— remained stained with oil and pigment, as though absolution lay in filth. He moved with the silence of one who expects footsteps behind him and spoke in whispers, wary that sound might stir some slumbering dread. Mirrors he avoided, not for age or vanity, but for the secret he feared his reflection would one day confess.

The hours passed with torturous languor. The fire in the hearth had long since withered to embers, and yet Lucien did not stir to replenish it. He lay there, his eyes unblinking, the crimson canopy above him a funereal shroud beneath which sleep dared not tread. It was not mere unease that gripped him—it was a pall, a disquiet that reached beyond the ordinary bounds of trepidation.

There was a presence in the manor. Not seen, nor heard—yet undeniably felt.

Each creak of the floorboards above, each soft sigh of the wind slipping between the windowpanes, pressed upon his heart like the fingers of some long-buried revenant. Somewhere in the depths of his consciousness, Lucien recognized the sensation not as fear, but as remembrance. As if the very house remembered him. As if the walls themselves exhaled a memory long suppressed.

By the time the first weak threads of dawn unfurled across the ashen sky, he rose from his bed with the stiffness of one who had wrestled specters all night. He dressed in silence, eschewing his morning tea, and descended once more to the lower halls. The great grandfather clock in the foyer had ceased its tolling, its pendulum stilled as if time itself dared not intrude further upon the domain.

The house, a gift from his uncle, bequeathed upon the old man's death, exhaled in murmurous sighs, its timbers groaning with a sentience most foul. And the air—ah, the air!—grew chill in phantasmal pockets, as though stirred by unseen wings. A disquietude settled upon him, for the door, sealed with rusted nails—yes, that somber slab of oak he had passed but yesternight—no longer bore the dumb stillness of abandonment. As he crept once more into the corridor's gullet, a scent assailed him—subtle, spectral—like wilted lavender pressed between the pages of a forgotten diary, its perfume clinging to the air like a memory unwilling to die.

He halted before the door. Though untouched, it seemed changed—more animate, somehow, as though aware of his scrutiny. A carved, wooden crest that rested upon it, though cracked, now gleamed subtly in the murky light filtering through a stained-glass window above. In that fleeting illumination, Lucien perceived a sigil carved in the crest he had not previously noticed—an ouroboros encircling a single, weeping eye.

He reached forth, his trembling fingertips tracing the furrowed grain of the ancient door, its surface marred by rusted nails driven deep in some forgotten rite. Beneath the fleshy whorl of his thumb, a subtle quivering stirred—a tremor so slight as to seem born of madness, and yet undeniably present. It was not sound, nor mere movement, but a sensation most profane—like breath exhaled from within the wood, patient and watching.

Lucien recoiled.

"I am not mad," he whispered, more to himself than to the silent hall. "I am not mad."

And yet, even as he said it, the certainty began to erode.

The days that followed passed in a stupor, each one more grey and lifeless than the last. The weather did not lift; the sun remained hidden behind a pall of leaden clouds, and a chill settled over the estate like a winding sheet. Lucien kept largely to himself, taking his meals in the library, where ancient tomes lined the shelves like tombstones, each concealing knowledge best left interred.

He found, amid his uncle's disordered papers, a leather-bound ledger of curious origin. The handwriting was delicate, almost feminine, and yet the contents were anything but gentle. The journal spoke of rituals and invocations, of ancestral debts and sacrifices made not in blood, but in memory. A single passage had been circled in ink grown brown with age:

"There are doors that open both inward and out—not all lead to chambers built by men."

Lucien closed the book with trembling hands.

That night, the murmuring intensified. It was no longer formless. The voice—if voice it could be called—had taken on cadence. Words lilted through the stone and timber like sighs from a distant room:

"Lucien . . ."

He bolted upright in bed. The fire was out. The room was steeped in shadows so complete they seemed to bleed from the walls. And yet, at the far corner, near the heavy drapes, a figure stood—indistinct, cloaked in the folds of darkness, eyes pale as frost.

"Lucien . . ."

He could not move, nor breathe. The figure did not advance, nor did it fade. It merely watched, and with that silent observation came a cascade of memories—his childhood visits to the manor, his uncle's locked study, the dreams of the crying woman in the cellar below.

He had dismissed them then as the fancies of a morbid child. Now, they returned with dreadful clarity.

When he found the courage to rise, the figure was gone, leaving no trace save the air—now tinged unmistakably with lavender and decay.

Mrs. Bettridge, that bent and brittle housekeeper, moved through the morning with a hush upon her lips and a tremor in her limbs. She would not meet his eye, nor would her foot dare cross the bounds of the east wing, where the ancient wood door stood like a sentinel of forgotten rites. When he pressed her, she spoke not to him, but to the air itself, murmuring, "Best not to wake what has only just begun to sleep."

That evening, Lucien stood before the sealed door once again, the lantern in his hand casting trembling shadows along the corridor walls. He had made a decision—born not of courage, but of compulsion.

He would open the door.

The Portrait Unearthed

Compelled by an insatiable curiosity that gnawed at the edges of his reason, Lucien resolved to unseal the forbidden door. Armed with tools procured from the manor's dilapidated workshop, he approached the wood barrier. Each strike of the hammer against the rusted nails echoed through the corridors like the tolling of a funeral bell.

As the last nail relinquished its hold, the door creaked open, exhaling a breath of air stale with the passage of untold years. A narrow staircase descended into a subterranean gloom, the steps slick with moisture and treacherous with age.

Lantern in hand, Lucien ventured downward. The cellar was a vault of shadows, the walls glistening with dampness, and the air thick with the musky scent of decay. Amidst the detritus of forgotten relics stood a singular object—a canvas draped in a tattered cloth, its form suggesting a portrait of considerable proportions.

With a sense of foreboding mingled with anticipation, Lucien removed the shroud. The lantern's feeble glow revealed a visage of haunting beauty: a woman of ethereal pallor, her raven hair cascading over slender shoulders, eyes of a penetrating gray that seemed to pierce the very soul. Her lips, though unsmiling, hinted at secrets untold, and her gaze bore an uncanny semblance of sentience.

"Who are you?" Lucien whispered, entranced by the lifelike presence captured upon the canvas.

There came no reply—naught but the hollow hush of the cellar's breathless gloom. And so, after a span that felt unmeasured by any earthly clock, Lucien turned his gaze from the painted woman's vigil. With limbs leaden and heart oppressed, he ascended the creaking steps, retreating from that subterranean abyss, and drew shut the ancient wooden door, as if to seal the darkness behind him—and perhaps some whisper of his own soul with it.

That night, his slumber was disturbed by visions of the enigmatic woman. She stood at the foot of his bed, her eyes luminous in the darkness, lips moving in a silent invocation of his name.

"Lucien . . ."

He awoke with a start, the echo of her voice lingering in the stillness of the chamber.

***

Sleep would not return to him. The shadows of the chamber seemed to lengthen and lean in toward his bed, as though listening for his breath, as though waiting for him to speak her name aloud. He lay still, frozen not with fear, but with an unease that permeated his every limb—an unease not born of dread, but of desire unformed, a yearning he could neither name nor dismiss.

He rose ere the sun had stirred, when the pallid gloom of pre-dawn crept like a specter through the shattered panes, casting its ashen glow upon a world bereft of hue or warmth. Without heed for sustenance or shroud, Lucien, lantern clutched in a whitened grip, descended yet again into the bowels of that accursed manor— drawn, as though fettered by some invisible chain, to the yawning mouth of the cellar that called to him beneath.

The portrait remained as he had left it. Yet there was something imperceptibly altered in the rendering of the woman's eyes. Where once they had merely watched, now they seemed to regard him—no longer inert but imbued with recognition, with longing. The corners of her mouth, which the night before bore the silence of marble, now gave the barest suggestion of movement, as if, at the precise angle, she might be smiling.

Lucien's heart thudded with a violence that startled him. He stumbled backward, colliding with a rusted wine rack that clattered against the stone. The sound reverberated like the clanging of chains in a crypt.

Yet still he did not flee.

He stood there in reverent silence, as if before an altar, and whispered again: "Who are you?"

No answer was issued from the shadows. And yet, the cellar no longer felt empty. There was a weight in the air, a presence hovering just beyond the edge of sight, of comprehension. He became aware of a soft rustling, like silk moving against stone, and the faintest scent—jasmine touched with something darker, the iron tang of blood or roses long since dead.

Thus, did he descend, day upon day, into the sepulchral depths of that accursed cellar, drawn as by a morbid compulsion to behold the woman imprisoned in pigment and shade—her gaze eternal, her silence a dirge that clung to the very stones like mildew born of grief.

Each descent into the cellar became a liturgy of obsession. He began to speak to her—not merely words, but confessions. Secrets he had buried deep within himself, grievances harbored from childhood, dreams abandoned, and desires unfulfilled. And always she listened. Or so he believed. The very air grew thick with his words, as though the walls themselves absorbed his torment.

Sometimes, he would pause, as if waiting for a reply, but none came—only the hollow echo of his voice, reverberating through the chamber like a mocking reflection of his own despair.

Days passed. Weeks. Time lost its linear march. Mrs. Bettridge, noted his worsening pallor, his tremors, the hollowness beneath his eyes, and implored him to eat, to sleep, to leave the cellar untouched. But her entreaties fell like raindrops on granite. Lucien was elsewhere, lost in the fevered labyrinth of his mind, and every return to the cellar only tightened the noose around his soul.

Then one morning, as the sun bled through the fog in dull streaks of crimson, Lucien found the cellar door ajar. His breath hitched. He knew with certainty he had closed it tight the night before—his hands still felt the coldness of its latch. Grasping a lantern with trembling hand, he descended the creaking stairs in fevered haste; yet upon reaching the dim cellar, he beheld the portrait unchanged. Yet, on the dusty floor, a single black hair lay coiled like a question. It was long and glistened wetly in the lamplight. It had not been there before.

He bent to touch it, but a sudden gust—impossible in the windless tomb of the cellar—extinguished the lantern. He was plunged into utter blackness.

He froze.

Behind him: the sound of footsteps descending.

Slow. Measured. Wet.

He turned—but saw nothing.

"Lucien . . ." The voice, unmistakable, barely a breath—closer than before, too close.

His blood ran to ice. He staggered backward, the darkness thick and suffocating.

Then—her face.

Not on the canvas.

Before him.

Her eyes opened wide, not painted now, but living, weeping, impossibly gray. Her mouth opened, and from it poured not words but a cold wind, a scream inverted, a breathless chasm that swallowed sound itself. The very air around her seemed to tremble as if the world itself had been split by her utterance, leaving only a hollow echo in its wake. The walls groaned in protest, the floorboards cracked beneath her ethereal presence, and the candles flickered, casting dancing shadows that writhed like trapped souls. Lucien, his breath caught in his throat, could neither move nor scream—he was bound to the spot, suspended between horror and awe.

All was swallowed by a suffocating darkness, absolute and unkind.

When consciousness at last returned, it did so in ragged breaths and shuddering heartbeats. He found himself prone upon the cold, unyielding floor—his garments clung wetly to his frame, his hair matted and damp, his face marred by streaks of grave-like filth drawn from the cellar's bowels. No woman, no trace of her. And the portrait—it had vanished, as though spirited away by hands unseen, or devoured by the very shadows he dared disturb.

Only the frame remained, leaning forlornly against the distant stone wall—its edges cracked, twisted, and scarred as though some malignant force had gnawed its way outward from within. The indentations were raw and recent, deep furrows that seemed to weep with an unearthly urgency as if some trapped soul had desperately sought release.

And upon the cold, indifferent stone behind the frame, scrawled in a hand foreign to his own, there appeared these words: "You opened the door. Now I am free."

Obsession Takes Root

D
r. Alton Grey arrived at Lucien's estate, his heart heavy with an unease he could not quell. The carriage wheels churned through the gravel path with a groan that seemed to reverberate through his bones, each turn a silent echo of some looming dread. Stepping out, his gloved hands trembled for a fleeting moment before he steadied them, the black fabric gleaming faintly beneath the indifferent light of the moon. The house rose before him like a decaying monument, its windows sealed tight in shadow, save for one lone flickering light that shuddered with a spectral pulse, as though mocking the life within. He lingered on the threshold, his strong jaw set in grim resolve, battling the growing suspicion that Lucien's summons heralded something beyond mere illness.

Within, the air clung to Lucien like a damp cloth, thick with an ancient grief that seemed to have been woven into the very walls. He sat in an armchair, slumped as if the weight of his years—and something darker—pressed him down into the cushions. His once-vibrant eyes were dimmed to a spectral gleam, like the last embers of a fire long extinguished. His skin had taken on an unnatural pallor, waxy and translucent, a faint sheen of death's advance creeping over him. "You've come, good Doctor," Lucien rasped, his voice a dry whisper that rustled like leaves crushed underfoot.

Grey, unflinching, nodded curtly. His voice was the crisp authority of one trained to dissect both the mind and the body. "Mrs. Bettridge wrote that it was urgent," he said, his tone clipped yet steady. "What is it you need, Lucien?"

Lucien's lips twisted into something that almost resembled a smile, but it was the smile of a man who had long since forgotten how to grin. It was grotesque, a hollow echo of the man Grey had once known. "It's not what I need," he murmured, his gaze drifting toward the corners of the room where the shadows clung thick and persistent. "It's what she demands."

Grey's brow furrowed, a mixture of skepticism and concern twisting within him. "She?" he echoed, his voice a thread of disbelief. He leaned forward, fixing Lucien with an intent gaze. "Lucien, you're unwell. I've seen you play at delusion before, but this—this is something altogether different."

Lucien's laughter emerged from him in a low, guttural sound, devoid of any trace of humor. It reverberated through the room as if drawn from some deep, desolate well within him. "Ah, you think me mad," he said, his fingers twitching against the armrest, as though reaching for something unseen in the room's oppressive silence. "But you'll see soon enough."

A chill slithered down Grey's spine, his scientific mind at war with the growing sense of unease that clung to him like a shadow. His gaze turned to the hearth, where the fire seemed to leap unnaturally, flickering in wild, unnatural spasms, as though it too were alive—watching, waiting.

Dr. Grey rose abruptly, his face hardening as he closed the distance between them, his voice lowering with an edge of authority. "Lucien, you're in the grip of something far worse than illness. This . . . this fixation you have with . . . her . . . it is consuming you. You must listen to reason. I came to help you."

Lucien's eyes, hollow and fevered, met his with a gaze that seemed to pierce through him as if seeing something far beyond the confines of the room. "Help me?" he repeated, a snarl of incredulity creeping into his voice. "You cannot help me, my good Doctor. None of you can."

Grey recoiled slightly, his brow furrowing in confusion and frustration. "I can see you are teetering on the edge, Lucien. This obsession—this madness—it must be stopped before it destroys you."

Lucien's lips parted, but no words came. Instead, his gaze slid to the shadows in the farthest corner of the room, as though something—or someone—beckoned from beyond. "You think you can save me," he whispered, his voice trembling with some unholy conviction. "But you cannot. This is not some passing ailment. This is fate, Doctor, fate woven into the very fibers of my being. Elira . . . she calls to me. You will never understand. You cannot help me. I think it best if you leave."

Dr. Grey stood rigid, his mind a maelstrom of frustration and disbelief. He took a step back, his eyes narrowing, and his voice was quiet, yet filled with an edge of finality. "If you continue down this path, Lucien, there will be nothing left of you. Nothing but a shell—haunted, hollow, and beyond saving."

Lucien remained motionless, his pallid face now betraying nothing but an eerie, resigned calm. "You are mistaken, my good friend. It is already too late for me. Please go. There is nothing more for you here."

A tightness formed in Dr. Grey's chest, his mind recoiling from the implications of Lucien's words. The man he had once known—his friend, his confidant—had been lost to some unseen force, drawn into the very madness that now consumed him. And now, he was beyond saving.

Without another word, Dr. Grey turned and walked toward the door, his feet dragging with the weight of defeat. He paused once, casting one last, sorrowful glance at Lucien, but the man did not stir. The fire flickered wildly behind him, casting grotesque shadows that danced in time with the pulsing rhythm of some unseen heartbeat. And, as he stepped into the cold, he knew that Lucien was lost—lost to something far darker than the sickness of the body.

Lucien closed the door upon Dr. Grey's departure with a finality that echoed through the vast and vacant halls like a tolling knell. The rain outside had begun to fall with a fervor most unnatural—thin, needling drops that scratched at the windowpanes as though some unseen talons sought entrance. Thunder, distant but persistent, rolled across the moors and reverberated in the marrow of the manor itself.

The moment Grey's carriage disappeared down the winding lane, Lucien returned to the cellar as though drawn by invisible cords wound tight around his limbs and heart. He descended the narrow stair with a mind fevered and eyes wide, the lantern's glow casting monstrous silhouettes upon the damp walls.

"Where are you?" he murmured, his voice barely a whisper in the stifling gloom.

The question echoed in the hollow space, unanswered as if the very air conspired to hold its secret. With a trembling hand, he began to tear the cellar apart, driven by an insatiable, frantic hunger. His eyes, wide and bloodshot, scoured every shadow, every forgotten crevice, until at last, beneath a heavy tarpaulin—its once-vibrant fabric now darkened by mildew and the slow, inexorable passage of time—he uncovered it. There, lying in wait like some forbidden relic of a past too painful to recall, was the original portrait—Elira, his silent enchantress, gazing back at him with those fathomless eyes.

He stood before her with reverence more fitting for a shrine than a canvas. Her gaze met his not as a painted illusion, but with a presence that pulsed, inexplicably alive. Though the air in the chamber was chill and motionless, he felt a warmth blooming behind him, as if someone—some thing—had entered unseen, breathing close at his nape.

"Elira," he whispered, and a sigh seemed to stir the dust on the stones at his feet.

The days that followed dissolved into a rhythm at once grotesque and divine. He partook of no sustenance save for meager crumbs and sips of water laced with brandy; his cheeks sank into shadowed hollows, and his voice—unused—reduced itself to a withering rasp. Then surprisingly, he returned to the studio, that dim sanctum of madness and devotion. Long had it been since brush had kissed canvas, but now—now he painted. Each stroke a supplication, each hue a litany. He spoke as he worked, voice trembling, invoking her name in desperate cadence, imploring her to answer, to unveil the cruel sorcery that bound her essence within the frame. The studio had grown into a consecrated cell, and he, its penitent captive.

Strange phenomena multiplied in both frequency and intensity. Music, faint and spectral, sometimes played at the edge of his perception—no source discernible, no instrument or melody he could later recall. Footsteps paced the corridors at night, though Mrs. Bettridge had locked herself in her attic rooms and refused to descend. Once, in the dead hour before dawn, Lucien awoke to find his sheets sodden and the name Elira scratched into the condensation upon the mirror in his chamber. His heart thudded with terror, but it was not a terror that repelled—it beckoned him further into the abyss.

On the fifth night of the full moon, the cellar door groaned open as if possessed by some unseen hand, though no breath of wind disturbed the stagnant air, which hung heavy with a suffocating silence. His trembling fingers grasped the lantern, its feeble glow flickering like a dying hope, and he descended into the depths below. His mind was a tumultuous storm, torn between exultant anticipation and a nameless dread that gnawed at his very soul.

Before the canvas, there stood a figure, a woman, neither born of shadow nor flesh, but something in between—a creature of spectral elegance, whose very form shimmered like the disturbed surface of a moonlit pond. Her edges were indistinct, wavering as though composed of liquid air, yet undeniably present in the heavy stillness of the room. Her eyes—twin abysses—glistened with a sorrow so profound that it seemed to tear at the fabric of his mind, yet within those same depths there danced a cruel, mocking delight. Her mouth remained motionless, but the voice—oh, that voice— seemed to slither from the deepest recesses of his skull, its resonance cold and distant, like the echo of some ancient wraith.

"Lucien," she intoned, her words a dirge of infinite weariness, as if they had passed through the millennia themselves to find his ears, "you have brought me near the veil."

He crumpled to the floor, his trembling limbs giving way beneath him, and fell to his knees. The weight of her presence was unbearable, an oppressive force that pressed down upon his chest, suffocating him with each breath. His voice cracked as he whispered, "Tell me how to free you," his tears, hot and stinging, carved tracks down his hollow cheeks. "Tell me what binds you to this place, this prison of pigment and silence."

The figure tilted her head, a motion so fluid, so unnaturally graceful, it could scarcely be called human. It was as if her neck bent in ways not meant for the living, a grotesque, beautiful thing that made his heart race with a terror both horrified and fascinated. "A portrait is but a gate," she murmured, her tone ethereal and disembodied, like the rustle of forgotten leaves in an ancient forest. "You must become the key."

"What must I do?" he gasped, his breath ragged, his throat tight with a strangled yearning.

With a movement that was as insubstantial as mist, her hand reached toward him. The fingers seemed to hover just above his chest, a pale suggestion of a touch that carried with it a chill so deep it was beyond human comprehension. When it made contact, it was as though the cold did not pierce his flesh but instead slipped through the veil of his very soul, an unbearable frost that burrowed deep within. His body stiffened, his mind screamed, but still, the touch lingered.

"Sacrifice," she whispered, her voice now a faint, final breath in the stillness of the room. "Blood for breath. Memory for form."

And with that as if the very air around her could no longer bear the weight of her presence, she vanished—dissolving into the shadows, leaving only the oppressive silence and the cold of her touch still burning in his chest.

"Where have you gone?" he wailed.

"Blood for breath. Memory for form," the whisper came to his ear.

Lucien curled himself upon the cold, unforgiving cellar floor, the darkness pressing down upon him as he gave way to grief—a sorrow so deep it seemed to rend the very marrow of his soul. His tears fell like drops of ash, staining the floorboards beneath him. The very air seemed to suffocate him, heavy with the scent of mildew and decay, as if the house itself mourned with him.

When at last he stirred, it was the oppressive weight of dawn that roused him from his slumber, the pale light creeping through the cracks of the cellar like the reluctant touch of some spectral hand. His limbs were stiff and cold, as though he had been entombed within the earth itself, and the lantern, once flickering with a feeble flame, now lay snuffed beside him, its faint glow extinguished by the encroaching dark. His heart pounded against his chest in frantic rhythms, each beat a violent protest against the horror of his surroundings. He struggled to rise, his frame quivering, limbs leaden and obstinate, as though his very bones had transmuted into ice. A dolorous ache writhed through his flesh, and his mind, enshrouded in a vapor of confusion, reeled—distorted—as though the flow of time itself had grown thick and spectral, suspended in that dreadful, death-invoking stupor. He could not fathom how long he had lain there, cradled in the cold embrace of oblivion, but the world around him now seemed distant, as though he had emerged from the abyss of some forgotten nightmare.

He looked up. The portrait of Elira had changed.

Her eyes, once fixed forward in solemn contemplation, now looked to the left—as though watching someone. Her lips, once passive, now bore the faintest, most terrible hint of a smile.

Lucien emerged from the cellar, his pulse quickened by a terror he could not name, a foreboding that clung to him like mildew on stone. He wandered the dim corridors, calling for Mrs. Bettridge—his voice raw, uncertain—but only silence answered, thick and unmoving, like a veil drawn over the house. Shadows lengthened as if to mock his search, and every doorway yawned with menace.

At last, he forced open the door to her attic quarters. The scene within chilled the blood: a chair overturned, the oil lamp shattered upon the floor, and across the boards a smear—dark, unholy—clung to the grain like something scrawled in haste by trembling hands. The air was foul, thick with the reek of iron and decay as if death itself had taken up residence.

And there she lay—poor Mrs. Bettridge—sprawled unnaturally among the wreckage, her garments soaked and torn, her body bearing the cruel testimony of many wounds. Her eyes, half-lidded and dulled, stared without focus, as though fixed upon some final, unspeakable revelation. The walls around her seemed to lean inward, listening still to her last cries, and the shadows danced in silence, as though mourning—or relishing—their part in her end.

"Blood for breath. Memory for form," came the whisper.

Lucien felt no grief. In truth, he felt nothing at all beyond a terrible resolve.

He understood, with a clarity both dreadful and irrevocable, the course his actions must take. Each day thereafter, he spilled a drop of his blood upon the base of the canvas and whispered words he did not recognize—fragments of a language that came to him in dreams, in fever, in the wild scrawlings he etched upon the margins of his sketchbooks. The house no longer creaked beneath its age but murmured. The walls pulsed with a kind of breathless expectancy.

On the seventh night, the wind howled as though all the hounds of the pit had been loosed upon the moors. Lightning burst across the sky in jagged veins, illuminating the manor in phantasmagoric flashes. Lucien stood before the canvas, his skin pale as wax, a knife in his hand trembling with anticipation. He gazed into Elira's eyes—eyes that watched him now with unmistakable intelligence. The air around him thickened, oppressive with a chill that pierced the marrow. Every brush of the wind seemed to echo her voice, a haunting, indistinct murmur that seemed to beckon him closer, urging him to complete the final, forbidden stroke.

"I come," he whispered, closing his eyes, and pressing the blade to his chest.

***

Lucien awoke to a soft rustling—not of fabric or paper, but the rustling of breath, of skin against skin. He opened his eyes to find Elira at his bedside—not the painted phantom, but the very woman, or something which wore her likeness. Her form shimmered faintly, as though suspended just beneath the veil of the world, yet her eyes—those unforgettable gray eyes—met his with a sorrow that burned like a dying star.

"You draw me closer," she murmured, kneeling beside him. Her touch, when it found his cheek, was cold, and yet it seared his flesh as if marked by frost and flame alike. "You must finish it, Lucien. Only the final stroke shall unshackle me."

He tried to speak, but his voice abandoned him. Only in his dreams did he find tongue, and even there, it was always her voice that prevailed. Her requests grew more precise with each visitation: the shadow beneath her jawline, the subtle curve of her clavicle, the scar—yes, a scar!—that marred the flesh just beneath her left breast. He had never seen her body, and yet he painted it with exacting detail. A scar he had never known yet could now not forget.

And with each hour, Lucien's vigor waned. He no longer ate, nor did he sip watered brandy. The skin beneath his eyes darkened, and the whites grew jaundiced. Still, he painted, his hand trembling not with fatigue, but with rapture.

Mrs. Bettridge—once merely the vessel of superstitious dread—now appeared to Lucien as one already claimed by some spectral realm, her figure wan and hollow, draped in garments that hung upon her like burial shrouds. She lingered outside the studio like a penitent at the mouth of the tomb, leaving behind strange tributes: vials of coarse salt, rusted nails black with age, and a crucifix laid trembling upon a table as if it too feared what dwelt within. She muttered incantations in fractured Latin, her voice dry as old parchment, and thrice she rapped upon any door before daring entrance. Her hands, marred by trembling, clutched her shrouds like a dying woman clutching her last breath, and her eyes—those hollow pits rimmed in scarlet—wept not tears but dread itself. The shadows seemed to know her, wrapping around her limbs like soot upon the dead.

"Her soul was cursed!" she wailed, her voice rising like a wind through crypt bars. "You have beckoned damnation, sir, with every stroke upon that canvas! Did you not see? That woman was never born of clay or cradle—she came from below!"

Lucien, whose form had thinned to that of a revenant, turned to her with wild, flame-fed eyes, and from his lips there burst a sound—a laugh, fractured and shrill, as though the breath of mirth had been exhaled through shattered glass. "Then let damnation cradle me," he whispered through clenched teeth, his voice a hiss not wholly his own—an utterance borne not from mortal throat but from some deeper chasm of despair. "If damnation hath delivered her unto me, then to damnation I shall bind myself in unholy wedlock."

Yet it was as though his voice dissolved into the ether, unheard and unheeded. She remained—motionless, spectral—her form fixed in a dreadful stillness as if sculpted from moonlight and sorrow, unmoved by his presence, untouched by time or supplication.

With trembling fervor, he lunged for the crucifix—intent to seize it, to cast it into the licking tongues of fire—but as his pale fingers reached out, they passed through it as through smoke. It did not move. It did not fall. It only shimmered faintly, as though already forsaken by the solid world.

The nights grew longer. Time lost all rhythm. Sometimes the dawn arrived too soon, and other times it tarried as though reluctant to lift the shroud. The trees outside withered prematurely, their leaves shriveling on the boughs though the calendar swore it was early October. A sour wind scraped at the windows, moaning like a grief too old for words. Shadows pooled in corners where no light dared linger, and the clock in the hallway stuttered, its pendulum faltering as if weary of its own motion. The air felt heavy with unseen menace, and every creak of the floorboards sounded like a footstep not his own.

In the waning days of his dreadful labor, the portrait began to emit a heat—not the benign warmth of life, but the feverish exhalation of some thing ill at rest. The very air before it quivered, as though disturbed by an invisible breath drawn from the bowels of the tomb. When at last Mrs. Bettridge, pale as moonlight and shimmering in a ghostly manner, approached the chamber once more, she recoiled with a strangled cry: "It watches! By the Almighty, it watches!" And with that she fled, entombing herself within the chapel, where no morsel passed her lips, nor any word escaped her throat.

Lucien no longer slept. Strangely, it seemed, he did not require rest. He took to standing before the canvas, whispering to it in hushed, adoring tones. He spoke to Elira as though she were present—sometimes apologizing, sometimes imploring her forgiveness, sometimes lapsing into long, ecstatic silences where he merely gazed at her face and wept.

Then came the final brushstroke.

It was no grand flourish. No decisive gesture of triumph. Rather, it was a subtle shade beneath the lower eyelid—an infinitesimal touch of ochre and umber that brought moisture to the eye and made it gleam with uncanny life.

And in that moment, the candles extinguished themselves.

The room fell into utter darkness, save for the portrait, which pulsed faintly, as though lit from within.

Lucien gasped. He reached for her, his hand trembling, inches from the canvas—

And the eyes blinked.

Not a trick of paint. Not illusion. Not madness. The eyes blinked. The mouth, parted in eternal sorrow, now curved into a terrible, exquisite smile.

Lucien staggered back, his legs failing him. He crawled toward the door, now sealed tight as if by invisible hands.

From behind him, her voice—no longer a whisper—rose clear and full:

"I am free, my love. And now, so are you."

The studio door burst wide—though not by Lucien's hand. There, upon the threshold, stood Mrs. Bettridge, spectral in aspect, her countenance ashen, pale as the linens that shroud the dead. Her fingers clutched a timeworn rosary, each bead trembling as if in prayer against some nameless dread. Her lips hung ajar in a silence more terrible than sound, as though some ancient scream, wrenched from the depths of her soul, had been stolen by invisible, pitiless hands. Her eyes, round and stricken with a horror too deep for utterance, were fastened to the easel, unblinking. Her breath caught—suspended in her throat by the grasp of phantoms. Shadows curled about her hem like serpents, sinuous and sentient. A breath of cold, grave-wind crept outward from the room's dark interior, though no window had been opened to permit its passage. The corridor's candlelight wavered, struggled—and perished. She recoiled, trembling, her voice swallowed by the black abyss that gaped just beyond the doorframe.

The canvas stood empty.

Only a solitary streak of crimson remained—descending from its heart, still wet.

And Lucien Harrow was never seen again.

The Silence Beneath the Floorboards

Widower's Fog

The sea wept that day.

It wept with a voice of grey salt and mournful wind, pressing its chill fingers against the rattling windows of the Wren estate, as though the ocean itself sought entrance, or else wished to confirm that all within had indeed perished. The manor, perched upon the cliff's edge like a broken tooth in God's jaw, exhaled a silence so dense it might have suffocated a lesser man. Yet Alaric Wren crossed its threshold once more, alone—wedded now not to any earthly companion, but to memory, and to the shadow she had left behind.

The great oak door groaned upon its hinges—a groan too sentient, too burdened by age and sorrow to be merely mechanical. He paused in the threshold, his valise suspended from one trembling hand, and peered into the foyer. The gaslight above seemed to sway without reason. Dust gathered like mourning veils in the corners. On the stair, a shawl still lay in a loose heap—hers—where she had flung it, careless and laughing, last spring.

That laugh had been her last.

"Evelyn," he murmured, though the air devoured the name before it could find any ears but his own.

He moved as one made of fragile wires, jerking and pausing, stiffened by cold and regret. His once-firm stride had softened, eaten away by weeks of vigil at the graveside, months of sleepless agony. And now, returned to the shell of his former life, he felt no welcome in these walls—only a kind of passive judgment, a wordless condemnation from the house itself. The house knew. The house knew everything.

Down the corridor, the study awaited, untouched since the day of her passing. The place where he had once transcribed forgotten alphabets, where she had read by the hearth with legs tucked beneath her, humming half-remembered melodies, always slightly out of tune.

A film of soot glazed the windows; it dimmed the afternoon into a parody of twilight. Within, the desk stood like a tomb. His manuscripts lay in stacks, yellowing. The inkpot had dried to a crust. And there, upon the blotter, as if placed by a gentle and mocking hand, was a single strand of auburn hair.

He sat.

He could not help the tremor of his hand as he reached for it. The strand of hair coiled like something alive, iridescent in the flicker of candlelight. He brought it close to his lips—not to kiss, not quite—but to breathe it as if her essence might remain, somehow preserved in keratin and time.

"Mr. Wren?"

Mr. Thatch stood in the doorway—stooped, his silhouette warped by the fog beyond. Quickly, Alaric placed the strand of hair between the pages of a book.

"You need not lurk, Thatch," Alaric said with a brittle smile. "Come. You are part of this mausoleum, too."

The old caretaker crossed the threshold, his weather-beaten hat gripped tight between trembling hands. His steps were uncertain—not from age nor affliction, but from a burden more spectral. A heaviness clung to him, palpable and unseen, wrought not of flesh but of memory—dark, lingering memory—or perhaps some ancient superstition that curled like smoke about his soul and made each footfall falter beneath its ghostly weight.

"The hearth's been cleaned, sir. And I've laid out the thick blankets in the west bedroom, as you used to prefer in winter."

"Very good," said Alaric, eyes still on the strand. "You've always been most attentive. Tell me—has the study been entered in my absence?"

"No, sir."

"You are certain?"

"I'd stake my soul on it."

Alaric lifted his gaze slowly. "Would you? Then you'd best be careful with so precious a wager."

Thatch looked down. "I've kept it as you asked. No foot has crossed this floor. And yet . . ." His voice caught, trailed away like a rope snapping under weight.

"And yet?"

The caretaker's mouth worked silently a moment. "It ain't my place to say, sir."

"I insist."

Thatch's eyes darted once toward the floorboards beneath Alaric's chair.

"There's been . . . noise, sir. From beneath. Of a night. Soft scratching. Like claws, maybe. Or fingernails."

Alaric laughed—but only with his mouth. "Surely we are not ruled by rats, Thatch?"

"No rat makes a sound so patient. Nor one that keeps to a rhythm. Nor one that pauses when you speak aloud."

Alaric's smile withered. "I take it you speak to the floor now?"

"I speak to her," Thatch whispered. "Sometimes she answers."

A silence fell between them, thick and disbelieving.

"She is buried," Alaric said at length. "And she will stay buried."

"Yes," said Thatch. "Yes, of course."

The old man turned to leave but hesitated. "Beggin' your pardon, sir . . . but if you'll heed a fool's advice: do not pry at the house. Not now. Not with her gone. The house remembers her. It don't want to forget."

And with that, he departed the study, drew his jacket close about him, and passed beyond the threshold of the house, vanishing into the fog as though swallowed by the breath of the sea itself.

***

The wind keened louder that night. Alaric, wrapped in Evelyn's old shawl, sat hunched at the study desk. He had tried to read—his mind rebelled. Tried to drink—his stomach sickened. Tried to sleep—but every time his lids drooped, he imagined her standing in the doorway, not as she had been, but taller somehow, longer-limbed, face pale and indistinct, eyes wide with mourning or hunger.

He pushed aside the book and teacup. Rested his fingers upon the wood of the desk, fingertips splayed like a pianist testing the first note of a requiem.

And then—he heard it.

A faint sound. So faint it might have been imagined, were it not for the strange halt in his own breath, the stutter of his pulse in reply.

Scratch.

Pause.

Scratch-scratch.

Pause.

He tilted his head, listening.

Silence.

He stood, moved around the desk, knelt on the rug, ear pressed nearly to the floorboards. He knocked once.

No reply.

He knocked again.

Scratch-scratch.

Pause.

He stood abruptly, his knees cracking, his mind thick with confusion and dread.

"Rats," he muttered. "Of course."

He lit another candle. The trembling flame danced along the shelves and tapestries, casting monstrous shapes that writhed upon the walls like tortured phantoms. The hearth stood cold as stone. He sighed—a sound more burden than breath.

The ink had dried. Evelyn was dead.

And yet—beneath him—the silence did not sleep; it lingered, it listened, with a patience that chilled the soul.

The Whispering Begins

It was on the ninth evening since Evelyn's interment—an interment carried out with all the funereal dignity of the age, and yet with none of its closure—that the scratching returned. Alaric Wren, hunched like a broken marionette over his manuscript in the dwindling lamplight of his study, felt again that thin tremor beneath his feet—a tremor too deliberate for wind and too patient for a rat.

At first, he had attributed the noise to the coarse scuttling of vermin, creatures emboldened by silence and rot. Yet now it came with an intonation—no longer mere claw or tooth, but something slower . . . measured . . . intentional.

He sat back in his leather chair—leather that creaked with ghostlike familiarity—and pressed his fingers to his temples. The study, ever his sanctuary, had grown unfamiliar in Evelyn's absence. The velvet drapes, once pulled back to reveal the moor and sea beyond, now hung as if in mourning. Books leaned in their cases like weary pallbearers. The air bore the bitter perfume of dust and ink, and the ever-present undertone of the sea's slow decay. Yet beneath it all, there lingered something else—a warmth—unaccounted for and unwelcome.

Then it came.

A sound.

Not a scratch. No.

A voice. A whisper.

Not spoken. Exhaled.

"Alaric…"

The name—his name—spilled out from beneath the floorboards, not spoken aloud but present, like vapor in the lungs or memory in the blood. He rose abruptly, chair screeching back across the uneven planks.

"H-Hallucination," he muttered, dry-mouthed, grasping at the air as if for balance. "The mind—yes—the mind, when chafed by grief, conjures nonsense. That is all."

Yet his ears, treacherous organs, strained downward toward the floor. A kind of trembling seized him, not of the limbs but of the soul. He stood motionless in the darkening study, with the lamp sputtering low, until the house—timbered bones and crumbling mortar—shifted audibly, as though exhaling with him.

The voice came again.

Closer.

Older.

"Alaric . . ."

It bore the cadence of Evelyn—not as she was, but as memory summoned her in its most fragile hour: her murmur when weariness softened her speech, when sleep hovered just beyond her breath. Yet it was wrong in its very perfection, not marred by mimicry, but rendered so precise it curdled the blood—like a ghost of wax, molded in sound, echoing with dreadful exactitude.

In a panic half-masked by scholarly pride, Alaric stormed from the room, robes flaring behind like wings of some disgraced seraph. His gait was clumsy, his boots uneven upon warped boards as he sought out the caretaker, the man whose silence had grown more suspect with each passing hour.

He found Mr. Thatch in the root cellar, hunched like a gargoyle over jars of withered pears and dust-mantled wine. The old man turned not at the sound of Alaric's descent, but only when addressed, and even then only partially as if reluctant to share his eyes with the world above.

"Mr. Thatch," Alaric barked, breathless. "You must come. There's—there's something beneath the study floor. You are to inspect it at once."

Thatch did not move. A long breath, with the sound of old paper tearing, exited his lips.

"You heard it, then?" he said, voice brittle, unsuited to the living.

Alaric's eyes narrowed. "What did you say?"

"I warned ye," Thatch replied, lifting his pale face. "Did I not? When she passed. Told you plain: do not disturb the bones. Let the house settle her. Let time and wood and worm take what they will."

Alaric clenched his jaw, hands trembling. "You speak in riddles, sir, and I have no time for superstition. There is some . . . thing—animal, spirit, or other—within the floor. I am not mad, nor dreaming. I require your aid, not your provincial murmurings."

Thatch stared, unblinking. "It is not an animal, Mr. Wren."

"What, then?"

"A reminder."

Alaric scoffed, a hollow sound. "I buried her with my own hands! I stood beside the grave! Are you suggesting she—that Evelyn—"

"I suggest nothin'," Thatch interrupted. "Only that some parts of the dead do not lie as easy as the flesh."

There was a silence between them. The kind of silence that does not rest, but perches.

Alaric stepped closer, jaw set like granite. "You will come," he said. "You will look beneath the floor and dispel this madness with reason. Or else I shall tear up the boards myself and find whatever remains."

Thatch flinched as though struck, the muscles beneath his thin beard twitching. "Don't say that. Don't invite it."

Alaric turned and ascended without reply. Behind him, the old man remained in the shadows of the cellar, mouthing something not meant for speech.

That night, the house would not sleep.

Alaric sat once more at his desk, quill abandoned, manuscript untouched. The lamp was full now, its glow feverish, casting malformed shadows upon the bookshelves—shadows that writhed, though the flame held still. The strand of Evelyn's auburn hair, which he had pressed between the pages of a book days earlier, now lay upon the floor beside his chair—as if drawn out by unseen hands.

He stooped to retrieve it. His fingers paused. The floor beneath was . . .

Warm.

From below arose a sound—not the rasp of claw nor the whisper of breath—but laughter, delicate as thistle-seed upon the wind, and possessed of a familiarity that curdled the blood.

He shrank from it, breath catching in ragged spasms, and lurched toward the wall where a slender decanter of sherry waited like a patient executioner. He drank greedily, too much and too swift, the somber draught escaping his lips to trail in rivulets down his chin. Its flavor was of salt and smoldered ruin, as though the sea itself had died in the glass.

And then, that impossible whisper coiled up from beneath, a voice no longer like Evelyn's . . . yet carried upon her intonation. Something had learned to speak through her shape.

"Alaric..."

Hours passed. Or minutes. Time had grown unreliable as if warped by the very presence that stirred below.

In the early gray of morning—when the fog clutched at the windows like desperate hands—Alaric dozed in his chair. And in that moment of weakness, of half-sleep, the voice came yet again. Not whispering. Calling.

"Closer."

His eyes snapped open. The room was unchanged. Yet in the floor's center, between the ink-stained rug and hearthstone, a hairline crack had formed in the boards—thin, sinuous, and smiling.

Reverie and Rot

No longer could he veil himself in the tattered shroud of doubt—for the presence had declared itself with a subtlety more terrible than thunder. By the twelfth night, Alaric Wren had forsaken all ventures beyond the confines of the study as if the very air beyond that chamber bore contagion. There he remained, hunched like a penitent shade among grimoires and archaic instruments, relics of sciences long eclipsed by madness. His form had grown gaunt, consumed by wakeful delirium; the methodical clarity of his mind disintegrated into a chaos of haunted conjecture. The hearth sputtered with weary breath, and the warped floorboards beneath him stirred with a sentient groan, as though some slumbering beast below shifted in restless anticipation.

The crack in the floor—thin as the thread of a widow's grief—had widened, not by hands nor tool, but by invitation. The grain of the wood darkened around it, warped inward as if drawn toward some breathless pull beneath.

He wrote in his journal:

It watches from below. Not by eyes as we understand them, but by something with memory. With patience. It waits not for its moment, but for mine—to tire, to weep, to kneel. It is not her, and yet it wears her intonation like a borrowed shawl.

He no longer dared to name the voice. The syllables that once passed his lips with reverence now curdled in his throat, unspoken, forbidden. A hush had settled over the house—not of peace, but of pact. There were laws now, unwritten and grim, born not of reason but of dread necessity—rules he demanded of himself and etched in the silence between heartbeats.

Do not look into the crack after dusk.

Do not answer when it speaks your name.

Do not weep in its presence.

Still, he wept.

It was the thirteenth night—a number he once scoffed at in lectures on the folklore of death—that he did what he had sworn against. He knelt.

The fissure had widened—nay, yawned—sufficiently to admit the passage of slender fingers pale as moonlight. And from that ominous aperture, there issued forth not merely the voice—velvet-toned, viscous as honey steeped in poison—but a scent most harrowing in its familiarity. It came subtle as a sigh yet struck the senses with unerring precision: the fragrance Evelyn had favored in the sepulchral chill of winter—bergamot mingled with the metallic taint of cold iron, like flowers laid upon a grave too long disturbed.

He bent his ear to the floor.

"Are you there?" he whispered.

There came a pause.

Then: "Alaric . . . "

His breath fled. His throat clenched.

"You should not speak," he muttered. "Not in this world. Your voice belongs to stillness now."

A rule, broken.

"Do you remember," the voice said, "the lake where we met? The rowboat with the cracked oar? You mocked my hat."

His eyes watered. "I remember."

"Then let us share it together," the voice said. "Open the floor. Let me remember with you."

He staggered backward on all fours like a beast, gasping. "No. You twist her sounds. You recite from my mind, not your own."

From the floor: a giggle. Childlike, wrong.

"You asked for her," the voice cooed. "You wrote poems. You begged heaven. You screamed her name until your throat split like fruit. And now that I have come . . ."

"I was mourning!" he cried, the sound raw as torn linen. "You are not she! You are but a shadow cast through the veil—a mimicry, twisted and blackened by night!"

Silence.

Then: "Shall I prove it? That I am her?"

And from the slender breach in the door, there slithered—not a hand, no—but a single finger, ghastly in hue, spectral in its pallor. A woman's finger, yes, delicate and marred by freckles, the nail gnawed down in that pensive, fretful way Evelyn once possessed in her darker reveries. It moved once as if testing the air. Then again, more deliberate, more dreadful. And then it vanished, curling inward like some loathsome creature retreating to its crypt.

He cried out—raw, unrestrained—but the house, old and deaf and monstrous, held his terror close, and no soul stirred in answer.

***

The following morning, the house was filled with flies.

They congregated not upon meat, nor waste, but upon books. They moved not as insects, but as if reading. Alaric watched them crawl across the spines of *Grief and Phantasm* and *The Ethics of Resurrection*. They landed upon his journal and smeared its ink into illegible madness.

Alaric, seized by a terror both sudden and unnameable, rushed to the door as though chased by phantoms only he could perceive. His breath came ragged, his eyes wide with the dread of understanding too late.

He grasped the knob—brass once burnished by time and touch—but it turned against him, alive with a malevolent heat. It hissed, a serpent's breath of steam, and sank its scalding teeth into his palm. He recoiled with a cry, the skin seared, the pain sharp and immediate. The house, ancient and brooding, made its will known in that searing kiss.

It would not let him go.

Alaric, trembling and half-mad with dread, fled from the cursed threshold and barred himself within the confines of his study—a dim, oak-paneled tomb lined with the spines of long-dead thinkers and their ink-stained lamentations. There, amid the wavering flame of an oil lamp, he nursed his ruined mind and whispered to no one, to nothing, save the ceaseless creak of the house that now seemed to breathe around him. Shadows pooled in the corners like watching eyes. Hours passed, or perhaps none at all, until the evening deepened into a suffocating velvet.

And then—precisely as the last light failed—there came a sound from the corridor: the hesitant tap of a cane upon old floorboards. Mr. Thatch had come, and there he stood at the study's threshold, framed in darkness, his old coat soaked with rain, his boots leaving prints shaped like hooves.

"I warned you," he rasped, each syllable frayed like parchment in flame, his breath trailing like the exhalation of some tomb-born wind.

Alaric did not stir, his form carved in stillness. "What is it that haunts me so?" he murmured, though the marrow in his bones already quaked.

Thatch stepped across the threshold. The hearthlight faltered as if recoiling from his presence.

"It is hunger," he said, voice low as a dirge. "A hunger untouched by death—a yearning that festers. That which you unearthed had no resting place. No grave, but a gaping maw, ever thirsting. It is a wound in the world that speaks."

Alaric laughed, a sound too dry. "I must let it starve."

Thatch approached the floorboard. "But you've fed it already. With tears. With memory. It knows your grief. That is its feast."

"What must I do?" Alaric asked.

Thatch stared at the crack, which now glistened as if wet.

"You must unmake her. Let go of the voice. Burn the house. Salt the bones. Bury your sorrow where no soil remembers."

Alaric shook his head. "I cannot. If I do . . . she is gone."

The crack widened.

Thatch stepped back.

"Then it will take more."

***

That night, the voice that had murmured with the spectral grace of Evelyn was no longer hers. It fractured into a multitude—each tone a revenant echo: the tender lilt of his long-departed mother, the plaintive cry of the child he could not save, the broken murmur of the grocer who last winter found the rope more forgiving than the world. Yet all these utterances clothed themselves in Evelyn's intonation like silk stretched thin over ossified bone.

With trembling breath and eyes alight with a fevered gleam, Alaric rose and took in hand a hammer—its head black with rust, its handle slick with old varnish and sweat.

He gazed upon the floor, where the boards had deepened in hue, a shade reminiscent of overripe fruit or the stain left by old wounds—plum-dark and pulsing as if the house itself remembered.

"So," he murmured, the words brittle on his tongue, "you hunger for memory? Then be sated."

With a cry torn from the hollow depths of his chest, he brought the hammer crashing down.

The wood shrieked as it splintered.

A stench rose, abominable and cloying—not the fetor of rot, no, but something far fouler still: a sweetness so thick, so sickly, it clawed down the throat like unseen fingers, wringing the breath from his lungs and stirring bile in the depths of his belly. With frantic hands and a cry half-choked, he tore at the board above the odor's source and cast it aside, his pulse drumming a dirge.

There was no earth beneath. No crawlspace carved by man's tool or design. Instead, a chamber yawned open before him—an abomination, not built but bred. The walls, pallid and slick, were formed of a ghastly substance, neither stone nor wood, but the interlocked gnashing of teeth, jutting and writhing as though still hungry. Above, the ceiling pulsed with a loathsome vitality, trembling as if stirred by breath too vast to hear.

And at the center—O God, the center!—there rested a cradle of bone, jagged and fused, like the ribcage of some titanic beast. Within it lay a thing swaddled in nightmare: a creature that might, once, in some blessed age, have borne the form of a child— but now twisted, malformed, a blasphemy of infancy.

The being stirred. Its eyes were not eyes but black hollows, vacant gulfs that drank in the lamp's light and gave nothing back— no reflection, no glint of life, only the void. Its mouth yawned open, cracked and lipless, a gaping wound where no sound should dwell. Yet from that awful chasm, there issued a voice—familiar, tremulous, and soaked in dread. It was Evelyn. Not her voice as he remembered it in life, soft with laughter or low with thought, but a twisted echo, stretched and soured, as though filtered through the throat of the grave.

"Alaric," it said and reached toward him with arms—too many arms, far too many—grasping, pulling, as though to tear him into the abysmal blackness.

He recoiled—nay, was hurled backward by the sheer, paralyzing enormity of his terror—as though some unseen force had thrust him from the edge of madness into its very maw. A scream, ragged and primal, tore itself from the vault of his chest, not born of the will but ripped loose by some ancestral dread. The hammer, once gripped with purpose, slipped from his hand and struck the floor with a cold metallic finality—clank, clatter—a sound made distant by the blood roaring in his ears, as meaningless now as the memory of sunlight.

The thing rose—not with the grace of the living, but with a ghastly deliberation, a crawl that defied reason, each motion birthing a wet scrape upon the pallid floor. Its limbs moved as if burdened by the weight of centuries, dragging behind it a shadow too immense, too animate, a stain that bled outward and seeped into the very seams of the chamber. And from the yawning pit of its throat—if throat it was, for no anatomy known to man could account for such unholy resonance—there issued a sound. Not a growl, nor a cry, but a chorus—a polyphony of names, his names, every tender syllable Alaric had ever whispered in sorrow. They poured forth in that dreadful voice: names spoken beside graves, murmured to empty cradles, offered in vain to absent faces. Every mourning word, every tear-drenched phrase he had breathed into the lonely silence of his grief came back to him now, defiled and monstrous.

Shaking—no, quaking—with a fear so absolute it hollowed his marrow, Alaric staggered from the blasphemous chamber. His thoughts reeled, a cyclone of dread and disbelief, yet amidst the chaos his hand found the journal—his only tether to sanity. He clutched it to his chest and fled, stumbling like a drunkard through the darkened corridors, the echoes of his own sorrowed voice still chasing him through the walls.

Through corridors that had shrunk, closing in as though to swallow him whole. Past paintings—paintings whose eyes had become sharp and hungry, like the jaws of beasts. The door, once sealed, creaked open this time, inviting him like some cruel gesture of fate. Without hesitation, he dashed into a storm, bare feet striking the cold earth as he laughed—a twisted, broken laugh— tears mingling with the rain, his body trembling as much from the chill as from fear.

Behind him, the house exhaled—a long, drawn-out breath—as though it, too, had awakened.

***

The moor swallowed Alaric Wren as if the very earth had taken him into its dark embrace. His footprints ceased abruptly at the cliff's edge, yet no trace of him was found—no shred of flesh, no hint of struggle. Only the journal remained, its pages scorched and sodden, ink bleeding into blood, the words now a grotesque blur of desperate scribblings.

The house yet endures, standing in hollow solitude. Empty. Or so it appears. The study's floorboards, once gnarled and cracked, are now smooth, as though they've forgotten their burden of years. At night, however, a warmth lingers, subtle, unsettling— and from the shadows, a sound emerges, soft and eerie: a lullaby, lilting through the air, though no mother ever penned its notes.

The Final Silence

The villagers did not utter the name of the Wren house, not even in jest, nor under the persuasion of drink or prayer. They passed it as one skirts a grave too shallow, crossing to the farther verge of the road with heads bowed and steps quickened, as though the very nearness of its threshold might leech from them some vital essence—be it memory, soul, or voice. Time had not ravaged the place so much as fed it. Moss clung ravenously to the eaves, an emerald blight. Ivy throttled the chimney, not like a vine, but a noose mid-tightening. And yet—the windows! O accursed windows!—remained untouched by grime or age, each pane a vigilant orb staring outward in spectral perpetuity, watching.

Upon the first night of frost, beneath a sky brittle with stars, a stranger arrived. His complexion was the hue of old ivory, and he walked with a stoop that spoke of either affliction or habit. Gloves, too clean for travel, adorned his narrow hands, and he bore a small suitcase that clicked, with every movement, like the rattling of bones in a reliquary. Upon the porch—boards moaning in complaint beneath his weight—he rapped once… then twice. The door responded not with welcome, but with a groan of its own accord, yawning inward.

No mortal hand had opened it.

"Curious," breathed the stranger, the whisper curling like smoke from his lips. "Just as they described."

He crossed the threshold, and the cold rose to greet him, embracing him not as a guest but as a possession.

The stranger—one Mr. Worthen Kell—was no common traveler, but an inquirer of rare and unnerving affairs, summoned not by edict nor ordinance, but by whispers, by rumor, by the low droning of dread that lingered in the mouths of those who feared what truth might do if named aloud. He had read the last entries of Alaric Wren—scrawled in haste, in tremor, in ink nearly torn by the fervor of the hand. He had seen the rendering Thatch had drawn before silence claimed him—a figure of impossible limbs and a voice drawn in lines that screamed. Thatch now sat, unmoving, in a cell deep beneath the asylum at St. Bellamy's, listening to that voice only he could hear.

Within the parlor, Mr. Kell struck a match and lit a single taper. Its flame sputtered as though reluctant, casting shadows that recoiled rather than danced.

He opened his journal—its spine crackling like dry bark— and placed pen to paper with the precision of a surgeon. "The house is silent," he inscribed. "Yet it listens. Not as an empty room listens—but as a mind does, restrained, biding. The silence is not absence—it is intent."

He pressed onward, drawn as if by fate's unseen thread, and made his way to the study.

There, the air thickened—became viscid, as though he passed not through space but through the breath of a dreaming beast. The very walls seemed to pulse, subtle and nauseous, as if alive with some slow, perverse respiration. The floorboards, too, were changed—darkened not by time, nor soot, nor rot, but by absorption. The grain drank the light. The timber swelled with that which had entered and never departed—not by door, nor window, nor cry. Here, everything remained. Here, all was steeped, steeped, and steeped again—until even silence fermented.

He found the boards—seamless, whole.

He found the hammer on the floor.

At the hearth, he sat—still as the dead, the fire's low breath casting eldritch reflections upon his gaunt cheeks. "You've played your games," he intoned, each syllable measured, deliberate, addressed not to the empty room, but to that which nested beyond its veil. "But I am not a man of grief. I come not with sorrow, but with curiosity. And I do not fear what I understand." His voice did not tremble, though the air grew cold, and the flames themselves seemed to recoil from his candor.

The fire sputtered then, as though choking upon its own embered tongue. He waited.

And then—it answered. Not in speech, not with the tongue of any known creature, but with silence inverted, compressed into a malign curve like the blade of a sickle pressed to the soul. The stillness thickened, shaped itself. The shadows conspired, not moved by light, but as though reassembling of their own volition— adjusting. Rearranging. Watching.

A single word, drawn out as if from the base of the earth: "Alaric . . ."

Kell closed his eyes, the lids trembling not from fear but from memory. "No," he said, softly but with finality. "I am not he."

The voice twisted, altered. A different pitch, a different wound.

"Mother . . ."

He opened his eyes. "You are hungry," he said, a whisper sharpened by disdain. "But you have grown careless. You think any wound will bleed for you."

A sound then—a movement beneath the floorboards—not a slither, not the sliding of a serpent, but something altogether more dreadful: a pulse. A heartbeat born of rot and memory, thudding in a cadence not meant for the living.

From his suitcase, he produced a mirror. Silver-framed. Oval. Worn by time and secrets. "This is not glass," he murmured as if reciting a prayer or curse. "It is obsidian, drawn from the chasm beneath the salt lake. It shows not reflection, but origin."

He set the mirror on the floor.

The creature faltered. The house—old and listening— groaned, then shivered as if something within its walls long buried now stirred.

"Now," Kell said, the firelight catching in his eyes like twin coals of defiance, "let us see what you are."

And the boards opened.

Not cracked. Not splintered. Parted—slowly, reverently, as though peeled back by unseen hands with fingers made of smoke and guilt. A mouth, circular and wide, yawned where once there was wood. From its depths rose not darkness but a suffocating saturation of color—blues bruised to black, reds like dried blood on parchment. Shapes undulated within, not forms but impressions: shadows of bones, sighs of the forgotten. Tendons of memory throbbed below. Threads of voice wove in and out like worms through loam, echoes honed to blades.

And at the center—it waited.

Not Evelyn.

Not the woman, not the memory, not the grief-made-flesh he had once dared to name.

But the thing. The hunger behind the mask. That which had worn her face, borrowed her voice, and now recoiled before the truth drawn from obsidian. A thing not born but conjured by mourning that had festered too long in a house that remembered everything.

Not Alaric.

Not any one soul.

A knot of devoured identities, all wearing the ones they had stolen.

It rose—not entirely—just enough to be seen and named.

"I see you," murmured Kell, his voice scarcely more than breath, as if uttered beneath the weight of a tombstone. "You are no specter conjured by the fevered mind, no fiend born of infernal fire. You are the residue of sorrow unspent, mourning left to ferment into monstrosity. You are grief—starved, then gorged—grown monstrous in its long feeding."

At this, the creature convulsed, its grotesque form shivering as if the words themselves had flayed it.

"No," it hissed, voice splitting and slithering like wind through mausoleum cracks. "I am love. I am the echo—a cherished lullaby that lingers after breath has ceased. I am what they would not bury, what they could not release."

"And now," spake Kell, with a solemn gravity born of reckoning, "you shall behold the image of your truth."

He lifted the mirror and turned it toward the thing.

Instant was the effect.

The being recoiled, not as one repelled by light, but as if wounded by recognition itself. Its unholy chorus faltered, a dissonant screech unraveling into silence. Its limbs—too many to name, too ill-born to count—thrashed in mindless protest. Faces bubbled forth and blistered upon its flesh: the eyes of a child innocent and new to weeping; the sagging visage of a mother drowned in lament; the gasping mouth of a man undone by solitude; the howl of a faithful hound whose master never returned; a stairwell echo—a whisper never meant for ears. All borrowed. All consumed. All worn like trophies.

"You are a parasite upon the sepulcher of love.," Kell intoned. "Yes. Parasite. You feed upon memory—you devour its marrow and leave only madness behind."

Then did the house scream—not with sound, but with pressure most infernal, a force that pressed behind the sockets of the eyes, that pulsed like a vice upon the temples, that forced the very air from the lungs like a drowned man's final cry.

The floor beneath Kell groaned—a tortured moan of timber and nail—and then cracked, not in descent but in separation, each plank tearing away from its brother like flesh riven from bone.

Kell staggered. The world lurched. And yet—yet!—his hand held firm. The mirror rose like a relic of justice against the tide of blasphemy.

The creature recoiled, contracting as if in agony not of body but of essence, folding inward like some profane blossom blighted in its bloom. Its limbs collapsed into its core; its face—if such a term could still be dared—dissolved into a shifting mire of grief and rage. It lost shape, lost voice; its form slackened, waned, until it was but a quivering blot of shadow. From beneath, the mouth— ah, that ghastly aperture in the floor—began to inhale, not with breath, but with a dreadful reversal of sound and soul, a vacuum that devoured not air, but memory and meaning. Silence poured inward like water into a drained tomb.

"No—no—do not take it from me!" it shrieked, voice unraveling into a wail that split through the air. "It is mine—mine! I remember it all! I am what they could not bear to lose—I am the echo of their yearning, the ghost of their love unspent!"

But Kell, steady as stone, replied, "You are the silence beneath the floorboards."

And with the slow solemnity of a priest laying down the relic of a shattered creed, he placed the mirror at his feet.

Then—then the thing vanished. Not in a flash, nor with thunder, but with a subterranean sigh, a final tremor, as though something vast and slick and unspeakably ancient had slumped into the earth's chthonic bosom. Beneath the house, the very foundations seemed to exhale, and with that breath, the fire guttered into cinders. The weight, that dreadful pressure which had pressed upon rib and soul alike, lifted—as though the air itself wept in relief. The boards, which moments before had buckled like a wound, drew themselves together with a groan both resentful and resigned, knitting closed the mouth from which no prayer had ever escaped.

Kell stood alone.

***

Weeks later—Kell's countenance drawn, his hand unsteady—he composed his final report, a document penned in a trembling scrawl:

The house remains. Yet its appetite—voracious, unspeakable—has at last been starved. The thing that dwelt beneath, that ancient hunger given form by grief and silence, has been named. And what is named may be banished, for its dominion lay ever in the unspoken, the unresolved. Let this stand as a harbinger to those who mourn: grief is no relic to be clutched, no pet to be fed in the shadowed chambers of the heart. It is remembrance, not sacrifice. Beware the things that breathe within sorrow's hollow—those phantoms shaped by longing, for once given form, they cannot be unmade by prayer nor undone by time.

And then he departed—silent as snow upon stone—from the village whose name he would never again utter.

The house still stands.

And if you find yourself upon that lonely road as the sun bleeds into twilight and the wind rides high upon the heaths, you may hear a sound beneath the timbers—not a voice, no, not now. That ghastly echo is stilled.

What lingers is quieter still.

A breath, faint and ceaseless, drawn in through splintered cracks—the hollow inhalation of a presence that once knew fullness, and now, in its barrenness, remembers only the shape of what it has lost.

ABOUT THE AUTHOR

Philip Mazza is a novelist with a boundless imagination, captivating readers with the epic fantasy series *The Harrow Saga*. Born in New York in 1959, he earned a degree in Business from LeMoyne College and an MBA, later holding leadership roles in human resources and operations. Now a professor at the Madden School of Business and Economics, Philip dedicates his time to his students and writing. *The Wicked Man Cometh* is his thirteenth literary work. He and his wife enjoy travel and continue to live in upstate New York.